Jaclyn Moriarty grew up in Sydney and has lived in the US and England. She spent four years working as a media and entertainment lawyer and now writes full time so that she can sleep in each day. She and her Canadian partner divide their time between Sydney and Montreal.

Also by Jaclyn Moriarty

Feeling Sorry for Celia
Finding Cassie Crazy

JACLYN MORIARTY

PICADOR

Pan Macmillan Australia

First published 2004 in Macmillan by Pan Macmillan Australia Pty Limited
St Martins Tower, 31 Market Street, Sydney

National Library of Australia
Cataloguing-in-Publication data:

Moriarty, Jaclyn.
I have a bed made of buttermilk pancakes.

ISBN 0 330 42137 9.

I. Title.

A823.3

Internal design by Melanie Feddersen, i2i design.
Typeset in 11.5/15 pt Bembo by Post Pre-press Group
Printed in Australia by McPherson's Printing Group

To Colin with love

Acknowledgements

I would like to thank the extraordinary people at Pan Macmillan, especially Anna McFarlane and Cate Paterson, for making the experience of publishing so delightful. Thanks also to my agent, Tara Wynne, and to my generous readers, Liane Moriarty, Nicola Moriarty and Corrie Stepan. My greatest thanks are to Colin McAdam who knows this book by heart.

1

THE HOT AIR BALLOON

Once upon a time there was a watercolour painter who thought he could invent a parachute.

This was in the early days of parachutes.

Out in the meadow with his easel and his brushes, he saw an early parachutist dripping from the sky.

'How was it?' he cried, jogging up to the gathering crowd.

'Oh,' cried the parachutist, tangled in the parachute: 'I feel *sick*.'

But this was in Paris, so they spoke in French.

Those days, parachutes had a design flaw: they did not float gently to the ground, they spun through the air at dizzying speed, and parachutists turned an olive green.

So, the watercolour painter went home and put up his feet for a coffee and a think. 'How can we stop these brave falling men feeling sick?' is what he thought.

After thirty-five years of thinking, he figured it out. He put down his coffee, picked up his sketchpad, and called to his wife.

'Look,' he said, calm with pride as he tilted the sketch towards her.

His wife squinted, and her eyebrows bounced, for his parachute was *upside down*! Instead of being shaped like an 'n', it was shaped like a 'u'.

'Will it work?' she mused.

'Of course!' he exclaimed. He made a parachute out of her handkerchief to prove it. The handkerchief flopped to the floor, but, as he pointed out, it didn't spin.

So convinced was he that *this* was the solution to the spinning parachute, he decided to make one of his own. He ran it up on his wife's sewing machine. Next he persuaded a friend to let him try it, by jumping from the basket of the friend's hot air balloon.

He was so excited that he didn't test it first with a dummy (or a cat), which would have been the custom in those days; he just strapped himself in and jumped.

He plummeted straight to the ground – like a vase knocked from a shelf – and was killed.

•

When she first heard this story, Maude Sausalito (aged eleven at the time) felt a cold gust of sadness for the painter. Then she imagined (yearningly) the things he might have landed on which would have saved his life.

A haystack; a pond; a freshly turned garden bed!

A vat of mulberries!

A gigantic banana milkshake.

A stack of blueberry muffins.

(She was hungry.)

If only, she thought – and she still thinks this often, even now – if only the stupid, overexcited man, could have caught an up-draught in his useless parachute! If only the up-draught could have carried him high into a zinging blue sky, over a hill of whipped butter, across a maple syrup pond. And finally, gently, deposited him on a buttermilk pancake bed.

Parachutes are vented at the top these days, and it is this which prevents them from spinning.

EXTRACTS FROM THE ZING GARDEN SHED (Burnt Fragments)

Imagine if you did not have knees!

When you walk downhill your body's natural tendency is to fall forward. Unconsciously, you lean back and bend your knees, contracting the quadriceps muscles as you do. The knees prevent you from falling.

Now, imagine if your quadriceps muscles are so weak that they cannot stop the knees from bending once they start! If the knees do not stop bending you fall flat on your face.

INSTITUTE FOR ARTHROSCOPIC SURGERY
OF SOUTH DAKOTA

THE SPORTS CARNIVAL

Cath Murphy (teacher, Grade 2B) holds one end of the finish line ribbon, and scans the carnival crowd for Zings.

Ah-hah. There's a Zing reclining on a picnic blanket and trying out the ring tones on her mobile phone.

Over there! A little Zing lining up to race.

That could be a Zing, that plump woman carrying the cranberry muffin –

No.

That's not a Zing.

That's Miss Heather Waratah (teacher, Grade 4C).

A year ago she didn't even know the Zings. Today, she gets a spasm in her right eye when she sees one. (The letter 'V' has the same effect.)

Also, she has lost her personality.

She lost the personality a few months back.

To be specific, it was burned to cinders in the Zing Garden Shed.

So, that's it for me, she thinks grimly as the finish line ribbon falls from her wrist to the feet of a tumble of children.

•

Fancy Zing pauses at the south-east corner of the oval. She has just collected bandaids from the glovebox of her car.

From here, she can see her daughter lining up to race. The starting gun cracks and Cassie takes off at the pace of Fancy's heart. The other children, Fancy thinks, move like frantic puppets. Cassie stretches smoothly away from them.

Fancy's gaze shifts to the finish line where Cath Murphy waits: her hair cut sharply across her neck; her excellent posture; her expression of mild exasperation. She feels a surge of love for the ribbon in Cath's hand. It has such power! A child need only brush against that ribbon and the adults must drop it at once.

Her eyes follow the lane markings beyond the finish line, to the other side of the oval where four blocks of colour have appeared. They seem to be enormous flowerbeds.

Amazed, Fancy turns back to watch her daughter's race.

•

Marbie Zing listens to the chanting of children. They have gathered into their four team colours to practise for the cheering competition. She sits on a nearby picnic blanket, sometimes pressing her fingers to her ears.

Her niece has just finished a race, and is catching her breath a few feet away from Cath Murphy. Cath says she's lost her personality. When Marbie heard this, she telephoned Cath to advise that she go for a drive. 'That's happened to me before,' she said. 'A lost personality. At job interviews and kitchen teas. But I always get it back on the drive home.' Cath hung up immediately.

On the oval, a girl is lining up for the long jump. The girl is so small she hardly exists, as far as Marbie can tell. Her arms and legs are slender to the point of translucence. She is wearing a sunhat tipped so low she has to tilt her chin upwards to see. Nearby, parents smile broadly at one another, about the girl. But the girl shakes out her limbs. She squats and stretches her knees. She squints down the sandpit, strategising.

Watching, Marbie thinks about how often children slip into adult worlds, and then – as a teacher rushes to measure the girl's jump – how frequently we find ourselves in theirs.

She is startled by two sets of footsteps thudding to a halt on her picnic blanket. It's her sister, Fancy, returning from the car, and Cassie, arriving from the opposite direction, a flutter of blue ribbon in her hand.

2

CATH MURPHY

A year ago now, Cath Murphy stood on the 2nd grade balcony, blinking and smiling in the morning sun, her hands in the pockets of her new baggy trousers, her neck feeling warm beneath her short blonde hair.

It was the first day of term, and the children were gathering downstairs.

The new guy, Warren Woodford, was at the other end of the balcony, outside the 2A classroom. He leaned his chin towards the railing and gave Cath a firm little nod: *Yes, there they are, gathering.*

She responded with her own solemn nod.

The new guy was sure to be a hit with the kids. He was very tall, so he would be able to reach up to touch the ceiling, or to tack paintings high on the wall. Also, he could pull down one side of his mouth while raising the opposite eyebrow. Kids think that kind of face, especially when done to tease them, is the essence of grown-up humour.

Cath looked back at Warren and he was making that exact face at her.

It was actually funny, and she surprised herself by imitating him. He smiled softly, looked away, and then called something that sounded like: 'From the highlands.'

'Pardon?'

'Aren't the highlands!'

'Yes,' she agreed, tentatively. Then she really wanted to know, so she ran a few steps along the balcony towards him. 'I'm sorry?'

He waved her back. 'I only asked if you were frightened! Are you scared?'

'Of course I am! Aren't you?'

Then she ran back to her spot to wait again, and felt awkward and foolish, but also she felt this: quirky, cocky, small, funny, wicked and extremely blonde.

In fact, she was not really frightened, more excited. But, as her mother liked to say, all meetings with new people, even locksmiths or seven-year-olds, can make you a little afraid.

Cath had been teaching for two years now, and had a reputation among the children as very nice and pretty, can be strict sometimes, but mostly nice. She was known to be generous with gold stars and SUPER WORK! stamps.

Among teachers, she had a reputation as *serene* and *conscientious*, perhaps a little shy, but prone to fits of giggling.

She ate a Granny Smith apple at lunchtime each day, and believed in smiles which continued for 5-4-3-2-clear! after corridor nods. She had a Mary Poppins glint in her eye, but not the Mary Poppins spots on the cheeks, or the carpetbag.

Now, as the children filed up the stairs, jostling and excited, chatting with each other and at her, she herself chatted back: *Good morning!* and *There you go!* and *Just leave your bag on the bag-rack, that's a good girl!* and *Oops! It's a bit early in the day to be tripping on your shoelace, isn't it, okay there?*

But she noticed, as she chatted, that the new guy, Warren, was welcoming his class in silence. He was holding one arm high in the air and using the other to wave them into his classroom. He was like a stately policeman. The children, she noticed, were obeying him in wide-eyed wonder.

Later, as she spent the morning playing educational welcoming games (Luke's name begins with the same letter as Lion! Scary!), Cath was conscious of long periods of silence in the classroom next door. The silence was interrupted now and then by storms of laughter.

The next day, Tuesday, Cath got a chance to talk to her friends Lenny D'Souza (teacher, Grade 6B, School Counsellor) and Suzanne Barker (teacher, Grade 1A). This was at recess.

Cath told them that, at the start of the summer holiday, she had broken up with her boyfriend from last year. Lenny and Suzanne said, 'Oh', sadly, but Cath just laughed and said she couldn't even remember his name. Suzanne reminded her what the name was. 'Thanks,' said Cath. 'I never thought he was right for you,' Suzanne offered. 'You didn't have the aura of someone *truly loved*.' 'Thanks,' said Cath again. Lenny told them she had been out to dinner with, guess who? And Cath said, 'Who?' and Lenny said, 'Guess,' etc. Then Lenny admitted it was *Frank Billson* (School Principal).

Cath and Suzanne shrieked and, when Lenny ran to get her sandwich, they lowered their heads and said, 'Oh my *God*' and raised their eyebrows: '*What is she thinking?*' Lenny came back and they straightened their faces and shoulders again.

Lenny asked Cath what the new guy, Warren Woodford, was like, and Cath was about to reply, but Suzanne interrupted to say she'd heard he studied *acting* before teaching.

And Cath found herself thinking: *Actually, Suzanne, the new guy belongs to ME.*

Because *she* was the 2nd grade teacher.

On Wednesday, arriving home late after a K to 6 Values and Goals meeting, and tossing her keys and sunglasses onto the table, Cath caught a glimpse of her busy, thoughtful face reflected in the dining room window. She paused to consider the face. 'You wouldn't know,' she said to the window, 'that my heart was broken not so long ago.'

The heart had been broken by last year's boyfriend, despite what she'd said to Lenny and Suzanne. He had left her for a job in New Orleans. He brought the job to her place one evening; it was in a small white envelope, and was very enthusiastic about the boyfriend's environmental science degree. 'When do you leave?' she asked, making her voice as amazed and excited as his was. 'Next week!' 'And how long is it for?' '*Indefinite!*'

He then spent the evening hunched over Cath's dining table, tracing scenic routes on a Louisiana Road Map with his thumbnail.

'Are you sure you can *see* in this light?' Cath had said, coldly.

But he was too excited about the alligators, and only seemed to remember her at the airport. By then, of course, it was too late. His luggage had been checked in.

Could he really have broken your heart? said Cath's reflection, skeptically. But then she thought of the nights after he left, how she cried herself to sleep in her empty apartment, kicked the telephone across the room, mistreated the flowers that he sent from New Orleans (she left them to die in their wrapping), cut her hair short, and enrolled in a part-time law degree. Whether or not he was worth it, he had certainly broken her heart. (He had added a '*Cheer up!*' note to his flowers from New Orleans.)

'But now,' she announced to her cat, Violin, as he twirled between her ankles, 'I am recovered!' The bell on Violin's collar tinkled faintly.

She gazed at herself in the window, thinking of how good it was to be single. Just last night, for example, she had made chocolate chip cookies at midnight, to celebrate the start of the school year! And tonight, she planned to have Vegemite and grilled cheese on toast for dinner. And then watch *MTV* for as long as she liked. (Most boyfriends get restless and want to try the cricket instead.) And then go to bed and stay up late reading a novel. Lovely!

And plus, said the tiny, secret voice at the back of her mind, *and plus, I am sure to get a new boyfriend now that I feel this way! Whenever I get to the stage of happy, independent, singlehood, THAT'S when I meet a new boy! It makes me ATTRACTIVE, being happy with JUST ME, I'm about to –*

'HUSH,' she said firmly, and turned away from her reflection. Then she found that she was jittery and had to take a walk to the corner store.

On Thursday, she thought: *I like being single!* as she walked around the classroom, complimenting children on the pompoms they were making. *I'm going to study law part-time!* Some of the children smiled back at her. A girl named Lucinda kept smiling for such a long time that Cath asked if she was all right. 'No, because I'm not allowed to call the teacher that,' said Lucinda.

'Call the teacher what?' said Cath.

But Lucinda kept smiling, and shook her head, whispering to herself. Cath crouched down to hear what she was whispering.

'Ms Murphy,' she was whispering.

'You're not allowed to call me Ms Murphy?' said Cath.

Lucinda nodded and her ponytail bounced.

'But Lucinda, that's my name!'

'I can't say Mzzz,' explained Lucinda, and then shook her head wildly as if she had walked through a spider web. 'Don't make me say that sound! I can't say any word with that sound! That *zzz* . . .' She gasped, and shook her head again.

Luckily, at that moment, the girl beside Lucinda said: 'Vagina, vagina, vagina'.

What was that child's name? Her name tag was on the floor.

'CASSIE SAID VAGINA!' shouted Marcus Ellison.

Cassie. That's right. Cassie had been five minutes late for school that morning and her mother had written an apology note, which was polite of her. *In return,* thought Cath sternly, *I should remember her daughter's name!*

But, to be fair, Cassie's name tag was rarely on display because she made dramatic speeches, waving her arms for emphasis and sweeping pencils and name tags to the floor.

'Vagina, vagina, vagina,' declared Cassie.

'That's enough, Cassie,' Cath said, firmly.

Cassie looked up in surprise. 'But I have to say it five hundred times!'

'Who said you have to?'

'I did.'

'Well then, tell yourself you don't have to.'

'Okay.' She nodded, and went back to her pompom.

On Friday, Cath sat on a wooden bench, waiting for Warren Woodford. They were going to have a Grade 2 Curriculum Meeting, but Cath had playground duty. So they would have it outside in the sun. She was swinging her knees to play her secret game in which she imagined she could lever herself up into the sky. She'd had a skiing accident as a teenager, and they used metal joints to reconstruct her knees. Since then, she had thought of her knees as a magic-levering-hoist.

As she levered, she called 'Hey there!' crossly, to a boy who dumped a salad sandwich in the bin, 'Ho there!' sternly, to a girl who pinched another girl's nose, and 'Hey *now*' lovingly, to a boy who approached to show a grazed elbow. Once she had dealt with the elbow, she leaned back to get the big picture (mainly games of elastics today and loud conversations about a new computer pet called *Mr Valerio*, which you fed by remote control), and to think.

It's great being single! is what she thought. But something was bothering her, and she stopped swinging her knees to confront what it was.

That's what it was. The one thing she liked about having a boyfriend: *the relaxed atmosphere when you meet a new boy.* In conversations with boys who might become friends, Cath liked to joke around a bit, maybe even flirt, but she had found that boys grew wary, and found a way to mention *my girlfriend.* This left Cath feeling irritated, put in her place, and wanting to explain: *I'm not making a move, I'm just making friends.*

It was much better when she had a boyfriend herself, so she could respond with *my boyfriend*, to redress the imbalance and get on with it. Or even better, say *my boyfriend* first.

'White, no sugar, yes?'

Warren Woodford's voice was behind her, and when she turned around, it was not just his voice, it was him. His left arm was pinning a bundle of folders awkwardly to his side, and his right hand stretched to hold two mugs of coffee, long fingers looped around the handles. He was staring ferociously at the coffee mugs, as if that would keep them from spilling.

He has noticed how I take my coffee! Or maybe that's how people take their coffee, as a rule.

She helped him to sort out the papers and mugs, then he straddled the bench, and now it was strange, because she was facing forward, while *he* was looking at her shoulder. Like a set-up for a photo shoot. Or like he was riding a horse the regular way, and she was riding it side-saddle. His nose was quite long, and his mouth was a bit big for his chin.

'I hear you're studying law?' he said, as if he didn't care that his mouth was too big for his chin.

He has heard things about me!

'Not yet,' Cath explained. 'I only just enrolled. The classes start next week.'

'Huh.' He nodded to himself, as if this was just as he'd imagined. 'Why would you do that? Study law, I mean?'

'Something to do.' Cath shrugged.

'*Something to do,*' he repeated slowly. And then, in a chant: 'Something to do; someone to sue; somewhere to queue. Hmm. Queue. Forgive me.'

He put down the mug and said, 'This is terrible coffee. And another thing, I don't know if I'm going to be able to work with the Principal here. What's his name? Billson. He seems a bit, I don't know, slow?'

'I think,' said Cath, 'that he is brilliant.'

'Well, *brilliant,* yes, of course. Frank Billson, eh? A remarkable man.' He took a thoughtful sip from his coffee: 'And this is *excellent* coffee.'

So far, in five days of school, and three brief chats on the 2nd grade balcony, Warren had not said *my girlfriend* once. Cath appreciated that. Either Warren did not have a girlfriend, or he did not see the need to mention her. Either way, it was respectful of him.

Cath liked being single, but she wanted to make friends with this man, this Warren Wishful Woodford. (His eyes had a wistful, wishful look.) She wanted to make friends and to do that, she might have to flirt.

FANCY ZING

The telephone rang like a rooster that was learning how to crow.

It was Grandma. She was on the walk-around phone. 'Why, it's my Cassie! How's my Cassie?'

She was fine.

'And how was your first day of *second grade* today? Was it exciting?'

A bit.

'And who will be your friends, do you think? Still friends with that nice little boy with the funny crooked leg? What was his name? Joey? Kaminsky? Kaminska?'

No, not really. Not since first grade.

'And what about your new teacher, Cassie? Miss Murphy! Was she nice? Was she nice to you today, sweetheart?'

Uh-huh.

'And were you nice to her?'

Uh-huh.

'And were the other children nice to her too?'

A bit.

'Well now, Cassie, can I talk to your mummy? Is she around?'

Uh-huh.

Cassie took Grandma down the hall, nestled in her arm like a soft baby duckling, and into her mother's study. Her mother wasn't there. She put the phone on the spare bed and sat at her mum's desk, to read some words from the computer screen.

Then she remembered, collected Grandma, and flew her down the hall like a kite without a string. Grandma got bumped against the wall once, and then Cassie saw her mum at the kitchen sink, and said: 'Grandma's on the phone.'

'All right,' said her mum, peeling off her washing-up gloves. 'Just put her over there for me.'

Cassie put Grandma down, gently, alongside the teapot and a saucepan lid.

Picking up the phone from the kitchen bench, Cassie's mother, Fancy Zing, announced: 'Today, Mum, the sky was *very* blue.'

At which her mother cried, 'Yes! Wasn't it? A beautiful first day of term! Cassie seems excited about second grade, doesn't she? I can't wait to hear more! I bet you had trouble getting her up this morning. She likes her sleep, that Cassie, doesn't she? Listen, as madcap as it sounds, I'm thinking of making a strawberry risotto for dinner.'

They discussed the merits of strawberry risotto, but Fancy found herself drifting to a day at the seaside, years before, when she had scolded a pair of seagulls. The seagulls were stretching their necks to bully one another. 'You *stop* that!' she scolded. 'You be *nice* to each other.' Curiously, the birds had glanced up at her, startled but also repentant, and she had longed to gather them into her arms and say, 'I'm so sorry for shouting, darlings, but you really *mustn't* fight.'

'And then,' said her mother, 'there's beef stroganoff. It's a good old stand-by, isn't it?'

'It *is*,' Fancy agreed, 'but I'd better go now, Mum – I think Radcliffe's at the door.'

Radcliffe was Fancy's husband and just that moment he had called from the front porch: 'Fancy that! My Fancy is at home!' This was his standard greeting from the porch, before he even opened the front door.

'I'm in my study!' called Fancy, and she hurried down the hall from the kitchen to her study, and sat down at her desk. She took a notebook from the drawer, and at the top of the page, she wrote:

Irritating Things About My Husband.

Then she used a ruler to draw a box.

Her husband leaned through the study door and said, 'Mwah!' which was his way of kissing her hello.

'Hello!' she replied, ruling boxes furiously. She realised he was still standing there, leaning against the doorframe, and she looked up at him. 'Hello,' she said again, and tapped the side of her glasses. He nodded calmly, and wandered off down the hallway, calling, 'What have you done with Cassie?'

Fancy ignored him, and began to write inside the first box.

IRRITATING THINGS ABOUT MY HUSBAND # 1

Well, in the mornings, he has this routine where he shaves at the bathroom sink while I take my shower. He uses a Valerio *Close-Shave!* which he keeps on a toothpaste-stained holding tray, and every few moments he taps it on the side of the sink.

Tap, tap, tap, and then a little while later: *tap, tap, tap.* Through the rush of shower water, and the snap of my shampoo bottle cap, I can hear it, the regular *tap, tap, tap.* Even as I step into my towel (which he hands to me from our heated rack, without looking back from his reflection), even then he taps: *tap, tap, tap.* Then he turns the water loud to wash his face, and to wash the little whiskers down the sink.

The whole thing drives me *wild*!

On Tuesday morning, Fancy dropped Cassie at school and came back to the smug, empty house. She sighed as she wandered its hallways. Its hall*way*, she corrected herself. There was only the one.

Then she changed back into her pyjamas and sat at her desk with a cup of tea and honey-on-a-crumpet. She was planning to write a prize-winning novel, and she thought she might write it in italics. Italics, she thought, had both gumption and mystique. Also, a particular italicised sentence was floating around in her mind these days:

How is your ocean bream, my love?

She was not sure what she meant by this sentence, but found it very moving. It would presumably be spoken in a restaurant.

IRRITATING THINGS ABOUT MY HUSBAND # 2

His family once owned a Rhodesian ridgeback, which was named Fancy, which is my name, and he cannot leave that coincidence alone.

On Wednesday evening, Fancy and Radcliffe were watching TV when Cassie walked in, damp-haired from the bath, in her summer nightie.

'Here's trouble!' This was what Radcliffe said whenever Cassie walked into the room. Or even if Cassie had just gone to the bathroom at a restaurant and was coming back to the table. 'Here's trouble!'

Cassie always looked worried when he said it, a bit suspicious, which Radcliffe had not noticed. Fancy wondered when he would. She regarded her husband carefully now, and then drifted back to his marriage proposal.

The marriage proposal had taken place several years before: she was now thirty-four; back then she had been only twenty-one. It was while they were walking a muddy trail outside Blackheath in the Blue Mountains. The mud was as black as shoe polish, and Fancy's head was filled with vaguely ominous yet sensual thoughts.

Radcliffe seemed to be concentrating on photography. He did not have a camera with him, but he kept backing up carefully from wild flowers or muddy twigs, squaring his thumbs and index fingers, squinting through the square and saying, 'Click!'

After one such photograph, he dropped his hands to his side, abruptly, and announced in an ordinary voice: 'I would like to marry you, Fancy.'

'Would you?' Fancy was surprised, even doubtful.

'I would like to marry you,' he confirmed. 'And everything about you.'

I would like to marry you, and everything about you.

Fancy drifted back to her own living room, and picked up the remote control to zip through the ads. They were watching a taped episode of *Law & Order*. But she realised as she zipped that the show was over. She had missed the end and was zipping into a whole new program. Radcliffe and Cassie sat quietly, pretending that nothing odd was happening.

'Well!' said Fancy, pressing STOP on the remote.

'No!' cried Cassie, frantically. 'Don't say "*well!*" like that! I don't like it when you say it that way!'

'How would you like me to say it?' asked Fancy, mildly. 'Well? *Well?* Well!!' She tried out different pronunciations. 'You choose, Cass.'

'I don't want you to say it at all,' explained Cassie. 'It means you want me to go to bed.'

'Oh ho!' Radcliffe swivelled around on his bottom. He was sitting on the floor cross-legged. 'Casso-tobacco suffers from clinophobia, does she?'

'What?'

Radcliffe grinned at his daughter.

'Clinophobia,' whispered Cassie, staring. Then she turned to her mother and explained: 'Just say it in a way that doesn't sound so happy, okay?'

'All right, darling, say goodnight to your father.'

'My little clinophobic!' Radcliffe gave Cassie a hug.

'It's a fear of going to bed,' Radcliffe confided later, leaning into Fancy's study.

'I'm trying to work, Radcliffe,' Fancy said coldly.

IRRITATING THINGS ABOUT MY HUSBAND # 3

During sex, he talks in this low, husky voice, which is nothing like his own. More like somebody hiding in the pantry, and phoning the police while a robbery takes place.

He uses the voice to say things like *do it to me, baby*, which is acceptable, though not to my taste. But he *also* uses it for ordinary things, such as: *Just move your leg slightly, honey? You're pinching my testicles?*

I am always clearing my throat, during sex, to indicate that he should clear his.

Fancy was a writer of erotic fiction. Of course, she was also planning to write a prize-winning novel: erotic fiction was her butter knife; the novel would be her tomahawk.

At fourteen, she had worked part-time in a hardware store and she still remembered fondly the counting down of change.

'Twenty dollars? Thanks. So, that's eleven, that's thirteen, that's fifteen, and *that's* twenty. Would you like a bag with that?'

No thanks, the men always said. But sometimes she gave them no choice, putting their screwdrivers straight into plastic bags. They never used the handles when she did that, grabbing the bag around the neck as if it were a hen.

On Thursday morning, Fancy felt that there could be nothing wrong with driving your daughter to school in your pyjamas. Also, nothing wrong with driving your daughter to school and quickly jumping out of the car on the way home to dump two garbage bags of second-hand clothes into the St Vincent de Paul blue bin. Nothing wrong with that at all!

Except that the man next door was having breakfast on his front porch as she emerged in her pyjamas, shouting: 'CASSIE! GET A MOVE ON! WE ARE *VERY VERY* LATE,' and spilling worn-out clothes from two garbage bags hopelessly clutched under her arms.

He was one of those dull Canadians, the man next door, the kind who speak slowly and with a polite, mild amusement about everything.

'Got your hands full there,' he declared from his porch, with his knife and fork poised over his bacon, and that little smirk of his. Their houses were very close.

'Yes!' Fancy agreed, and then she had to pause, for the sake of politeness, before shouting at Cassie again.

The neighbour returned to his bacon and pancakes – *bacon and pancakes!* – and Cassie emerged from the hallway with a comb and scrunchie hanging from her mouth, the car-keys looped around her finger, her hair falling into her face, dragging an enormous garbage bag behind her.

'What on *earth* are you – Cassie, darling, that's the bag of books! We're not bringing that one.'

Cassie took the comb and scrunchie from her mouth. 'Why not?'

'Darling, we're giving that one to the school fete, not to St Vincent de Paul. But *thank* you, that must have been *very* heavy on the stairs.'

Cassie raised her eyebrows and turned to drag the bag back inside.

'No!' Fancy panicked. 'Just leave it by the door there. No need to take it back upstairs.'

'Okay.'

'Have you got your lunch?'

'What is it?'

'It's peanut butter. On the second shelf of the fridge; run back in and get it, quick.'

'*Peanut butter!*' shouted Cassie, and stamped her foot. She had loved peanut butter yesterday, but sometimes her taste took an unexpected swerve.

'In Newfoundland,' said the Canadian from his porch, 'the kids swap lobster sandwiches for peanut butter.'

Cassie stared at him.

'Gosh!' Fancy said, politely.

'That's how common lobster is,' confirmed the Canadian, 'in Newfoundland.'

'Cassie,' Fancy said after an agonising pause for politeness, 'quick, honey, go and get your lunch.'

The news was already starting its triumphant drumbeat as they pulled into the bus zone at Cassie's school. 'Vagina, vagina, vagina,' said Cassie, counting on her fingers. 'Uh-oh.' She pointed at the radio. 'The news is on.'

'Here –' Fancy craned into the rear-view mirror, and brushed Cassie's hair behind her ears. 'Pass me the pen from the glove box. I think I'd better write you a note.'

Dear Ms Murphy,

Please excuse my daughter, Cassie Zing-Mereweather (better known as Cassie Zing – her choice!), for being late today.
I had to take some second-hand clothes to St Vincent de Paul.

Yours sincerely and VERY best wishes!
Fancy Zing

On Friday night, Radcliffe and Fancy drove to a Zing Family Secret Meeting. Cassie was in the back seat with her first week of 2nd grade piled all around her.

'They are going to be *amazed* about this, aren't they, Mum?'

Cassie leaned forward in her middle seatbelt and waved a butterfly painting around in front of them, blocking Radcliffe's view of the road for a moment.

'They sure are!' agreed Fancy.

'For Christ's sakes!' snapped Radcliffe, at the same time.

This threw Cassie back into her seatbelt for a moment. Then she recovered. 'First I'm going to show my Mentals book with the gold star, next I'm going to show my pompom, *then* my painting and then – no, *wait* –'

'We must be just about due to have the Samsons and Bellamys for dinner, eh?' Radcliffe said to Fancy, tapping on the steering wheel. He had the habit of talking over Cassie when he found her boring.

'Yes,' she agreed. 'But Cassie's birthday's coming up soon.'

'Well then, sixth I'm going to sing and – did you say something about my birthday, Mum?'

'Hey Cass-kid.' Radcliffe glanced in the rear-view mirror at Cassie. 'Let's hope you don't suffer from alektorophobia, eh?'

There was silence from the back seat for a moment. 'Pardon?'

'Alektorophobia.'

'Is it something for my birthday?'

Radcliffe chuckled. He pulled up at a red light, and Cassie sat quietly, waiting.

'It's a fear of chickens,' Radcliffe explained to Fancy, in a low voice. 'Alektorophobia. A fear of chickens. We'll probably have roast chicken for dinner tonight, eh?'

'Well, tell Cassie then! Cassie, honey, don't worry about Dad, okay? He's just being silly.'

'Leave it,' said Radcliffe, accelerating off as the light turned green. 'This is how she learns.'

'Learns what!'

'Electra,' murmured Cassie from the back seat. 'Alektro? Electro.'

Fancy felt as if a mosquito had just bitten her chin. She decided to calm herself: drift to the seaside, soothe the angry seagulls, drift, Fancy!, drift!

Radcliffe turned on the radio.

MARBIE ZING

After midnight, the apartment waited, still in the moonlight and the heat. It shifted slightly, trying to find a cooler position. A moth touched a wing on the front porch light and the apartment cleared its throat sharply.

Inside, the apartment was a sleepy confusion of boxes, paint tins, sandpaper, buckets, and bananas. A wooden ladder, flat on its stomach, stretched the length of the hallway.

A young woman, perhaps twenty-eight years old, emerged from a bedroom at the end of the hall. She stepped over the rungs of the ladder, one careful rung at a time, seeming to float as she did so, in a mist of long hair and white nightie. When she reached the entrance to the living room, she paused. There was a crocus-shaped scar on her forehead.

The moonlight followed, intrigued, as the young woman drifted to the kitchen.

Next, a young man stepped into the hallway. He was ruffle-haired, sleepy-eyed and dressed in nothing but boxer shorts. He too paused at the entrance to the living room but this was to yawn and stretch. The muscles of his arms and his chest rippled just as if they had been put into place, specifically, for this stretch. He disappeared into the kitchen.

When he emerged he had his arm through the elbow of the woman and was speaking to her, gently, 'No, Marbie, there's *no* green turtle in the kitchen.'

The woman gazed up at him, and he nodded encouragingly, 'Okay? Okay now? Ready to go back to bed?' But the woman was looking past his face to the wall on the far side of the room.

'I can *not* believe it,' she murmured. 'Again! How many nights is this?'

'What?' said the man, looking around uneasily. 'Are you awake?'

'Watch your eyes, Vernon,' she ordered. 'I'll take care of this.' She marched across the room, muttering, 'Oh, you think you can just drop by, do you? Little alien starships! Putting up your elevator shafts on *our* –' She stopped as she reached the wall, and stared at its smooth pale surface.

'It was just here –' She turned back to her boyfriend, who was waiting patiently.

'Yes?' he prompted. 'The elevator?'

'Hmm,' she said slowly, 'there *is* no elevator shaft.'

'Are you awake now?' said the man.

'Sorry,' said the woman.

'That's okay.'

They both stood still in the moonlight.

'It's hot, isn't it?' said the woman, after a moment. 'I wonder if we should –'

'It depends on whether Listen is awake,' agreed the man, peering into the hallway.

'Yes.' The woman raised her voice slightly. 'I wonder if she *is* awake?'

'COULD SHE BE AWAKE?' boomed the man.

'I HOPE WE HAVEN'T WOKEN HER!' shouted the woman.

They both paused, hopefully.

At last, a twelve-year-old girl appeared at the entrance to the living room, blinking into the darkness.

'Oh no!' cried the woman. 'We didn't wake you did we, Listen?'

'It's hot, isn't it?' said the girl.

'Exactly,' said the man.

A few moments later, all three walked out of the apartment door to the porch, down the driveway, and onto the street. They walked beneath the street lights and the charcoal starry sky, their bare feet silent on the asphalt. The man brushed a mosquito from the woman's shoulder. The girl kicked her toe, hopped for a few steps, and then recovered completely.

After ten or fifteen minutes, they passed a row of suburban houses, each with a small front lawn. One particular inoffensive blond-brick house caused all three to crouch and scurry past.

Just beyond the inoffensive house, the small front lawns gave way to a tall dark hedge. Set into the hedge was a wrought iron gate, which carried a black and white sign:

BELLBIRD HIGH SCHOOL
To strive itself is to succeed.
Please Close the Gate.

The woman looked up and down the street, and then nodded to the others. All three climbed over the gate.

On the dark front lawn of the school, they began to run. They ran through a courtyard and a car park. They ran across a netball court, and along the stone walls of various school buildings. Occasional security lights flickered.

At the back of the school was a sloping lawn, which fell into patches of long grass and tangled bush. A narrow dirt path wound through this bush, and ended at a gate. They climbed this gate, and then they stopped.

They were standing at the edge of a swimming pool. Across the pool was a bank of wooden benches; alongside the benches, several neat piles of yellow boards, each stamped in fluorescent white: 'Training Device

Do Not Remove'.

A signboard stood on an easel beside them:

SWIMMING POOL RULES
• NO RUNNING
• NO JUMPING
• NO BOMBING
• NO SPLASHING
• *NO SWIMMING WITHOUT TEACHER*
  SUPERVISION (MEMBERS OF SENIOR SWIM
  TEAM EXCEPTED)

Without a word, all three dived in.

The woman in the pool was Marbie Zing. The man was her boyfriend, Vernon. The twelve-year-old girl, floating on her back and gazing at the stars, was Vernon's little sister, Listen. The three of them had just moved in together.

Later that night, Marbie and Vernon lay sleepily in bed, wet hair tangled on their pillows, hearts still pounding from the midnight swim. Marbie said to Vernon, 'I think I'll go check on the pot plants.'

Vernon rolled over and gazed at her. 'You're awake?' he said.

'I'm awake,' she confirmed.

'Stop being so beautiful,' he said, and he fell asleep.

Meanwhile, Listen Taylor was down the hall, sitting on the floorboards by her bed. Her nightie had dried in the breeze on the walk home, but her hair spilled occasional water drops down her neck.

It was 3 am, but she was wide awake and she was thinking about her name. 'Listen Taylor,' she said, and then in its place she tried: '*Listen Zing*'. Only that was a question: *Listen Zing?* Because she was considering: *Am I now a Zing?*

If you and your brother move in with a Zing, go shopping with a Zing, paint the walls with a Zing, go swimming in the middle of the night with a Zing, go along with a Zing to Zing Family Secret Meetings each week – do you, eventually, become a Zing yourself?

Maybe.

To be fair, only Vernon knew the Secret – Marbie had told him when they bought the apartment together a month ago. So only Vernon went *inside* the garden shed for the Zing Family Secret Meetings. Listen stayed in Grandma Zing's house and watched movies with little Cassie.

Also, and more importantly, the name *Listen* worked better with *Taylor*. The Taylor part relaxed the 'Listen', or gave it an approving tick. 'What's your name?' 'Listen Taylor.' 'Oh. Okay. Well, hi.'

'What's your name?' 'Listen Zing.' The stranger, already skating on Listen, would whack her head hard against the Zing. 'It's *what*?'

You had to think about these things when you were about to start high school next week.

Primary school had already gone back for the year – the Zings were excited about Cassie starting 2nd grade that day – but Listen had another week of holidays. *In just one week,* she thought, *it will all be different.*

But it was already different: she and her brother had moved out of the caravan and into an apartment with a Zing.

She sat up to look around at the boxes. It was not possible to open the boxes because they were so well taped you needed scissors or a knife to get through. Meanwhile, the scissors and knives were packaged up inside the boxes.

Listen wondered which box had her new school uniform inside. It would be funny if they still hadn't figured out how to unpack by next week. Vernon would have to write a note to the school:

To whom it may concern.

We are very sorry but Listen Taylor will not be able to attend Year 7 this year. Her uniform is stuck in a box.

Fondly,
Her big brother,
Vernon
XXX

It was just as Listen was smiling sleepily to herself, at this idea, that she noticed the book. It was sitting on top of a box.

It was a flimsy book, lime green with huge white letters on the cover: 'SPELL BOOK'. It looked like one of those early school workbooks, in which you have to do things like draw diagonal lines between COLD and HOT, or BUSY and CALM. But when she opened the first page of the book, that's not what it was at all.

Congratulations! You have found this Spell Book!
Hooray for you!

Listen gave the book a skeptical look and noticed, when she did, way down at the bottom of the page, a disclaimer:

Disclaimer

This Spell Book will only work if you follow the instructions VERY CAREFULLY. For example, you may only turn a page when we say you can. If you skip ahead, it WILL NOT WORK. Right now, you have to put the book under your pillow. You can only turn the page on Wednesday, at 5 pm.

At that moment, Listen jumped because Marbie was knocking on her window and calling, 'Listen? Can you let me in?'

•

Marbie Zing was the kind of person who wandered outside in the middle of the night to check on pot plants, forgetting to bring her keys. Marbie also was the kind of person who walked around with this sentence in her head all the time:

It was a decision she would regret for the rest of her life.

Because she was so excited by her good luck in meeting Vernon and his little sister Listen, she feared she would take one tiny wrong step and lose them.

For example: Let's say Marbie is running late for work and she opens her wardrobe and sees her short blue dress hanging alongside her long floral skirt. Which one should she wear? Hurriedly, she chooses the long skirt. *It was a decision she would regret for the rest of her life* – because later! On her way to work? The skirt gets tangled in her sandals and trips her up! And she breaks her ankle! And she has to go to hospital! And Vernon comes to visit with flowers for her, and the nurse says to Vernon, 'What lovely daffodils,' and he says, 'Actually, they're tulips,' and then their eyes meet, and they *fall in love, and Vernon leaves Marbie for the nurse.*

The next day, Tuesday, running late for work, Marbie chose her long floral skirt (*it was a decision she would regret for the rest of her life*), and then with a shiver she replaced it and picked the blue dress.

'Vernon,' she said, waking him with a kiss on his bare shoulder, 'Vernon, what would you think of a woman who didn't know the difference between daffodils and tulips?'

Vernon opened his eyes and said: '*There is no such woman.*'

Marbie worked in insurance, third party recoveries, and along with her colleagues, played car crash on the edge of her desk. Second party car enters roundabout *here*, third party car is reversing *here*, family of elephants distracts attention *here* (these doughnuts are the family of elephants), *our* car heads straight through the middle and boom! Little plastic people go zipping through the air.

She read their explanations for their sorry little smashes.

'I sneezed and lost control and hit a fence.'

'I sneezed, hit a pothole and ran into a tree.'

'I sneezed and collided with the rear end of an elephant.'

She sent out the mercantiles to bang their doors at midnight (mercantile agents never got a cent); she smacked them with Intentions to Sue. She hushed angry customers and *redirected* hostility: 'Don't speak to me like that, please . . . I'm hanging up now. I'm just about to hang up the phone.'

On Tuesday evening, they ate takeaway Thai, sitting on boxes on the living room floor. Then Vernon found the stereo, and Listen taught Marbie how to dance the modern way while Vernon made them chocolate bananas for dessert. Listen had her hair pulled back from her forehead and tied into a single, high-swinging plait. She wore her T-shirt and sweat pants, and she was a patient and dexterous dancing teacher.

Later that evening, Marbie called goodnight to Listen from her bedroom door, and Listen looked up from her pillow with sleepy eyes, her hair about her shoulders now, the collar of her nightie looking frayed, and Marbie went into the room, and sat down on the edge of the bed like a mother.

Marbie wrote a Letter to the Editor inside her head as she fell asleep that night.

Sir:

I am writing with respect to my boyfriend. He has a younger sister, Listen, and the three of us, I should explain, live together.

To be frank, it is difficult to capture (with words) the magic of the Taylor siblings: their eyes are like maple syrup! They are very quiet, observing the world with their maple syrup eyes, but now and then they chatter, like unexpected fountains. Also, they are musical: Vernon sings along with every single song on the radio, no matter the musical genre, and Listen likes to dance wherever she goes.

Furthermore — and this is the point of my letter — Vernon is an extraordinary lover. When he makes love to me, I find myself in rooms filled with tiny, vibrant empires. Orgasms come at me, really, from every direction.

Yours sincerely,
Marbie Zing

Marbie Zing was a slippery person. In restaurants, serviettes slid from her lap to the floor. Hairclips never stayed in her hair, they slipped to her shoulders where they perched like silver butterflies. And her shoes were always falling from her feet. (It was because of this that she was first — aged six and a quarter — stung, on her toe, by a bee. 'You ran right out of your thongs,' scolded her mother, who was always cranky when they hurt themselves.)

On Wednesday morning, running late for work, Marbie tripped out of one of her high-heels. A bicycle courier had to hold the lift door open while she reached a stockinged foot back to collect it.

Later that morning, boiling the kettle for her ginger tea, Marbie watched the kettle (it always boiled, even though she watched) through narrow, sultry eyes as it bubbled quietly to itself. She watched as it gathered its excitement about it, and then, in particular, she watched as the bubbling reached the quiet point: the point at which the kettle seemed to disappear deep within itself. After that moment of stillness, there was the explosion of boiling and then the click! as it turned itself off. *I know just how you feel,* thought Marbie.

It turned out to be an excellent, efficient, document-stamping sort of a day. She sipped from her tea, used the 'DRAFT' stamp, and the 'PRIVATE AND CONFIDENTIAL' stamp, and then she made photocopies and added the 'COPY' stamp. She did this all day with occasional breaks to chat to the others about how much she enjoyed stamping documents (they thought she was being ironic, and laughed), and when she looked at her watch it was almost five o'clock.

She phoned Listen to fill in the last five minutes.

Obligingly, Listen chatted to her, explaining in detail how she felt about starting high school next week. She thought there would be a *fundamental shift in the universe* but her old friends, Donna Turnbull and them from Primary, had made an *eternal pact* to stay friends to keep the universe stable.

'Hey,' said Listen, interrupting her own philosophising, 'What time is it, Marbie?'

'It's five! It's the end of the day!'

'Gotta go,' said Listen. 'Gotta go do something.' And she hung up the phone.

Hooray for you! You waited until 5 pm on Wednesday! You can clearly follow rules, and that's just what you need to be able to do, because otherwise *this Spell Book won't work*!

Here are the rules:

1. You have to do *every single* Spell in the book, one at a time. You can't skip ahead!
2. Usually, you won't even know if a Spell has worked or not! But *never mind*! Trust us! It *has*.

You can turn the page now.

Okay!

Now put the Spell Book *back underneath your pillow* and DON'T GET IT OUT AGAIN until 4 PM this FRIDAY.

YOU WILL THEN BE ABLE TO DO THE FIRST SPELL!!!

(Note: take great care not to say the word '*walnut*'
from now until then.)

•

On Thursday morning, running late for work, Marbie almost stepped
into the path of a semitrailer. A pencil-seller shouted a warning just in
time.

Later that day, she phoned Vernon at the Banana Bar, to tell him
about it. She liked to phone Vernon at work, especially when he was
busy, surrounded by customers. It was then that his voice took on the
cool restrained edge that it had way back when she first met him.

Actually, when she first met him, his voice had been jocular, like
someone playing tennis. They had met in a hotel lift in Melbourne, and
had spent the next few days drinking coffee together, while Listen
danced around their table.

It was not until they were all back home in Sydney that he began to
telephone.

He carved off an edge of his voice for the phone calls, making it cool
and restrained, which caused her to press her forehead into the wall,
hushing even her breath so she could hear.

'Are you there?' he would say, in his nonchalant voice.

'Uh-huh.' And then she would fall silent, at once, so that his voice
would go on in that way.

On Friday, Marbie met the aeronautical engineer.

Tabitha (Marbie's supervisor) had arranged for an aeronautical engineer to visit the small boardroom, the one with the views of Darling
Harbour and the bowls of mints on the sideboard. He was there to
demonstrate the tendencies of airborne cars.

They were always dealing with airborne cars in their work. Cars
seemed to leave the ground at the slightest suggestion: a little tap from
a semitrailer; the bark of a dog on the side of the road. One claimant
even said that her car took flight when she changed the radio station.

Marbie and her colleagues tended to be dubious about these claims, but *perhaps*, they often said, *we are wrong.*

Fridays at work, everyone was cocky and buoyant, saying cheerful things with their heads tilted sideways. The aeronautical engineer arrived with his swinging paisley tie and his plump, petal-pink face, and right away he recognised their Friday mood. He put both hands on his almost bald head (which was actually covered in very slight spikes) and said: 'To begin. The aeroplane!' Then he asked for a page from Marbie's notepad and showed them how to make a paper plane.

They spent the afternoon making paper planes, paper fans or paper swans, and drinking all the wine from the small boardroom fridge, while the aeronautical engineer wandered around with his hands behind his back. He praised Marbie's fan, exuberantly.

Toni got the key to the big boardroom, and came back with seven half-bottles of white wine, and the aeronautical engineer praised her, which made Marbie slightly jealous, so she showed him the paper turtle she'd been working on. He didn't understand what it was, but still praised it. Then Rhamie interrupted with a handful of toy cars, and the aeronautical engineer remembered why he was there and made them throw the toys at one another to demonstrate the tendencies of airborne cars.

It was wonderful.

At four o'clock, everyone decided they had done enough work for the day, and they invited the aeronautical engineer to join them at the Night Owl Pub for their Friday drinks. He said he had to run and move his car because he had just that moment remembered it was in a one-hour parking spot! *Oh no*, they cried, *you could have parked in our building!* They wanted him to park in the building now, but he wondered if there was any point, as he had a meeting in Chatswood and maybe didn't even have time to have a drink? But he said he'd try to join them for five minutes or so, once he had moved his car.

Marbie ran to phone Vernon at the Banana Bar and tell him she was having a drink but would be back in time for the Zing Family Secret Meeting.

'Don't get hit by a semitrailer on your way,' instructed Vernon.

'Okay,' agreed Marbie. 'Where's Listen?'

'Well,' said Vernon, 'I suppose she'd be at home.'

•

HELLO AGAIN! YOU DID IT! IT'S 4 PM ON
FRIDAY!

You can go ahead and do the First Spell now. The
First Spell is simple. You probably already know this
one, but you still have to do it, I'm afraid. You know
what I'm talking about?

The Spell To Make Someone Decide To Take A Taxi.

Of course! That old favourite. You know the drill.
Take two lemons and cut them in half, take five
bananas and peel them. Fill up the bathtub with
lukewarm water, toss in your lemons and banana
peels. WAIT UNTIL 5 O'CLOCK AND THEN say
the magic words – 'Bob's your uncle' – and *Bob's your
uncle!* The Spell is done.

Now put the Spell Book back under your pillow.
Don't turn the page until Thursday week!

•

At the Night Owl Pub they were all a little depressed because the aeronautical engineer had not shown up. They had made aeroplanes out of
beer-damp coasters and wanted to show him. And now Tabitha and Toni
had to go to their step class, and Abi and Rhamie had their husbands
waiting, so Marbie said goodbye, and she would just stay and finish her
beer and take care of their coaster aeroplanes, and then she'd go home.

'You've all gone home!' It was the aeronautical engineer. Standing beside her in the Night Owl Pub.

'Have *I* gone home?' said Marbie, rhetorically.

'May I?'

He was carrying half a beer and tilting his chin at the seat opposite.

'Of course.'

He sat down and nodded to himself, as if agreeing with a thought.

'My car got towed,' he said sadly. 'That's why I was late. So now I'll have to take the train to my meeting. And look at this, I've missed everybody.'

He looked around sadly at the empty beer glasses and soggy aeroplanes.

'Am I not *somebody*?' said Marbie.

'What time is it?' he asked.

'Five o'clock.'

'So late!' cried the aeronautical engineer. 'I've got to *run*!'

But he moved his chair closer, and smiled.

CATH MURPHY

In the early light of a birthday once when she was small, Cath woke to the shapes of presents huddled by her bed. One was a short-fat-barrel-shaped present, wrapped in bright pink paper.

I know what that is. She sat up from her pillow with a whisk of excitement. *That's a pair of rollerblades!*

Only rollerblades would come in short-fat-barrel-shaped presents like that. Under the pink wrapping, there would be a barrel. The barrel would be silver. She would prise the lid open with her fingers and inside, wrapped in bubble-paper: sleek black rollerblades.

Cath had never tried rollerblading before, so she lay in bed thinking about how she could learn. On the front lawn first. Maybe her father would mow the lawn, leaving a trail of grass clippings, so she could build grass castles to fall on?

Opening her presents on the verandah that morning, Cath saved the rollerblade present until last. Her father ate his bran flakes, and her mother peeled an orange with her fingers, wiping her sticky hands now and then on a roll of paper towel. They watched while Cath opened each present until there was nothing but the rollerblades left. All the time, she had been tempering her reactions, conserving energy for this particular gift. Now she regarded its pink wrapping. What would she do when she saw the rollerblades? She would let out a high-pierced squeal. She would shout: 'NO WAY!' She would jump to her feet and dance.

She felt intensely nervous as she opened the wrapping. Then the paper fell away.

It was not rollerblades. It was not even a silver barrel.

It was a wastepaper basket, with pink plastic butterflies sewn into the straw.

Cath held the basket for a moment. It was shaped like a barrel.

'Butterflies,' she whispered. She had one of those moments of disso-ciation: *can this be happening? Am I really here? Is it a dream?*

Then she rallied: 'Butterflies! Hey, Mummy, you know how I've got birds on my curtains? You know what's going to happen? The birds are going to fly off the curtains and play with the butterflies on my new basket!'

Her parents laughed happily.

Cath joined them at the table feeling shaky at the knees. 'Okay there?' said her father. 'You look kind of white.'

Her mother explained that it was just the excitement.

Cath sat quietly, feeling strange and wise. She had been tested. She had passed. For here was an important lesson in life, and one she had never suspected:

sometimes you get a bad surprise, but you have to act calm and un-amazed.

●

The first few weeks of the school year seemed to Cath to be stage-lit. She was always shading her eyes from the sun, blending her squint into a smile. Often, she threw back her head in laughter; or tilted her chin as if struck by an inspired thought. She smiled warmly or ironically at children, and she told quick quirky stories to Lenny and Suzanne, who obliged her by shrieking, 'Cath! Cut it *out*!'

While they hooted – or while she shaded her eyes or tilted her chin, opened her car door or adjusted her rear-vision mirror – Cath would glance around quickly, and sometimes, there he would be:

Warren Woodford.

Watching her.

He often had a single eyebrow raised.

In the first few weeks of the school year, also, Cath and Warren became friends. This was only natural – they were the 2nd grade teachers and had to hold curriculum meetings after school. When they held their meetings, one or the other of them would run across the highway in the heat to bring back iced café lattes. Then they would have a break and Warren would ask Cath's advice about difficult children. This was his first year of teaching, whereas it was her third, so she had wisdom to share. He also liked to hear about her part-time law classes, and she would memorise the best cases to describe to him. As she talked, he would gasp slightly at surprising facts, and ask innocent questions, and she would explain the law to him, feeling articulate and smart. It was good revision too, reciting the facts of cases like that.

Meanwhile, Warren quickly gained the reputation, among teachers, as a charming and light-hearted young man, quick to give an inquisitive look whenever someone said something silly. 'He cuts through the crap,' Lenny declared to Cath, and she nodded, feeling proud to be his friend.

Among children, Warren had a reputation as VERY funny, and you never know what he's going to do next, and sometimes he doesn't make sense, but he's nice if you hurt yourself.

It was now acknowledged by Lenny and Suzanne that, so far as information was concerned, Warren Woodford belonged to Cath. 'Hey, did Warren do any acting work before he became a teacher?' Lenny might say. 'He's so funny with that face of his at staff meetings!' And Cath would explain: 'No, he only did two years of drama training – then he transferred straight into Education.' 'How come?' Suzanne would ask, humbly.

'Well, one day,' Cath explained, 'he was doing this practical drama exercise with a bunch of kids, and he realised he just loved working with them, and he thought: *what if I could do MORE than entertain them?*'

'Huh,' Lenny and Suzanne would say, impressed, and then move on to other topics.

Sometimes, Cath would watch their faces, waiting for some hint that they expected romance between herself and Warren. Had they not noticed how he *watched* her? Did they not think she was *good enough* for him?

But there was never even a suggestion; instead, the three talked about the romance between Lenny and Frank Billson (School Principal). Suzanne liked to suggest new hair colours for Lenny, to help the relationship along, and was pushing for a rich dark red to bring out Lenny's cheekbones, but Lenny thought blonde with candy lipstick. Sometimes, Cath thought wistfully: *shall I die of boredom?* But she was pleased for Lenny.

The late afternoons were sultry and hot, and, once all the other teachers had gone, Cath and Warren would sigh in the heat of the staffroom, leaning forward over their work, elbows sliding out in either direction so their chins were low above the table. They would flick sweat from their foreheads, and open all the windows. Or agree that the windows were only letting in hot air, and close them.

Once, Warren slid an ice-cube along the back of Cath's neck to cool her down.

During school days, they held joint singing or arts-and-crafts lessons, with all of 2nd grade in a circle on Assembly Hall floor. Warren had a surprisingly deep voice when he sang, which made the children stare and sometimes giggle.

One brightly lit Thursday, Cath sat on the edge of her desk in her classroom, swinging her legs and looking around at the room full of small, fidgeting people. *I'm pretty happy, you know*, she thought. She was the Queen of Her Own Life! She had so many little kingdoms! Her classroom, the staffroom, her car, her apartment! And in between the kingdoms, she went to law classes, or had iced café lattes with friends.

'Let's talk about the *environment*,' she said to her class, happily. 'Anybody here know what the environment is?'

They all nodded, and many said, 'Yeah.' Anthony McMasters said, contemptuously, 'The *enviroh-ment*?!' and put his fingers in his ears.

'Take your fingers out of your ears, Anthony.'

Lucinda Coulton said, 'I know, Mssssss Murphy, because do you know why? My dad's a biological engineer.'

'Hands up, Lucinda,' chided Cath. 'Is he *really*?'

Marcus Ellison said, 'My dad's an astronaut.'

'He is *not*.' Cassie Zing turned to Marcus in a fury.

'You don't have to put both hands in the air,' Cath explained to Lucinda.

'My dad *is* an astronaut. He already went to Venus, okay for now?'

Cassie Zing lifted the lid of her desk and slammed it down hard. The slam ruffled her hair and surprised her eyes.

'We'll do careers then, shall we?' Cath said smoothly, imagining her voice through the wall between the classrooms, imagining how gentle and sensible it might sound. 'We've had biological engineers and we've had astronauts. Anybody know another career?'

While the children listed careers for her, against a background of Cassie slamming her desk-lid, Cath imagined a knock on the classroom door. She imagined Mr Woodford leaning into the room, and bumping his head on the doorframe (he was that tall). 'Ouch!' he would say, quietly to himself. Then: 'Word with you for a moment, Ms Murphy?' She would nod and then explain to her class: 'Keep it down, guys? I won't be a moment,' in a firm yet casual voice. Then she would sidestep to the door, where she would look up at Warren with her short, smart hair, and say, 'Hi.'

What would he say in reply?

Cassie Zing put her desk-lid down and announced: 'My mum is a writer of erotic fiction.'

'Anthony,' said Cath, 'take your fingers out of your nose.'

Driving home, Cath wondered again why Lenny and Suzanne never mentioned Warren as a potential boyfriend for her. Did they not realise how good-looking he was? Did they not see that he was sexy?

Or were they, like her, simply waiting? Perhaps they sensed that this would be romance of a different kind – romance so fine it was as fragile as crystal, romance unfurling delicately, like a silken bud, or a cygnet hatching. It had to be watched through binoculars with steadiest hands.

Cath changed gears, and her hand seemed to tremble on the gearstick. Perhaps, when she was not looking, Lenny and Suzanne glanced at one another, and held the glance a moment, silent and steady, glad for their young friend, Cath.

At home that night, Cath phoned her mother across the country and her mother said, '*Darling!*' and wept a little. It was a recent habit, this weeping, and must have been hormonal. After all, it was not her but her parents who had moved interstate, leaving Cath with no home, no Mum, no Dad, no my-room-become-sewing-room, no Sunday baked dinner, no cappuccino-Sunday-afternoons.

After her mother had wept, she called: 'Dad! It's Cath! Pick up!'

Cath's parents were named 'Mum' and 'Dad', even when she was not around. She had paint-stripped their names, and now they existed only so long as she herself existed. *Too much power for one girl to have*, she sometimes decided, grimly.

'I was just reading that the child you love best is the one who is far away,' said Mum. 'And aren't you far away, Cath, darling?'

'Yes,' agreed Cath. 'So you love me best.'

Cath was the only one. There were no siblings. But anyway.

'Cath, you all right, love? How goes the new school year? Any little monsters in your class?'

That was Dad on the extension, his voice a layer closer than Mum's.

'Yes,' said Mum. 'Yes, I also read that the child you love best is the one who is ill.'

'What's that?' said Dad.

'Well, I'm perfectly healthy, so where does that leave us?'

'Who knows!'

'Breaking any hearts over there?' said Dad.

'Any young men on the horizon?' agreed Mum, returning abruptly to her more familiar, businesslike voice.

Breaking any hearts was funny. Cath got her own heart broken so often it was just about a write-off. But she always considered the horizon, obediently, for her parents, and there he was on the edge of a sunset sky: Warren Wishful Woodford, a little self-conscious, damp with drops of ocean mist.

'No,' she explained. 'Not really.'

She shook the horizon gently, tipping him off the edge. Let him climb back up in his own time.

•

'Hey, Cath,' whispered Warren, sneaking into the Assembly Hall and sitting down beside her, late on Monday morning. Mr Billson was giving a lecture on punctuality, so a lot of kids pointed at Warren and said: 'WAH – HAH!'

'Hi,' she murmured. 'How was your weekend?'

'Oh, fine, fine. Kind of a strain, you know? Eh, cut it out,' sternly, to some kids who would not stop pointing and trying to get the Principal's attention.

'Kind of a strain?'

He nodded, distracted, and she raised her eyebrows, watching him. His shirt was already patched with sweat: he must have run from his car to the Assembly Hall. He must be in some kind of trouble – *kind of a strain* – and mentioning it like that, he must want to talk. She would find a gentle way to ask him later.

For now, she looked down at the folder of papers on her lap; at Monday assemblies, she always pretended to be making notes of what Billson was saying, but in fact she was catching up on class records. She was ticking through last week's lesson plan when she came across this word: *Environment*.

She put a tick beside it. Then she thought, hmm, and changed it to: ½ √, before writing at the end of the list: *Careers*: ½ √.

'Did you know,' she whispered to Warren softly, 'that Cassie Zing's mother writes erotic fiction?'

'As you do,' agreed Warren, nodding.

'And Marcus Ellison's dad is an *astronaut*.'

Now his nod became a slow, impressed tilt: 'An *astronaut*?' He looked at Cath admiringly, as if she were the astronaut.

She returned to her class plan, and flipped the page. This week she was going to start reading *The Lion, the Witch and the Wardrobe* to the class, and they would build their own wardrobe, and talk about the worlds you might reach through the wardrobe door. Let's say the worlds included a variety of environments: ocean, canyon, *etc*; and let's say each world contained various occupations: sailor, orthodontist, *etc* – well then! She could then change the ½ √s to √s.

At that moment, Warren leaned slightly into her shoulder, took the pen from her hand, turned a page in her notebook and wrote:

THIS FRIDAY, THE CAROTID STICKS WILL BE PLAYING AT THE BORROWED CAT.

(1) Does Cath like the Carotid Sticks:
    (a) Yes   ◯
    (b) No   ◯
    (c) Do not know them   ◯

(2) Will Cath come along with Warren to see the Carotid Sticks:
    (a) Yes   ◯
    (b) No   ◯
    (c) Do not know him   ◯

She leaned forward and marked the boxes 'yes' and 'yes'. Warren studied her answers, and then he put a √ alongside each 'yes'. Underneath, he wrote the word: *Excellent.*

The next day, Tuesday, wandering her classroom aisles like a queen, Cath remembered that she didn't actually know 'the Carotid Sticks'. She had them mixed up with 'the Clotted Creams'.

She felt strangely embarrassed, yet also excited, to realise this, as if she had cheated in an exam. Also, she had a sort of heart-pumping moment of terror, remembering how close she had come to getting caught – she had almost mentioned to Warren how much she liked the goldfish in a small glass bowl that the drummer brought along to his shows. (She had seen the Clotted Creams a couple of years back.) She had almost *drawn* a *sketch* of the goldfish on her notes, and shown this to Warren! Showing off her knowledge. Imagine if she had! Warren would have frowned in confusion, and she would have tried to explain, and realised her mistake as she did so, and then she would have tried to cover up, and got flustered.

She must look up the Carotid Sticks in HMV and listen to a CD, so she could prepare for the Date. *Not a Date. You don't know it's a Date. Who said it was a Date?*

'Scrotum, scrotum, scrotum.'

'Cassie?'

Cassie Zing coloured by numbers, and murmured: '*scrotum.*'

'Cassie? You want to keep quiet for us? Or see if you can find a new word?'

Cassie looked up and blinked once. She leaned onto her elbow and spoke into her fist.

I really should mention this habit to her parents. It's been going on for weeks now. And her mother sends so many notes! Really, an amazing number of notes from that Mrs Zing. I wouldn't even notice that Cassie was late if she didn't bring notes from her mother. Maybe I shouldn't have written back the other day? I've probably just encouraged her to write more. She may be a loony. Of course, the compliments are nice.

I hope I'm not late on Friday. I'll have to go straight from my law class to the Borrowed Cat. I'll wait until Friday night to ask him what he meant by that comment about his weekend being 'kind of a strain'. He will open up to me then, after we've had a few drinks, and I will listen sympathetically, and make him laugh with little jokes. Perhaps he'll even cry on my shoulder!

Okay, but it's not a Date.

What colour should I wear? What colour is the Borrowed Cat? I should try not to clash with the walls.

It was a strange week then, for Cath, waiting for Friday and the Clotted Creams. Then remembering that it was not the Clotted Creams but the *Carotid Sticks*. (She found them at HMV and they were kind of bluesy. She didn't like *blues*, but whatever.) She walked around under a spotlight, but a secret, private spotlight, because she didn't mention the invitation to anybody.

Not even Lenny and Suzanne, even when Suzanne suggested the two of them see a movie on Friday night. 'I'm busy Friday,' is all she said, 'how about Saturday?' Because here it was: the invitation. The first fragile step in the unfurling. She would not even *whisper* his name.

•

On Wednesday afternoon, Cath and Warren were working on a class plan.

'I am,' said Warren, '*extremely* hungry,' and he looked around the room.

Cath opened the fridge and found her cheese and pickles sandwich. She hadn't eaten it at lunch, on account of buying a sausage roll instead. 'You can have it,' she offered generously.

Warren was pleased with her, opening up the sandwich from its grease-proof paper, as if it were a birthday present. But then he paused and said, 'Imagine if this were toasted.' He held out the sandwich towards her.

'Are you saying you want me to toast it for you?' demanded Cath. 'Because I won't.'

'It's ten to five!' Warren slid back his chair and leapt to his feet. 'We will *buy a sandwich maker.* Quick! Let's go!'

They ran across Castle Hill Road together, amongst the lanes of traffic; skidded to the department store; scanned the directory for kitchen appliances; ran down the up-escalators accidentally; and got there just in time.

They went halves in a Breville Sandwich Maker, and carried it back in its box. They were sweaty from the heat and the excitement, and the fading sun blinked in their eyes.

'We keep it here,' said Warren, showing Cath the second shelf of the corner cupboard. 'And it's for us, and us alone. We alone get toasted sandwiches for lunch. Is it a fact? Is it a pact? Is it a *tac*-tic?'

On Thursday night, she felt jittery, and had to go to the corner store. The corner-store girl had such long plaits they drew attention to her hips. 'Hello there, *you*!' she always said to Cath, who felt she could never live up to this greeting.

'You know what *I* dreamed last night?' declared the corner-store girl as she reached for Cath's 60-watt light bulb. 'I dreamed I was in a bath-tub, right? With an antelope! What did you dream?'

'Hmm,' said Cath. 'Can't remember.'

'Come on! You always have the *best* dreams! And it's been so hot lately! Doesn't that make you dream? It makes me dream. Look at the time! It's so late and it must be what? Thirty-six degrees? Any nightmares?'

'Well, okay, I had this great dream where Doctor Carter from *ER* wanted to cure me of this disease which made me pale and beautiful, and I was hoping I'd get to stay pale and beautiful even when I was cured. Also, I've been dreaming a lot about extra rooms for my apartment. In the dreams, I keep finding doors in my hallway which open out into things like sewing rooms or saunas. I'm so happy when that happens. Maybe I think my apartment's too small? So. Those aren't nightmares, I guess.'

'How *is* your health anyway, Cath? I notice you've picked up some lozenges there. Sore throat?'

'Just hayfever,' explained Cath. 'It makes my throat itchy. How about you?'

Sometimes the corner-store girl liked to chat, but often she was vague and glassy-eyed when asked about herself.

When she got home, Cath was still jittery so she got out the bucket, the Windex and a roll of paper towel, and washed all the windows in the apartment.

On Friday afternoon, she was sleepily supervising children whose penalty was to hunt down apple cores, orange peels, paper bags, and ice-block wrappers – that is, rubbish – after school. She would let them stop soon because she wanted to get home, shower, change into a summer dress, get to law class, and *then* to the Borrowed Cat to meet Warren.

Warren, striding past, his arms and legs moving like the spokes of a wheel, slowed to a helicopter hover.

'Still on for tonight?' His eyes went straight into Cath's.

There was a whisk of excitement in her stomach. 'You bet,' she said.

'Breanna might be a little late,' explained Warren.

Cassie Zing, walking past at that moment, swinging her school bag in circles, said 'Ms Murphy?'

'Yes, Cassie?' said Cath. Also, to Warren: 'Breanna?'

'I wanted to tell you something important,' said Cassie.

'Breanna,' said Warren. 'My wife?'

'Did you, Cassie?' Cath turned smoothly. 'What did you want to tell me?'

'That it's my birthday tomorrow,' whispered Cassie.

'If she misses her train from the coast,' Warren explained, 'and she says that she might.'

Cath had bent forward so she could hear Cassie Zing. She kept her eyes on Cassie's face and said, 'Your *birthday* tomorrow! What are you going to do? Will you have a party? Happy birthday! That's *so* exciting.'

Cassie nodded. 'I know. And I'm having a party at my auntie's place tomorrow.'

'Wonderful!' said Cath, still leaning forward. 'We'll have to sing 'happy birthday' on Monday, but you know, we could have sung today. Why didn't you tell me sooner?'

Then there was a HONK, and Cassie cried, 'My mum!' and skidded away.

Cath straightened up and looked at Warren. 'Your wife?' she said, with a friendly smile.

'She lives up the coast during the week,' he said, 'so we only get the weekends? Which is a strain. Which is a drain. Which is a *brain drain.*'

Cath considered him.

'You didn't like that one?' he said. 'Fair enough. But anyway, I hope *you're* not planning to be late?'

'No, Warren, that's not what I was planning.'

'Great!' he said. 'See you there!

FANCY ZING

In the afternoon light of a summer day, Fancy, a teenager then, sat on her beach towel and watched Radcliffe's toe. The toe sprouted from his foot like a plump little table tennis bat. It also sprouted hairs, like an unkempt hedge. The toe was writing in the sand:

Radcliffe Mereweather

LOVES

Fancy Zing

The toe took a long time to write this.

Next, Fancy was distracted by Radcliffe's hands. The hands were thin and knobbly, and were clutching at her sunburnt shoulders. *I should put some suncream on those shoulders*, Fancy thought. But now was not the time.

Radcliffe's hands clutched tightly. He had a tear on the edge of each eye. 'I don't want to hurt you,' he was saying. 'I never meant to hurt you.' She stared at him. He was hurting her shoulders, but, apart from that, it didn't really hurt.

'I appreciate you telling me,' she said, feeling pleased at her own maturity.

Radcliffe had kissed another girl. He had gone to the surf club party the night before, leaving Fancy at home with an asthma attack.

'Did you meet a girl?' she teased the next day, side-by-side in the sun.

'Well, kind of,' he replied, alarmed.

'Did you kiss her?' She did not think for one moment that he had.

'Well . . .' and then he was silent, and the odd feeling started, her face stretched out, and she thought: *perhaps he did!*

And he had.

Radcliffe! Her First True Love! Her long-lashed boy with the sneakers and guitar! Radcliffe, who bought her marzipan and chocolate, had kissed another girl! They had only been together for a month.

'I don't want to hurt you,' he said, fervently, and his toe had just proved it by etching in the sand: Radcliffe Mereweather LOVES Fancy Zing.

They sat solemnly, looking at the words, their legs stretched out to the sun. A man shouted, 'Turkey! Win a turkey in the raffle!' Nearby, Marbie shook her towel and Daddy growled, 'Marbie! The sand!' Mummy called, 'Look, everyone! There's a skywriter!' and an announcement warned about the dangers of the rip.

'If you will only forgive me,' Radcliffe was anxious, 'I will love you forever and ever. Even, say you get old and wrinkled? I will love you. Even, say you get as fat as your mother?'

At that, Fancy pounced. '*Don't* call my mother fat!'

'Sorry.'

'I mean it. That's a stupid thing to say.'

'Sorry, I didn't know,' he explained. 'I didn't know you were sensitive about your mother's weight.'

'That's *not* the point! You don't know a *thing* about my mother.'

'What do you mean? What's to know?'

Strange. How she told the whole story, in a flood, right then. Radcliffe stared, the sun burned freckles onto Fancy's shoulders, and the Zing Family Secret ran straight into the letters of:

Radcliffe Mereweather

LOVES

Fancy Zing

•

The first few weeks of the school year were hot, and, as usual when the sun burned white, Fancy remembered the day at the seaside when Radcliffe revealed he had kissed another girl. Fancy had trumped him with the Zing Family Secret.

Also during the first few weeks of the school year, Fancy wrote seventeen notes to her daughter's 2nd grade teacher. She was just finishing the third of these notes –

Dear Ms Murphy,

Thank you so much for teaching Cassie (and the rest of your class, I suppose) that lovely song about the sparrow and the ironbark tree etc etc. She has been entertaining her father and me with the song (on and off) all week, and it is such an unusual tune!

Just thought I should let you know.

Best regards,
Fancy Zing

– when her husband, Radcliffe, arrived home from work.

'FANCY THAT! MY FANCY IS AT HOME!'

Fancy sat up straight and waited patiently for the sound of his key in the front door, the scraping of his feet on the welcome mat, then the little 'huh!' of pleasure as he put his umbrella in the stand. He had given Fancy the stand for a birthday, and he used it assiduously, taking his umbrella back and forth to work each day, even during heatwaves.

The footsteps approached. Fancy scraped a wisp of hair out of her bun.

'Mwah!' said Radcliffe, at the study door.

'Hello,' she replied. 'How was your day?'

Radcliffe leaned into the room and smiled around at the bookshelf, the scanner, and the corkboard. He looked at the printer next and gave a little chuckle. 'What have you done with Cassie?' he said, wandering away down the hall.

'I haven't done anything with Cassie,' murmured Fancy. She opened her desk drawer and took out her secret notebook.

IRRITATING THINGS ABOUT MY HUSBAND # 4

In the early days, when we were teenagers, he used to like to touch me all over. Knees, nose, fingernails. The line that runs from the throat down the valley of the bosoms and ends with a jump across the belly button. But over the years he has reduced his touching to *the* most obvious places. As if he had edited me down to three main points:

- The right breast.
- The left breast.
- The special private place between the legs.

They had frozen quiche for dinner, and watched *Hot Auctions!* and the next day, the moment she woke up, Fancy remembered this: *it is possible to change a person.*

Fancy had always believed this, even though people went around warning her: *never imagine you can change someone, for people NEVER CHANGE.* Then they talked about leopards and spots. Forgetting altogether about chameleons. Or that octopus which lives on the ocean floor and can change its shape to become a stingray, a sea anemone, or even an eel, depending upon its fancy.

Furthermore, Fancy recalled, she herself had changed. There had been a time when, after a shower, she would leave the shower curtain where it was when she stepped onto the bath mat: crowded together, pressed against the bathroom wall.

Radcliffe explained, a month or so after they were married, that this was unhygienic. 'The shower curtain should be drawn closed,' he explained, demonstrating, pulling the curtain all the way along its metal bar as if somebody were taking a shower. This would help to prevent mould.

Just like that, Fancy changed, and began to close the shower curtain tight.

Stepping out of the shower that morning, and drawing the curtain closed behind her, Fancy regarded her husband, shaving at the basin.

Tap, tap, tap, said his razor.

'So, that's how you get the whiskers out of the razor, is it?'

He turned to her. He had a white towel around his waist, a white smear of shaving cream around his chin, and he was squinting in the steam from Fancy's shower.

'Is there another way you could get the whiskers out?' she suggested.

'We should change this routine,' he replied, turning back to the steamy mirror. 'Me shaving, you showering. Same time, eh? Look at the mirror here. Can't see a thing.'

She leaned around him and flicked the switch on the overhead fan, so the room was filled with its buzz.

'What's with that rash on your arm there?' he said, shouting now over the buzz.

'I know.' She reached for her skin cream. 'I feel like a fish. It's just dry skin. I burned my skin too often as a teenager.'

'Wouldn't be that, would it? It's eczema. Or what? Psoriasis?'

'No,' said Fancy, coldly. 'It is not.' But Radcliffe was picking up her arm, turning it this way and that to catch the light, and whistling through his teeth.

•

'Here, Cassie, don't forget to take this note to your teacher, okay? Where are you going to put it so you don't forget?'

'In my pocket.'

Cassie stood on the footpath, next to the open car door, and showed her mother her open pocket.

'Good girl. Will you remember it there?'

'Yes, because I'll sneeze and then I'll have to get out my hanky, and then I'll find it there and I'll go, I HAVE TO REMEMBER TO GIVE THIS TO MS MURPHY.'

'That's my girl,' said Fancy.

'See over there.' Cassie pointed to a bench just inside the school gate. 'That's Lucinda.'

'So it is! We'll have to invite her over again one day soon. What do you think?'

'Okay,' agreed Cassie, nodding. She walked through the school gate and, without turning back, raised one hand to farewell her mother.

•

'Eczema, eczema, eczema.'

Cassie had a new word. It was a disease which made your skin fall off and then your blood went everywhere, like a laundry flood. Then you turned into a fish. Then you died.

'Eczema, eczema, eczema.' Cassie sang her word, eating her Vegemite sandwich before school had even started.

'Eczema?' Lucinda put her elbow in Cassie's side. 'I've got eczema.'

'No you haven't.' Cassie rolled her eyes at an imaginary person on the bench alongside Lucinda. She looked back from her imaginary person to Lucinda and saw that Lucinda was also eating her lunch before school. Lucinda's lunch was brown bread with soggy tomato. It was disgusting.

To change the subject, Cassie pointed to the ground and said, 'See that? That's a stick insect.'

'No,' said Lucinda. 'It's just a stick.'

It was a stick insect though.

Lucinda pointed to her wrist: 'See that? That's eczema.'

'There is no *point* in our having this discussion,' Cassie announced.

'Yes there is.'

'Eczema's when you turn into a fish, actually, *Lucinda*.'

'Do I look like a fish? No. I don't think so.' Lucinda swung her legs and ate her tomato sandwich.

The word, Cassie realised, was spoiled now.

'Eczema, eczema, eczema,' she said listlessly. She had her eye on the stick insect, but so far it was just asleep.

•

When she got back from taking Cassie to school, Fancy knew that she ought to be working on her erotic fiction. She had promised thirty thousand words to her editor by tomorrow, and she had only written eleven. Specifically:

His penis smelled like a pappadam: sweaty, salty, strange and strong.

Her editor would cut that line.

She reached for the phone and selected the button for MARBIE AT HOME.

'Hello,' said Marbie's voice.

'You're at home! Why aren't you at work? I was just going to leave a message. Well, if you're home, let's go out for a coffee!'

Marbie agreed, explaining that she and Listen were taking a day off because they had ticklish throats, which could be the start of colds.

'Or hayfever,' suggested Fancy. 'I'll call Radcliffe and let him know, in case he was thinking of coming home for lunch. And then I'll come right in.'

Marbie looked fine when Fancy saw her, although Listen appeared to be weary. Also, she was behaving strangely: wearing sunglasses inside the shopping centre; walking backwards wherever she went.

Marbie was excited about buying a tennis racquet, and wanted to talk about something that the tennis racquet had which was called the *sweet spot*.

After the coffee break, Fancy did not feel ready to go home, so she shopped for Cassie's birthday, even though it was a month away. At home again, she stood before her computer and decided she ought to do some housework.

'Oh, *Cassie*,' she said aloud to herself when she put on the washing-up gloves. Cassie was always putting soapy wet hands into the gloves, and leaving them wet, cold, clammy and unpleasant on the inside.

Luckily, by the time she had finished washing up (with a fresh pair of gloves), it was just about time to fetch Cassie from school.

Dear Ms Murphy,

This is just a note to thank you for keeping an eye on my daughter (Cassie) yesterday afternoon. I noticed that you were on 'bus duty', and I also noticed that you are very good at keeping all the children within your 'radar'. As I waited for Cassie, this is something I observed, and, as a mother, I was pleased.

I do hope our Cassie is behaving herself. I know she can be a little erratic, but she has a good heart.

Kind regards,
Fancy Zing

At nights, staying up with her erotic fiction, Fancy felt afraid sometimes when she went to the bathroom. While she was washing her hands, for example, she would glance back at the shower cubicle, with its curtain tightly closed, and think: *there is somebody in there!*

She supposed she would see a shadow through the curtain, but it was a thick forest-green material, and she was short-sighted, not wearing her glasses in the bathroom generally (preferring to see herself, in the mirror, as somebody blurry and unmarked).

Sometimes she swung the curtain open quickly, to catch the intruder out. But so far, there had never been anybody there.

CHAPTER 2

'Beauty spots,' he said, cocking his head at the two or three moles on her arms. He cleared his throat slightly, so that his voice was strong and powerful, and, cocking his cock at the special, throbbing place between her legs, he said: 'Beauty spot.' She raised one eyebrow and teased, directing her words to the cock: 'Coming in?' 'Are you kidding?' he declared, answering for his cock. He climbed onto her naked body. But, without entering her, he began to stroke her forehead, her shoulders, her stomach, hips, shins. All over! 'Certainly not! Not today!' he said. And she laughed and groaned, feeling the cock almost casually hard against her thigh, like the handle of a tennis racquet. She hoped he didn't mean it.

Radcliffe, she noticed at 3 am, had left the bedroom light on for her, and was lying asleep in the brightness. Making a point about how late it was. Or perhaps he just accidentally fell asleep.

When she climbed under the sheets, he opened his mouth slightly, as if to say something, but it was only a gentle snore.

•

'You look tired,' remarked the Canadian from his porch next door. He was eating sliced mango and kiwifruit this morning.

'It's funny you should say that,' said Fancy, 'about me looking tired. Because I just saw myself in the hallway mirror without my glasses on and I thought, "I look *awful*", and then I thought, "isn't it lucky I wear glasses so that nobody can see my eyes?" I put my glasses on and felt safe. And now I come out here and you notice right away.'

The Canadian took a pensive sip of coffee.

'Cassie, honey!' Fancy called, as usual, through the screen door.

'Mum, I can't find my shoes, where are my shoes? What did you do with my shoes?' came a panicky little call from upstairs.

'I didn't do anything with your shoes. They're right here by the front door where you left them.'

'To be honest,' said the Canadian from his porch, 'I didn't notice that you look *awful*. If you look *awful*,' he continued, and peeled the foil lid from a boysenberry yoghurt, 'your glasses are hiding that well.'

Fancy looked at his wide white breakfast plate, with its elegant butterflies of fruit, and tried to think of something to say besides *isn't it hot?*

'Kiwifruit is very good for you,' she declared. 'Vitamin C and zinc.'

'You don't say?'

Cassie clattered down onto the front-door mat to put on her shoes.

'I'll do one lace and you do the other,' offered Fancy.

'No, Mum. I'll do them both.'

'Bye now,' called Fancy to the neighbour as she tightened the straps on Cassie's satchel, her keys at the ready to open the car door.

'It is possible,' called the Canadian, his voice melting distantly against their car windows, 'to be both beautiful and tired. A sleeping beauty. You see?'

Fancy adjusted the rear-view mirror and reversed with the regular bump of the fender on the steeply graded drive. Cassie, meanwhile, wound down the window slightly, and gave the Canadian a stare.

●

Dear Ms Murphy,

Please excuse Cassie for being late today.

It was all my fault! I was up late last night, working, and then overslept this morning.

Best regards,
Fancy Zing

Dear Ms Zing,

Thank you very much for your note!

I'm sure that Cassie was not more than a few minutes late – some of the children are much later than that, and we seem to get along all right. It is very kind of you to write notes of explanation, but please do not trouble yourself.

I look forward to meeting you at the Parent-Teacher Night later this year, when we can discuss Cassie properly. She certainly does seem to have a good heart, and is quite popular (I often see other children gathered around her while she entertains them with funny little stories – I wonder what she tells them!).

Best wishes,
Cath Murphy

●

Turning into her driveway one day, Fancy looked across at her neighbour's verandah and saw that there were two of them. Her neighbour had become two.

She got out of her car, and glanced over quickly. Yes, there were now two men sitting at the breakfast table, slicing up kiwifruits, sipping from their coffee mugs. She kept her back straight, and hurried across the burning driveway to the soft, cool grass. She never wore shoes to drive.

'– coyote fuck,' she heard from the porch next door, just as she reached her front door. And then a chuckle.

She couldn't help it. She turned and stared.

'Fancy,' said her neighbour, 'hello there. This is a friend from Canada, visiting for a couple of days. Bill. Meet Fancy.'

'Did I offend you?' said Bill with a friendly nod. 'You heard what I just said? Coyote fuck?'

How direct the Canadians were. 'Well . . .' she began.

'It's an expression – *coyote fuck*,' he explained. Meanwhile, her neighbour looked down, slicing up another kiwifruit. 'You know when you pick a girl up at a bar – or, I guess, in your case, when you pick up a guy – anyhow, you pick someone up at a bar, right, at the end of the night, so you're blind drunk and you don't know what you're doing. You take them home, you sleep with them, the next morning, there they are in your bed, fast asleep, lying on your arm, you're thinking *what the fuck?* You're thinking: *how do I get OUT of here without waking up this chick?* What are you going to do?'

Fancy tilted her head to the side. 'What are you going to do?' she asked.

'You're going to chew through your arm.'

The visitor nodded to himself and picked up a slice of kiwifruit.

Fancy waited.

'It's what coyotes do when they get caught in a trap,' he explained as he slurped at the fruit. 'They chew through their leg to free themselves. See?'

Her neighbour offered her a cup of coffee.

'No thank you. And thank you for the story, Bill. Nice to meet you.'

She opened the screen door to her house, and it let out a long, thin squeal.

•

Dear Ms Murphy,

How kind of you to write! I, also, look forward to meeting you at the Parent-Teacher Night.

I'm so pleased to hear that Cassie is popular! I hope she does not give you any trouble.

You know, I just thought I would let you know that I was talking to Barbara Coulton the other day — she is Lucinda's mother — and she told me that Lucinda is happier than she's ever been at school! Barbara is delighted with the standard and variety of work that Lucinda brings home, and is especially pleased that you correct Lucinda's spelling mistakes — such a rare thing in modern teaching.

Take care, and
Best wishes!
Fancy Zing

•

'Write this down,' Fancy said to Radcliffe on Sunday afternoon: '*Toilet paper.*' Radcliffe wrote it down. 'Follow me down the hall,' she instructed, taking out the vacuum cleaner from the hall closet. Obediently, Radcliffe followed, writing the list.

'The vacuum cleaner's broken, you know.'

'I don't want the vacuum cleaner,' said Fancy, patiently. 'I just want the bucket from behind it. *Paper towels.* I've decided to wash the glass doors. Or will Cassie just run through them? Okay: *butter, self-raising flour, Kangaroo Cookies, Valerio Pies.*'

'I think she'll run through them,' agreed Radcliffe, writing carefully. 'Don't wash them. Let's go for a walk instead. Anything else?' His pen at the ready.

'Yes. *Spaghetti.* Okay. Good. Let's go for a walk. Radcliffe, what do you mean it's broken?'

'What's broken?'

'The vacuum, you just said it was broken. Since when?'

'Oh,' he said vaguely, 'since the other week. I came home to surprise you at lunchtime and you weren't here, so I smashed a glass, then I tried to vacuum it up, and the vacuum cleaner jammed, and now it seems to be broken.'

'So you smashed a glass? Because I wasn't here? Where was I?'

'That came out wrong. I think you were having coffee with your sister in Castle Hill. Remember that day? And Marbie brought Alissa along, you told me. They both had colds. Or at least Alissa did. That's how you put it.'

'She prefers to be called Listen, you know.'

'Anyhow, let's go for a walk and, tell you what, I'll take the vacuum into that new repair shop by the hardware store.'

•

REDEEMING FACTOR ABOUT MY HUSBAND # 1

He can spit a cherry pip from the front porch of our house all the way to the road. I can only spit a cherry pip to the edge of the porch.

•

On Saturday, it would be Cassie's birthday. It was a secret, almost scary, wonderful fact which she carried around each day, like a big smile about to happen on her face.

But what Cassie was actually realising today (Thursday) was that it used to be better than this, back when she was a kid. Maybe when she turned five or six, it was more than just a smile: it was like everything was whispering and just about to skip. Now, turning seven, her excitement felt a bit wrong.

It's because I know you can get disappointed, she realised to herself. One time she got too excited on her birthday and jumped on the table where the grown-ups were sitting and at first they laughed but then she knocked over their champagne bottle and champagne spilled onto her dad's lap and she got into trouble. She cried, and you should never cry on your birthday.

•

It was Thursday already, and tomorrow she had work to do for the Friday night Zing Family Secret Meeting, and then Saturday it would be Cassie's birthday, so that really only left today and Sunday to finish another thirty chapters of her erotic fiction. Fancy stared at her computer in wonder.

She decided to write to Cassie's teacher.

> *Dear Ms Murphy,*
>
> *Just wanted to let you know that Cassie has a loose tooth*

But then there was a knock at the front door.

She opened the door and, in the sun-shadow, there stood a handsome stranger. Tears sprang at once into Fancy's eyes. She blinked them away.

The stranger was carrying a plate, covered in a tea-towel. He was wearing a loose T-shirt and jeans, and worn sneakers without socks. His shoulders were broad, his face was darkly tanned, and his eyes, behind small, wire-rimmed spectacles, were glinting.

'*Hello* there,' he said.

At that, he transformed into the Canadian-next-door.

She was so disconcerted, she did not open the screen door. She stood and simply stared.

'*Not* in any way intending to bother you,' he continued, in a slightly formal voice. 'But I've baked you an *apology* cake. My buddy from Canada. Bill. The other day. I just wanted to apologise for him. He's a good guy but not exactly the most tactful, and I just about died when he told you that story of his. I just about died, and now I am here to apologise.'

'Oh!' cried Fancy, in a flutter. 'The coyote fuck story! I wasn't offended at all! I liked it even! I write erotic fiction. That's my occupation. So, see, nothing like that bothers me at all! It's my career! I know it must sound strange to you, me, a mother in the suburbs, writing erotic fiction, and the only person I ever slept with my whole life is my husband!'

There was silence for a moment.

Fancy opened the screen door, and it let out its usual squeal.

'I could fix that for you.' He was looking at the door.

'No! No! I can do that! All it needs is a bit of WD40!'

'I agree,' he said, with that odd little smile. 'I still think my friend was inexcusable, so please take this maple cake. Okay?'

He used one foot to hold open the screen door as he passed the cake towards her. She took the cake, and he withdrew his hands, palms upwards. She saw that his palms were calloused. Then he saluted, with that same glint in his eye, and ran down the steps of her porch.

Rather than crossing directly to his own porch, he took the driveway, walked along the street, and then walked back up his own driveway. She found this extremely moving.

CHAPTER 3

The palm of his right hand, when she turned it, to kiss it, was calloused. 'From the tennis racquet?' she guessed. He nodded, and then suggested that she take off her dress. 'You don't like my dress?' she teased. He chuckled, and then mock-growled: 'Into the bedroom, wench!' She reached for a Chux, wanting first to clean up the cracked egg that was dribbling towards the edge of the counter – remnant of their cake-baking efforts. But he intercepted, taking her wrist. 'Let it spill,' he said, calmly. 'Leave it. I'm going to have you. And now.' 'I'll do that,' he said, calmly. 'Give me the cloth.' Then, when he had cleaned the whole kitchen, he repeated, with a droll little glint in his eye, 'Into the bedroom, wench.'

Driving to the Zing Family Secret Meeting the next night, Fancy felt very happy. She felt excited about dinner that night – it would be roast chicken, as usual – and about the meeting afterwards (there was lots to discuss, and she had prepared a slide show). She also felt excited about Cassie's birthday tomorrow. How wonderful that Marbie and Vernon were hosting it! She might go to the gym before the party. How thin she was these days, now that she was going to the gym regularly. She leaned back into her seat, humming along with the tune that Cassie was singing in the back seat.

And then Radcliffe said what he said. 'You remember Gemma in the pay office?' he said, changing lanes.

'No,' said Fancy.

'Come on! You must remember Gemma. She's the one who spilled her drink everywhere at the office Christmas party? Remember?'

'No,' repeated Fancy.

'Well.' He shrugged. 'Well, trust me, there's a Gemma who works in my pay office. She works afternoons only, lucky duck. Anyhow, turns out she had some kind of laser treatment done on her moles. You know, you'd call them freckles, but they're really moles. Anyhow. Extraordinary. She got about ten of them zapped.'

Fancy could not believe it. She lowered her chin to check the freckles on her bare shoulders: nicely spaced, attractive freckles. *Beauty spots*, really.

'What exactly do you mean by that?' she said coldly, after a moment.

Radcliffe turned swiftly towards her with a hurt, confused expression on his face. Then he looked back to the road.

MARBIE ZING

In the hot noon light of a summer day once, Marbie, nine years old at the time, was almost killed by an umbrella.

She was distracted at the time.

The day before, her sister Fancy had walked in to the beach house at sunset and announced that she had done something incredible.

Marbie was supposed to be washing the sand off her feet, but hearing this, she ran inside. She made herself invisible by placing herself, side-on, in the narrow open space between the bubble-glass sliding doors. She had to turn her head to see what was happening.

Fancy was standing in the centre of the main room, her hands on her hips, waiting for her parents. Mummy leaned in from the kitchen, where she was making a beetroot salad. Daddy leaned in from the bathroom, where he had just had a shower.

'What incredible thing did you do, sweetheart?' called Mummy.

'What's up, Fance?' said Daddy.

'I told Radcliffe the Secret.'

Now there was a stampede of parents – Mummy's purple hands flying, Daddy's bath towel flapping – and they gathered around Fancy. Daddy straightened the towel around his waist.

'You did not!' cried Mummy.

'I did,' said Fancy, defiantly. 'I told you it was incredible.' She looked up at her parents and folded her arms, but her mouth trembled. Marbie, in her door-space, thought of the episode of *Charles in Charge*, when the good sister tries to be bad, but she can't pull it off because of her nature.

'When?!' cried Daddy.

'Oh, darling,' said Mummy, gently. Fancy's hands fell to her side and she sat down at the table.

It turned out she had told him *everything*. She did not know why.

'Tell us again what you told him,' ordered Daddy, over and over. 'Why did you tell him?' murmured Mummy, also over and over, until Marbie grew bored and climbed onto the side of one of the doors so she could slide with it, very quietly.

'Marbie!' snapped Daddy. 'Go and get changed out of your bathing suit!'

'Okay,' agreed Marbie, looking down to the floor where there were little splatters of sea water from her bathing suit. Quietly, she walked into the room and sat down on the couch.

'Oh, Fancy,' said Mummy, in a low, shivery voice.

'Tell us what you told him,' Daddy commanded. 'Tell us exactly.'

'Well, I told him about Ireland and about the cherry pies –'

'Oh never mind,' grumbled Daddy.

He looked at Mummy and she looked back. It was quiet.

From the couch, Marbie murmured to herself, 'Should I tell them that I never told anyone the Secret? Should I say that out loud?'

The others turned to her. 'GET OFF THAT COUCH!' Daddy shouted.

'Radcliffe's not going to tell anybody.' Fancy's voice collapsed into her arms, and her next words were tangled in a sob: 'He promerr ewerd terl *any* obee.'

Mummy and Daddy were quiet, figuring out what she had just said. After a moment they both breathed in an 'ah' of comprehension.

'Well,' said Daddy, 'if he promised he wouldn't tell *any*body, I suppose we have to trust him.'

'But heaven help us when the two of you break up!' fretted Mummy.

'We're not going to break up,' Fancy wept. 'He loves me! He said that he loves me forever!'

'There now,' said Mummy, apologetically. 'Of course he does.' She put her arms around Fancy and said, 'Of course he does, hush now, of course he does, sweetheart.'

So the next day, in the high noon sun, Marbie was distracted.

Fancy was sitting on her beach towel under the umbrella, one arm curled around her knees, gazing moodily down at the sand. Daddy was trying to tune in his transistor to hear the cricket. Mummy was on her fold-up chair, reading *New Idea*. The seaside noises and the radio fuzz and the magazine pages turning were only there to heighten the quiet of the family.

From her towel in the sun a few metres away, Marbie was able to observe her family and, in particular, Fancy. It seemed to Marbie that Fancy, who was usually smart, had now been stupid in two ways. First of all, it was stupid to tell her boyfriend the Secret. Second of all, it was stupid to tell her *parents* that she had told her boyfriend the Secret. In fact, and this was what interested Marbie, the second stupid thing was a whole new level of stupidity.

She stared out to sea, thinking hard about the two different levels of stupidity. Soon the levels began to shimmer in the air. Just above the horizon was the first level; somewhere a little higher, striking through clouds, was the second. Marbie stared at the first level, then looked up at the second, down at the first, up at the second, down and up, down and up, until an umbrella hit her smack in the forehead.

It was a beach umbrella, snatched out of the sand by a random gust of wind. It had streaked through the air like a javelin while men shouted 'HO!' and leapt after it. The sharp end hit Marbie in the forehead and knocked her out cold.

While she was in the hospital, there was a lot of talk about how lucky it was that it hadn't hit her just over to the right. Or just up a bit. Or a tad lower. Or a smidgeon to the left. And imagine if it had hit her in the eye! She was that close to death, but all she got was ten stitches, two black eyes, and one night under observation.

Fancy was very emotional so Radcliffe held her hand and nuzzled his nose into her shoulder, for support. That Friday, Radcliffe came along to his first Zing Family Secret Meeting, and was quiet and polite, but couldn't stop looking at Marbie, who was on the couch surrounded by pillows, and whose forehead was a thunderstorm of purple. The fol-lowing week he had relaxed enough to point out that the circles of black around her eyes made her look like a racoon. 'See you later, racoon girl,' he called as he left the garden shed that night. Everybody laughed.

Afterwards, Marbie took over responsibility for putting up the family beach umbrella. She alone knew the full extent of the risk. She had a strict routine: first, dig a hole as deep as your arm; deeper; dig until you have to lie down on your side to reach the bottom of the hole and scrape the damp sand with your fingertips; next, take the *bottom half of the umbrella* and plunge it into the hole, then twist to the right leaning with all your weight; *next!* pack the hole with firm sand; finally, pile sand thick and high around the base of the umbrella, twist on the top half, and bury three sea-grapes at random spots for good luck.

She was left with a crocus-shaped scar on her forehead, and a life-long fear that long sharp items (such as umbrellas, or fence posts) would somehow end up in her eye.

●

One Friday morning, Marbie stood on the porch of their new apartment, drinking her berry-and-banana shake and saying goodbye to Listen.

'Don't walk too fast,' Marbie suggested. 'You'll need your energy for the Walkathon. Why don't you skate to school today? Or I could give you a lift.'

Listen just laughed, and strode off at her regular high speed.

'You look good,' called Marbie. 'You look great. Like a really *hip* walker is how you look.'

Listen laughed again, and changed her walk to something hip and groovy for a few steps, then continued in her normal way. Because of the Charity Walkathon that day, she was not wearing her school uniform, but hipster jeans and a tank top that showed off her stomach.

Marbie herself locked up and set off to her car which was parked down the street. Halfway to the car, the neighbour's black cat crossed her path.

Every day since the day they had moved in, the neighbour's black cat had crossed her path. Sometimes it made an elaborate effort to do so: a triple backflip from a tree followed by a high jump over Marbie's head, for example. But that Friday morning, it didn't even try, it just walked on across her path.

'Oh, for heaven's sake,' Marbie said aloud. 'You don't scare me, you know that, Gary?'

Gary was the name of the cat, and in fact, his name alone scared her.

But it was a perfectly nice day at work: a lot of chatting; stamping documents; a plate of leftover sushi from a conference on another floor. Toni went to stationery and came back loaded with gifts, so, also, a lot of time setting up her new magnetic paperclip holder.

She spilled some of the paperclips onto the carpet, and picked up a handful, deciding to leave the rest on the carpet there. *It was a decision she would regret for the rest of her life.* (Let's say, one day, Marbie knocks over a vase of flowers. The water seeps into the carpet, while flowers roll under the desk. She gets down on her hands and knees and crawls under the desk to retrieve a flower or two, and, *without her noticing*, a paperclip sticks to her knee. Unaware, she leaves work, travels home, meets Vernon, playfully knees him in the thigh, and *the paperclip somehow sticks into his skin, and he gets lead poisoning, and dies!*) (Her eyes filled with tears at the thought.)

So she crawled under the desk and picked up every single paperclip, afterwards brushing her knees carefully for remnants. Then she wrote replies to all the e-mail in her 'FRIENDS – MUST REPLY' folder.

That evening, at the Night Owl Pub, the others had just left and Marbie was finishing her beer when the aeronautical engineer appeared.

'I have just enough time for one beer,' he informed her, sitting down opposite.

'What makes you think that I have time for one beer?'

'Sure you do! What's the rush?'

The Zing Family Secret Meeting was the rush.

'Okay. Just one.'

'Where *is* everyone?' said the aeronautical engineer, frowning around at the empty seats.

'I wish you'd stop doing that,' said Marbie.

The aeronautical engineer went to the bar and returned with a pitcher of beer, which they began to share.

'Aeroplane wings are supposed to shake,' said the aeronautical engineer after a pause in conversation.

'Okay,' agreed Marbie. He would know.

The aeronautical engineer said: 'Play a spot of tennis?'

On the train home, Marbie wondered why she had agreed to play tennis with a stranger. They had arranged to meet at courts close to her place, the following Saturday.

Arriving at her station, and walking through the balmy night to her car, she wondered next if she was sober enough to drive. She stepped up onto the parking lot fence, put one leg in the air like a ballet dancer, and held that position for a moment before she fell. That was a good sign.

She drove to her parents' place, imagining her arrival in time for dessert, hopefully some kind of cherry pie tonight, and also imagining her excuses: *Tabitha told this really long story about her pregnant sister, who has started having fits. It's awful; she was really upset. The train was one of those slow, all-stops ones. My car was in a different part of the parking lot from where I parked it this morning! I'm sure it was. I'm sure somebody moved it.* All of these things were true, even though they were not the reason for her lateness.

By the time she got there, dinner was already over, and the Meeting had begun. Listen and Cassie were watching a movie, as usual, in the living room. 'Hello!' she called to them, running through on her way out to the garden shed. 'How was the Walkathon, Listen?'

'Fine,' said Listen, her eyes on the TV.

In the garden shed, Marbie sat next to Vernon, and leaned over to whisper in his ear that she had just agreed to tennis with a stranger. Before she had a chance to whisper, Vernon kissed her. He quietly passed her an extra copy of her mother's handout, which she immediately made into a paper aeroplane. Vernon took the aeroplane from her hand, held it up, and said a dismissive '*tch!*', at which Marbie giggled, and her mother, at the front, said, 'SHH.'

She and Vernon were always getting into trouble at Meetings.

Then Vernon reached under his chair and he had a plate of cherry pie hidden there for her, with a spoon.

After the Meeting, they drove home in Vernon's car. Marbie, feeling sleepy in the passenger seat, took her paper aeroplane out of her pocket, straightened out the crumples, and said: 'What do you mean: '*tch*'?'

'It'll never fly,' he declared, glancing over at her plane. 'Crash and burn.'

'It'll fly.'

'Show me,' said Listen, leaning forward. Then, sitting back again: 'Vernon's right, Marbie. That won't fly.'

'An aeronautical engineer showed me how. It will fly.'

'Crash and burn,' repeated Vernon. 'Which aeronautical engineer showed you how?'

'I don't know. Just this guy.'

The paper aeroplane had a sharp point, which hit Vernon smack in the cheek.

'It flew,' proclaimed Marbie.

'It never.'

'It hit you in the cheek!'

'It never flew.'

'Well then *how* did it get to your cheek?'

'You threw it at me. Throwing isn't flying.'

Marbie sat back and pulled on her seatbelt. 'Hmm,' she said.

'Hey, Listen,' said Vernon, checking his sister in the rear-view mirror. 'How was the Walkathon today? We forgot to collect your sponsorship money from the Zings.'

'Fine,' said Listen. 'It was fine.' She didn't say any more than that.

●

The Walkathon was fifty-five times round the oval to raise money for an international mine-clearance charity. They got their purple sponsorship cards ticked each time around. Every five times they got a cup of orange juice, and every ten times they got to stop and have a Vita-Weat, and the teachers laughed and said things like, 'Come on! Pick up the pace! Hup-two!'

They walked in groups with their friends, and Listen walked with Donna Turnbull and the others, from Primary.

After eight laps, Donna said, 'Raising money for mines, eh? What do you reckon we should do with the mines when we get them?'

'Depends on what kind of mines,' said Sia. 'If they're diamond mines, we should get out the diamonds. If they're gold mines, we should get out the gold. If they're silver mines . . .'

The others were all laughing, so she stopped.

'We should plant them in the Science labs,' suggested Caro. 'So we wouldn't have to go to Science anymore.'

'Yeah you would,' said Gabrielle. 'It'd be cool, because Science'd be like a mine field. So you'd have to get someone to go into the lab first and, like, test out the path to your bench.'

'You'd get Caro to do it,' said Donna.

'You would NOT!' shouted Caro, and they all laughed again.

'Let's run now,' Donna said, when they'd stopped laughing. 'You wanna run for a while?'

Then she counted. 'One, two, three, and four,' she pointed as she counted, Joanne, Caro, Gabrielle and Sia, and pointed at herself, 'and five.'

She didn't point at Listen.

'Just us five,' she said, without looking at Listen: 'Let's run.'

They had funny sparks in their eyes, and smirks, and they all began to run.

Listen was confused for a moment. She thought that Donna had just forgotten to point to her, and she started to run too, but then saw that they were running faster, and looking at each other as they ran, like: 'She's coming with us! What will we do?!'

She slowed down for a moment, to see if they would stop.

They didn't stop, they kept on running into the distance, and around the corner of the oval. Then they slowed to a jog, without looking back. Then they kept walking, fast.

Okay, thought Listen, the idea is to catch up with me on the next round?

Listen walked alone then, forty-seven times around the oval, slowly, to give them a chance, but they never caught up with her once.

The Monday after the Walkathon, Listen watched Donna and the others out of the corner of her eye, waiting to see what would happen. At first she thought: *well, if they don't want me around, that's fine with me,* and she went to the library at lunchtime. You weren't allowed to eat in the library so she saved her lunch and ate it walking home. In classes, she decided to concentrate on what the teachers were saying. *It's pretty interesting anyway,* she told herself sometimes, but actually it wasn't.

Meanwhile, the others were getting on with life, talking to each other about ordinary things.

The same thing happened Tuesday, but on Wednesday morning, Listen woke up and thought: *this is all a mistake! They think that* I'm *the one who's ignoring them!* How terrible! But such a relief, and she practically ran all the way to school to clear things up.

Caro was arriving at the school gate at the same time as her, so Listen called, 'Hi!'

Caro looked around and said, 'Hi-i-i,' sort of comical and musical, like the 'hi' you might say to a big blue beetle that landed on your plate at a picnic. Everyone would laugh and you'd shake the plate and the beetle would fly away.

'What's going on?' said Listen, walking in step with Caro.

'No-o-thing,' said Caro, quickening her pace.

'SIA!!!' shouted Caro suddenly, and she waved at Sia, who was down in the teachers' parking lot. Sia turned and stared, and Caro sprinted away from Listen, pounding down the driveway. Listen paused, and watched as Caro reached Sia and seemed to hunch over, gasping and talking rapidly, until Sia hugged her as if she needed comforting.

Listen walked on quickly then, in a different direction.

Later that day, packing up to go home, Donna spoke to Listen in a kindly voice. 'Can I just explain something?' she said.

'If you want.'

'It's just that we all agreed on this, okay? It's no offence or anything. See, we decided things are kind of different now we're in Year 7, and you have to kind of like make the tough decisions? If you're going to survive. And we think you're not kind of right for survival, okay? And it was a good example at the Walkathon, when we were all making jokes about mines and that, and you were *laughing* but you weren't making jokes yourself. You were kind of like *taking* because you were laughing, but you weren't giving anything to us. And you know, things change, and we all agreed, kind of like. Okay?'

'O-ka-a-ay,' said Listen, trying to give her 'okay' a lilting, comical edge.

The next day, Listen took a day off school. Marbie was staying home with a ticklish throat, and she suggested Listen might need a break too. After clearing her throat several times, Listen decided she had a tickle too. 'I'll write a note and say you've got pneumonia,' offered Marbie. So that was settled.

Marbie was reading a novel in the sunny part of the kitchen, and Listen went into her bedroom and stared around the room, and then she remembered: *it's Thursday week! I'm allowed to do the next spell!*

It was A Spell To Make A Vacuum Cleaner Break.

'Well,' she said to herself, 'that's a pretty stupid spell.' But then she remembered that their vacuum cleaner was already broken. It got broken in the move: Mr Zing dropped a wardrobe on top of it, in the back of the ute. Maybe A Spell To Make A Vacuum Cleaner Break would have the reverse effect on a broken one? You never knew.

These were the instructions:

1. Wear sunglasses all day. From now on. Quickly, go and get the sunglasses and put them on.
2. Walk backwards but every few steps skip a bit and say 'oh!', as if you've just remembered something.
3. Phone up a Tae Kwon Do class and sign yourself in, then phone again ten minutes later, and cancel.
4. Peel fifteen potatoes and sticky-tape the peelings back together.

NOW YOU HAVE TO WAIT SIX WEEKS PLUS ONE DAY BEFORE YOU CAN TURN ANOTHER PAGE! (You'd better put the date in your calendar.)

These were challenging things, but Listen did them all. Even when she and Marbie went out with Marbie's sister Fancy, for a coffee in Castle Hill. It was difficult wearing sunglasses inside and walking backwards, but she explained that her theory about the flu was to disguise herself, and run away from it, so it wouldn't find her. Marbie and Fancy were impressed.

And the next morning, she checked in the hall closet, but the vacuum cleaner was still crushed, as she had known it would be.

•

On Saturday morning, Marbie explained to Vernon, through the bathroom door, that she was going to her parents' place to look through decorating magazines.

'Hey, sporty girl!' said Vernon, coming out of the shower and seeing Marbie dressed up in her sports gear. He pretended to box with her a bit, but Marbie did not have the time.

On the way to her parents' place, she stopped and bought a tin of tennis balls. She stayed at her parents' place for ten minutes, and then she drove to the tennis courts. There was a new tennis racquet hidden in the boot of her car.

The air was still under a low hazy sky, except for vague swarmings of pollen and speck-shaped black bugs. Crossing to the tennis courts, Marbie felt the dry grass crunch beneath her sneakers, and then, in the distance, she saw the aeronautical engineer. He was already at the court, unzipping his tennis racquet and staring at her. He was dressed all in white, including little white ankle socks and bright white sandshoes. The only other colour on him was the black of the hair on his legs and arms. The hair seemed very thick.

She herself was wearing the following: black, shiny lycra shorts; lemon-yellow T-shirt with a faded blue announcement: BEAR HUGGER; pink terry-towelling elastic in her ponytailed hair; and Reeboks.

From a distance, the aeronautical engineer looked troubled and plump.

As soon as she arrived, he said: 'Here, I'll spin my racquet.'

'Ah!' *Why does he want to spin his racquet?!*

The aeronautical engineer spun the racquet, asking: 'Rough or smooth?'

'Rough!' panicked Marbie. She waved at a swarm of bugs, and sneezed: once, twice, three, four, five.

'Phew!' he said (about her sneezes) and the racquet hit the court with a low-level thud. 'Rough it is!'

Marbie served into the net, twice, clicked her ticklish throat, annoyed, and wanted to blow her nose. The bugs touched her tongue and the edges of her nose, and she scratched at her ears and her knees.

'Love-fifteen,' called the aeronautical engineer, helpfully.

'Thank you.' She stamped one foot at the itches and the bugs, and agreed: 'Me too! Love it too!'

The aeronautical engineer said: 'What?' and then he laughed once: 'Ha'.

Arriving home, sweaty, Marbie explained to Vernon that she had decided to go for a run around the oval after she visited her parents, and that was why she was sweaty, and so now she would just have a shower.

'Listen's gone shopping,' Vernon said, following her down the hallway, 'but she wanted me to tell you something as soon as you got home. She wanted me to tell you her idea. Okay, let me remember the idea. The idea is this: she thinks we should have Cassie's birthday party here as our house-warming party. She tells me it's Cassie's birthday in a few weeks.'

'Does she tell you that, does she?' said Marbie, taking off her sweaty sports clothes and stepping into the shower. 'I think it's a lovely idea, and I think Listen is beautiful, and I think that you are too.' The last part she gurgled through the shower water.

'Thank you,' said Vernon, pulling his shirt over his head, unbuttoning his jeans, pressing them down his legs and over his feet, and stepping into the shower with her. Marbie stared at the fine, light brown hair on his chest, and at his lovely muscular shoulders and arms. He was well-built because he was always lifting boxes of bananas. As he kissed her in a warm, wet, shower-water way, Marbie began to draft a Letter to the Editor:

Sir:

I am writing to inform you that I have, just this morning, had an affair with an aeronautical engineer.

I have written to you before to discuss my good fortune in having met the Taylor siblings, and to describe what an excellent lover Vernon Taylor is. I can verify now, as we speak, that Vernon really is a sensational — really, a remarkable —

Anyway, the affair took the form of a game of tennis: 6-0, 6-1. I lost. And my single win in the second set was a result of his double faults. 'Blast!' said the aeronautical engineer, after every single double fault, and wiped a little sweat from his sideburns.

I was appalled to be having an affair with such a man. Actually, I got quite bored, which is why I am mystified by what happened next.

What happened next was that I arranged to have a second affair! I arranged it for next Wednesday, during my lunch hour, at the Sydney University courts. Let me just emphasise though, because this is what is so mystifying, this is really ironic — let me just emphasise that Vernon is really an excellent —

The following week, Listen joined a new group, Angela Saville's group, and she sat with them on Monday and Tuesday and asked questions. For instance, she asked everyone what they did on the weekend, whether they watched the Valerio movie last night, whether they liked it, what subject they had after lunch, whether they liked that subject, and so on. She listened to their answers.

On Wednesday, she ordered her lunch from the tuckshop, and it arrived in the basket at the front of the room, in a brown paper bag with her name: LISTEN TAYLOR. GRADE 7A. It was a Cornish pastie, hot and damp, plus one can of Sprite, plus one Freddo Frog.

The paper bag was fat and lumpy, and she held it by the ruffled bend at the top, along past the Year 7 balcony bars. The lawn was set with its garlands of girls.

She saw Angela Saville's group and she walked the grass carefully toward them, ready with a smile. The circle felt funny. Angela and the others saw her coming; their heads bobbed down and their eyes giggled slyly at each other.

Listen, from not far away, saw that the circle was perfect, and tight. She stopped. She was not going over.

She stood on the lawn among the garlands of girls, and she felt, for a moment, like a fading Christmas tree, awkward and bulky in the centre of a room, when Christmas had finished weeks before. She was foolishly conspicuous and perfectly invisible, both at once. Coloured lights, she thought, were blinking down her legs and hanging loose across her waist. Her arms were branches slung with rusting baubles, and strings of stale popcorn dangled from her hair.

●

Sir:

I am writing to provide you with an update.

Today is Wednesday, and, as planned, I had a second affair with the aeronautical engineer.

Three things occurred which were of note.

First, when he arrived at the University tennis courts, A.E. mentioned that he has read Madame Bovary, *in the original French. 'Have you?' I said. 'Yes,' he replied.*

Second, halfway through the first game, A.E. stopped and took off his right tennis shoe and sock, to check on a blister. The blister was so bad that he had to PEEL the sock away from his foot. It was disgusting. I noted that his toes are very hairy.

Third, and perhaps most importantly, after he had applied a bandaid to the blister, and replaced his sock and shoe (and tied the shoelace), he stood up, turned to me, and said: 'You want to come to my place, and, you know, fool around?'

Fool around!

I said: 'I have a boyfriend!'

He shrugged. I'm not sure whether his shrug meant 'so what?'

about my having a boyfriend, or 'oh well' about my not wanting to fool around.

Whatever it was, we played a set of tennis, I lost every point, and then, of course, I went back to work.

Yours sincerely,
Marbie Zing

●

The following week, Listen was a sentry.

In most of her subjects, she had found places to sit away from Donna and the others, although in Science, she was not allowed to change benches. So she still had to sit with Donna and Caro, and when they did experiments together they were very polite.

At lunchtimes she hovered around the tuckshop door, like a sentry. She stood on the tips of her toes, scanning the crowd at the counter. *Where are my friends?* her facial expressions said. *Why so slow?* She had to open up her Vegemite sandwich and eat it, all the time watching and guarding the door. Then, finally, when she had finished her sandwich, she gave up and went to the library until the end-of-lunch bell rang.

●

Sir:

Can I be honest? I am really sick of tennis. I'm so bad at it. What do you think we should do? Should we try squash instead or should we diversify? Should our next affair be a lateral move into a different sphere? Like a dinner or trip to the zoo? Only I hate the zoo. There are so many animals.

We have had two more affairs since I last wrote, both of them tennis and always the same result: 6-0, 6-0.

You remember I told you that my aeronautical engineer suggested that we 'fool around'? And you remember how I gallantly refused?

Well, since my refusal, there has not been even a murmur in that direction. I keep planning the tone of my rejection (reproving; annoyed yet kindly; exasperated but faintly amused; and so on), but it is all for nothing.

Why hasn't he asked me again? Do you think he's lost interest? And in that case, why does he keep asking me to tennis? It can't be for the game.

Your sincerely,
Marbie Zing

•

'Do you think we should be worrying that Listen isn't talking about school anymore?'

'No,' said Vernon, serving up the soup. 'She's always been quiet.'

'She's not quiet around me,' said Marbie. 'Not usually. Or around my family.'

'Well, maybe tomorrow when the family's all here for Cassie's birthday, she'll talk again,' suggested Vernon.

'Remember her first week of Year 7, she didn't stop talking?' said Marbie, nostalgically. 'Remember? She told us about the Geography teacher who ran around the room pretending to be the monsoon wind, and about the Science teacher who said they had to dissect frogs, and how Caro said she would get a note from her mum saying she didn't have to and the teacher said, "Notes don't count!" and Caro said, "Notes *always* count," and the teacher said, "Have you —"'

At that moment, Listen walked in and sat at the table, saying, 'Cool. Pumpkin soup.'

'Have you read *Madame Bovary*?' Marbie said to Vernon, smoothly. 'In the original French?'

'No,' replied Vernon. 'I've only seen the movie.'

'I've read *Charlie and the Chocolate Factory*,' offered Listen. 'But I haven't seen the movie.'

'You haven't seen the movie!' Vernon and Marbie cried in unison, and Vernon rain danced around the table. The telephone rang and he incorporated the answering-of-the-phone into the dance, so that his head was upside down for most of the conversation.

'Yes . . . yes, there's a Listen Taylor here, let me – . . . okay, sure, you're from where? . . . From the Kenthurst School of – really! Uh-huh. Uh-huh. She did? Well no, I didn't . . . I mean, of course! Well, I'm sorry about that. You know what? I'm going to call you back in five minutes. Okay. Can I get your number? Okay, okay, I'll call you back.'

He wrote a number on the back of the electricity bill, which he swiped from under a magnet on the fridge, and then he turned his head right way up to hang up the phone.

'Hey, Listen,' he said, sitting back at the table. 'Why didn't you tell us you wanted to do Tae Kwon Do?'

'Because I don't want to do Tae Kwon Do.' Listen took a bite of her bread roll.

'Well, the guy on the phone says a few weeks ago you joined his class, and then you phoned back ten minutes later and cancelled.'

They both looked at Listen. She dipped her roll into her pumpkin soup, studying the soup to do this, and then she looked up from under her fringe, saw they were still staring and said, 'What?'

'Could it have been a different Listen Taylor?' suggested Marbie. 'There would be a lot of them around. *Listen* is a very common name.'

'Okay, shut up. You can talk. *Marbie Zing*. I wanted to do Tae Kwon Do but then I didn't want to. I changed my mind.'

'In the space of ten minutes!'

'I decided it would be too expensive. Hey, should I sand the kitchen cupboards tonight, ready to repaint?'

'Don't try to change the subject. Vernon, call the man back and enrol Listen in his class.'

'What do you think I'm doing?' Vernon was reaching for the phone.

'Oh no, that's okay. I changed my mind. I *seriously* don't want to do Tae Kwon Do, guys. Do we have enough sandpaper?'

'Because it's too expensive!' cried Marbie. 'Listen! You must do *anything* you want. You should be learning Portuguese and auto-mechanics and candle-making, and *definitely* Tae Kwon Do! Fancy learned the drums when she was your age and she is now a more interesting person than I am! Because I don't play the drums! Money is no *object* where *interest* is concerned! Would you like to play the drums?'

' 'Well, but I'm not really *interested* –'

'Shush, Listen, it's ringing.'

'You don't need to turn upside down again, Vernon.'

'Is this the Kenthurst School of Tae Kwon Do? Yes, we just spoke. *I have a new member for you!* I know. I know! I know.'

•

Sir:

It's after midnight and I'm lying awake staring at Vernon, and thinking of how lovely he is to his little sister, and how I have never even seen the movie of Madame Bovary, *let alone read the book.*

And also, you know, of course, that I don't mean a word. I have had no affair. I have only played tennis with a stranger, four or five times. A perfectly pointless stranger. And he did ask me to fool around but maybe he was talking about PlayStation.

The only reason I have called it an 'affair' is that I have not told Vernon about the tennis. But, paradoxically, the only reason I have NOT told Vernon is that it is NOT an affair. It is nothing, nothing at all, and maybe I'm just looking for intrigue.

Tomorrow, Vernon and Listen will spend all day helping to prepare for Cassie's party. And I know Vernon thinks our Family Secret is dangerous and wrong, but he still accepts that it's part of my life, and he comes along every Friday night, and he's much more punctual than I am.

And guess what, he just woke up and asked if I'm okay and can I sleep? Should we go for a swim at Bellbird High? he said, even though he has a cold and an early start.

I told him I was writing a letter to the editor, and he kissed my elbow.

I would never do anything with the A.E. except tennis, you know.

I have decided not to see him again.

Yours sincerely,
Marbie Zing

CASSIE'S BIRTHDAY PARTY

Neighbourhood children were playing a skipping game on the street. Occasionally, the game would pause as the sun-heated tarmac became too much for one or another of the children. That child would shout and hop about until another child turned a garden hose onto the burning soles. Then the game would continue.

Across the street, Marbie said, 'Hmm', Vernon took a sip of beer, and Listen shook her head and murmured, 'Why no shoes?' They were sitting in a row on their front porch, waiting for their party guests.

'If this front driveway belonged to us,' said Marbie, 'instead of to the entire apartment block, what do you think we would do with it?'

'I would put in a duck pond,' said Listen. 'And gentle, grazing horses.'

'I'd build a university,' Vernon said. 'Educate the youth around these parts.'

Two cars of party guests arrived, and the neighbourhood children had to clear off the road.

'Look at that!' cried Grandma Zing, bustling out of the first car. 'We all arrived at once!'

Grandpa Zing got out more slowly, and saluted the hosts one at a time.

'We're HERE!' cried Fancy, climbing out of the second car. 'And we've got the birthday girl!'

The birthday girl opened the back door, twisting her mouth around to make her face casual. She stepped out and brushed down her dress.

'HAPPY BIRTHDAY, CASSIE!' Vernon, Marbie, Listen and Grandma Zing shouted, and Cassie looked up with a shining smile.

'I've got Lucinda too,' she remembered, and everyone said, 'Oh!', as another little girl emerged from the car.

'What's Radcliffe doing?' said Grandma Zing, squinting through the window of Fancy's car. 'Why isn't he getting out? Radcliffe! What are you doing in there?'

'He's just trying to figure out the air-conditioning,' explained Fancy. 'He couldn't get it to work.'

'Fancy, darling, tonight's good, between seven and ten. I've got the new code; it's in the mint.'

'All right,' agreed Fancy, but her mother had already turned away, and was rapping on the window with her keys, calling, 'Too late, Radcliffe! You're here now!'

In the living room, everyone exclaimed about the multicoloured beanbags and the table covered with treats. There were banana fritters, chocolate bananas, banana tarts, banana bread, a pavlova covered in bananas, and jugs of banana smoothie. Also, there was a large bowl of punch in which bananas and strawberries floated.

'Look at all the strawberries in the punch!' cried Grandma Zing. 'Cassie, do you know, I almost forgot to bring your presents! Can you imagine?'

'Not really,' said Cassie.

'Your place is looking gorgeous,' said Fancy.

'A *garden apartment* is such a lovely find!' declared Grandma Zing.

'What kind of a security system do you have?' said Radcliffe.

'Does it have a bathroom?' said Cassie's friend Lucinda, politely.

'You got a pest inspection done, right?' said Radcliffe.

'That's not termite damage, what you're looking at there, Radcliffe,' said Grandpa Zing. 'That's just regular wear and tear.'

'Haven't they done it up nicely,' said Grandma Zing. 'They've put silver covers on all their electrical outlets. Isn't *that* a nice touch?'

'Nice painting job here,' said Radcliffe. 'Professional or . . .?'

'This is not just a house-warming party,' said Cassie, 'this is also a *birthday* party. As far as I recall.'

After Cassie's presents had been opened, they toured the apartment, establishing, several times, that: there were six apartments in the building; that this one was on the *ground floor*; that they were almost finished renovating; and that Marbie had only been joking when she said they were going to tear down the outside bathroom wall and bathe *al fresco*. Then Cassie suggested they play Pass the Parcel.

They played Pass the Parcel, Musical Chairs and Pin the Tail on Grandpa Zing. Cassie had painted a picture of Grandpa Zing for the purposes of this game, and Grandpa Zing was a good sport about it.

Later, they sat down, still breathless from the games, and ate banana treats.

'I'll never get out of this beanbag,' said Grandma Zing, now and then.

Vernon took Radcliffe and Grandpa Zing onto the roof of the apartment building, to see where the air-conditioning vents came out. Grandma Zing remembered she had a house-warming present and returned from her car with a fig tree. Fancy remembered she also had a house-warming present and returned from her car with a cocktail shaker. Marbie watered the tree and Fancy made cocktails. She used vodka, vermouth, apple juice and apple gratings, then she put a curl of apple peel on the edge of each glass.

'Look,' she said, carrying the glasses carefully, as the contents tended to lap over the edges. 'I've invented an apple martini.'

Listen took Cassie and Lucinda into her bedroom so they could play Cassie's new game of Valerio Rock. You took turns composing melodies on the keyboard, sang into the microphone, and then waited while the game added beats and back-up singers, so that you were, for a moment, a rock star. After that, the game became complicated and you had to spell, mime, draw pictures and do the hokey-pokey.

'Hang on a minute,' said Cassie, and she ran into the living room, where she announced to the room: 'Listen is *such* a great dancer, everyone', before running back into the bedroom. 'Keep dancing, Listen,' she ordered, 'until everyone comes and sees.'

In the main bedroom, Grandma Zing admired the curtains, and then took them down so she could redo the hems.

The game of Valerio Rock ended, and Listen said, 'Cassie, your nose is bleeding.'

'It'll stop in a minute,' said Cassie. 'It's because it's summer.'

'She just needs a hanky,' explained Lucinda, 'and I have to put a key on the back of her neck.'

Listen gave Cassie a handkerchief and the front door key, and left the girls to work on the bleeding nose.

In the living room, Marbie put on a Red Hot Chili Peppers album and asked Listen to teach Fancy how to dance. Listen jumped on the spot to the music, shaking her head wildly, and Fancy obediently copied.

Quietly, Grandpa Zing and Radcliffe retreated to the porch.

In the bathroom, Cassie leaned over the tub and allowed her nose to bleed. She tried to write her name but it just went: spot . . . spot . . . spot, each spot leaking in a different direction.

Lucinda sat on the edge of the tub, holding the key against the back of Cassie's neck, and watching the blood with interest. Every now and again she reached to turn the taps on and wash the blood away.

Later, Grandma Zing asked Listen what she thought of her new school, and whether she had some new friends.

'She likes her old friends, don't you, Listen?' Vernon said affectionately when Listen hesitated. 'Tell everyone about the teachers, Listen. She's got some funny teacher stories.'

'Well,' said Listen, slowly. 'There's a Food Technology teacher who taught us how to make lamingtons. It's not a funny story, but I can make some now?' She was walking backwards towards the kitchen.

'But will you need eggs?' said Marbie. 'Because I used them all in the pavlova.'

'Yes,' said Listen, hesitating again. 'I'll need eggs.'

Fancy looked at her watch. 'Gosh,' she said. 'It's eight o'clock. Let's go to the corner store and buy some eggs for Listen. Marbie?'

'Tell us about 2nd grade, Cassie, while they're gone,' said Grandma Zing. 'How's your new teacher, darling? What do you think of your teacher?'

'I prefer Mr Woodford to our teacher,' chatted Lucinda. 'He's the other second grade teacher? And he's REALLY funny. I wish I was in his class instead.'

'Do you?' Grandma Zing regarded Lucinda, and then turned back to Cassie.

'I like *my* teacher,' declared Cassie. 'She's nice.'

'That's my girl,' said Grandma Zing. 'Come here and give me a hug.'

Cassie gave her grandmother a hug.

'We might be a while, okay, everyone?' said Fancy, drawing a black chiffon scarf from her handbag. 'Because I think we should go into Baulkham Hills for the eggs, don't you, Marbie?'

'I agree,' said Marbie.

'Be careful, eh?' said Vernon, reaching for a handful of peanuts.

●

'Over there, behind that station wagon,' Fancy pointed, and Marbie pulled over.

'Have you got it?' said Marbie.

'It's in my scarf.'

'And the new code?'

'Apparently it's in the mint.' Fancy opened the back door, and reached into a wicker basket. 'Got it.' She fell into step alongside Marbie.

'Final check,' said Marbie, drawing out her pager, and tapping in a number. They walked on side-by-side, until a cat gave a faint 'miaow' from Marbie's pocket. 'That's it,' said Marbie. 'You okay?'

'You bet,' said Fancy, and they separated smoothly, Fancy floating into the distance. Her earrings glinted in the moonlight.

●

Lucinda had fallen asleep on her beanbag when Fancy and Marbie returned.

'Here we are,' said Fancy, opening the front door.

'All right?' said Radcliffe.

'All right,' agreed Fancy.

Listen reached out for the eggs.

3

THE HOT AIR BALLOON

At the time when Maude lay in bed for several weeks, loss and pain were put into context. Broken hearts, blisters, papercuts, scaldings; all grains of sand pouring regularly through an hourglass. She was used to them. But here was this sharp rock, lodged in the neck of the hourglass, choking the flow. No time, no breath, just monolithic pain holding everything still. If only she could pick up the glass, shake it loose, lose the pain as she had lost that life.

Occasionally, she dreamt herself out of the hourglass, into the basket of a hot air balloon. But then she could only watch helplessly as an inverted parachute fell from the basket and crashed through the air to the ground.

This was years after she first heard the story of the watercolour painter.

4

CATH MURPHY

It was well known at Redwood Primary that Warren had a wife up the coast. He just hadn't mentioned this, specifically, to Cath.

In fact, in the weeks after the Borrowed Cat, it seemed to Cath that 'Warren's wife, Breanna' was the subject of constant conversation at Redwood, *even among her friends*. For example, Suzanne would say to Lenny, 'What are you up to this weekend, Len?' To which Lenny would reply, 'Going up the coast to Terrigal, I think.' To which Suzanne would declare, 'Terrigal! Isn't that where Warren's wife, Breanna, lives?' To which Lenny would demur, 'No, Warren's wife, Breanna, lives at Avoca. It's the next beach around.'

Or, for example, Mr Bel Castro (teacher, Grade 5A) would say, 'These muffins are delicious!' To which Miss Waratah (teacher, Grade 4C) would reply, 'Oh, thank you! The recipe is Warren's wife, Breanna's!' To which Mr Bel Castro would say, 'Gosh.'

That's how it seemed to Cath in the weeks after the Borrowed Cat. *Warren's wife, Breanna* was like one of those new phrases you learn and then find that it's been kicking around for years.

Of course, the night of the Borrowed Cat itself, she only knew that Warren had kept the wife a secret, and then sprung it on her, cheerfully, like a novelty mousetrap. Driving home that afternoon, she felt a flash of terror at how stupid she had been. Then the terror became a fierce blush of self-loathing at how VERY <u>VERY</u> STUPID SHE HAD BEEN.

The blush lasted almost all the way home, and blazed up again when she found her favourite dress set out neatly on the ironing board. Also, her black opal necklace, whimsically looped around the fridge door handle as a reminder to herself to wear it. She opened the fridge and slammed it so hard that the kitchen shook.

Then she opened the fridge again and poured herself a glass of apple juice, in order to calm down. 'So what? He's married. Big deal.' She wandered carelessly into the dining room where she stamped once and flung the juice at the window. It dribbled over her reflection.

At her law class, tears began to well in her eyes. She realised, drawing sad little squiggles in her notebook, that there would be no shy, meaningful glances tonight, no bluesy conversation. No! There would be Warren-and-his-Wife-Breanna. They would sit opposite her with their hands intertwined.

Actually, now that she thought about it, it would be *more* than just Warren-and-his-Wife. It would be the whole gang!

'Come along' he had written in his quiz at the Monday assembly. 'Come along to see the Carotid Sticks *where we will meet a jolly circle of my friends, my wife, incidentally, among them*!'

That's what he had meant. It was so obvious she was blinded by her tears, and her breathing became tangled. Doctor Carmichael, the lecturer, leaned towards her from his podium and his turban almost fell off.

Warren's friends, she realised, would stand up noisily when she arrived, their ashtrays and drinks in a clutter. There would be a shortish woman in a large-collared blouse, who would swap a cigarette to her left hand, and squint a smile at Cath through the smoke. There would be two skinny men in corduroys, each saying 'hi!' in a witty friendly way. Also, a little later, breathless from the Central Coast train, there would be Warren's wife, Breanna.

By the time Cath reached the Borrowed Cat, she was furious with Warren and his gang. *Don't you smoke in my face*, she commanded, angrily, as she pushed open the door. And: *What's with the corduroy, boys?* she sneered as the waitress welcomed her.

The Borrowed Cat was in a basement. An unexpected spotlight roamed the room, but otherwise it flickered darkly like a shaded candle. The waitress led Cath to a corner table where Warren was sitting alone.

She gave him a vicious, complicated smile, which he returned with a dazzling beam, stretching out his arms in welcome.

'You're not late at all!' he said.

'Yes I am. I am *fifteen minutes* late.'

'It's okay, they're not starting for another hour,' he reassured her.

'Where's your wife, Breanna?' she said archly. 'And everybody else?'

'There is nobody else,' he apologised. 'And Bree just called. She's not going to make it and she's disappointed. She wanted to meet you. She said to say "hi", okay?'

Cath was so shocked she sat down and snatched the menu from Warren's hands.

That night, their knees touched under the table several times, and each time she moved away, abruptly. She drank a reckless pitcher of sangria, and she made a little monster out of Warren's bread roll, so he couldn't eat it. Also, she told him the facts of some brutal murder cases, all the time glaring and glowering at him, while he leaned forward, delighted.

When the Carotid Sticks began playing, she turned her chair around so she could see the band, and fell asleep against his shoulder.

When she woke, she told Warren that the band was *crap* and that was a word she never used. 'I only agreed to come,' she said, 'because I was thinking of the Clotted Creams.' He shouted with laughter and suggested they see the Clotted Creams together some other time. 'No,' she said, 'because you have a bony, uncomfortable shoulder and I hardly slept a wink.' He shouted again, and then apologised sincerely.

While the band packed up, she asked a lot of ironic questions about the wife. *What does she do for a living? Oh, and why does she live up the coast? Uh-huh, and where did you two meet?*

The wife was a psychologist, and was having trouble finding work in Sydney, so she lived up the coast during the week. She did relationship counselling up there. They had met through friends or something dull like that. Breanna had a late appointment that day, and would come down on the early train tomorrow. Usually, she arrived, Fridays, on the seven fifty-three.

'Ah,' agreed Cath, 'the seven fifty-three.' She felt wonderfully cutting.

The next day, Saturday, she felt so vicious and vengeful that she phoned Suzanne and cancelled their movie. But Suzanne called back and said she had been *so* looking forward to a night without the kids, and her husband was all set to babysit and had the *Finding Nemo* DVD ready to go. So Cath agreed, and sat through the movie with her eyes half-closed, pressing her fingernails into her palms, imagining each palm was Warren's face. Suzanne, beside her, ate a choc-top.

But the following week, back at school, Cath discovered the wife's renown, and felt contrite. It was not Warren's fault. He must have assumed that she knew about the wife! He had just kept her out of conversation!

The weather shifted one shade down: the sky cast a light that was cautious and reserved, and the air took on a disapproving chill. Cath walked around in cardigans and in a dull private shame.

With Warren, she became gentle and polite, as if she had discovered he had a terminal disease rather than a wife. Sometimes he tried to liven her up, doing things like jogging on the spot in the playground and crying: 'Cath! What's happened to my legs? They're moving too quickly!' But Cath just gave a sad little smile and continued walking, while the children fell about in hysterics. Some of them grabbed at Warren's knees to help him stop.

Often, he looked at her in a puzzled and disappointed way, as if to say: what has happened to my friend?

But, she cried in the middle of the night, *he is married! How can I continue as his 'friend'?* At the same time, she wondered what had happened to their friendship. Could it just end like that?

Coincidentally, the day after one such sleepless night, Cath attended a law class on:

Principles of Statutory Interpretation: Lesson 1

She always began her law notes with a flamboyant heading. Begin as you mean to go on. After a while, though, the lecturer's voice would drift, taking its own meandering path, and her notes in turn would grow drowsy. Today, Cath's notes paid attention, at least for the *first* principle of statutory interpretation.

> *Generalia specialibus non derogant*: if a special Act is followed by a general Act, the special Act remains as an exception to the general.

Doctor Carmichael explained: 'For example. Let us say Parliament enacts the *Care for Pigs Act*. This is an Act requiring all pet pigs to be dyed a lurid shade of orange.'

He paused, but nobody ever laughed in law class.

'E.g.,' Cath wrote in her notes: '<u>Care for Pigs Act</u>. Must dye pigs orange.'

'And one month later,' continued Doctor Carmichael, 'Parliament enacts the *Care for Animals Act*. This Act requires all *pets* to be dyed blue. Okay, guys, let's say you have a pet pig. What colour do you dye your pig?'

'1 mnth ltr,' Cath wrote. '<u>Care for Animals Act</u>. Must dye pets blue.' She waited with her pen poised for the lecturer to give the answer.

'Come on, come on,' said Doctor Carmichael, looking around the room. 'Take a guess! Do we dye our pig orange or blue?'

Ask the pig, thought Cath, *which it prefers*.

'Orange,' said Doctor Carmichael, calmly. 'You must dye your pig orange.'

'Dye pig orange,' wrote Cath, and drew a little doodle of a pig.

'You see?' Doctor Carmichael had bright blue eyes and little wisps of orange hair escaping from the edges of his turban. 'The first Act was *specific*, so it stays on as an exception to the second. Your dogs and cats and turtles must be blue, but your *pig* has *got* to stay orange.'

At this point, Cath's notes faded into half-finished words – 'dog, cat, turts, bl'. Then she wrote: *Surely it is wrong to dye a pig any colour at all?*

She drew a circle around the question mark, and added petals to the circle. The petals made her think of Warren. *We have bought a Breville Sandwich Maker together*, she remembered sadly. *If I can't have an unfurling romance, why can't I at least have the friendship?*

But she knew that the special little act, the purchase of a Breville Sandwich Maker, had been eclipsed by his announcement: 'My wife.' She could never be friends with him again.

Generalia specialibus non derogant.

Ah-hah! Cath realised, with a sudden thumping heart: *if a special Act is followed by a general Act, the special Act remains as an exception to the general!* So it's all right! Her face was burning. The sandwich maker is allowed to carry on! It remains as an *exception* to the Wife!

So then, with some relief, Cath returned to her jocular ways with Warren, and he also seemed relieved to have her back. They started having takeaway lattes again, and sometimes hot chocolates with marsh-mallows. And they spent a lot of time kneeling in front of the staffroom radiator trying to turn it up.

Since their sandwich-maker friendship had never included discussion of the Wife, Cath did not raise her in their conversations now. Nor did Warren.

One Wednesday afternoon, they worked in the staffroom until the sky was heavy with darkness. Walking to the parking lot, through the empty, echoing school grounds, cold fog curled around their ankles. 'Like my cat,' suggested Cath. Warren gave a chuckle, and kicked a pebble towards Cath. She kicked it straight back.

'Don't our cars look lonely?' said Warren. 'We should park them next to each other when we work back like this.'

'So they can get to know each other,' agreed Cath.

They were now at the edge of the parking lot – Cath's white Mercedes Sports gleamed from the far right corner; Warren's rusting Corolla glinted from the left.

'Holy baloney, I love your car,' breathed Warren. 'Remind me how you scored that again? Some wealthy former lover?'

'I won it in a competition.'

'Lucky girl,' whistled Warren, and then swiftly: 'Remind me when you were planning to take me for a ride in it?'

'Right this moment,' said Cath, clapping her hands together once like Mary Poppins. 'You don't have any plans, do you?'

'*Plans*,' said Warren, sadly. 'I'm as lonely as our cars are tonight. I was going to see a movie actually. But what kind of a fool would choose a movie over a ride in *your* car, Cath? What kind of a fool, what kind of a tool, what kind of a *drool*ing mule? Eh?'

'I could drive you to the movie if you like. I'll see it with you.'

Warren leapt into the air. He was tall enough already: Cath imagined his leap would take him right into the stars.

Then, suddenly, Katie Toby (teacher, Kinder A) was standing beside them. Cath gave a little shriek, and Warren said, 'Holy *jacaranda*, woman, where did *you* come from?'

They both stared down at Katie Toby, who was little, with a dimpled round face and a reputation, among parents, teachers and children alike, as: *sweet as a toffee apple*.

'Hi, guys,' she giggled. 'Sorry to scare you. I've just come from my classroom. Going to a movie, are you?'

Cath nodded, uneasily.

'What movie?'

'Ah, the Valerio retrospective at the Chauvel,' said Warren, after a beat. 'It's *Pie in the Sky* tonight.'

'Oh yeah, *great*. I'd love to see that again. What time? On your way right now?'

'Well,' said Warren, 'it starts at nine.'

Then there was a silence as Katie dimpled at them, until Warren said, 'You want to come along?'

'Oh *no!*' cried Katie. 'I'm off! My bicycle's just over there! Stay joyous!' and she skittered away into the darkness.

Cath and Warren approached Cath's car in silence, but as soon as they had each pressed the car doors closed, Warren said, 'Thank Christ she didn't accept,' and Cath felt such a gust of relief that she fell into a fit of giggles. She couldn't get the keys in the ignition she was giggling so helplessly. Warren sat beside her, laughing happily and looking around at the upholstery.

Then, just as Cath had calmed enough to sniff and wipe her eyes, Warren's phone rang.

'WHERE *ARE* YOU?' cried a tinny voice.

It was Breanna. Inside Cath's car. Cath gave a little shiver.

'I'm in a beautiful Mercedes Sports car, next to the lovely Cath, and we're going to the movies,' Warren explained promptly. 'How about you?'

'I'm *here!* At *home!* I've come down for a surprise visit! I've got candles and *everything!*' Breanna's voice rushed along in a high-pitched gabble. It was unnecessarily loud, and was filling Cath's car. She opened her window.

'You're joking,' said Warren, his voice deepening and softening at once. 'You're here? My beautiful Bree, within *minutes* of me? On a weeknight?'

'I was starting to worry about you! What kind of a job does he have, I thought. I thought he was a teacher! A laugh of a job! I was wrong! Come home! Come on! I've got Indian!'

'I'll be there in five.'

He returned his phone to his pocket. 'Sorry, Cath. Another time?'

As he walked toward his own car, he blew a passionate kiss her way, which she almost took for herself. Then she realised it was for her car.

Driving home, Cath passed the ice-cream van that was always parked across the street from her apartment block, and thought: *That van is NEVER open.* What if she wanted an ice cream right now? Even if it *was* after eight, and a cold, foggy, blustery night. She would, in fact, like an ice cream.

She walked into her apartment and the silence seemed to catch her like a hangnail.

•

I like the way he walks, thought Cath, one late afternoon, watching Warren cross the playground. *I like the way he kind of lopes along, scuffing at the fallen leaves. See how his head sits way up on top of his body there? I like that. He looks good in that linen suit, too, with the open collar. I wonder when I'll get to kiss his collarbone?*

Of course, I didn't mean that. I know nothing is ever going to happen. He is married to the beautiful Bree.

She watched as he approached their building. He had stopped to lean over and pick up a toy car.

Still, I don't think it's wrong just to THINK about kissing him. That's probably quite healthy, actually. You have to have sexual fantasies about SOMEONE, don't you? It could be Brad Pitt, let's say, and you know you're never going to kiss HIS collarbone. So why not dream about Warren's?

Warren was now running up the steps to the 2nd grade balcony, and Cath thought fiercely: *Turn right, turn right towards my classroom.*

He did. He leaned in to her open classroom door and said, '*There* you are! I've been looking for you everywhere!'

'How come?' She busied herself away from the window. 'I'm just taking down these pictures of polar bears.'

'Because I want to take you out to dinner tonight,' explained Warren. 'I've got a reservation at Tetsuya's, and Breanna was coming down especially, but she just cancelled, if you can believe it, so you're not allowed to say "no", okay?'

Cath regarded him.

'And also,' said Warren. 'It's my birthday today.'

'Okay,' said Cath. 'I'll come.'

After Tetsuya's, they took a taxi to the Shangri-La for cocktails. The taxi nudged through traffic and gathering rain clouds, and Warren Wishful Woodford unfurled his long thin body, and unfurled his words ('How much?' to the driver), and his body and his words were like a banner, or a long royal carpet, thought Cath, gazing through the steamy taxi window. He was standing on the footpath waiting for her, and she was inside the taxi thinking that his words were like a pathway through the woods.

As she gathered up her handbag, he opened her door, taking the steamy taxi window with him, and letting in the traffic and the cold. She walked beside him silently, her legs moving smoothly like the wheels of a cart through the furling ferny fronds of a forest. (At Tetsuya's there had been a nine-course *degustation* menu, with a wine to match each course.)

At the cocktail bar, it was so crowded they had to lean in close to hear one another. They talked for a while about how wicked it was of Breanna to cancel on Warren's *birthday*, even *if* a pair of clients had phoned her to say they had made a joint suicide pact and were having trouble with the catch on the gun. 'Birthdays come but once a year,' said Cath, sternly, 'but suicide pacts?' She gave a dismissive shrug. 'A dime a dozen,' agreed Warren.

'Hey,' said Cath, changing the subject, and looking up at Warren from her frothy strawberry cocktail (she reflected that her eyes would be shining in this light). 'I need your teaching advice. You know Cassie Zing?'

'How could anybody not know Cassie Zing?'

'Well, today she said the c-word five hundred times.'

'The what?'

'The *c-word*.'

Warren leaned in to her ear and whispered, 'Cunt?'

'Warren! You're not allowed to whisper that word into a woman's *ear!*'

'Well, you don't want me to say it out loud, do you? So . . .?'

'Well,' agreed Cath, doubtfully. 'What should I do about Cassie? She does this all the time, you know, she chooses a word to say five hundred times, and sometimes I think the best thing is to ignore it, and she'll get over it, but she doesn't. And today, it turned into a kind of crisis, which I didn't really handle very well.'

'What other words?'

'You know, bad words. Like *eczema* or *scrotum* or the *c-word* — you *get away from my ear* — and now I think about it, maybe she's casting a kind of spell over the classroom, I mean a *good* spell, where she's taking all the evil out of the world by chanting it away, so there's nothing left for us but *good*, so maybe I should just, you know, let her cast her spell. Or, do you think maybe I'm drunk?'

'Well, she's either casting a spell or she's obsessive compulsive, and you are gorgeous when you're drunk. Do you want me to ask Bree about Cassie? She used to work with kids before she got into relationship counselling.'

Bree was in the conversation a bit too much tonight, Cath thought, disgruntled.

'Oh no,' she said, 'I'll ask Lenny. Good idea! Professional help! I always forget that Lenny's the school counsellor as well as the 6th grade teacher. I'll ask her advice.'

'She'll be distracted,' said Warren, signalling for the bill. 'Screwing Frank Billson must be very — distracting.'

'You can't pay for this too, Warren. This will be me paying. This will be your birthday present from me. Watch me pay, okay? And HEY, HOW DO YOU KNOW ABOUT LENNY AND BILLSON? IT'S A SECRET!'

Warren slid the bill from underneath her hand and said, 'You coming out with me tonight? *That* is my birthday present from you. And I know about Lenny and Billson because Lenny and Billson are blindingly obvious. Everybody knows about them, Cath Murphy.'

'Do they?' Cath said, wonderingly, enjoying the way he just said her full name, and scraping at the sides of her cocktail glass with the straw.

'Maybe not Heather Waratah,' conceded Warren. 'Heather Waratah probably doesn't know about Lenny and Billson. She's too busy baking muffins. Don't forget your jacket there, eh? Here, let me take your arm.'

Later that night, Cath lay awake replaying Warren's sentence: 'You coming out with me tonight? *That* is my birthday present from you.' Sometimes she rewrote it to say, 'You getting a room with me tonight? *That* is my birthday present from you.'

Even later, she sleepily, drunkenly, wickedly, replayed him whispering the c-word in her ear.

The next day Warren passed on Bree's 'eternal gratitude' to Cath, for taking care of Warren on his birthday.

•

Zooming from school to her law lecture, and then from the lecture to Feminist Discussion, Cath felt she had a full life. Her windscreen wipers dashed back and forth, trying to keep up with her full life.

She ran through the rain to the café and sat in the comfortable plum-purple chair. 'Hi,' she whispered, and, 'Sorry to be late', and Leonie mouthed back a quick, 'No worries!'

Leonie Marple-Hedgington was an old friend of Cath's from university. She had purple hair, polar-white skin and the settled, mistaken belief that Cath was the kind of person who would want to go to Feminist Discussion. Cath did not like to correct her, and so attended every session.

Leonie leaned forward, bonily, cardigan pushed up to her elbows, to say, 'I thought today,' (a little shy to start), 'I thought today we might find a way to deconstruct the rational/irrational duality?'

Everybody nodded, including Cath, but as she nodded she thought of Warren Woodford and his own special nods. His own sideways thinking nod, his own hearty, rapid nod, his own slow *perhaps* nod, his nodding nod–nod.

'As you know, there's a crit group who call themselves the *irrationalists* so as to reclaim the word irrational, and invest it with something powerful and good,' continued Leonie.

Irrational, thought Cath, and she thought, immediately, of the word: *affair*.

How irrational an affair would be! Even, let's say, if Warren planned such a thing. I would NEVER let it happen! It would be wrong, but more to the point: IRRATIONAL. I've read the books, I've seen the movies, I've read the magazine problem pages! Don't even worry about it. He'll keep promising to leave his wife, but he NEVER EVER will.

'Doing no more than exploring the boundaries of the admittedly nebulous notion of sense, of course.'

And of course, I wouldn't WANT him to leave his wife! That makes no SENSE. Because, see, if he's the kind of guy who leaves his wife, he's not a nice guy, and why would I want a not-nice guy? Plus, I would never want to hurt another woman like that. I'm at Feminist Discussion! If I had an affair with Warren, I would betray my own KIND!

'What we still have to do, you know, is to pin down the power/knowledge paradigm, and colonise Foucault, make him our own. Keeping in mind the Balkanisation of the issue, of course,' finished Leonie.

'Hmm,' agreed Cath, nodding along with the others.

•

In the last week of the school term, Cath sat on her living room floor, wrapped in her quilt, and played with the hole in her tooth with her tongue. It was so cold that the windows had fogged over, and her small electric heater did not know what to do. It made hysterical hissing noises.

Cath had to make a dentist appointment. She leaned out of her quilt to write in her Filofax, choosing the second Tuesday of the holidays to:

Make dentist appointment. Then, efficiently, she closed the Filofax. So, that was done.

'Now, I'm sure you will *all* have noticed that Sydney is experiencing *record-breaking* lows this winter,' the weather man interrupted her. She looked at the TV and nodded, 'Uh-huh.'

'And you might *also* have heard some buzz around that *snow* might come to Sydney. You know what? I'm going to put my eggs in that basket too.'

'Snow!' said Cath, scornfully. 'It doesn't snow in Sydney!'

But still, imagine if it did! The weather man was waving an arm over his map, and talking about ground temperatures, a cold front and moisture on its way. 'Or,' he was saying, 'let me go out on a limb here – I would not be at all surprised if this turned out to be *freezing rain*!'

'Freezing rain,' wondered Cath, imagining a sky filled with long thin streaks of ice. Dangerous. But what was 'freezing rain'?

'If you don't know what that is,' the TV was saying, obligingly, 'take a look at these shots from the film *The Ice Storm* – see the ice and the icicles everywhere? Turns out they used *hair gel* for those shots. But if it happens here in Sydney, it won't be a result of film tricks – no, it will be the result of these zero-degree temperatures we've been having. See, rain falls from the warmer sky, hits the colder surface of the earth, and instantly freezes. That's any surface – cars, letterboxes, rooftops, trees, you name it.'

'Zero degrees!' said Cath. 'No wonder I'm so cold!'

'Brrrr,' agreed the weather man.

She changed the channel to MTV, and waited for a song that would make her cry. Crying would warm her up. She had an apple, but eating made her feel unbalanced, her left cheek aching from all its chewing, and the right side begging for some apple. But if she relented, let the right side of her mouth have some apple, she was sure to hit the tooth with the hole and make it shriek.

She set the apple on the carpet.

There were Things-To-Do clumped all around her, and her cat, Violin, trod from Thing to Thing; disrespectful, indiscriminate, like the weather. She took Violin beneath her arm, the bell on his collar jangling, and surveyed her Things-To-Do.

1. A toppling pile of egg cartons for art and craft at school. (Cut out the egg cups so that the kids can colour them and glue them to paddle-pop stick rafts. Think up a reason why.)
2. *Cases and Materials on Torts.* (Read Chapter 7: Trespass and Assault.)
3. Letters from her Staffroom Pigeonhole. (Open.)

She decided to begin with the Letters from the Staffroom. The first envelope was addressed in swirling pink:

Cath Murphy, Teacher, Class 2B,
Redwood Primary, Hillside Street,
Mount Montmart

Dear Ms Murphy,

Thank you for your note enquiring about my daughter (Cassie's) loose tooth. She has lost it now! And the tooth fairy has come and gone.

I hope you will forgive me for writing again so soon, but I have a small favour to ask. I have just learned that Cassie's 'cousin' will be 'attending' Redwood next term — she is one of the <u>Year 7</u> students from St Carmel Catholic Girls, where, as you may have heard, there has been a flood! So, after the holidays, she and her classmates are being 'shipped out' to your school for a month or two.

I say 'cousin', by the way, rather than cousin, for this reason: I have a sister, Marbie, who lives with a man named Vernon, and they take care of Vernon's little sister. Do you see? And it is this little sister (Alissa Taylor, better known as 'Listen' Taylor) — she is the 'cousin' of whom I speak.

In any case, I am wondering if you might keep an eye on Listen for us? She is a quiet little thing, and good-natured. If you could just look in on her, once or twice — make sure she is not lost in the system — I would be so grateful.

Again, thank you for being such a delightful teacher to our Cassie, and again, I am longing to meet you at Parent-Teacher Night!

Best wishes,
Fancy Zing

Well, said Cath, rereading the part about what a 'delightful' teacher she was. She had heard something about Year 7 students using the new demountables at Redwood next term, but she had only thought, wisely: *Billson would never have allowed this if it wasn't that he's distracted because he's so in love with Lenny.*

Now she drafted a polite reply to Fancy Zing, agreeing to look out for 'Listen', and pointing out (for the sake of something to say) that she herself had a toothache today, and wished it was a matter for the tooth fairy! (*Who ARE you, Cath Murphy?* she scolded, as she wrote.) Then she turned to the next letter in her pile.

Cath Murphy
c/o Redwood Primary

Dear Ms Murphy,

<u>*The Harvey K. Whatsmeyer and Dorothy P. Ruckleman*</u>
<u>*Scholarship in Part-Time Law*</u>

It is with great pleasure that we inform you that you have been awarded the Harvey K. Whatsmeyer and Dorothy P. Ruckleman Scholarship in Part-Time Law.

This scholarship covers the full cost of tuition for your part-time law degree, and offers a textbook and photocopying allowance each term.

It is awarded to students at the Barhill University School of Law, who are studying law part-time, and seem to be particularly brilliant. Congratulations! We are very glad to have you join the 'prestigious' and 'exclusive' club of Harvey K. Whatsmeyer and Dorothy P. Ruckleman Scholarship in Part-Time Law holders!

Your tuition will be paid directly on your behalf, and we now enclose your first textbook cheque.

Kind regards,

The Trustees,
Harvey K. Whatsmeyer and Dorothy P. Ruckleman Scholarship in Part-Time Law

Cath read the letter five times, maybe six, noting that the paper was thick, that the font was elegant, and that a bank cheque was pinned to the back. Her cheeks began to ache from the smile of it all. She turned the TV loud, danced with her cat, and danced into the kitchen to make celebration chocolate-chip cookies. This is wonderful, she danced, wonderful!

Still, she thought, in a more reasonable voice, *it's not all that surprising.*

Chocolate chips spilled in a shower to the floor. What did she mean by that? Why should it not be surprising? Certainly, she had never applied for the Harvey K. Whatsmeyer and Dorothy P. Ruckleman Scholarship in Part-Time Law. She had never even heard of such a thing.

But she had to admit that, in fact, she had won a scholarship like this every year of high school, and every year of her Education degree. So that, even the other day when she was talking to Warren and Suzanne about how worried she was about the cost of tuition – even then, she was more *impatient* than actually concerned.

Violin skidded among chocolate chips as Cath reflected that this sort of attitude – *impatient to win a scholarship!* – was both conceited and spoiled. Furthermore, such an attitude – *unsurprised when she actually won one!* – was likely to ruin the excitement of almost *any* happy event. So she collected her excitement about her again, danced the chocolate-chip cookies onto the top shelf of the oven, and danced back to the TV.

There was one last letter waiting for her, an *internal* letter, a two-word CATH MURPHY envelope, in handwriting that she knew. She had known that it was there all along, actually, and *partly*, the careful piles of Things-To-Do and the chocolate chip excitement at her scholarship letter – partly all those things were nothing more than self-imposed suspense.

Cath,

This is just something ridiculous that I made for you. It's to say thank you, because you helped to make my birthday so special the other day.

How about we have dinner this Thursday night? In honour of the end of the term. I have a favourite Moroccan restaurant which would do the trick. The 442 takes us to the door if you don't want to take that Merc of yours.

Warren

Cath looked at the letter as a rectangle of paper. She looked at the letter as geometry, at the handwriting as angles and curls, and finally, she looked at the enclosure. It was a cross-stitched bookmark (stitched with a crescent moon and three stars, all in midnight blue).

No, well, of course I cannot go. A Moroccan restaurant! The idea! This Warren Woodford had such tall skinny legs that his head was stuck up in the sky. She grew angry at him for a moment, because what did he think he was playing at? What was he doing to her face and her cheeks, and her forearms and the space behind her knees, WHAT DID HE THINK HE WAS DOING, when he sent her the *moon and the stars*?

She would, of course, say NO. Sternly and firmly: NO.

But Warren Wishful Woodford had long skinny legs and wishful flecks of gold in his wistful eyes. Warren Wishful Woodford was as *good* as *gold* can be, and his long thin fingers had taken up a needle and some cloth. These long thin fingers had taken *her*, Cath Murphy, and threaded her, like cotton, through the needle. He had thrust her (Cath Murphy) straight into the cloth (her eyes closed tight against the shock) – then gently, his long thin fingers had tugged her through the other side. Then down again, and gently, up above the cloth, always gentle but firm, these fingers had taken Cath Murphy and transformed her into Moon and into Stars.

Cath Murphy had a beanbag and a slender cat. She had the Harvey K. Whatsmeyer and Dorothy P. Ruckleman Scholarship in Part-Time Law. She was *delightful*, she was *brilliant*, she was lucky as a cat, and everything was sewn in midnight blue.

She took up her pen to reply.

•

On Thursday night, at dinner with Warren, Cath leaned forward and told him it was her *destiny* to be a lawyer. He poured her another glass of wine, and she explained that each year in high school she had received a special award, and it had *always* turned out to be a book about *justice* or the *law*.

'Every single time?' said Warren.

'Every single time.'

'Well,' said Warren. 'Who chose the books? It was probably the legal studies teacher or something.'

'I don't know,' said Cath, confused, 'I don't know who chose them, but listen to this!'

'Listen to what?' He poured himself some wine, and held the bottle above the glass allowing it to drip, drip, drip, until a waiter saw and said, 'Shall I bring you more?'

'Yes please,' they both said together.

'Every single career guidance counsellor I ever had told me I HAD to study law!'

'Hmm,' said Warren.

'And once. Once! A palm-reader told me I was going to be a lawyer. And my star sign *often* tells me that. And Chinese fortune cookies – no . . . But once I had a swimming coach, Ella her name was I think, she was some former Olympic champion or something, anyway, Ella told me I did backstroke like a lawyer. "Forget the swimming," she said, "you go straight to law school, little one." I was only ten or eleven at the time. And plus, I just remembered, I got offered a scholarship to study law in my last year of high school! Without applying for one! What do you think about *that*?!'

She ate a mouthful of couscous.

'But you still became a school teacher,' said Warren, admiringly. 'You know what you are? You're a *destiny fighter*.'

'Thank you,' she blushed.

'So what happened? How come you started law this year, Cath Murphy?'

'That doesn't count,' she explained. 'I had a broken heart. And then I got this leaflet in the mail about a new law school, and the classes were at convenient times, and it was easy to fill in the application form. But, you know, I had a broken heart so it doesn't really count.'

'You can't fight destiny if your heart's not in it,' agreed Warren. 'But what I want to know is, what brain-dead moron broke your heart? Look at you! Would you just look at you? And tell me, *who* could break that heart?'

She laughed and looked down at her food. 'Do you believe in omens?' she said, to change the subject.

'Yes,' he said. 'Don't you?'

Their eyes caught for a moment, and held, and continued to hold, until Cath felt her whole body tremble.

'Why?' said Warren.

'I don't know. It's just that we got the 442 tonight, and the Friendly Bus Driver was driving.'

'The *friendly bus driver*?'

'Yes, didn't you notice him chatting to me when we got on the bus?'

'Cath, I'm sorry, but who is the friendly bus driver?'

'You don't *know* the Friendly Bus Driver!? He comes by Redwood every afternoon – he drives the Glenorie bus? And he always leans out and chats to me while the kids get on board, and he is *so* friendly, Warren.'

'And so,' said Warren, gazing at her. 'And so, it's an omen that he drove us here tonight. An omen of what?' He leaned forward on his elbows and stared at her, waiting, while she stared back.

'Guess what,' she panicked, suddenly. 'I'm always cutting competitions out of magazines!'

'Are you?' said Warren, archly, leaning back into his chair again and straightening the serviette on his lap.

'Yes, and guess what else? I practically always win.'

'Like what? Like what competitions?'

'Like, I won a free flight to go see my parents in Perth last year, and that's from a coupon I cut out of a magazine. Always cut them out, Warren. Okay? I don't mean from big newspapers like the *Herald* – I never win those competitions but small ones, like *Travel Schmazzle*.'

'Small ones like *Travel Schmazzle*?'

'Right,' she said, nodding excitedly. 'Or *Cat Nap*.'

'Never in my life have I heard of a magazine called *Travel Schmazzle*.'

'Or *Cat Nap*?'

'No, not *Cat Nap* either, as a matter of fact.'

'The *Journal of Dreamy Window Boxes*?'

'Cath Murphy, you are priceless. Come home with me tonight.'

'Well, how about *Elf Epistles*? I won a blender from them. Just the other day.'

'Cath, you are beautiful. Come home with me. Please.'

•

The next day, the last day of term, Cath watched Warren through the window of the classroom, and felt the chill of the ice storm in her chest. Because: *what if that had been her only chance?*

She had not gone home with him. She had ignored his invitation. At the end of the night, she had held her head haughtily and climbed into the taxi, while he watched her through narrowed eyes. Then he slowly pressed her taxi door closed, took one step back, turned his shoulder to the wind, and flagged down a taxi of his own.

At first, in her taxi, she had felt proud, but she quickly found herself appalled. Her lips ached from not having kissed. She held her arms around her body to comfort it. Because the next day it would be Friday! Breanna would be down from the coast! Then two whole weeks of school holidays, during which time Cath would be alone with the empty space where his body should be. Two whole weeks during which time Warren would forget their flirtation and remember himself and his wife.

Cath, you are beautiful, come home with me, please. It had been her last chance. If she had just stepped back from the taxi for a moment, and kissed him, just that, the kiss might have held him for the holidays.

She watched him now in the lunchtime playground, through the iced-over windows of her classroom. He seemed to have agreed to referee a game of rounders.

Marcus Ellison took the bat, Severino lined up with a tennis ball, and then, in a whirl out of nowhere, there was Cassie Zing. She was sprinting on the iced-over asphalt, in a wildfire skid towards Marcus. Cath, behind the window, gasped.

But Warren Woodford, calm as snow, took two long strides toward the wildfire. He lowered his body, caught her in her skid, straightened her up, and dusted the ice from her hair. Then, crouching crookedly, he turned and spoke to Marcus. Cassie's fists relented, her hands fell by her side. Marcus shrugged and turned back to the game. Cassie hopscotched towards her friend Lucinda, who caught her just before she fell.

From the window, Cath watched as Warren Woodford stood and smiled like a gentle king, and clapped his hands once, meaning: 'Right! Play on!'

Later, sharing bus duty with their shoulders close against the cold, Cath pressed her fingers together through her gloves, and tried to think of something to say. What could she say that would hold him until next term?

'What are you and Breanna doing tonight?' she tried, hopelessly.

Warren cried: 'Don't *tell* me you haven't heard! How could you not have heard?'

'Heard what?'

'Lenny D'Souza is *leaving*, and wait, there's more, she's leaving *today*!'

While Cath stared, Warren explained that Lenny and Billson had had a HUGE fight about ABSOLUTELY NOTHING, in front of EVERYONE, in the STAFFROOM, at the end of RECESS that day.

'And she *resigned*?' whispered Cath.

'She resigned! But she left a message saying she's having a farewell party at her place tonight, and everyone's invited.'

'Including Billson?'

'No, Cath. Not including Billson.'

'Well!' said Cath, importantly. 'Lenny's my *friend*. I have to get over there, right away. She must be wondering where I am. And she must not realise that you can't have a farewell party and then change your mind about resigning. I have to stop her!'

'Don't stop her,' said Warren. 'I feel like going to a party tonight.'

'You're coming?' cried Cath, startled, and almost giddy. Then she said, lightly: 'So you'll bring Breanna along? I finally get to meet her!'

'Cath Murphy,' said Warren. 'Where exactly have you been all day? Has it passed you by that the weather is *really weird*? That this is Sydney's first *ice storm* on record? That the whole public transport system has been *completely shut down*? Have a look at these school buses here, Cath, and tell me what's happened to their tyres. They have *chains* on their tyres, Cath. School buses are the only ones allowed to travel today, to get the kids home, and that's *it*. Do you think they'd let trains run today? How exactly do you think Breanna's getting down from the coast tonight? And another thing, how exactly did you get your class to talk about anything *other than weather* today? You're a better teacher than I am, that's for sure.'

Cath giggled, pleased, and said, 'I wonder how we'll get to Lenny's party?'

Then she explained, casually, that she lived down the road from Lenny's place, and that Warren might as well share a taxi with her. After the party, he could take a taxi to his home, and she could walk back to her own place.

Warren was pleased with this idea.

•

Lenny wept into Cath's neck. 'Oh my God, Cath! I *loved* my job! I *loved* that man! I will *miss* you so *much!*'

Cath, on the couch beside Lenny, tried to balance a gin and tonic around her sobbing shoulders. Also on the couch, sipping a cup of tea and turning the pages of Lenny's photo albums, was Heather Waratah (teacher, Grade 4C).

'Lenny,' murmured Cath. 'You know you could just change your mind and come back? You want me to call Billson for you right now?'

'I can't,' sniffed Lenny, shaking her head. 'But you have to keep in touch,' she sobbed again, drank from her beer, and dribbled beer alongside her tears. 'You have to *promise* you'll keep in *touch*!'

'Ha!' exclaimed Miss Waratah, pointing to a photo of Lenny and her brothers dressed as reindeers.

'All right,' said Cath. 'I promise.'

●

Warren was as plastered as a wall, he said. Cath said that she was too.

They caught one another in the kitchen, and made some rude sentences with the magnet words on the fridge. Katie Toby (teacher, Kinder A) and Jo Bel Castro (teacher, Grade 5A) wandered into the room, and Katie Toby said: 'Ice? Where's the ice?'

Jo Bel Castro put a friendly arm around Katie's shoulder and declared, 'Where *would* a person find ice?'

Warren opened the dishwasher and took out the cutlery container. 'Not here,' he shrugged, and put it back.

Katie Toby stared and frowned. 'Thank you, everyone,' she said, and left the room. Jo Bel Castro raised an eyebrow, and walked in the other direction.

Cath giggled and fell against Warren, on purpose more or less, by the fridge. Warren held her up, with his arm around her shoulders, and pressed his face into her hair. He was saying something.

'What?' she said, not wanting to let go. 'What are you saying?'

'Thank you,' he murmured, in his muffled voice. 'I'm saying thank you for last night. For not coming home with me. Cath? I don't trust myself around you anymore.'

Cath stayed still. His nose was pressed just above her ear and the warmth of his face was in her hair. 'Well,' she said, eventually. 'What does that mean?'

'It means,' said Warren, 'that I'm relying on you. You have to be the stronger one, okay?'

'Right,' said Cath. 'Right.'

She pressed her whole body against his for a moment, as hard as she could, and then she stepped clean away.

'Right,' she said. 'I'm going to the bathroom.'

Lenny's bathroom had an apricot theme and an art nouveau pattern around the tiles. Cath looked at herself in the mirror and immediately knew that she was drunk: it was just as she'd suspected.

'Nine times seven is sixty-three,' she said to the mirror. So she was not all that drunk. She was still there, inside her head, doing her nine times tables. *But that woman there, that woman in the mirror? Who is that, Cath Murphy, who is that?*

Seven times nine is —

In reverse, it was not so good.

•

'You'll never get a cab in this.'

It was snowing outside.

'Freakish weather!' whispered Katie Toby, gazing through the window. Then, to the room: 'Snow in Sydney! I mean, maybe a few flakes, once in a blue moon! But *heavy* snow! I mean, it's really kind of *heavy*? You know? In the hippy sense. Ha ha!'

'Promise me something,' said Warren, who was holding his phone to his ear. '*Never* lose that sense of humour.'

'Okay,' said Katie, dimpling. 'I'll try. Thanks.'

Importantly, Cath explained to the room: 'Warren is going to get a cab.'

'He'll never get a cab in this,' said Lenny.

Warren had decided to go home, and was holding his mobile phone patiently to his ear. Lenny looked up at him and repeated: 'You'll never get a cab in *this*!'

They looked through the window at the glow of white, and Cath turned back to watch Warren. 'Nobody's answering,' he mouthed at her. And she nodded, solemnly, with her face and her heart singing over and over: *do not answer, do not answer, do not answer.*

Cath's boot tap danced the icy path home. One boot, *thud*, one boot, *tap*.

'I have a couch that turns into a bed,' she told Warren, proudly. 'It's in the living room. I have linen too. One hundred per cent cotton. It might even be *Egyptian* cotton, you never know. Plus I have a spare feather quilt.'

Snow feathered about them. Warren's head was hunched into his shoulders. 'I'm hungry,' he said. 'Let's get some food.'

'It's midnight,' said Cath, 'and you're *always* hungry.'

'This corner store,' suggested Warren.

'It won't be open,' declared Cath.

But it was. They bought chips and salsa for a midnight snack, and behind the counter, the corner-store girl with the plaits to her hips said, 'Hello there, *you!*' as usual to Cath, and 'Hey!' in a friendly way to Warren.

'Hey,' said Warren, friendly back – and Cath thought: *I like a man who's friendly to strangers, and friendly to corner-store girls!*

'Right,' she said aloud and confused. Warren and the corner-store girl looked at her.

At that moment, Warren's mobile phone rang, and Cath panicked, thinking it might be the taxi company calling to try to take him home. She and the corner-store girl watched in suspense as he answered and said, 'Bree! Hey! Do *not* worry yourself. Couldn't get a taxi so I'm staying at Cath's place tonight, okay? We're just on our way there now. You okay? Keeping warm? It'll all be melted by tomorrow, trust me on that.'

'My wife,' explained Warren, when the conversation finished, smiling at the corner-store girl.

'Crazy, huh?' Cath jutted her shoulder at the window while she paid.

The corner-store girl flung her plaits over her shoulders and said: 'You bet! But you know what? I'm *out of here!*' It turned out that tomorrow she would take a week's vacation to Byron Bay.

'Lucky!' Warren and Cath said at once, and the corner-store girl began to nod her plaits, as if to say more, but stopped, becoming distant and glassy-eyed. Warren and Cath quietly gathered their things to leave, but just as they reached the door the corner-store girl called, 'You guys, you want to know what? While I'm away, I plan to collect some sea water and bring it back!'

'Do you?' said Warren.

'For my fish tank,' she explained.

•

'Look!'

Cath wanted to show him everything, suddenly, frenetically. Photos of her mother, her father and the family Alsatian. Photographs of Violin, her cat. Violin, the cat in living form. ('Violin! Come here and meet Warren! Violin!') A new ceramic casserole dish she bought a month ago. The rewind button on the VCR, which was jammed. The new DVD player she had won in a contest just last week! Warren moved his legs carefully, amongst her books and chairs. At each thing she showed him he said, '*Mmm*,' with fascination and a crunch on a cornchip.

'This window is all smeared,' Warren observed, standing by her side in the dining room.

'Oh,' she agreed. 'I threw some apple juice on it. A few weeks ago.'

They both stood and stared at the smears.

'Hang on,' said Warren. He went into the kitchen and came out with a glass of water, splashed water at the window, and then rubbed the window with a cloth. It squealed, but soon was crisp and clear, and their reflections leapt out at them, sharply. Vaguely, beyond the reflections, was the eerie white world of snow outside.

'Gosh,' said Cath, in awe. 'Shouldn't we be building a snowman?'

She gazed up at Warren. Then she ran back into the living room and sat down on the couch, leaving space for Warren to sit beside her. But he chose the armchair.

She lifted her foot onto her lap and looked to see what was making her boots go thud, tap, thud. 'Look!'

It turned out a pebble had embedded itself deep within the rubber of her heel. Cath showed Warren and then tried to dig the pebble out with her fingernail.

'Here,' said Warren. 'Let me try.'

He swooped a cornchip full of salsa, ate it in one go, and then took her foot onto his lap. He scratched industriously at the pebble.

'Wait,' said Cath in a moment. She took her foot back, unlaced the boot, and took it off.

'This will make it easier. I should have taken them off right away anyway. I'm walking snow all over the apartment.'

She passed him the boot, which he took with one hand, gulping his beer with the other.

He put the beer down, placed the boot beside it, then took her foot onto his lap.

'Yes,' he said, 'that's better,' and he began to press the sole of her foot.

'No,' explained Cath. 'That's not what I meant.' But she left her foot there in his lap, safe in its short black ankle sock, and had a sip of beer of her own.

'Look!' she cried suddenly, taking back her foot and leaping to her feet. 'You want to see my Criminal Law essay, Warren?'

'Not really,' said Warren, frowning. 'Give me back your foot.'

Cath flicked through papers on the dining room table. 'Warren, look at my Criminal Law essay.'

'All right,' accepted Warren. He looked:

LEGAL STUDIES: AN INTRODUCTION
(UNIT: CRIMINAL LAW)

'THE LISTENING DEVICE AND THE LONG-LENS
CAMERA: ADMITTING ILLEGALLY OBTAINED
EVIDENCE IN CRIMINAL PROCEEDINGS'

BY CATH MURPHY (STUDENT NO. 7893332)

'Side-by-side with the major technology of the telescope, the lens and the light beam, . . . there were the minor techniques of multiple and intersecting observations, of eyes that must see without being seen; . . . secretly preparing a new knowledge of man.'[1]

1. Foucault, *Discipline and Punish: The Birth of the Prison* (Trans by Alan Sheridan, Penguin Books, Harmondsworth, 1977), p. 171

'Lovely,' said Warren. 'Where's the rest?'

'That's it. I've only done the cover page. I did it weeks ago.'

'That's it!' Warren cast aside the page. 'Give me back your foot.'

Cath sat down and gave him her foot. Warren began with her instep.

'But don't you think it's wonderful?' she said, after a few moments. 'I've got alliteration in my title. *L*istening and *L*ong and *Llll*ens.'

Warren confessed that he was not the alliteration type, but accepted that other people were. He moved on to her toes, one toe at a time.

'Massage the bit that matches my knee,' Cath suggested. 'You know the way you can cure yourself by massaging certain bits of your feet? Like the bit for the liver and the intestines and that? Get the bit for knees.' She crunched on a cornchip and added: 'Please.'

'Because I've got a problem knee,' she explained, when he ignored her, continuing with her toes. 'I had two operations in high school and my knee's got metal bits in it now, but they've never set off the x-ray machine at the airport.'

'Hmm,' said Warren. 'Okay, listen. I'll rub every part of your foot and you tell me when you feel your knee begin to heal.'

'All right. But let's talk about my essay some more.'

'It's a cover page! What is there to say?'

'Foucault!' countered Cath. 'Didn't you see I used a quote from *Foucault*? I don't have to write another word. Not another word. That's a high distinction, right there. It's all about the small things, you know. Like my little toe, just press my little toe and my knee is cured.'

Warren ignored her, and peeled off her sock. 'You probably have to kiss it anyway,' he suggested, and kissed one toe.

'Warren! I've had *boots* on all day. Don't kiss my *toes*. Put my sock back on.'

'Maybe I have to kiss the knee directly?' said Warren. 'Maybe the foot won't do?'

'I don't know,' admitted Cath.

'I do,' said Warren. He stopped for a moment and stared at her. He put her foot onto the carpet, moved to sit beside her on the couch, and kissed her.

'That's my mouth,' said Cath, blinking at his face, 'not my knee,' but she kissed him back in a fury of relief.

FANCY ZING

IRRITATING THINGS ABOUT MY HUSBAND # 5

Let's say it's an ordinary weeknight, I'll be cleaning up the kitchen, and I've *just* about finished – the dishwasher stacked, detergent neat in its compartment, only the large baking tray left to rinse – when Radcliffe, right on cue, will step into the room and announce: 'Leave it' (grandly) 'I'll do the rest.'

Fancy closed her secret notebook and leaned back in her desk chair. She would now spend twenty minutes working on her prize-winning novel. It was 10.23 am.

Having read several prize-winning novels, Fancy was confident that she now knew the recipe:

1. Write a simple narrative.
2. Make a long list.
3. Scatter the contents of your list throughout your narrative.

So, for example, in the prize-winning novel that Fancy had just read, the author had done the following:

1. He wrote a simple narrative in which two people fell in love, then the man left the woman, and the woman cried.

2. He made a long list of leaves.
3. He scattered the story with his leaves.

So, 'Tears fell from her eyes' had become:

> 'Tears the shape of sugar maple leaves fell (like so many blackjack oak leaves falling on an autumn day) from her eyes.'

Voila! A richly-textured (prize-winning) novel all about love and leaves.

There was no harm in mixing the recipe around a little, Fancy believed. (She had flair in the kitchen.) She would begin with the *list*, and then write the narrative around it. Although she was not yet at the stage of making her list, she was well underway with her list of things to list.

This was on the back of an old phone bill which she carried in her handbag wherever she went. It was stained with splats of cranberry juice.

LIST OF POTENTIAL LISTS
- sounds
- things that are very hot
- delicious things to drink
- foreign currencies
- fish

'Hmm,' she said, running her fingernail down the list. 'Fish?' She had a slight zing of excitement then, and picked up her pen, quickly scribbling:

> 'Tears the shape of trout fell (like a school of those darting glassy fish that you see in tropical waters) from her eyes.'

Pleased, she turned to her computer and typed the word 'fish' into the word processor's thesaurus. 'Angle', it suggested promptly. And 'trawl'.

'No, no,' she chided gently. 'I meant it as a noun.'

She sat back frowning, murmured 'of course!' and typed the word 'Fish' into Google. For a few minutes, she excitedly scribbled down fish names – dottybacks, pufferfish, clownfish and tangs – but then she discovered an extremely comprehensive website. It broke fish down into categories (such as marine fish and fresh fish) but then it expanded each category into several more. Sub-category collapsed into sub-sub-categories, and these slid on into sub-sub-subs. There was a veritable flood of fish. No single fish would sit still: even *goldfish* became blackmoor, fantail, lionhead and red cap oranda. For heaven's sakes. Not to mention the latin names. *Carassius auratus*, she transcribed carefully, and then she said *pfft!* and put her pen down. Really, there were too many fish to fit on the back of a phone bill.

There were also too many references to streams, wetlands, bays and aquariums, which reminded her of something. She reached for the phone and dialled the Castle Hill Gym. A man with a husky voice answered.

Clear your throat, thought Fancy. But aloud she said, 'Hello. I'm just ringing to enquire about the hours of your swimming pool there. I'm hoping you might tell me when the pool is quietest.'

'The *quietest* time,' said the man with the voice, 'would be Friday mornings from nine-thirty to eleven-thirty, but then . . .'

As he talked, Fancy circled the first word on the list ('sounds'), and tapped it with her pen, frowning. That category, like fish, was much too broad.

The man on the phone was laughing in a rasping, unpleasant way.

'All right,' she said briskly, 'thank you.'

Then she hung up, crossed out 'sounds' and replaced it with 'UNPLEASANT SOUNDS!!!' She looked at the clock on her computer, which said 10.42 am. After she had watched for a while, it said 10.43 am.

'So, that's that,' she declared, pleased.

•

In the back seat of the car, Cassie wore the middle belt so she could lean forward between the two front seats and talk to her dad or mum.

Her mum was driving and her dad was changing the radio stations. Dad tipped his head sideways to listen carefully to the news. Mum was behind her glasses, and you couldn't tell if she was listening to the news or not.

Cassie looked through the groceries in the box beside her, which they had just picked up from Coles. They were extremely boring. Celery sticks and milk, cauliflower and toilet paper.

'Mum?' said Cassie.

'Shh,' said Dad, listening to the news with his head on his shoulder.

'Radcliffe,' said Mum, 'it's just the weather.'

'I want to find out if there'll be good sailing weather this weekend, *actually*,' said Dad, with his calm voice.

'We can't *possibly* go sailing this weekend!' said Mum. 'There's the Bellamys and the Samsons coming for dinner on Saturday. Not to mention your parents on Sunday!'

'We don't need to see the Bellamys and the Samsons,' said her dad. 'We can cancel.'

'I think you'll find that we do, actually,' declared her mum.

'You know I don't like *routine*, Fancy.'

'It's not a *question* of *routine*, Radcliffe. It's a question of *manners*. You can't *invite* people and then *uninvite* them because you feel like going *sailing*. And, besides, what do you *mean* when you say *routine*? It's been *ages* since we had the Bellamys and the Samsons!'

'That rhymed, Mum,' said Cassie from the back seat. 'What do you *mean* when you say *routine*?'

'I also don't like being told what I can and cannot do,' said her dad, coldly.

'Radcliffe, would you not be ridiculous? Please?'

'There is no point in our having this discussion,' said her dad, shrugging. 'I just *do* and *don't do* exactly as I please. Thank you very much.' He switched off the radio, so he could be angry in peace.

'No point in having *what* discussion?' muttered her mum.

Cassie thought she should be quiet, but first she had to murmur, softly: 'What do you *mean* when you say *routine*? What do you *mean* when you say *routine*? *What* do you mean when you *say* routine?'

'The light's green, Mum,' Cassie interrupted herself.

'Thank you, Cassie,' and her mother made the car jump forward.

•

IRRITATING THINGS ABOUT MY HUSBAND # 6

Let's say we've just had the Bellamys and Samsons to dinner on a Saturday night. Let's say, after a night of booming storytelling, buttoned shirts, swishing skirts *etc*, the Bellamys and Samsons set off, leaving behind, in their wake: candle wax, salad bowls, bread knives, eggshells, stacked plates and beetroot on the floor. *Well*, after such a party, closing the front door, I like to take a garbage bag from beneath the kitchen sink and begin with the dirty serviettes.

Behind me, at once, the bleary port breath! Radcliffe with his gravelly voice: 'Leave it,' he murmurs, 'leave it for now,' his hands on my shoulders ready to steer me to the bed.

Leave it! As if he were a king, offering the wondrous treasure of *himself*.

•

Fancy flipped open a notebook, took the lid from a thin black marker, and instructed: 'Radcliffe, tell me some sounds that are unpleasant.'

'Right then.' Radcliffe leaned back in his television chair to think. The TV commercials blazed away.

'The sound of a fingernail on a blackboard,' he declared after two commercials had gone by.

Fancy replaced the lid on her marker. 'I'm not writing that down.'

'Why not?'

'It's very common, Radcliffe. I think I need something original.'

'Too common? Well then.' He thought again, but had to pause to watch a humorous commercial for margarine.

'Heavy footsteps,' he suggested eventually, 'walking around upstairs.'

From the floor by the couch, Cassie said, 'That's a good noise.' She crawled around toward them. 'I think that's a good noise if you hear footsteps upstairs, because you wonder to yourself: *who's upstairs?* You wonder if maybe it's a ghost, or maybe Santa Claus, or maybe Grandma, or anyone.'

'What's Grandma doing upstairs?' wondered Radcliffe.

'I agree with Cassie,' Fancy said. 'Sorry, Radcliffe, I need you to think again.'

'Ah!' sighed Radcliffe, exasperated. 'The sound of your voice!'

Fancy and Cassie both cried, 'HUH!' and Cassie said, 'Mum's got a *beautiful* voice!'

Radcliffe shrugged: 'Show's back on.'

'You have no imagination,' Fancy declared, closing her notebook.

'No need for one,' Radcliffe replied, amiable, tilting his wineglass towards his mouth. 'That'll be the telephone,' he announced next, as it had just begun to ring.

As soon as she picked up the telephone, a voice said, '*His penis smelled like a pappadam?*' So she knew it was her editor, Tanya.

'I knew you wouldn't like that line,' Fancy said jauntily. 'Go ahead and cut it.'

'*Seriously*, Fancy, shouldn't he take a *shower*? If his penis smells? He's dirty. I'll write in a shower scene if you like.' Tanya always worked at night, while watching Japanese kung-fu movies, so the sounds of rapid breathing and occasional yelps filled the background of her calls.

'I said you could cut it,' said Fancy, sinking down to the hall floor, where she sat, cross-legged, leaning against the wall.

'Okay. Great. Let's cut that, but Fancy, honey, what's this about a special private place between your legs?'

'Mummy,' whispered Cassie, tiptoeing down the hall towards her, 'do you want me to bring you a jumper?' The heater was on in the TV room but the hallway was icy cold.

'Okay,' mouthed Fancy, nodding at Cassie, who accepted the nod as permission to take a noisy skidding jump down the hall.

'It's not between *my* legs,' declared Fancy.

'Whoa!' said her editor. 'Check it out, Fancy. This one guy just put his *elbow* in the other guy's *mouth* and somehow it came out the *back of his head.*'

'Huh,' said Fancy.

'So, listen, Fancy, whatever happened to pussy? That was your word of choice, wasn't it? I open up your manuscript ready for your sweet little brand of pussy, and what do I get? *Special private place between her legs.* Now, would you call that – I don't know – *pithy?*'

'No,' admitted Fancy. 'But it's *rhythmic*, don't you think?'

'It's what you might call a crock of shit. If you're over pussy, choose something new and I'll do a global search and replace. Go ahead and choose. You've got ten seconds on the clock. Ten, nine – fuck *me*, that was his *toenail*!'

'I still think we should do that rotating cardboard wheel thing that my sister suggested,' said Fancy. 'You know, let the *reader* decide what she wants. Put all the potential words for private parts on a wheel and you could spin the wheel to your favourite one.'

'Ah yes, that brilliant idea. Well, Fance, okay, I loved the book. The tennis player is a *dude*, and the scene with the tennis ball tin? Wow. Why not back to pussy? Or, any other ideas?'

'Well,' Fancy lowered her voice. 'I was thinking about "cunt".'

'Who-ahhh,' cried Tanya, and Fancy waited patiently, but then she said it again, 'Who-ahhh, Fancy, that is *not* your *readers*. You can't use that word. It's offensive, Fancy, it's one of those words that brings down the whole female race, or whatever.'

'I was thinking,' said Fancy, 'that it might be time we reclaimed it. You know, made it our *own*. Can't women of the world decide to get street smart and refer to each other as *cunts*?'

'You're going to have to let me think on this one, Fancy.'

'Hang on,' said Fancy, 'that's call-waiting. Can you hold on a moment?'

'It's okay, just get it, I'll call you back. See ya.'

Fancy pressed the disconnect button and found her sister Marbie on the phone.

'Dressed in black?' said Marbie.

'Oh really, *tonight*? What for? It's *cold*!' As she said it, she looked up and there was her daughter, holding out her favourite black jumper.

'*Thank* you, Cassie,' she said. 'Marbie, have you met my beautiful, generous and thoughtful daughter, Cassie?'

'She's *met me, Mum,*' giggled Cassie, 'she's my *auntie!*' and skidded away down the hall again.

'For the maintenance,' explained Marbie. 'It's blurred, remember? We can do it easy if we leave right now. Meet you at the ice-cream truck?'

Marbie was not at the ice-cream truck when Fancy arrived. She was already in the tree above the truck.

Fancy pretended to consider the range of ice creams (single cone, double cone, single dipped in chocolate with a Flake on the side *etc*), and then squinted briefly up into the darkness.

Marbie gave the sign for 'all set' (both hands flat on the head). She almost lost her balance and had to grab noisily at clumps of leaves.

Fancy gave the sign for 'great, and I've remembered all the tools' (a playful twirl of her handbag) then clipped across the road to the apartment block. Without pausing, she firmly pressed in the security code, and entered the building.

She and Marbie had both learned to pick a lock when their fingers were fresh and nimble. She got into the apartment in less than three seconds, smiled at the cat, and slid silently from room to room in a quick Emptiness check. (There had once been a plumber in the bathroom, but Fancy, ingeniously, recruited him on the spot. He was now one of their best.)

In the dining room, she opened her handbag, reached in for the nailfile, and accidentally took out her telephone bill. The cat miaowed.

'Hmm,' she murmured, and sat down at the dining table, turning over the telephone bill. There was a clutter of papers there, which she shifted slightly so she could study her List of Potential Lists.

- ~~sounds~~ UNPLEASANT SOUNDS!!!
- things that are very hot
- delicious things to drink
- foreign currencies
- fish

Except that the word 'fish' was now a tangle of skinny lines, linking 'fish' to various fish species. *Objects in a family home*, Fancy wrote at the end of the list. The cat miaowed again and Fancy said, 'Hello,' and added *cats* in a flash of inspiration. Beside it, she scribbled: *(include lions, tigers, panthers, etc!!! also, basic domestic cats?).*

Miaow, miaow, said the cat.

'Are you hungry, is that it?' Fancy murmured soothingly, reaching out her left hand to stroke the cat, but not being able to find it.

She looked up and the cat was standing way across the room in the doorway, its collar bell whispering faintly.

'How —?' began Fancy.

Then she gasped, took out her beeper (which *miaowed* at her even as she pressed the message button), and read: GET OUT NOW.

At which exact moment, a key turned in the lock.

•

On Friday night at the Zings', after dinner, Fancy sat on the carpet next to Listen and said, 'Tell me some sounds that you don't like to hear.'

'The sounds of cars crashing,' offered Vernon from the dining room table.

'Not you,' Fancy said, but she wrote it down in her notebook. 'I'm asking Listen now. I'll ask you later.'

Listen thought hard.

'You have to think outside the box,' advised Radcliffe, dryly. 'Other-wise, she cuts you to the quick.'

'Oh!' cried Grandma Zing. 'Radcliffe! Was she mean to you?'

'Utterly cruel.'

'The sound of a puddle,' Listen said now, 'going splat when you just accidentally stepped in it with your sneaker.'

'Good!' Fancy wrote fast.

'The sound that our school library computer makes,' Listen said, calmly. 'Kind of a mean-sounding BLEEP? When you return your book and it turns out it's overdue. Does that count?'

'Perfect!' Fancy scribbled frantically.

'Come on, Fancy!' Grandma Zing called. 'We're all going out to the shed!'

'Fancy,' beckoned Radcliffe, at her mother's shoulder, 'come on, hon.'

From the slightly raised platform at the far end of the shed, Grandma Zing frowned at her clipboard.

'Have you got the beeper issue?' Fancy called to her mother, who nodded with a little smile, so Fancy turned to her sister. 'Marbie,' she said, opening her notebook again. 'Tell me some sounds that you don't like to hear.'

'I think your mother wants to start the meeting.' Radcliffe sat straight in his chair. He had his reading glasses on and had already replaced two of the bulbs in the halogen track-lighting.

'No, no,' said Grandma Zing. 'Carry on, I'll just be a moment.' She flipped through documents piled in a box.

Marbie thought. 'Some people,' she said, after a moment, 'make this kind of grunting sound. This sound kind of like *uh*, and they don't even know that they're doing it. They just do it while they're reading or thinking.'

Fancy wrote the word: UH.

'I imagine the sound of a *key* in a *lock* might be a sound you don't like to hear!' called Grandma Zing, with a mischievous glint.

There was a clamour at this as everyone cried, '*Yes*, Fancy, what did you *do*?' and '*How* did you make it out the *window*?' and 'That was *such* a close one', and Radcliffe said, bossily, 'We should discuss this at the appropriate time in the meeting, shouldn't we?'

'Oh *God*,' said Fancy, closing her notebook again. 'How did I let it happen? I think I must have lost my touch!'

There was another clamour as everyone assured her she had not lost her touch.

'Look at the way you opened the window, closed it behind you, jumped into a tree, and climbed down without being noticed!' cried Marbie. 'I think you're amazing. And anyway, Fancy, it was all my fault – I didn't notice the car coming down the street until the last moment.'

'Why didn't you see it?' said Radcliffe, pointedly.

'I was distracted.'

'Distracted by what?'

'But still,' interrupted Fancy, 'it was so lucky that she switched on the TV right away like that, and just stayed in the front room – if she hadn't . . . who knows?'

'Gotta change that beeper sound,' said Radcliffe.

'And we all thought that it was the cat's *miaow*,' offered Vernon.

Everyone groaned and Marbie hit his leg, but then she embraced him proudly, while Grandma Zing said, 'Shall we start the meeting? We have an *edict* today!'

'Worn out brake-pads,' whispered Grandpa Zing, leaning over to Fancy, 'make an awful squealing sound.' He pointed at Fancy's notepad, and she mouthed, 'Thanks, Dad,' and noted it down.

•

'I will.'

Cassie had seven hundred hands in the air; her shoulders were stretched like string. Her head could fall off any minute. Marcus Ellison, meanwhile, had his chin on his hand, and his other arm slumping from the desk into the air. His hand wobbled like a puppet.

Ms Murphy had already nodded and smiled at Marcus when Cassie said 'I will' in an almost-shout, and put seven hundred hands into the air. Ms Murphy lifted her nose in surprise.

'Cassie!' she said and everybody murmured, '*Cassie* wants to do it' and '*Now what?*'

Ms Murphy moved her neck in a straight-up swivel for a moment, and then she said, 'Thank you, Cassie, that's very generous. But what about if you write the play for the next big assembly, and we'll have Marcus write the end-of-year one. Seeing as he just volunteered, and he's always writing such great plays for us. Don't you think?'

'No,' said Cassie, and put her hands down.

'He *is* so,' was the outcry all around.

'Ms Murphy?' said Cassie. 'That's sex discrimination. Choosing Marcus instead of me. Sex discrimination.'

'Sex discrimination,' said Ms Murphy. 'Interesting, Cassie. Maybe we should talk about *discrimination* for a while. Who can tell me what that word means?'

Cassie lifted her desk-lid and slammed it down.

'Cunt,' she murmured, 'cunt, cunt, cunt.' Then she leaned forward and began to count on her fingers, whispering to herself.

Ms Murphy kept her neck in a straight line and her eyes on the Solar System poster up the back.

'Anybody?' she wondered. 'Discrimination?'

'Ms *Murphy*,' cried Elaine Yin. 'Can't you *hear* what *Cassie* is *saying*?'

'Do you know what?' Ms Murphy exclaimed. 'I have a wonderful idea. I think we should have a play with *two* parts, and I think we should have Marcus write one part and Cassie write the other. All right, Marcus? All right, Cassie?'

Cassie looked up from her feverish counting in surprise. 'All right, I suppose.'

Marcus Ellison opened his whole face in fury, but Ms Murphy pretended not to notice.

'What are you going to write for your play, Cassie?' Lucinda asked as they walked out of the classroom at lunch.

'I haven't decided yet,' explained Cassie. But, in fact, she had decided. It was easy. Erotic fiction.

'I'll *get* you, Cassie Zing,' whispered Marcus Ellison.

'I'll get you first,' said Cassie, with a tilt of her head.

•

Hanging up the phone after chatting with her sister, Fancy walked into the TV room, and said to Radcliffe: 'We *never* go out.'

'Where are they off to now?' He was lethargic in his reclining chair with the retractable corduroy footrest.

'Who?' said Cassie. 'Who's going where?'

'Marbie, Vernon and Listen. They're going to the Blue Mountains to see the snow. Did you know it was snowing in Katoomba? They were calling from the train; they're on their way right now. At this hour. On a Wednesday night! Remember when we used to go to the Blue Mountains, Radcliffe?'

'As the actress said to the bishop,' murmured Radcliffe.

Fancy stared. 'WHAT?'

'Of *course* I remember!' he collected himself, and Fancy explained to Cassie: 'That's where your dad proposed to me!'

'It's going to snow right here,' said Cassie from the floor by the TV. 'It's a waste of a train ticket.'

'Darling, you sit too close to the TV, you know.'

'It's not going to snow here, Cass.'

'Yes, Dad. It's going to snow. I heard it on the news.'

'It don't snow in Sydney, kiddo.'

'Cassie, honey,' Fancy fretted, 'I read somewhere about an experiment where they put these bean trees in pots and made them watch TV, right up close like you are, and the bean trees grew up pale and slender, and with hardly any beans.'

'I'm not a bean tree.'

'Cassie's not a bean tree,' agreed Radcliffe.

'Yes, but she still sits too close to the television.'

'She's going to ruin her eyes, I'll grant you that. She'll cost us a fortune in *optometrist* fees one of these days. Cassie, will you pay your own optometrist fees?'

'Yep.'

'Well, that's settled then. Stop fretting, Fance, and sit down.'

•

Cassie was growing up pale and slender, a very fast runner, but with hardly any beans.

•

At the Zing dining table, on a Friday night, with one week left of school before the holidays, Fancy, who had just been chatting with Listen, declared that they all had to help choose a topic for Listen's school assignment: 'Choose two creatures of the sea,' recited Fancy, while Listen nodded encouragingly. 'They may be mythical creatures and *they need not be fish.*'

'They *need not be fish,*' murmured Grandma Zing, impressed.

'Ocean bream and rainbow trout,' suggested Grandpa Zing at once.

'Mullet and mermaids,' tried Grandma Zing.

'Blowfish and stingrays,' said Vernon.

'Fish and chips,' declared Cassie, giggling.

'Blue-eyed cod and . . .' Radcliffe clicked his fingers a couple of times.

'Pickled herrings and lobster mornay,' said Marbie. 'Oysters and mussels.'

'I was thinking that I would try to do something kind of opposite,' said Listen. 'Like one thing very very big, and one thing very very small.'

'Whales then,' said Vernon.

'Definitely whales,' said Listen.

'Do a little bit of seaweed,' said Cassie, 'or a tiny teeny little sea-grape.'

'Good idea, Cassie, but I was thinking of the sea*horse.*'

'You already know what you're doing,' Grandpa Zing observed. 'Whales and seahorses. See that everyone? Whales and seahorses. So why is she asking us?'

'I *didn't* know until this moment,' argued Listen. 'You all just helped me decide. Thank you very much.' She looked around and everybody nodded, except Fancy, who was thinking.

'Does it have to be creatures of the sea?' said Fancy. 'Can't it be, I don't know, *dragons* and *cows*?'

'I don't think so,' Listen said, apologetically. 'It's for our Ocean unit. But the other day, at Tae Kwon Do, we learnt about this Grandmaster who was the first person to knock over a cow with a flying side kick. I could have put that in the project if I was doing dragons and cows.'

'He knocked over a cow! Why would he do that?'

'It wasn't a cow,' Listen remembered. 'It was a bull.'

'Vernon,' whispered Marbie, 'read out the letter. Everybody quiet now. Do you have it with you, Vernon? Good. Everybody listen. Vernon's going to read.'

Vernon held his fork in one hand while he took a piece of folded paper from his pocket. He cleared his throat as he unfolded it.

'But a bull is a cow, I guess,' said Listen to herself. 'Or is it?'

Fancy leaned towards the gravy. 'Can you –?' she said. 'The gravy?'

'Shh,' said Marbie, and passed her the gravy. 'Vernon's trying to read.'

Vernon smiled kindly at Fancy, to show that he forgave her and also to show that he knew he had not yet begun to read. Then he cleared his throat again and began to read.

'Dear Parents,' he read. 'Dear Parents – this is a letter from Listen's school I should add.' He looked around the room and everyone nodded except Listen, who said coldly, 'Vernon, why are you reading out a letter from my school?'

'Shush,' said Vernon, and looked down at the letter again. 'Wait and see, Listen. Wait and see. Okay. We regret to inform you that an unexpected crisis has occurred here at St Carmel Catholic Girls.'

'A crisis!' cried Grandma Zing, excited.

'Due to a faulty connection,' Vernon continued, nodding, yes, a crisis, 'due to a faulty connection, a water pipe has burst and many of the Year 7 classrooms have been flooded.'

'A water pipe!' burst Grandpa Zing. He had to shift his chair back as if to show his serviette around. 'Does your school not ensure that *water pipes* don't burst?'

They all looked at Listen for the answer.

'Well, I guess they don't!' cried Radcliffe. 'Since one just burst!' Everybody shouted, except Listen, who gave a polite little breath of laughter, and blinked.

'Did you see it burst?' said Fancy. 'Did your feet get wet?'

Listen explained that it had happened the previous Thursday, while she was away in the Blue Mountains, so her feet didn't get wet. She also explained that they had been taking classes in the Science labs or outside ever since, even though it was freezing cold.

'You should take along a little knee rug,' suggested Grandma Zing.

'Unfortunately,' read Vernon solemnly, 'technicians could not be located in time to stop excessive damage occurring to these classrooms. Year 7 lessons are currently being taken in the Science labs, and where possible, in the school grounds –'

'We already know that,' Grandpa Zing interrupted. 'Listen just told us.'

'However, it has been decided to transfer Year 7 students for the winter term, while the damage is repaired. From the first day of term after the holidays, could you please ensure that your daughters report to –'

Vernon paused, dramatically.

'Report to where?' Grandma Zing shifted in her chair. 'Marbie? Why doesn't he finish reading?'

'Because you won't be quiet. Vernon. Tell them where.'

Vernon read: 'Redwood Primary.'

Radcliffe cried, 'Huh!' and everyone was silent, looking from face to face.

'That's *Cassie's* school!' cried Grandma Zing, unnecessarily.

'But my school's a primary school.' Cassie was astonished. 'Listen's in *Year 7*.'

'Exactly,' said Listen. 'How can I go there? I can't.'

'Mum,' Cassie cried, 'Listen's in *Year 7*!'

'I think I should just not go to school next term,' said Listen, then more kindly to Cassie: 'Not that I wouldn't love to come to school with you, Cassie.'

Fancy looked around and saw a newspaper on the sideboard. She reached out and ripped off a corner. 'Anybody have a pen?' she said.

'Mum!' Cassie persisted. 'Listen can't come to my school, can she?'

'No,' agreed Listen.

'Radcliffe, give me your pen.'

Radcliffe reached around to the jacket on his chair, and took a pen from his inside pocket. 'Don't forget to return it to me,' he instructed.

'Isn't it amazing?' Marbie bounced on her chair. 'Listen is going to Cassie's school!'

'Mum!' pestered Cassie. 'Mum!'

Fancy wrote on her newspaper scrap: '*Peas on a fork can look, sometimes, like an abacus!*' She folded the paper and put it next to her plate.

'*Mum*,' Cassie wailed.

'Hush,' said Marbie.

'Darling?' said Fancy.

Everyone talked about floods and technicians, primary schools and high schools, teachers and fire engines. Grandma Zing and Radcliffe began to gather plates.

Radcliffe scooped up crumpled napkins. He scooped up Fancy's paper corner and now it was on a plate, drenched in gravy: '*Peas on a fork can look, sometimes, like an abacus!*' He scraped the plate into the bin.

•

Later that night, Fancy sat at her desk and began to write a letter.

Dear Ms Murphy,

Thank you for your note enquiring about my daughter (Cassie's) loose tooth. She has lost it now! And the tooth fairy has come and gone.

Then she stopped and *tch*ed. She needed a *reason* to write.

She had already written about Cassie's asthma, her allergy to bees, her aversion to gingham, and her preference for Vegemite over Marmite. What else was there?

Cassie sat on the floor behind her, threading plastic beads onto a string and saying now and then, 'Mum? Will Listen *really* come to my school next term?'

Fancy swivelled around and looked at Cassie. 'Any more loose teeth, darling?'

'No,' said Cassie, sadly. 'Wait.' She tested each tooth with her tongue. 'No. No loose tooths.'

'Teeth! Cassie, anything *interesting* happening at school?'

'No,' asserted Cassie, confidently.

'Hmm.' Fancy turned back to her note and stared at it for a while, while Cassie continued to chant, 'Mu-um, will Listen *really* come to my school after the holidays?'

'Right then,' Fancy said suddenly. 'I'm trying to work, Cassie, and you should be in bed!' Then her eyes roved over the pink plastic beads scattered on the study floor like sugar drops. 'Sorry, Cassie! Yes. She will go to your school. After the holidays, Listen will be at your school for just one term. Because her school is flooded.'

'Thanks,' said Cassie solemnly, and stood up at once, ready to go to bed.

Fancy had a happy flash of inspiration then, and continued her letter:

I hope you will forgive me for writing again so soon, but I have a small favour to ask.

•

Cassie was climbing under the covers, and her mum was picking clothes up off the floor.

'*Cassie*, this is your sports tunic! You should have put it in the wash!'

Cassie said, 'Whoops!', slid under the Harry Potter quilt, and squashed her cheek against the pillow. Her mother shook out the uniform, frowning at it. She folded it over her arm, pulled the curtains tightly closed, patted Harry Potter smooth, and switched off the light.

In bed, Cassie imagined her own school flooded. She thought of papers, teachers, desks and bottles of White-Out bobbing along in a river. Ms D'Souza in a life raft, Mr Woodford in a row boat, Ms Murphy treading water. She thought of blackboard dusters, whiteboards and pink chalk; overhead projectors, flower vases, cardboard boxes. She thought of the school turtle, swept out of his pond, paddling and honking in alarm.

The whole thing seemed suspicious to Cassie, and also, absolutely strange.

•

On the Monday of the final week of term, Fancy found an unlidded purple texta in the pocket of Cassie's sports tunic. A purple butterfly bloomed at the hip of the tunic, but Fancy attacked it with Pre-wash Stain Remover, and watched as the wings began to dribble.

In inky purple texta, on a piece of tissue paper, she then listed as follows:

OBJECTS IN A FAMILY HOME: THE LAUNDRY
Domestos
oatmeal soap
a blue bucket containing a pink sponge and Ajax Spray & Wipe
a small puddle at the base of the washing machine
washing machine

On the Tuesday of the final week of term, Fancy found a coffee filter, filled with ageing coffee grounds, quietly wilting in her coffee-maker. 'Oh, *Radcliffe*,' she said aloud, and then *'ew'* as she lifted it out and dropped it in the garbage bin.

On the MESSAGES board beside the telephone, she then listed as follows:

OBJECTS IN A FAMILY HOME: THE KITCHEN
clock
calendar with photos of Canadian Rockies
collage of family snapshots in silver frame
exercise book
name stickers
doll's underwear
port decanter
collapsed birthday card display
on the table: spots of candle wax
also on the table: a ceramic bowl filled with this and that

On the Wednesday of the final week of term, Fancy sat at the kitchen table to scrape at the candle wax. After a moment, she reached for a notebook and a pen and listed:

OBJECTS IN A FAMILY HOME: CERAMIC BOWL FILLED WITH THIS AND THAT, SPECIFICALLY

drawing pins
elastic bands
empty film canister
business card
Valerio Sore Throat Gargle
cotton
AAA battery
bobby pin
Hong Kong two-dollar coin
large black button
blue pen lid
glue stick
nailfile
a tube of sample Musk perfume
a safety pin
a paperclip
a token for a locker at Baulkham Hills Shire Council library
Moisture Absorbent in white paper wrapping: DO NOT EAT, DO NOT EAT, DO NOT EAT

On the Thursday of the final week of term, Fancy felt she could not possibly go on. She reached for her handbag to choose something new to be listed: she would strike through *Objects in a Family Home*.

Her List of Potential Lists was not in her handbag.

'Ah,' she sighed, moving into her study and checking on her desk. It was not there. It was not in the desk drawers either. *Hmm!* she said, with a jaunty frown.

She was not concerned because she remembered exactly what was on the list. It would be easy to rewrite on the back of another phone bill. Nevertheless, she began a thorough, cheerful search of the house: the kitchen, the laundry, the bedrooms, the garage, the car. She found herself running up and down the steps, searching in random places such as the cutlery drawer and the liquor cabinet.

It's probably in a pocket somewhere, she realised. *Now, when did I last have it?*

And then it came to her. The last time she had it was at the Intrusion. The *near-disastrous* Intrusion – when she had failed to notice Marbie beeping her, had come within a cat's whisker of getting caught, and somehow had climbed out of the window. *So, it would be in the pocket of my black pants, of –*

But there was the strangest sensation in her cheeks: as of automatic doors closing slowly towards her nose. Because there were *no pockets* in her black pants.

She had left her List of Potential Lists on the dining room table by the window inside the apartment. And her phone bill was on the back.

Her mother, when she telephoned with shaking hands and teary voice, was remarkably professional. 'There was a pile of papers on the dining table there?'

'Yes,' Fancy quavered.

'Chances are it's still exactly where you left it,' said her mother contentedly. 'I'll put out a Request for an urgent Distraction. You let Marbie know what's going on. And we'll have an Intrusion underway before the end of the day, you mark my words, my dearest.'

'I'll sit by the phone,' promised Fancy.

'Don't worry so much, darling. Just go about your day as planned but keep your beeper with you. We may have just a slight margin.'

Of course, Fancy could not possibly leave the house. She was agitated and hysterical all day, gasping whenever the phone rang, and whenever she heard leaves rustle (that was the new beeper sound). She called Radcliffe and asked him to fetch Cassie from school as she was too overwrought to drive. Radcliffe tried to reassure her but the excitement of disaster bristled in his voice. She called Marbie several times to confirm that she would leave work early: Marbie laughed and was serene about the whole thing when Fancy first told her, but even she seemed to grow a bit tetchy after Fancy's fourth phone call.

When their mother's alert finally arrived, Fancy's heart was playing some kind of thrashing rock and roll song.

But it went surprisingly smoothly.

There was nobody around; Marbie climbed her tree safely; the code worked; the apartment was empty and dark; and the List of Potential Lists was sitting safely on the dining room table, underneath some kind of legal assignment. Once she had folded the List into her handbag, Fancy was so relieved that she decided to do the maintenance work she had not completed on the last Intrusion.

'Sleep well,' said Marbie, kindly, as she dropped Fancy back at home. 'And have a nice, relaxing day tomorrow, you poor thing. Get an aromatherapy massage.'

But the next day, the Friday of the final week of term, Fancy woke in such a state of jitters that she had to spend some time deep breathing. *It's all right, it's all right, it's all right*, she chanted.

Her hands fluttered from her mouth to her elbows to her ears, and sometimes to nothing.

'Are you all right, Mum?' said Cassie, as Fancy drove her to school.

'Yes, darling, perfectly fine! Have a nice last day at school! Holidays tomorrow! Hooray!'

Cassie looked back at her suspiciously.

Driving home again, Fancy knew that she must *take action* against this hysteria. Otherwise, it would manifest itself in some physical way such as a heart attack or hives. She needed exercise – it was far too cold to go jogging, but she could go to her gym. *Swimming*, that was what she needed. The serenity of gliding through the water!

And how about that, it was Friday morning, and that man on the phone had told her that *this* was the quietest time for swimming. She would go home, gather her things, and drive directly to the gym.

The Canadian was standing on his porch.

'I haven't seen you for a while!' she chatted as she reached her own front door. 'I guess it's been too cold for your breakfasts on the porch. I never got a chance to thank you for that *delicious* cake! Cassie *loved* it, by the way. I froze a couple of pieces for her so she could take them to school as a special treat with her lunch.'

'Never too cold for me,' he said, 'to eat breakfast on my porch. I've been away, is the explanation. And that is the nicest thing I've heard in a while, that Cassie took a piece of my maple cake to school as a special treat. Thank you.'

'Tell me,' said Fancy, suddenly. 'Now, a sugar maple leaf, that would be a Canadian sort of leaf, wouldn't it?'

'They have sugar maples elsewhere as well,' said the Canadian, formally. 'But yes, the maple leaf is on our flag. So, you could say it's Canadian.'

'Then tell me,' Fancy repeated, 'would a teardrop ever look like a maple leaf?'

The Canadian considered this for a moment. 'I would have to say,' he said slowly, 'I would have to say, I'd choose a different sort of leaf if I wanted to describe a teardrop. I would choose a leaf with your more traditional leaf shape. Such as that eucalyptus leaf, right there. Now, I suppose that a teardrop might fall *splat* onto a page – say you were reading a book and having a little weep – a teardrop might fall *splat*, and the mark that it left on the *page* might, if you were lucky, resemble a sugar maple leaf. But otherwise, I would say no.'

Fancy felt a rush of love for the Canadian-next-door.

'Thank you,' she said, blushing, and walked into her house.

Driving to the swimming pool, Fancy felt calm and happy. She allowed herself to imagine that she had invited the Canadian along. And he had said, *Swimming, I love to swim!* And she had said, *Me too!* And he had run inside and returned with his swimming costume. Perhaps even wearing it! To prove that he was Canadian, and could get about bare-chested in such grey and icy weather. (It was close to zero degrees, the radio told her.) And then she had driven chattingly along, her bare hand on the gearstick, so close to his bare, hairy legs! (The hair on his legs would be fine, not thick.) And then, at the pool, there would be nobody else! Just the two of them! And he would shake his head in wonder at the grace of her stroke.

Fancy, unlike Marbie (who was a high-speed swimmer), swam exceptionally slowly but with grace; so slow that she tended to hold up even the slowest fellow swimmers if she had to share a lane. That was why Fancy had called about the quietest times to swim.

Calmly, she entered the gym and explained that she wanted to use the swimming pool.

'Sorry,' said the man behind the counter – and it was the man with the rasping, unpleasant voice who had answered her call – 'Sorry,' he said, 'the swimming pool's closed for cleaning. Nine-thirty to eleven-thirty every Friday.'

'No,' said Fancy, emphatically. 'No, I phoned a few weeks ago, and I was told that this is the *quietest* time to swim.' She intended to stand her ground.

'That was you calling about the quietest pool times? What I said,' declared the man, with a leering grin, 'was that the swimming pool is *quietest* at this time! Of course it is! There's nobody here! They're cleaning it!'

Fancy stared at him. That a person could play such a trick! She felt entitled to continue staring, with amazed, accusing eyes, for as long as she liked.

'I did explain,' he said, defensively, 'I did go on to explain why this was the quietest time. You mustn't have heard me.'

'If the swimming pool is being cleaned now,' said Fancy with a proud swing of her head, 'then I don't *imagine* it's all that quiet. I *imagine* the cleaning equipment makes quite a racket!' Then she flounced out of the gym.

Behind the wheel again, Fancy felt so foolish that she had to cry a little. The rain was strange on her windshield: it seemed to land with an icy skid rather than a normal, sugar-maple-leaf-shaped splat.

She felt especially foolish at the idea that the Canadian might have been with her. How she would have wasted his time if she'd brought him along. She was cold with fear at the thought. Of course, he might have found her error adorable, and suggested a hot chocolate instead. The car skidded and slipped on the road, and some of her jitters returned.

Back in her own home, the day seemed endless. She tried phoning her mother, and they had a brief chat about whether to cancel the Zing Family Secret Meeting that night, because of the weather. They decided they should cancel, so then her mother had to hang up to let the others know. Fancy wandered from room to room, picking up objects from the floor and then letting them slide back down in a different place. She took books off shelves and replaced them, and flicked through the pages of photo albums. As she did this, she wept to herself: about the man at the gym with the awful voice; about how close she had been to getting caught at the last Intrusion; about how stupid she was to have left her *phone bill* behind when she got out! About her well-meaning husband Radcliffe (because look at him in this picture with his worried expression; and what if he got killed while driving home?). About her beautiful daughter Cassie. (She was so little. Look at her here in her cosy red mittens!)

And all the time, that sad little sentence played itself over in her head: *how is your ocean bream, my love? How is your ocean bream?*

Meanwhile, Cassie was asking her friend Lucinda to hold her lunch and was skidding to the far side of the playground. Lucinda watched with interest as Cassie straightened her mittens.

The playground was so slippery it was perfect: all she had to do was run, as fast as she could, from as far away as this, and the slipperiness would do the rest. It was better than the trolley ramp in the Castle Towers car park, where you could take a run and skid almost all the way down.

Cassie bent forward, concentrating, jumped on the spot and then ran. She was fast. She was faster than she had ever been. Ice-cold wind ran along with her excitedly. Marcus Ellison was a small dark figure with his cricket bat and his frown, but he was growing bigger. She was hurtling into the midst of the game and the kids around her were a blur!

Then, Mr Woodford caught her. It took a minute for her to stop panting. The blurriness calmed down around her.

'Cassie,' Mr Woodford was saying in a solemn voice, 'the stride you had going then, as you ran, was the stride of an Olympic runner. Do you understand me? Do you understand that this run of yours, with this pace you had going, was the start of an Olympic run? Do you under-stand?' Everyone was used to Mr Woodford joking, so they waited. But then they realised he was serious. Mr Woodford was being serious. Everyone paid attention.

Cassie glanced over at Marcus – he was staring at her, pale and trem-bling: he had seen what she was willing to do. She was willing to *take an Olympic run straight at him across the ice, and if Mr Woodford had not stopped her –* He looked back down to his bat.

'Do you understand?' Mr Woodford said again.

Cassie nodded her agreement, and skidded away to Lucinda. She had got Marcus Ellison, she knew that from his face. So that was finished.

The unfinished thing, she realised, as Lucinda returned her lunch to her, was the run. Her legs had to finish that run.

•

Anything but this. Fancy jumped up from the living room floor, tripping over photo albums, and strode down the hall to the front door, throwing it open.

She stepped onto the porch and something whacked her face like a leather glove: *that's how cold it was.* The mat, when she stepped on it, crunched with ice. A shudder spiralled through her and pinched her shoulderblades. The sky was low, pale and plaintive, like Cassie when she was coming down with something. The Canadian's porch was empty.

Back inside with the door firmly closed against the cold, Fancy stared down the hall. What if she were to make gingerbread? What if she were to try a little mosaic? What if she were to do some of Cassie's mending? What if she were to –

But no, no, she panicked, and strode back to the front door. The sky was still looking sulky, and the Canadian's porch remained empty. She held the door open a moment as an icy breeze shifted twigs on the lawn, scattering dried leaves on the porch.

'Oh no!' said Fancy, her eyes glinting as a leaf or two skittered past her ankles and into the house. 'Now I'll have to vacuum!' Then she remembered that her vacuum cleaner was in the repair shop.

I wonder if the Canadian has a vacuum cleaner I might borrow? she thought, suddenly and earnestly. At that moment, the Vacuum Repair Truck turned into her driveway. Fancy accepted the repaired vacuum with cold politeness, and, as soon as she had closed the door, she plugged it in.

She vacuumed: the hall, the lounge room, the TV room, Cassie's room. And now she was in the main bedroom. Her lower back ached, the room roared with vacuum cleaner groans, she used her knees to shove the bed to the side, and she busied herself with the skirting boards. Crouching down to the floor, she fed the nozzle way under the bed, but then there was a gasping choking sound and she switched the vacuum off. There was something caught in its mouth, which she gently removed.

It was a dusty purple sock. Stitched at the back of the ankle with a simple purple daisy.

She held it up and frowned at it. This was not Fancy's sock. Nor was it Cassie's sock. Certainly, it was not Radcliffe's sock. So now, whose sock would be deep under their bed like that?

In the post-vacuum quiet, Fancy rocked back on her heels, looking from the sock to the window to the ceiling to the vacuum. The vacuum had no reply, but there was something wide-eyed about the room.

This sock belongs to another woman, Fancy whispered to herself. *Radcliffe is having an affair.*

Immediately, crouching on the floor by the bed, she laughed to herself. Radcliffe, having an affair! It was so unlikely that the word ('affair') was immediately surrounded, in her mind, by a circle of witty prompt cards. Each card contained a rhetorical question, such as: *When would this affair take place, Fancy, given that you work at home each day?*

I know, I know! *When?* (She laughed along.) Although still (she noted, politely) I often *do* go out – on Zing Family Secret business, for instance, or for coffee with Marbie or Mum. He's only ten minutes away and often slips home to surprise me for lunch. He could easily slip a pretty woman home.

But, FANCY, what sort of a pretty woman would have sex with Radcliffe? I mean, seriously.

Me, for a start (she thought, tartly). He's not that bad. He has an unexpected charm. And there are plenty of women at his work. There's *Gemma,* for instance, in the pay office, who spills her drinks at Christmas parties, and gets all the moles zapped from her arms.

Yes, but a purple sock? Why would she leave a purple sock behind?

Here, Fancy had to pause. She had never believed for a moment in bits of gossamer lingerie or single diamond earrings. No woman would have a dalliance with someone else's husband and then flit off in a taxi without her underwear and earring. No woman! The wind would blow cold against her buttocks! Not to mention her diamond-less ear.

But a purple sock. This she could believe.

Let's say Gemma (it might as well be Gemma) – let's say Gemma only works afternoons. (Gemma does only work afternoons – Radcliffe mentioned that.) All right, so let's say one morning Fancy calls Radcliffe to tell him, 'I'm going to have coffee with Marbie today, so I won't be home!'

Radcliffe makes a furtive call to Gemma: 'Are you still at home, my darling? Haven't left for work? The wife's gone out. Meet me at my place in ten.'

Gemma, dressed in jaunty morning attire of shorts, sneakers and purple socks, arrives breathless. Her work clothes are in a gym bag over her arm. They hurry up the stairs for a few moments of passion; Gemma showers steamily; then she throws her work clothes on (stockings, skirt, lipstick); and off they rush to work. So easy to forget a purple sock!

Well, but really, why would you imagine that Radcliffe is having an affair? You've never thought a thing like that before.

The question (frostily) is why have I *not* considered it before. Recollect that Radcliffe cheated on me when we were fifteen years old and had only just begun going out. If he could not last a single month, why do I imagine he can last a lifetime?

And now she found the word 'affair' gleaming and proud, surrounded by fallen cards. It waited patiently for her to fill in the details.

It *was* with Gemma! Of *course* it was! Remember how Radcliffe spoke of her? So tenderly, so fondly. 'You must remember Gemma,' he had said. 'No,' she had replied. And then he had explained how Gemma had the moles zapped from her arms. Why should he know that? Why would Gemma from the pay office tell Radcliffe about her moles? Didn't people in the pay office stay behind closed doors, filling up envelopes with pay?

He must have brought her home on the day Fancy met Marbie and Listen for coffee in Castle Hill. On that day, Radcliffe had come home from work to 'surprise' her for lunch. *But*, she realised now, *she had phoned to let him know she was not there*. He came home *BECAUSE she was not there*. He came home with Gemma in purple socks! And on that day, she recalled in a rush, he had broken a glass. He had broken the vacuum cleaner trying to clean it up. Trying to clean away *the evidence of his affair!*

No! It was *Gemma* who had broken the glass. Gemma was clumsy. She spilled drinks at Christmas parties. He only mentioned his sojourn home, and the breakage of the vacuum cleaner, *weeks* after the event. It was a slip! How strange and awkward he had been when he told her. And then how kind and loving as they carried the vacuum in to be repaired.

All this time, her vacuum cleaner had been trying to let her know about the affair. First, it choked on the broken glass; then it caused Radcliffe to slip up and reveal he had been home that day; and now, today, it had come home to her from the repair shop. *On purpose, to swallow the purple sock.*

Fancy lay flat on her back on the bed, and thought with clarity: *Radcliffe is having an affair.*

Oh *stop* that, she cried, sitting up with a final burst of scorn. *It's just a sock!* She looked at it on the palm of her hand, so flimsy and frail. How could this mean something so immense as an *affair?*

But then she thought of her recipes: an accidental touch of egg yolk in her meringue; one-eighth of a teaspoon of cayenne pepper in her mango dressing – these tiny things had such an impact! Small things, she realised, *can* mean something immense.

Suddenly the sock felt moist in her hand, a scaly, alien thing, and she flung it back onto the floor. It lay there seeming to wriggle, like a fish too small to eat.

MARBIE ZING

The Monday after Cassie's party, the neighbour's black cat crossed Marbie's path and tripped her up in such a way that she stumbled underneath a ladder. The ladder was leaning quite deliberately against the neighbour's house. She stood under it for a moment, trembling. As far as she could recall, it was the first ladder she had ever walked beneath. There was now no point going to work.

'Are you up yet?' she called, knocking on Listen's bedroom window. Listen was going to school later and later these days. She appeared in her frayed pyjamas, rubbing her eyes.

'You look tired,' said Marbie.

'I just woke up,' explained Listen.

'Still,' said Marbie, 'you need a break. Let me take you to the seaside and buy you a sarong. This week autumn will begin and the sun will start to fall from the trees and become little shadows at your feet. We should wear sarongs until that happens.'

'Okay,' said Listen, 'good idea.'

'I'll write a note and say you've got rabies.'

While Listen found her beach towel, Marbie phoned work and explained about the cat and the ladder. Tabitha was very understanding. 'You stay right where you are,' she said. 'Don't take a step toward the office.'

Then Marbie phoned the aeronautical engineer and said she could not meet him after work that night.

'Can't meet me?' said the A.E., with a slurping sound. 'I'm sick anyway. Hear this? I'm sucking a lozenge. So, better off not meeting me, but aren't you the one who arranged this?'

It was true she had arranged the meeting. It was so she could formally explain: *no more tennis*. Anyway, either that or invite him over for a cocktail, so she could alter the tone of the thing: 'Here, Mr Aeronautical Engineer, meet Vernon and Listen! The A.E. is a sort of colleague of mine. Listen! Show the A.E. some Tae Kwon Do! *Look* at her, A.E., she's a natural! I think it's because she can dance.'

Afterwards, A.E. would drive away, and she would hold Vernon's hand on the doorstep, already talking about something else, such as dinner.

Marbie was silent on the phone, thinking about this, so after a moment the A.E. made a crunching sound and said, 'Ouch. Bit through the lozenge and it's got sharp edges. What say you to Wednesday instead?'

'I say okay to Wednesday instead,' agreed Marbie, and put down the phone. She had a habit of simply hanging up rather than making some conclusive remark such as 'Great! See you then. Keep smiling!'

On Wednesday, A.E. arrived at the pub in an unusually chatty mood, declaring that his cold had been cured by Butter Menthols.

He sat down and chuckled to himself, picked up his beer and made a *brmmm* sound as he flew the glass towards his mouth. Foam spilled over the edges. 'Here comes the aeroplane!' he said. Then he told Marbie that his father used to be a pilot.

'Huh,' said Marbie.

'So this is how he always fed me,' he explained, 'when I was a baby. And *that's* why I studied aeronautical engineering!'

'Hmm,' said Marbie, wondering if she should mention that babies all over the world were fed by aeroplane spoons.

Instead, for the sake of politeness, she told him she had been to several festivals of hot air balloons. She picked up her beer and floated it towards her mouth like a hot air balloon. He chuckled, then remarked that hot air balloons were 'terrifically significant' in the development of the principles of aeronautics. She said she once heard that Leonardo Da Vinci figured them *all* out, *all* the principles of aeronautics, in sketchbooks five hundred years ago. He said that this was a common myth, such as the myth that William Shakespeare wrote his own plays.

So then Marbie said she thought that myth was actually true, that William Shakespeare did write his own plays. And even if somebody else *had* written the plays, did it matter? Who really knew William Shakespeare these days? He could be a compilation of people, couldn't he, and it would still be William Shakespeare?

'Whoa!' said the aeronautical engineer, making his eyes sparkle to show his fascination and confusion at her point.

Also, she continued, talking about William Shakespeare, she herself came from a family of writers. For example, her father once travelled to Ireland for a year to write a novel (although he then threw the manuscript, one page at a time, into the ocean); and her sister, Fancy, was a writer.

Aeronautical Engineer looked almost shifty at the news of her family of writers. He did not express environmental concerns when he heard that her father threw his novel to the sea. (That was the usual reaction.) And he did not ask what *kind* of writing Fancy did, which was also a common reaction. Instead, he shifted (shiftily), looked into his beer (sadly), then looked up at Marbie (sharply), and said: 'I don't know if I should tell you this or not.'

'Of course you should,' said Marbie, emphatically.

'I don't know,' he said, 'I don't know', shaking his head and trying to get something out of his eye for a moment.

'Just count to ten and then tell me,' suggested Marbie.

He looked embarrassed, and gazed at her with unexpectedly vulnerable baby eyes.

'I'm a writer myself,' he breathed eventually. And looked back down.

'What?' she said, although she had heard him.

So that's when he told her. He said he had invented a new form of poetic self-expression which he called the 'vision'. He said he had written exactly 1449 of these 'visions' and that he intended to publish them, as a collection, once he had reached 2000. He had never told anybody this before. Also, he had a selection of his favourites in his pocket right at that moment.

Politely, Marbie said, 'Can I take them home and read them?'

And he said, 'Okay, but promise you won't lose them?'

'I can't promise that,' explained Marbie, 'because it's in my nature to lose things.' She suggested he make photocopies before he loaned them to her.

'These *are* copies,' he admitted. 'It's just I'm scared they'll get lost and someone'll steal the ideas, and, you know, *publish* them.'

Marbie said, don't worry, ideas can't be stolen, that's illegal.

So he let her borrow them to take them home.

'By the way,' she said as she pressed the visions into her handbag, 'there was something I wanted to say —'

At that, her handbag miaowed and her hand jumped out in surprise.

'UP FOR SOME MAINTENANCE?' said the message from her mother. 'CONFIRMED 3 HR MARGIN AS OF NOW.'

'Got to go, sorry.' She looked up at the aeronautical engineer. 'Got to phone my sister and then leave!' She slid out of her seat and floated away from the table.

Left behind, the aeronautical engineer watched as she approached the pay phones, and idly turned back to his beer.

Marbie read the first of the A.E.'s visions later that night, while sitting in the tree above the ice-cream van. She had watched Fancy safely enter the building and had surveyed the empty street for a few minutes. There were never any problems on Intrusions these days, and being Look-out was boring. Also, they were well within the '3 hr margin' and her mother never sent them in without confirmation.

So Marbie opened her handbag for a Mini Mars Bar, and her hand found the A.E.'s scroll of visions. The first, curling at top and bottom, was vision # 263.

THE VISIONS OF AN AERONAUTICAL ENGINEER
VISION # 263

Deep on the inside of my fried egg brains I see:
This! I see this, I see this.
I see a fence along a roadside (an iron railing fence),
sharp arrow tops are snipped along the fence,
And deep on the inside of my fried dead brains I see:

> This! I see this, I see this,
> I see this fence with its sharp arrow tops and
> I trip on a scuffle of my boot-lace heel,
> and I fall *eye-first* atop an arrow top!
> Firm atop an arrow top atop an iron fence!
> BUT:
> *deep on the inside of my fried vanilla brains I see:*
> This! I see this, I see this.
> I see myself jogging, calm,
> alongside the fence,
> *And I'm breaking off the arrow tops, one by one,*
> and the arrows snap away *just right,*
> like fresh asparagus.

Marbie felt curious. She shook her head, trying to shake herself back into herself. She read the vision again, and felt even more curious. For she had *never told the aeronautical engineer* about her lifelong fear that long sharp items (such as umbrellas or fence posts) would somehow end up in her eye. *She had never even told him about the event with the flying beach umbrella.*

And yet here, curling in her hand, was a *vision* containing not only her fear, but also the *solution* to her fear. He was going to break the arrow tops *off the fence!* Like the ends of fresh asparagus..

Her hand, which was holding the travel torch, trembled violently, and the torch slipped and rustled through the branches to the ground. She looked down. And there was the car in the street beneath her, turning in to the apartment garage.

GET OUT <u>NOW</u> Marbie typed into her pager, fingers shaking. She sent the message thirteen times before Fancy finally acknowledged it. A few moments later, she saw Fancy leaping smartly from the window to a tree, and elegantly stepping down its branches.

Marbie phoned the A.E. from work the next day and expressed wonder at his vision. He did not seem surprised at her wonder. In fact, he seemed despondent because, it turned out, he *hated* writing his visions. He said that, as a writer, one felt a *compulsion* to write, much like the compulsion that some people have to tear out their own hair. He would give anything, he said, *not* to be a writer, for writers have *expression* in their soul, which is tearing and scratching to get out! Worse, he said, far worse, to tear something out of your soul than simply to tear it from your head.

It was his secret anguish, his writing of visions, and it surprised him, too, this anguish, given that he was generally: practical, objective, logical; just as an *engineer*, a *scientist!* should be. But the artist, sadly, was in him.

THE VISIONS OF AN AERONAUTICAL ENGINEER
VISION # 1232

Deep within the catacombs of piezoelectric plate,
I see this, I see this, I see this.
I see laminated beams that are strung with plates and shells,
In a loft in a barn in a farmyard in a wood.

Also, the A.E. said that he found his visions were at their best just before he fell asleep. So each night when he hopped into bed, he set his alarm for ten minutes hence. Then he let the visions scratch their way out (the agony!) as he fell asleep, and the alarm ensured that the latest visions were not lost in his dreams forever.

He said he got this idea, of setting the alarm, from a particular genius of the past, whose name he could not recall, who used to tie bells to his fingers and sit down for a sleep. The bells would wake the genius just as he began to doze and he would quickly scribble out the ideas he had had while falling.

Marbie said that there was a famous composer who used to tie weights to his little fingers to strengthen them, for piano playing, but often this just broke the fingers.

THE VISIONS OF AN AERONAUTICAL ENGINEER
VISION # 47

Deep within the cobwebs of my avocado dip,
I see this, I see this, I see this.
I see *me* as a *child* with a *curdle* and a *kite*,
I see *me* and I *cuddle* with my *curdle*!
Oh, you do not know what a curdle is?
Nor do I!
You do not know how I cuddle with my curdle,
how my kite swings high on the telegraph wire,
how my curdle tastes of orange juice
question-marking milk,
how my cuddle is of curdle and a kite!
You fool!

After her telephone conversation with the aeronautical engineer, Marbie did not hear from him for two weeks. She read the other visions he had given her, but none of them spoke to her in the same direct way as the one about the sharp fence posts. That particular vision she pinned to the corkboard above her desk, and read each morning like a mantra.

It is curing me, she thought to herself, in wonder. Whenever she feared a long sharp item these days, she would close her eyes and imagine the aeronautical engineer, prancing plumply alongside a fence, snapping off the sharp bits one by one. In her imagination, he turned to her with an armful of fence ends clutched to his chest, and he blushed, and lowered his head.

One Tuesday afternoon, Marbie looked at the phone on her desk and thought: *well!* Because why had he not called?

She had not had a chance to say: *no more tennis*, so why had *he* decided no more tennis? All of his own accord. (Did he have a *vision* that she had meant to say it?) Of course, the weather had turned grey and chill, so maybe tennis was no longer appropriate. Bare legs would goose bump as they ran towards the net. Still, he could have called for a chat.

Marbie wandered out of her office and found Tabitha and Toni gasping in the corridor. It turned out that Abi and Rhamie had joined an A-grade netball team, abandoning the office comp. 'Call me old-fashioned,' said Toni, hotly, 'but Abi is just *not* an A-grade player!'

'Let's have some wine from the small boardroom fridge,' suggested Marbie, 'and discuss it.'

They slipped in to the boardroom, one at a time, and closed the shutters so that Abi and Rhamie would not find them. Then they discussed what a bad netball player Abi was, although, they conceded, now and again Rhamie was an excellent shooter.

Later, they moved on to the Night Owl Pub, where Abi and Rhamie found them and said, 'What's going on?' Toni explained, with a strong but occasionally trembling voice, that she and Tabitha felt betrayed. Abi and Rhamie were shocked, and it turned out it was all a misunderstanding! Because Abi *had* sent an e-mail around about the A-grade team, inviting Tabitha and Toni to join too. But Tabitha and Toni had both deleted the message, thinking it was that virus going around. So it was nobody's fault. They all congratulated each other on being such good netball players, and Toni cried.

Marbie herself was not on the team, so she could be objective, and they thanked her for that, once the dispute was resolved. 'You're so *tall*,' said Rhamie, as usual. 'You'd make a great keeper!' But the others just laughed because Marbie always let the ball slip through her fingers.

At that, Marbie put down her frothy Irish ale and said, 'I don't feel so good.'

'That's because you had wine before beer,' declared Abi, and then she chanted: 'Wine before beer, and you'll feel queer; beer before wine, and you'll feel fine.'

'Is that true?'

'Of course it's true,' said Rhamie, 'it rhymes.'

Then Abi and Rhamie remembered their husbands, gathered their handbags, and made a joke or two about netball.

A moment after they had gone, Marbie gasped with realisation, and whispered to the others: 'How did Abi know I had wine before beer?' Tabitha and Toni also gasped, for they had kept their meeting in the small boardroom a secret.

After they had analysed this for a while, Tabitha and Toni had to run to their step class, and Marbie thoughtfully finished her frothy Irish ale. She was just about to pick up her own handbag, so she could get the express train home, when two hairy hands fell on her shoulders.

●

Sir:

I am writing this while riding the 73 bus. There is a largish, sweaty man beside me and his bottom is taking up more room on the seat than it ought. It is Wednesday, 2 pm, and I should be going back to work. But it is impossible. I'm going home.

This is what has happened.

Last night, I went to the Night Owl with the girls from work. There was a lot of crying and gasping, to do with their netball team, but it was all fine and I felt refreshed. The girls left – Rhamie and Abigail to their husbands, Tabitha and Toni to step. I had my Irish ale to finish, and there I sat, and behind me? Leaning over my shoulder, breathing beer into my cheek, two hairy hands on my shoulders? The aeronautical engineer.

I hadn't seen him for a fortnight, at least. Not since he gave me his visions. I had almost forgotten him.

Anyhow, there he was in the Night Owl Pub.

'Hello,' he said, leaning over me, a murmur of a smile around his beery lips.

'Hello,' I replied.

'I have a suggestion,' he said.

'Not tennis,' I said.

He pretended to look shocked. He did a mime, as if a tennis ball had hit him in the stomach, but recovered quickly, and the smile was less a murmur, more a shout.

'All right,' he agreed, 'not tennis. I had this idea, is all.'

Then he leaned closer and murmured in my ear: 'Come to my house, tomorrow at 1, and you know what we'll do?'

'What?' I whispered back.

'We will take off our clothes,' he explained, in his low, soft voice.
'We will take off our clothes, and we will lie on my bed, and you know
what we'll do? We will look. We will not touch. We will lie together,
for no more than three minutes, and then we will get dressed again!'

I stared at him and said, 'Will we?'

'We won't touch,' he said again. 'So there is no betrayal. I know
you have a boyfriend, but this can hardly hurt him. And I'll get to
see your body without these things.' Then he touched my shirt with
a contemptuous wave.

And here is the extraordinary thing: 'All right,' I said. 'We will.'

'Take the 73 bus at 12.45,' he said, 'it stops right outside my door.'

And that is what I did; and that is what we did; and that is
what happened; that is: nothing; nothing except nakedness; and now
I am on my way home.

I hardly looked at him; I felt very cold, I have to say, and I felt
very pale and strange and I wondered: what are you doing?

He set his clock radio for precisely three minutes, and then, when
three minutes were up, a toothpaste ad filled the room, and he sat up
and looked for his shirt.

So, you see, I could not go back to work.

I am on my way home, to fix this.

Yours sincerely,
Marbie

THE VISIONS OF AN AERONAUTICAL ENGINEER
VISION # 1450

Locked within the golf balls of my enterprising wit
I see this, I see this, I see this.
I see tennis balls toss in noctilucent cloud,
(Ace! By *deuce*! Forty-thousand love!)
I see hail stones that clatter on kennels!
('Help!' cries a puppy. 'The insurance!')

I see how my fingers press buttons on blouses,
I see how my tongue's like a bouquet that rouses,
I see how my tongue's like the snake in my trousers,
(Harmless. A carpet snake. Quicksand! A rattler!)
Stop me! Stop me! I am *wonderful* today!
Somebody fetch me a drink!

●

On Wednesdays, before recess, they had Food Technology. Recess was the most difficult time because there were fifteen minutes to fill, and you were not allowed into the library. You were never allowed into a classroom; everybody had to sit outside on the lawn even though it was so cold these days that girls huddled together, or rubbed each other's hands between their own to make them warm, or sometimes groups of girls got up and did the Can-Can in a row.

The point was, there was nowhere to hide, and there were fifteen minutes to fill.

Sometimes, Listen thought about just going out onto the lawn and joining a group of huddled girls. If she was quiet, they might not notice.

Sometimes, also, she thought about going out there onto the lawn, amongst the garlands of girls, and simply sitting on the grass. She could sit alone, eat an apple, read a book, and *who cares what anybody thinks?*

There was never a single person eating lunch on the lawn alone. *I am the only one in the entire school with no friends*, she realised. Or if not, where do they go? Where are the other lonely people? Why can't we join up and be friends?

On this Wednesday, they had made cheese soufflé in Food Technology, and Listen was hopeful. The bell had rung for recess, and they had not even washed up! The other girls groaned, while Listen quietly filled her sink with slow, soapy warm water.

'Never mind, girls!' cried the teacher, generously. 'Out you all go! I'll clean this up later!'

Listen pretended not to hear, and concentrated on the cheese chunks in the grater.

'Come on, Listen, I'm sure that's clean,' called the teacher, ushering the last girls from the room. 'Go along and get some fresh air!'

Outside the classroom, Listen checked her watch. It was ten forty-six. There were still fourteen minutes to fill. She leaned over, untied her shoelaces and retied them, went to the end of the corridor and retied them again. Then she took the long route to the bathrooms, around the back of the building, always hurrying, sighing and checking her watch, so that if anybody saw her she was just rushing off to meet her friends.

At the bathrooms, she washed each hand with soap, and dried them at the heaters with great care. Now it was ten fifty-one. There were still nine minutes. She hesitated outside the bathrooms, looking both ways along the empty balcony. One direction would take her into the admin office, where she could pretend she had lost something and fill in a lost property form. The other took her to the Year 7 classrooms, where they were not supposed to be. Her eyes wandered the locked doors of Classes 7A, 7B, 7C and 7D, and then stopped at the next door along. She had never noticed that door before.

It was a darker grey than the other doors and did not have a number or letter. As she watched, it was slowly opening. A school handyman was emerging, his arms stretched wide around a large cardboard box. Once out of the room, he looked both ways, kicked the door closed behind him, and grunted. Then he disappeared down the fire escape. She did not even make a decision. She just strode along the balcony, opened the grey door, and walked inside.

It was cramped, dark and smelled like mushrooms. She could see the shadowy shapes of boxes stacked precariously, shovels, rakes, and shelves lined with aerosol cans. Also, against the far wall, a tiny bulb illuminated a panel of switches. *Fuse box*, she thought, and felt pleased with herself. Growing up in a caravan with nobody but a big brother, she had learned how to change fuses, tyres, and halogen lights. She had helped Vernon install a dishwasher once.

She had a moment of pleasure at that thought, and then the pleasure faded like a pilot light burning out. *What if the handyman came back?* What reason could she give for being here? She could be practising her

Tae Kwon Do. She could say that she had a grading right after recess and this was the only place to practise.

For authenticity, she tried a spinning hook kick. Then she swivelled and tripped on a tangle of cords. She fell against the fuse box and slid to the ground with a sound like someone flicking through playing cards. She stood back up in a panic and flashed her eyes over the fuses. Some said OFF and some said ON – which ones had she knocked?

They should probably all be ON. She flicked them all, breathing hard, and backed out of the utility room, closing the door behind her.

There was nobody on the balcony. There were distant sounds of girls laughing and chatting on the lawn. Somewhere, teachers were also chatting, in deeper, more sardonic voices. She used up the last five minutes of recess standing at the bag rack outside 7B, and leafing through the contents of her school bag.

Walking home from school that day, hunched against the pale cold sky and the thin waves of rain, Listen thought: *don't worry, there are only two more days until the end of the week.* Also she thought: *don't worry, soon I'll find a new group to join.*

As she stepped around the edges of muddy puddles, Listen tried once again to go through the different groups of girls in her form, but instead found herself remembering a particular day from a weekend a few years back. On that day, she and Vernon had taken a ferry ride on the harbour. Alongside a ferry wharf she had seen a large yellow sign, which announced, in black letters:

Caution:

Submarine cables.

Reading the sign, she had shivered with delight. *There was a submarine right beneath her!* She imagined it must be slender and silver, and inside, a group of harried sailors hunched over long low tables, sipping black coffee and studying maps. The submarine would be tethered to the sea floor with a cable which might trip you up.

Later, Vernon explained that 'submarine' just meant 'below water'. The sign was saying 'Caution: underwater cables'.

As she stepped up onto the apartment porch, Listen thought: *there is nothing magic in the world. There are no flying motorbikes, just aeroplanes. There are no shooting stars, just satellites. There are no submarines, just underwater cables. There are no eternal pacts.*

Then, as she found her key in her pocket, she thought: *I don't think I can make it to the end of the week.*

Inside the apartment door, she had to stop as the weight of her school bag had become too much for her shoulder. There was a noise down the hall. 'Hello!' called Marbie's voice. 'Is that Listen or a burglar?'

Marbie was sitting at the kitchen table, and the radiator buzzed at her feet. The room was so warm it was like a woollen hug. 'It's my beautiful Listen!' cried Marbie, leaping to her feet and throwing her arms into the air. 'Look, I've got you a welcome afternoon tea!' She swept her arms back and forth across the table, which was set with a lace cloth, a chocolate bar arranged in pieces on a saucer, wedges of orange in a bowl, and a steaming cherry pie.

'Wow,' said Listen, dropping her school bag. 'How come you're not at work?'

'Do you think you could take the rest of the week off school?' said Marbie, ignoring the question and pushing the saucer of chocolate closer to Listen. 'I'm about to call Vernon and see if he can close the Banana Bar. Because guess what? I heard on the news that it's snowing in the Blue Mountains! So I've arranged the Deluxe Package for the three of us at the Hydro Majestic. There'll be flowers and chocolates on arrival! And there are fireplaces in the rooms! And we can build snow-men, and toboggan down gentle slopes, and then we'll come inside for spa baths, and hot chocolate, and marshmallows, and we'll all play Pic-tionary or whatever game you like. What do you think? Would you like to take the rest of the week off school? I'll write a note and say you've got a brain tumour!'

Listen laughed so hard she started crying.

The following week, Listen arrived at school with a snow tan, and found that the Year 7 classrooms had been flooded. Everyone was excited like a holiday, and they had to take their lessons in the Science labs or even outside on the lawn. The teachers laid plastic sheets on the grass to stop them getting chills in their kidneys.

•

Vernon reached under the driver's seat to adjust it back. 'You must be shorter than you look,' he commented to Marbie, who was in the passenger seat beside him.

They were driving home after a Zing Family Secret Meeting.

'How was the meeting?' said Listen, from the back seat.

'Okay,' said Vernon, 'how was your movie with Cassie?'

'Fine,' agreed Listen. Passing headlights striped all three in turn. 'Vernon, how come you read out that letter from my school tonight?'

'Sorry.' Vernon glanced in the rear-view mirror. 'I thought you wouldn't mind. It was just for fun.'

There was silence in the car, except for the tching of the indicator as they waited in a right-turning lane.

'How's school anyway, Listen?' Marbie said.

'Fine.'

Vernon and Marbie each sighed slightly. They had discussed Listen's recent habit of answering questions this way and concluded that now she was a teenager with a new private world inside her head.

'Looking forward to the holidays?' Marbie tried next.

'Yep,' said Listen.

Then she surprised them, as Vernon took the corner, by asking, 'Marbie, can you tell your swimming pool story again?'

'Well,' said Marbie, at once. 'I was five years old and this was a hot summer day. I was playing on the swing that Dad had hooked up for us, as a goodbye present when he left to go to Ireland, you know, the swing that hangs from the big gum tree down the back of the yard? So, I was swinging back and forth trying to pick up a breeze to cool me down, so higher and higher I swung, and the higher I went the more I could see: Mummy's flower beds, our old trampoline, the tops of small trees, the tops of taller trees, and the roof of the garden shed. Higher and higher I swung until I could even see the roof of our own house, and then of course, I started to see the neighbourhood – the empty school yard of Bellbird High next door, their netball court and its goal posts, their tennis courts, their old stone buildings, the sloping lawn at the back of the school, how it falls into scrub and forest, and then, with one final *swing* of my knees, I went higher than I ever had before. And that's when I saw the spark of something blue in the bush there.

'That night, I waited until everyone was asleep, and I climbed out of my bedroom window, and ran down the back of our house. I found a gap in the fence between our place and the school, and I ran down into the bush, and there were rocks and dried grass that hurt my feet, but I didn't notice because I wanted to find out what it was. And what it was, of course, was the school's new swimming pool. I was hot and dirty from running through the bush so I jumped in and swam around a bit. Then I went home and went to bed.'

'And then for the rest of that summer,' prompted Listen, sleepily.

'And then for the rest of that summer, every night, after midnight, I would slip through the gap in the fence and go for a swim in the pool. I thought it was my own secret pool. Of course, after a couple of years I stopped being able to fit through the gap in the fence, which is why –'

She turned around to the back seat, but Listen was fast asleep.

●

Sir:

I am writing to you from my office where, I am pleased to inform you, it is Wednesday afternoon. Soon it will be the weekend! Tabitha and Toni are gasping through the plexiglass there, and, in a moment, I will join them to find out about the latest netball drama.

But this is to inform you that I have not seen the A.E. since that nakedness fiasco. It is like a nightmare in my memory, that fiasco, and I prefer to regard it as simply that: a dream. It never happened.

Something that lasted only three minutes, and that did not

involve touching or words (or almost no words anyway) – something
so fleeting can surely be erased?

I won't even meet with him to tell him: No More Tennis.
Anyway, we couldn't play, it's so cold, it's like another country.

Also, I will soon be very busy. Listen will be on holidays starting
this Friday, and Vernon and I will probably take some time off work
and take her on another trip.

So! No time for the aeronautical engineer!

I am just about to take down his vision from my corkboard, by
the way. Do you know what it is? It's a coincidence. It has nothing
to do with my umbrella experience or my fear of long sharp objects.
Nothing at all!

Sir, I must ask you to excuse me for a moment – an intriguing
pink envelope has just been tossed on to my desk by the mailboy.
My name appears on the front in swirling purple!

I will see what it is.

Kind regards,
Marbie

Inside the intriguing pink envelope was a large piece of paper bearing two yellow sticky notes. The first sticky note said in scratchy pen: *Just wrote this and you came to mind. So here it is for you.*

On the large piece of paper, vision #1451 was neatly typed.

THE VISIONS OF AN AERONAUTICAL ENGINEER
VISION # 1451

Deep within the icicles of muddy, cruddy space
I see this, I see this, I see:
Gosh!
I see your face! Your own precious face!
I see black cats, umbrellas, and streaks of spilling milk.
I see a footpath crack, a burning ear, a ladder and a wooden door –
A necklace clasp is glinting from beneath a dimpled chin!

The second sticky note said: *Tomorrow night. My place. Let's go all the way.*

The next day, Thursday, Marbie sat at her desk and unwound paper-clips. A little pile of ragged wires formed on her desk. Every now and then she took one from this pile and tried to bend it back into paper-clip shape. It was never possible.

The yellow sticky note was on her corkboard: *Tomorrow night. My place. Let's go all the way.* Each time she read it, she felt a chill breeze waft through her mind: *You must not go! You must not go! You must not go!*

Of course not! She gave a contemptuous laugh. But she continued to unwind paperclips. Then the telephone rang. It was Fancy.

'Marbie!' said Fancy, urgent and breathless – and Marbie felt at once that Fancy knew. *You must not go!* Fancy would instruct her. 'Of course not,' Marbie would reply.

'Marbie, something terrible has happened! I left a *phone bill* of mine on the dining room table at the last Intrusion! I just realised! I have to go back in and get it! But what if it's too late? I can hardly breathe! I've called Mum and she's put out an Urgent Request for a Distraction. So, if we get one, is tonight okay?'

'Of course,' agreed Marbie. 'I'll leave work early and wait for your call. I'm sure it's not too late or we'd have heard something. Just calm down and breathe and have a foot massage.'

Well, she said to herself, hanging up after several minutes of calming Fancy down. *So that's that then. But a phone bill! Why did she take a phone bill along to an Intrusion?*

She sent a brisk text message to the A.E. ('Can't make it'), took down the yellow sticky note, and scraped the misshapen paperclips into the bin.

Then she got on with her day's work.

•

Listen was allowed to do the next spell on the last Friday of school before the holidays. She would do it as soon as she got home: like a beginning-of-the-holidays reward. On that day, they had Science first, and the teacher made an announcement: 'Guess what, girls, I've just got word that all Year 7 students are allowed to go home at the end of this lesson!'

Everyone said, 'Wha-a-a-at?!' and 'No way!' and the Science teacher explained: 'It's obviously much too cold to take lessons outside' – he was interrupted by noisy agreement – 'and the weather, as you will no doubt have noticed, has become, shall we say, quite strange. The bus companies have hinted that they may be shutting down in the next few hours – so – hush, hush, no need for hysterics – so, we're arranging a staggered collection throughout the day, and you poor little homeless Year 7s, yes, yes, I know – you poor little homeless Year 7s have been selected as the first lot to go!'

After that, of course, the lesson was upbeat and hilarious, with nobody paying much attention to the teacher. At Listen's bench, Donna and Caro passed each other's homework diaries back and forth between them, writing the names of unlikely movie stars in large red hearts. Then they would show the other what had been written in her diary, and the other would shriek and try to scribble out the name. *Well really*, thought Listen, *why do you keep letting each other write in there if you know you're both going to write something stupid?*

'Hang on, hang on,' said Caro, 'I *promise*, this time, I *promise* I'm going to write something normal.' Donna passed her diary back, and Caro wrote, in large letters: 'Be alert. The world needs more lerts.'

Listen, reading over Caro's shoulder, giggled. At this, Caro grimaced as if she had been asked to dissect a frog. She closed the diary and slid it back along the bench towards Donna, who gave her a sympathetic pat.

'Excuse me for living,' murmured Listen, and shifted her stool a little further from them.

As the period drew to an end, the teacher's voice rose again. 'Okay, guys, the bell's about to go, so, while I have your attention, *two* things! Obviously, I don't need to remind you that you must all report to *Redwood Primary* at the start of next term! I know! I *know* that it's a primary school, but I expect you will survive. And I *also* expect to see your assignments that *very* day! I assume you've already got it *well* under way!'

Everybody laughed.

'Well, you've had a *whole* week! Who can remind me what the topic is? Nobody? Choose two creatures of the sea. They may be *mythical* creatures and they need not be fish!'

Donna raised her hand and said, 'How can they be creatures of the sea and not be fish?'

With an elaborate sigh, the teacher declared: 'Donna Turnbull. Is it possible that you have not heard a single *word* of what I have said today?'

Donna shrugged and said, 'It's possible,' and beside her Caro made a snorting noise. Donna kept a straight face but it crinkled around the edges.

'Donna,' said the teacher, 'have we been talking, this lesson, about *whales*?'

'Have we?'

'And, Donna, is a whale a type of *fish*?'

Donna stared, while Caro grabbed at her arm. The bell rang shrilly for the end of the lesson.

'Okay! Nobody steps out of that door until someone has told Donna what kind of animal a *whale* is!'

Then half the class shouted, 'It's a *mammal*,' while Donna opened her mouth wide, and Caro slithered down in shrieks of giggles. Next thing they were all tipping their stools backwards, talking, and reaching for school bags, and leaning for pens which had dropped onto the floor.

Listen Taylor, however, sat at her bench for a moment, as if she had forgotten where she was, watching the girls packing up to go, and also watching Donna and Caro helping each other through the classroom door, both by now crippled with laughter.

•

Marbie stood in the corridor with Tabitha, Toni, Abi and Rhamie, and watched Tabitha talk about her pregnant sister. The other girls were gasping and shaking their heads, so Marbie joined in when they did. But what she was really thinking was: *I am the luckiest girl in the world. I* am so lucky that Fancy called yesterday and we had to do another Intrusion last night, so that Fancy could get her phone bill back. Because that meant I couldn't go to the A.E.'s house. I can't believe I was even considering it. Just because he sent me a vision about my superstitions. A lot of people are superstitious, you know. I am SO lucky.

'That's your mobile, isn't it, Marbie?' said Tabitha.

'Sorry!' said Marbie, and slid into her office.

She had missed the phone call and there was no message. But as she stared at the '1 MISSED CALL', a text message arrived: '2day then, my plce, 1 pm. Lv wk nw.'

She stared at this for a while. 'Lv wk nw.' *Lv wk nw.* What did that mean? Love wake new? But what did *that* mean?

Leave work now, she realised.

At which moment, Tabitha leaned into her office and said, 'Leave work now, Marbie! It's all over the news! They're expecting *freezing rain* or *snow*, and if we don't leave now, we will *never get home!* They're about to cancel *all public transport!'*

•

HELLO AGAIN! said the Spell Book. 'Hello,' said Listen, automatically, and then stopped.

> *Hasn't it been ages? Well, and how do you feel today? I hope you feel fine. I myself feel JUST fine. Here is the next Spell.*
>
> *This is A Spell To Make Two Happy People Have A HUGE Fight Over Absolutely NOTHING!*
>
> Here are the instructions:
>
> 1. Do twenty star-jumps.
> 2. Take a piece of paper, write the heading 'Things That Make Me Sad', then fill the page with the *things that make you sad.*

3. **Put the piece of paper at the bottom of a full box of tissues (bury it carefully under all the tissues!).**

Close the book, put it under your pillow, and we'll see you again for the next Spell TOMORROW!

Listen lay on her bed, on her side, and read the spell over twice. And what she was thinking was that this spell was easy, and quite good exercise. She was thinking that she wouldn't mind writing out the things that made her sad and burying them in the bottom of a tissue box. She was thinking that *tomorrow* was an unusually short time to wait for the next spell.

But what she was *really* thinking was: *why would anybody do a spell to make two happy people have a fight?*

Before she got time to think of an answer she was already on star-jump number five.

Things That Make Me Sad. Listen poured herself a glass of juice, sat at her bedroom desk, and stared at the heading she had written on a blank piece of foolscap paper. Then she moved her pen to the line beneath the heading and began.

'Donna has a table tennis table in the basement of her house,' she wrote, 'and once Sia's mother made us all eat spaghetti squash. The first thing that makes me sad is that I'll never get to play table tennis at Donna's place again. Caro and I used to be the best team when we played doubles. The second thing is that I'll never get to eat spaghetti squash at Sia's place again, even though I actually don't like it.'

She continued writing until she had filled both sides of the paper, and had reached 'the 33rd thing that makes me sad is that I don't see any point in my existence.'

•

The aeronautical engineer met Marbie at his doorway with one red rose and a kiss. He was on his front verandah, waving at the No 73 bus.

Marbie was skidding on the icy path to his doorway. The red rose was waving in his hand, clutching at rain and dipping at wind. The kiss was quick, and met Marbie's lips.

Too soon! thought Marbie. *Too soon!*

The aeronautical engineer took her by the hand into his hallway, where she said, 'Wait a moment,' and took off her coat. She sat on the cold of the tiled hall floor to unlace her boots, one by icy one, and he crouched beside her, took both her hands in his and said, 'Cold hands, Marbie, my princess!'

Princess, thought Marbie, *well!*

He murmured in her ear, in a tickly way, 'You are cold, my princess, let us to the fire!'

'Oh, well,' Marbie explained, 'I haven't taken my boots off yet, you see?' She showed him the one boot on and the one boot off.

He caught at her hand. 'Come along!' he said, shrugging expansively at her one boot, and took her tripping to the fireside, where he made her sit on the floor.

Too soon! thought Marbie.

He seemed to sense her owlish tune, and he paused at her feet. Marbie sat, demure by the fireside, her arms around her knees. He unlaced her boot, crisscrossing down amongst the eyelets. He went too far. He slid the entire lace out until it leapt from the boot. Surprised, Marbie said, 'Do you not understand how shoelaces work?'

But he was ignoring her. He was sliding off her boot, which was easy with the shoelace gone. He took a glass of champagne from the mantelpiece and in one smooth move had the cold glass in her hand.

'Champagne?' said Marbie. 'What's it doing on your mantelpiece?'

She took a sip while the aeronautical engineer hit the PLAY button on the CD.

'Jazz,' said Marbie. 'A lot of people like jazz. Not so much myself. I'm not what you'd call a *jazz* kind of person. Fancy is. My sister Fancy? You wouldn't think it because –'

'All right,' interrupted the aeronautical engineer, leaning back to the CD player, 'no jazz then.'

The CD tray slid open slowly, presenting the CD like a waiter with a plate.

'Oh well, *that* jazz,' cried Marbie. 'Switch it back on. *That* sort of jazz I do like. Not so much Fancy. That's not her kind of jazz. I think.'

He replaced the CD.

'Lovely,' said Marbie. 'Jazz.'

'Marbie,' said the aeronautical engineer, sitting cross-legged next to her. 'How long do you have?'

'Just the lunch hour, really,' she lied. 'I'll have to go back to work.'

She tapped her stockinged toe to the jazz. 'It's tricky, isn't it?' she chatted. 'Tapping to jazz? Maybe that's why I don't like it. What do you think?'

He moved towards her, in a sort of slide across the carpet on his bottom.

She felt alarmed.

He said, 'Let's take these stockings off, no?'

She was not sure if that was possible. 'You mean without me taking my skirt off first?'

'Lie down,' he suggested.

She was worried she would knock the champagne over and hovered it about in the air until he took it and placed it back on the mantelpiece.

She lay down flat on the carpet now, and sneezed, once.

'Perhaps I'm allergic to the rug,' she chatted.

He unbuttoned the skirt, at the side.

'Yes,' she agreed. 'That will make it easier.'

He reached both hands underneath her skirt. He looked at her face as he did so, and concentrated, his head tilting, reaching along the sides of her thighs as if he was a burglar working in the dark, reaching for the wires to cut off the alarm. He found the waistline of her stockings, and began to roll them down, with great caution, over her hips, over her thighs, across the knees, down to the toes. 'There!' he said, holding up the crumpled stockings.

Marbie lifted her head and saw her legs looking white on the carpet. 'Shall I sit up?'

'No.'

He wanted her blouse off now, and was reaching for the buttons, and taking them one by one until the blouse fell open around her, and she lifted her head from the floor and saw her breasts standing up in their bra.

'Isn't my bra lovely? My sister gave it to me for my last birthday. I only wear it on special occasions such as Fridays. I'm talking about Fancy a lot, aren't I?'

'Your bra is beautiful.'

He had decided to take off her skirt, which was easy enough because it was already unbuttoned, but she had to lift her hips in the air to help.

'Sit up,' he asked her.

'Oh well, now you want me to sit up? I kind of feel like I'm at the dentist.'

He burst out laughing and said that this was not flattering.

She sat up and he slid off the unbuttoned blouse, too.

'Lie back down now.'

'Oh well. All right.' Although the carpet felt prickly on her back and she believed it would make her sneeze. Her throat itched too, and she clicked at it, once.

'Aren't my underpants nice too? They match the bra, see?'

'So they do.'

He was standing up and looking over her, white upon the carpet in her white bra and underpants. He was wearing tracksuit pants and a T-shirt, both of which are very simple to remove, and he did so. Now he was in his boxers.

'Oh gosh,' said Marbie suddenly.

'What?' He had been reaching for his champagne again but stopped.

'We're not going to play that game, are we? Where we don't do anything? We just be naked?'

'Maybe,' he said, sipping the champagne, calm again. 'Maybe not.'

'If we are,' said Marbie, 'I'm going back to the office. I don't want to.'

'All right then. We're not. You see?'

From the mantelpiece he slid a small blue square, which Marbie had not noticed before. *Protection*. She felt as if her vision were speckling. *What are you doing?* she thought suddenly. Somehow, until this very moment, it had all been a game. Now she saw that it was real.

'All right?'

'All right,' she whispered. And then more loudly, 'All right, but for heaven's sakes, let's just *do* it! Hurry up!'

He dropped the blue square package to the carpet, and knelt slowly by her side. He took her arm and kissed the inside of her elbow.

Intriguing, thought Marbie, relieved at the distraction.

But then he lifted his body so he was lying on her, his chest against her bra, his boxers brushing her thighs.

'Well –' began Marbie.

But he leaned down and stopped her with a kiss.

●

He had his shower and bathtub all in one, which is common, he said, or did she not know?

'May I watch you shower?' he asked.

'Oh well, if it were a *normal* shower. But this is a shower in a tub, you see?'

'Ah then. Shall I make us an omelette or some bacon and eggs?'

She said, 'That would be breakfast, and this is afternoon.'

'Ah then,' he agreed, and: 'Must you really go back to work?' And she said, 'I know. It's terrible. Have you got a towel for me?'

He had a towel for her, a great, soft, white towel, a cosy, hotel towel, the sort that Marbie always dreamed of, for burying her face in, or for drying herself.

'I can't watch you shower then?' he tried again.

'Oh well,' said Marbie, 'not really', and she closed the bathroom door.

She stood in the bathtub and filled up the room, which was pink, with steam.

●

'Look at it on the trees.'

He stood at his door with a towel around his plump waist, and a cold and hairy chest, and pointed. 'That's freezing rain is what that is.'

'You'd better get inside,' Marbie told him. 'You'll freeze.'

He said, 'Look at the ice on the trees. Have you ever seen a Sydney winter like this? No, you wouldn't have. Nobody has. That's your bus now, at the lights on the corner. I think they should cancel the buses. I bet they do any moment now.'

'You'd better get inside,' Marbie said again. 'What happens if the freezing rain hits your chest? The hair will turn into curly icicles and you'll have to snap them off.'

'I'll watch you onto the bus,' he said. 'You be careful on that ice, won't you? It'll be a skating rink out there. Deadly.'

'Don't wait for me,' said Marbie. 'You'd better get inside.'

'Kiss me,' he said.

This was only fair.

Freezing rain crackled on the edges of the twigs, and shark-toothed its way along the turrets and the grooves. The ice was like lace, or like Spanish moss, or like hand-blown glass on the trees.

Marbie sat at the kitchen table later that day and waited for Vernon to get home. He was driving Listen to Tae Kwon Do. When he returned, she would tell him. She was surprised at how simple this was. She had thought it would be anguished indecision: should I tell him, should I not, should I tell him, should I not? But at once, as she stood in that bathtub pink shower, at once as she filled up the room with its steam, at once as she reached for the change for the bus, as she stepped from the bus to an iced-over puddle that soaked through her boots to her toes, at once! she had known.

She sat at the kitchen table with a Twix chocolate bar and a glass of lemonade. These were for Vernon.

After a moment, she opened the wrapper and ate the Twix bar. She had never eaten a whole one like that before, in big greedy bites, like a starving Charlie before the Chocolate Factory. Then she drank the glass of lemonade in one thirsty, greedy gulp. She had never done that before either. The fizziness, for a start, would have stopped her in the past. Now her mouth was chocolate sugar and her eyes were startled red. She was so frightened it made her want to giggle.

She reached into the kitchen drawer and took out the corkscrew, and then she began to play with it, rotating the top so that its arms rose up and then down, up and then down, like a person crying out for help. Giving up, crying out, giving up, crying out, the long thin body in an anguish of perpetual twisting.

There was the sound of a key in the door. She dropped the corkscrew with a clatter. But then there was a tumble of voices in the hallway: *Listen was home.*

'What happened?' Marbie called down the hallway. 'What happened to Tae Kwon Do?'

'Cancelled!' cried Listen. She danced, excited, and Vernon seemed excited too.

'Teacher left a note on the door,' he explained, opening the fridge. 'We should have thought of it. The traffic was hell. We were skidding all over the road. There's *ice* out there, Marbs, you should go have a look. Still, we weren't the only ones, were we, Listen? There were other kids hanging around there waiting. They hadn't seen the note. They were all trying to hit on Listen. Hey, Twix. I love Twix.' He was staring at the wrapper on the table.

'I know you do.' Marbie felt terrible guilt. 'I'm sorry. I ate it all. I'll get you another one tomorrow.'

'Ah well,' said Vernon, turning back from the table to the fridge.

'I'm *hungry*,' Listen danced. 'They were not *hitting on me*, Vernon.'

'Well that kid with the giraffe tattoo on his wrist was,' said Vernon, pulling up a kitchen chair. 'He's got it for you bad, kid.' To Marbie, Vernon indicated how the giraffe's neck ran from the boy's wrist to his elbow.

'That's Carl Vandenberg. He's going for his black belt. No way he likes me.'

'What say we go out for dinner,' Vernon said. 'We can walk down to that new Indian restaurant, to celebrate.'

'Celebrate what?'

'The ice storm. And the Zing Family Secret Meeting being cancelled. Not that I don't enjoy the meetings, Marbie, of course. It's just a reason, see. And Tae Kwon Do being cancelled,' suggested Vernon.

Listen pirouetted. 'But I like Tae Kwon Do.'

•

Alone in the kitchen again, Marbie thought sadly about buying another Twix for Vernon, only it was too dark and icy outside. She had pretended she was too cold to join them at the restaurant, but now she was too frightened to do anything. She couldn't even make herself a curried egg sandwich for dinner.

•

'Come on to bed.'

Vernon sat up against his pillow, and Marbie stood at the foot of the bed, staring at him.

'You know how Arnold Schwarzenegger can kill a person by applying pressure to exactly the right part of their neck?' she said eventually.

'He's just an actor, Marbie,' Vernon said gently.

'Well, but he plays characters like that sometimes, and the thing is, Vernon, you know how I sometimes give you a neck and shoulder massage?'

'Not very often.'

'But *sometimes* I do, and the thing is, what if I accidentally pressed that bit that kills you and accidentally killed you?' Her voice broke.

'Marbie, I would tell you if you started killing me and then you could stop. Okay? There's nothing to cry about. Look out the window, why don't you? I think it's snowing. I think I can see something white, and if I'm right, we should wake Listen and go outside.'

'It doesn't snow in Sydney,' said Marbie tragically, tears now streaming down her cheeks. 'But I could accidentally kill you with one little touch of my finger. Or what if you developed a spontaneous allergy to seafood, and I gave you a stamp to put on an envelope, and you got a reaction from licking the stamp because they use tiny fragments of fish bones in the glue on the back of the stamp. They do, Vernon, I read that. Or anyway they used to. And that could happen, you could die from a postage stamp.'

'I'm sure that's snow.' Vernon was leaning forward. 'Open the curtain.'

'It doesn't snow in Sydney,' Marbie said again, listlessly.

Finally Vernon paid attention. 'What's up, Marbie? Tell me what's wrong.'

'Okay, I'll tell you,' said Marbie, through her tears, and she did.

5

EXTRACTS FROM THE ZING GARDEN SHED (Burnt Fragments)

- *Mrs Z asks: 'how do we get rid of her?'*
- *Radcliffe makes a joke: 'a broken ankle or wrist might do the trick' (e/body laughs).*
- *General talk.*
- Resolved *that sub-committee be formed, consisting of*

6

SNOW STORM

The first day of the winter holidays, Cath woke up in a ruffled, empty bed and thought: *of course, he has already left.* She wondered if there would be a single red rose on his pillow as a poignant goodbye but there was not. Instead, looking around her bedroom, she noticed a strange, almost exquisite light.

Then, as she watched, Warren Woodford appeared in the doorway. There was snow woven into his eyebrows.

'I've been for a walk,' he said, hesitating. 'If you can believe it, there's still snow on the ground outside.'

He was carrying a cardboard tray of takeaway coffees. His face was grey and frightened.

'It doesn't mean a thing,' Cath reassured him, sitting up against the bedhead. 'We were drunk and it didn't mean a thing.'

Warren raised an eyebrow.

Then he moved into the bedroom, closing the door with his boot. He put the coffee cups onto her bedside table and sat down on the side of the bed. He placed one cold hand on her forehead, as if he was checking her for fever, and his gaze was so troubled and so searching, she realised that it did mean a thing.

•

The first day of the winter holidays, Fancy woke when Cassie jumped onto her bed.

'There's *snow* outside! THERE'S SNOW OUTSIDE! MUMMY! THE WORLD'S GONE *WHITE!*'

Radcliffe muffled his voice straight into his pillow: 'Cassie, just lie down, honey, and have a little sleep.'

Cassie bounced on her father's ankle and he yelped.

Fancy blinked in the strange, almost secretive light of the room. Could there really be snow outside? Her daughter's shouts faded into a curious middle distance, and Fancy stretched her arms like a ballerina. Why did she feel so poignant and so graceful? Then she remembered: *my husband is having an affair.*

She had not yet confronted her husband about his affair. He had arrived home early the night before, and found her sitting on their bedroom floor, the sock hidden safely in her pocket. He stage-whispered, 'If you're working on a book idea, I'll leave you to it,' and tiptoed out of the room.

One day, soon, she would tell him that she knew. In the meantime she would consider this poignant, graceful mood. Actually, she recognised the mood. It was the same strange, detached feeling that she had experienced at all secret yet significant times of her life: *I am not a virgin any longer; I am on the Atkins diet!; I think I may be having a child.*

'COME OUTSIDE AND PLAY IN THE SNOW, MUMMY!' Cassie's shouts began to penetrate. 'MUMMY, CAN I GO OVER TO LUCINDA'S PLACE AND THROW SNOW AT HER AND SHE COULD THROW SNOW AT ME?!'

'Well,' began Fancy, slowly, and gracefully, but then the telephone rang.

•

The first day of the winter holidays, Marbie woke to a strange, almost haunting light which clouded her vision. For a moment she lay flat on her back, trying to see.

A buzzing sound gave her a flurry of hope: *it was all a dream! I never had sex with the aeronautical engineer! I never told Vernon about it! Vernon and Listen are out in the kitchen making banana milkshakes!* But then she realised it was the sound of a leaf-blower somewhere outside.

Slowly, she wandered the apartment, gazing at the empty spaces: the doorknob where Listen's coat belonged; the shower rack where Vernon's shampoo should be standing. How thoroughly they had packed in the middle of the night!

She opened the front door and gasped at the strange little patch of white on the porch. It must be a message from Vernon. But what did it mean? She crouched down and touched it: it was icy cold. Had he hacked at the ice in the freezer, scraped it into a bucket, then tipped it out on the front porch? Meaning what? That her heart was as cold as an ice-patch? That he would return *when the ice had melted?*

Then she looked up and around the neighbourhood, and, for the first time, saw that the white patches were everywhere. The white had dabbed at fence posts, letterboxes, tree branches. It sat on car roofs and bonnets, spread itself across front lawns, and tipped over the edges of the gutters. Across the street, two little girls were aiming at the white with a leaf-blower.

Panicked, Marbie backed through the door into her hallway and reached for the phone. Her fingers shook as she dialled her sister's number.

'Can you meet me at Mum's place,' she whispered, 'right away?'

In Grandma Zing's kitchen, Marbie hyperventilated, her mother baked a carrot cake, and Fancy sipped wisdom from her coffee cup.

'He will return,' was Fancy's wisdom. 'He won't be long.'

'I suppose he will.' Grandma Zing measured a teaspoon of dried ginger. 'But Marbie, darling, what were you thinking?'

'That's the thing.' Marbie sat back up, wide-eyed. 'I don't think I was thinking.'

'Someone as special as *Vernon* —'

'Stop it, Mum,' interrupted Fancy. 'Vernon will come back eventually, Marbie.'

'No, he won't,' murmured Marbie, turning to her sister. 'You didn't see his eyes. He was so *calm*. He listened to what I said, and then he got out of bed, and took out his suitcase and packed. He folded his clothes like they were going on display in the window of a shop. And then he slept on the couch, and in the morning when I got up, he and Listen were gone. *And the snow was here.*'

'Never mind,' Grandma Zing comforted, 'the carrot cake won't be much longer now. I'm about to put it in the oven.' She glanced over to confirm that the oven was preheating. 'We'll leave your dad in the TV room for the moment. He loves that game show of his, doesn't he? And he's spent all morning in the shed.'

'Look,' said Fancy, firmly. 'It was just once, wasn't it, Marbie?'

'Yes,' agreed Marbie. 'Just the once.'

'And you don't plan to see him again, do you? This aeronautical engineer of yours?'

'No,' insisted Marbie. 'Never again.'

'Well now!' It was settled. 'Vernon will come back.'

'No, he won't.' Marbie shook her head, with tears blurring her eyes. 'No, he won't.' Then she dried her eyes, looked thoughtful for a moment, and added: 'I admire his resolve.'

●

'Gosh,' said Fancy, 'it's still *here.*'

They were standing at the front door staring at the snow which was just like icing on a wedding cake. It stared back at them, a little defiant, as if it knew it shouldn't be there at all.

'Honestly,' said Grandma Zing, 'I think you should both stay put now that you're here. I think it was dangerous of you to drive over unless there was an emergency.'

Then she looked at her two daughters and added, politely, 'Of course, I understand that this *is* an emergency, Marbie.'

'If you drive slowly it's okay, I found,' said Fancy. 'Although I was skidding all over the road. Really, everywhere.'

'It's safe,' declared Marbie, 'because no-one else is driving.'

'Yes, well, they're saying all over the news that you should stay in your own homes, and only come out to get necessary supplies such as torches and blankets and so on,' Grandma Zing confirmed.

They all stood quietly on the porch for a moment, considering this, while up and down the street children and adults shrieked and played in the snow. Snowmen grew, snow fights flourished, and one or two people wandered around their gardens in their skis.

'I might stay here for a while,' conceded Marbie, eventually.

'Well, I just arranged to meet Radcliffe for lunch,' Fancy declared.

'I'm going to go and lie down,' said Marbie.

'What are we going to do with that girl?' said Grandma Zing in the driveway, at the window of Fancy's car.

'Look at that!' said Fancy, surprised. 'The windscreen's completely frozen! The wipers aren't making a difference. I suppose people in cold countries have some kind of a *scraping* device for situations like this.'

'Let me see if I can get it with my fingernails,' offered Grandma Zing. 'Ouch, turn off the wipers will you, darling? Fance, who on earth is this aeronautical engineer? And Vernon will forgive her, won't he?'

'I don't know,' admitted Fancy. 'Vernon's so nice and sensible, so — then again, men can be funny about affairs.'

Her mother gave a sharp breath of laughter, and said, 'Still. At least we don't need to worry about Vernon and the Secret.'

Fancy was playing with the vents in the dashboard, but at this she said, 'I completely forgot about the Secret! It must be because you're right. Vernon's not that type.'

'It was going along so nicely,' sighed Grandma Zing, 'what with Project 78 getting under way. Oh, and Fancy, I suppose I shouldn't bring this up now, but you know, it happened again. Just last night.'

'Again!' exclaimed Fancy. 'It's blurry?'

'No, it's just slipped. I don't suppose you and Marbie would be interested in another Intrusion for some Maintenance just now?'

'Not in the middle of a snow storm,' said Fancy firmly. 'We'll wait until it melts.'

Fancy drove away from her parents' place, skidding on the snow and listening to the radio. It was a State of Emergency, the radio said, the roads and public transport were in chaos. Also, some areas had lost power, and there were concerns about homeless people freezing to death. Still, things were in hand because Sydneysiders were battlers. 'If there's one word to describe a Sydneysider,' the Premier was saying in a recorded message, 'it's the word *battler*. I didn't say bull-headed there. We're not too proud to turn to our countrymen for advice — Aussie battlers in colder climes than ours. Tasmanians. Canberrians. We're not too proud to turn to *other* countries for advice either. Norway. Finland. Trust me. We have this in hand.'

'There you have it, people,' said the announcer, coming back on air, 'I think the message is clear! And let me say this one more time: have as much fun as you can in your own back gardens, but stay *off* the roads!'

'Oh blah,' said Fancy, stabbing at the radio buttons. Four centimetres of snow! What must *immigrants* be thinking about this hullabaloo! She blushed to think of the Canadian next door — how he must hoot as he sliced his kiwifruit.

Fancy kept her own secret, Radcliffe's affair, buttoned up tight in her cardigan. She hadn't told anybody yet, but it was affecting the way that she moved. Her elbows, for example, as her hands gripped and skidded with the steering wheel, stuck out at a curious angle.

●

'What's happened? What's happened?'

Radcliffe was excited as the waiter led them to the table. The restaurant's lunchtime crowd was spilling out the door. It was the only place open in the neighbourhood and people wanted to bustle into public spaces, and chat with strangers about snow. 'Magic, isn't it?' a man said to Radcliffe, shaking his head at the picture windows. But Radcliffe only half nodded: he wanted to know Fancy's news.

'Something has happened,' Fancy had said, mysteriously, when she phoned from her parents' place to suggest that they meet for lunch.

'Well!' said Fancy, then paused as the waiter took her coat for her, and paused as he drew out the chair for her, and paused as he swooped out the serviette for her.

'Well!' she repeated. Then the waiter jutted the menu at her nose, and she had to pause again.

'Can I start you off with a drink?'

Radcliffe ordered champagne.

The waiter allowed her a moment to continue, by setting off to fetch their drinks.

'It's not a *celebration*!' she remonstrated, on account of the champagne. 'Something *awful* has happened!'

'Well, I wasn't to know,' Radcliffe grumbled. 'You didn't tell me what it was. You *sounded* like it was something exciting on the phone. Besides, we could celebrate the snow. Look at it out there! With the sun sparkling! It's like diamond-flavoured ice cream, isn't it? Don't you think?'

'Hmm.' Fancy straightened her serviette on her lap, pressed the hair behind her ears, and announced: '*Vernon* has *left* Marbie!'

'He has not!'

He was so perfectly sure of this, that Fancy began to doubt.

'He has!' she exclaimed, remembering. 'Marbie's been crying all morning. It turns out that she's been having an affair.'

'Ah,' said Radcliffe, 'that I would believe.'

'Radcliffe!'

But Fancy had to stop because the waiter was back and wanted them to decide what to eat. Radcliffe chose Braised Lamb in Oyster Sauce. Fancy wanted the Atlantic Prawns.

'It wasn't an affair, really, anyway,' Fancy said, as soon as permitted to continue. 'It was just once, yesterday. With an aeronautical engineer, if you can believe it. And she told Vernon about it right away, that very night. Last night.'

'Good for her,' said Radcliffe.

'Yes,' agreed Fancy, staring at him carefully. 'It's the right thing to do. To tell. You should always tell.'

Radcliffe smiled slightly and looked down, which at first set off a panic in Fancy's chest (*he's about to tell me!*) until she realised he was thinking back in time. He had always been proud of himself for telling Fancy, when they were teenagers, that he had kissed another girl.

'But he *left* her!' Radcliffe exclaimed. 'Whatever for?'

Fancy regarded him shrewdly. 'You know,' she said, 'confession isn't everything.'

Radcliffe nodded.

'He moved out right away.' Enthusiastically, Fancy tore her bread in half. 'And she thinks they've moved back to the caravan where they used to live. You know, the one behind the Banana Bar?'

'Good God!' Radcliffe was impressed. 'Back to the *caravan*?'

'Yes,' agreed Fancy. 'Just when the renovations were practically done.'

The waiter interrupted with their food.

A little later, Fancy said idly: 'Who do you think you'll work with on Monday?'

Radcliffe had his mouth full of crunching snow peas, but he tilted his head sideways to show confusion. 'The usual, I guess,' he said, once he had swallowed enough to speak.

'Gemma?' said Fancy, staring at him carefully. 'Will you work with Gemma?'

'Gemma?' he frowned. 'Gemma.'

Fancy squinted scornfully. 'The one who had her moles zapped,' she reminded him, and peered at his mouth, his cheeks and his eyes.

'Oh, *Gemma*, yes. She works in the pay office. I wouldn't usually work with someone from the pay office, Fance. The moles! I remember. She also got her eyes zapped. You know, that laser operation where they burn open your eyeballs and scrape away whatever makes you short-sighted, and then you don't need glasses anymore? She had that done.'

This conversation was not actually part of Fancy's plan, and was suddenly exasperating, so she stopped and looked around for the waiter.

'I think I might drop by the Banana Bar,' she changed the subject as she looked, 'and see how Vernon and Listen are. Or is it too soon?'

'Ah-hah,' nodded Radcliffe. 'Remind Vernon of his responsibilities vis-à-vis the Secret, eh? Remind him of all those confidentiality documents he signed?'

'Well, no, Radcliffe, we don't think Vernon's the vindictive type. We're not worried about him and the Secret. I just want to see if he's okay.' She raised her eyebrows at the waiter as she spoke, and wrote her signature in the air, including the flourish she always added to the 'g' in 'Zing'.

'Ha ha,' chuckled Radcliffe, 'not worried, eh? Because he seems like such a nice guy, such a gentle, laid-back, easy-going guy? You mark my words, Fance, it's the *quiet* ones you've got to worry about. Underneath all that *gentle wit* is a seething mass of resentment.'

'Well, I don't know about *that*.' Fancy frowned at him sternly, but also with a flicker of unease.

'Aren't you going to have dessert?' said Radcliffe. 'I was thinking of a coffee and now it's too late. You've gone and asked for the bill.'

'It's never too late,' said Fancy, mysteriously. 'Nothing is *ever* too late, Radcliffe.'

'Okay,' he agreed, and when the waiter put down a slender leather wallet containing two chocolate mints and the bill, Radcliffe said, 'Might I add a flat white to that, do you think?'

'Easy,' said the waiter, and smoothly whisked it back.

•

Fancy skidded along in the afternoon light having dropped Radcliffe back at home. She was listening to a pair of excited radio announcers. In their excitement, they were cancelling flights, trains, ferries, parties, fetes and festivals, all on account of the snow. They were cancelling Harbour Bridge Walks (indefinitely), but replacing them with sleigh rides down the sides of the Opera House (hilariously). They sympathised with a caller who had never seen snow before, and had been saving the experience for her fortieth birthday: now it was too late! She had seen it! ('Still,' the next caller pointed out, 'I suppose she could have stayed inside and kept the curtains closed.') They were warmed by a caller who phoned to say she had opened her house to strangers, on account of her pot-belly stove. 'It heats the whole house!' They were fretful about what would happen when the snow melted. There would be floods, wouldn't there? They invited callers to confirm or deny.

'Hello!' said Fancy, brushing snowflakes from her jacket as she jangled the Banana Bar door. 'Busy today?' She sounded odd and bright.

'Nope,' said Vernon. 'Not one single customer. The weather, I guess.'

'Well,' (she could not stop the brightness) 'I'll be your first! I'll have a banana milkshake, thanks.'

'On the house.'

'No! No!'

And then Fancy looked at him meaningfully, to indicate that she knew, and Vernon shrugged to himself.

'So,' continued Fancy, building on her meaningful glance, 'I just wanted to see how you *were* – see if there's anything I can – and about the caravan – isn't it a bit too cold?'

'We won't sleep in the caravan. We've got a generator for the shop, so we'll sleep out the back there. And also, if your mother's worried. I understand about the Secret. The Zing Family Secret. I would never –'

'Vernon! No! Of course we're not worried about *that*. I'm just hoping it will work out again. I mean, Marbie . . .' She was going to say that Marbie was a brat, a fool, a wicked witch, but one with the right sort of heart – only there was something about Vernon's eyes when she said the name 'Marbie'. So she changed the subject. 'Where's Listen? How is she?'

'She's not so happy.'

'Did you tell her about – about Marbie – about . . .'

'I just said that Marbie and I had a fight. I said I didn't think we'd ever get over it. The fight. I said that was most probably it between Marbie and me.' He took Fancy's milkshake back from her, although it was not quite finished, and dumped it in the sink.

'Ah,' said Fancy.

Their eyes met for a moment and they both looked up at the giant plastic bananas hanging from the ceiling.

'She's out the back now in the caravan, I think. Practising her Tae Kwon Do.'

'Okay,' said Fancy, standing and gathering her purse. 'Well, lovely to see you, Vernon. Make sure you call if you need anything. Or if you want to talk . . . And give Listen my love, won't you? Tell her to –'

But she didn't know what to tell Listen, and simply waved.

•

It took years before you could do a proper flying side kick. Carl Vandenberg could do one, but he was a black belt, and even he looked messy in the air. The other day Listen had been one of the four people who crouched on the floor in a row, so that Carl could jump over them and kick the piece of board held by the master.

Listen had decided she would secretly teach herself the flying side kick. Out in the cold, she ran, leapt and fell onto her face. Her feet were bare. She wore summer pyjamas. She ran, leapt with her leg tucked under and she fell face-forward in the snow. She leapt and fell; leapt and fell.

When she got up, she could not feel her face, except her nose, which ached. Her hands were purple, her fingers were stinging, her knees and elbows were bruised or grazed, and all the time she thought: *I deserve this.*

Because she had ruined everything. She was a stupid, selfish person and she stamped her bare feet in the snow to prove this, and found herself stamping up the stairs into the caravan to burn the book.

A SPELL TO MAKE TWO HAPPY PEOPLE HAVE A HUGE FIGHT OVER ABSOLUTELY NOTHING.

She could not believe she had done a spell like that. She could not believe it meant Vernon and Marbie. She never thought these spells even worked.

She took the Spell Book from her backpack and slapped a hand scornfully against the lime green cover. She would *never* open it again. Excuse me, but why had she even bothered? The spells were useless. A spell about making somebody catch a taxi. A spell about breaking a *vacuum cleaner*. And then, the first spell that actually worked was an evil spell to make two happy people have a fight.

She was supposed to do the next spell today but she was actually going to throw it away, burn it, tear it up, or maybe just throw it in the recycling bin.

She would drown the book. She slammed it down into the tiny caravan sink, although it just made a slow popping sound, not the THWACK she wanted, and she reached for the tap, but of course nothing happened. The water pipes had frozen.

It was then, looking down into the sink, that she saw the inside flap of the back cover. She had never noticed it before, since she had been careful not to turn the pages. But it had slipped out in the caravan sink now, and she could see a square of print:

> **This Book really truly works! You've got to do all the Spells of course but boy oh boy! Until I did those Spells, I was the unhappiest girl in the State. I didn't think I'd make it through another day! I thought I'd maybe peg myself to the clothesline and hang myself out to dry. Praise be for the Spell Book is all that I can say — it saved my life!'**

> *Elinor Daisy Weaver, Jacksonville, Alabama*

Listen took the book out of the sink and read the endorsement again. And then she noticed, at the bottom of the back cover itself, in tiny silver italics, this:

> *This Book will make you Fly, will make you Strong, will make you Glad. What's more, this Book will Mend your Broken Heart.*

Her face throbbed cold and goose bumps pricked her pyjama sleeves. She opened the Spell Book and read the next spell.

> **A Spell To Make Someone Give Someone A Rose**

> **Put your finger on your nose and say: 'Golly!'**

> *This Spell will work in about eight weeks, or so. You can do the next Spell next Saturday!*

•

'Cassie, honey, you know you don't need cushions and things for the snow. It's okay to fall on it. It's soft.' Fancy explained this as she drove

Cassie home from Lucinda's place, keeping the car in low gear and skidding to the wrong side of the road occasionally.

'Not soft enough. See, there's not enough snow so you have to get the pillows and take the cushions off the couch and put them around on top of the snow so you can fall on them.'

'Hmm. Well. I'm sure that's wrong.'

'And we used Lucinda's mum's cake tins and frying pans to slide on, but you had to push yourself along with your legs because they don't really have any kind of hills in Lucinda's back yard.' Cassie drew a picture of herself on a cake tin in the window steam. 'See, Mum? This is how we pushed ourselves along.'

Fancy glanced over and said, 'Oh!', then, a few moments later: 'I suppose that's okay, about the cake tins. I suppose you can't really hurt them.'

'But I think we broke their VCR.'

'Oh, Cassie, I thought you were outside playing the whole time.'

'We were. We broke the VCR when we were sliding on it.'

'Cassie! Did Lucinda's mother know about this?'

'No,' explained Cassie. 'Lucinda hid the VCR under her bed. They should get a DVD anyway.'

'Well,' said Fancy, 'I suppose so.'

Then they listened to the radio together for a moment: all over the city, people were tripping over, tobogganing down Martin Place, catching skis on parking metres, and leaving ski poles outside shops.

'Brrrrrrrr,' said Cassie as they walked through the front door.

'Here's trouble,' exclaimed her father. 'Cass, you're walking snow into the house, kiddo. I think you ought to take your shoes off. Call me old-fashioned.'

'Come and sit on the steps beside me,' her mother offered. 'I bet this is what they do in cold countries. They take off their shoes on the steps. Radcliffe, shouldn't we put snow chains on the tyres?'

'I'll ring up the *Living With Snow* Help Line,' agreed Radcliffe.

'Gosh,' said Fancy. 'There's a Help Line? So they think the snow's going to last?'

'I think we should have chicken noodle soup for dinner,' suggested Cassie, 'and then roast beef and roast potatoes, and then cherry pie, and then we should get a fireplace with a fire and marshmallows and games. That's what they do in cold countries when it snows.'

Over the next few days, the snow slowly melted, but the weather stayed exceptionally cold and everyone expected more to fall. Just in case, the City of Sydney commissioned a series of television ads under the slogan *Living With Snow*. The ads advised on such things as shovelling the driveway and not wearing slippery shoes. Also, they pointed out that snow was designed to be 'fun' so nobody should panic if it did happen again.

Meanwhile, the Bureau of Meteorology cautioned that more snow was *highly unlikely* since snow in Sydney was a *freakish event*. It could not resist adding now and then: *but still, you never know!*

Each morning, the Canadian sat on his front porch, dressed in his overcoat and a black woollen hat, drinking coffee and breathing mist as he answered Fancy's queries about cold.

•

Each morning, Marbie woke at her parents' place, tangled in her childhood bed. She could not bring herself to go home, or to go to work. She took long hot baths and showers, left phone messages for Vernon at the Banana Bar, and asked her parents whether he had called while she was in the bath. He never had.

•

On the first Friday of the two-week school holidays, Fancy visited her parents for morning tea.

'Marbie's still asleep,' explained Fancy's mother, sitting down and taking the teabag out of her cup. 'And your dad's in the shed. He's taking it hard, this break-up of Marbie's – you know how fond he was of Vernon – and really, I wonder what Marbie thinks she –'

At that moment, Marbie walked into the kitchen, wearing slippers and her mother's pink dressing gown.

'Hello,' said Marbie, seeing her sister. 'Did you bring Cassie?'

Fancy raised her chin towards the kitchen window, and Marbie turned around. In the back garden, Cassie and her friend Lucinda were stamping around in the mud.

'Oh,' said Marbie vaguely. 'I felt like talking to her.'

'Never mind, darling. Have some ginger cake with us. It's still warm!'

'Why aren't you at work, anyway?' Fancy wanted to know.

'Well,' explained Marbie, 'I phoned Tabitha on Monday, she's my supervisor, and I told her what happened and she said I should take as much time as I needed.'

'You can't stop working,' interrupted Fancy, pointing her teacup at Marbie, 'just because you've got a broken heart. It's no excuse. It's like when you have a hangover. You have to go to work even then.'

'I would think it'd be pretty quiet at Marbie's office these days,' their mother soothed, 'what with this funny weather.'

'Actually, imagine how many claims are coming in with all the skidding cars,' Marbie admitted thoughtfully.

'Cassie and Lucinda have been outside playing every day,' said Fancy. 'They've adapted to the cold, and my point is, Marbie, there are some things you just *have* to do.'

'I'm going to have a bath,' Marbie said to her mother. 'See if you can find out what's wrong with Fancy. She's gone all right wing and Protestant.'

'Well,' said Fancy, 'if the *children* can get on with their lives . . .'

•

'Vernon? Is that you? It's me. I'm calling from the bath.'

'Marbie, you'd better stop phoning me, okay?'

Marbie was quiet.

'Marbie? Did you hear me?'

'You prefer me not to call?'

'That's right. Please stop leaving messages. Okay? This is not going to work.'

'I can't even leave messages to say I'm sorry?'
'Not even that.'
'But it makes me feel better.'
'That's not really a concern of mine.'
'Can I speak to Listen then?'
'No, you can't. She's at the library working on her assignment.'
'Choose two creatures of the sea?'
'That's the one.'
'Is she still doing seahorses and whales?'
'I'm hanging up now, okay?'
'Really?'
'Marbie, I'm hanging up the phone.'

•

SEAHORSES
A seahorse is a member of the pipefish family. A lot of people don't know this about seahorses, but they are 'monogamous'. That word means that they stay together with their one true love for their entire lives. Each day, the seahorses link tails and go for walks along the ocean floor. Then the male seahorse gets pregnant.

WHALES
It is commonly known that a whale is a mammal, not a fish. Some scientists even think that whales used to live on land, and that they had legs and fur, like enormous wolves. They waded into water, their legs turned into tails, and their arms turned into pectoral fins. If that is true, it was not the best decision the whales ever made – they can't breathe underwater, and they have to spend most of their lives thinking about that. If they ever fell asleep, they would forget to breathe, and they would die.

•

On Friday night, Marbie drove to the Night Owl Pub but the only person there was Toni.

Tabitha couldn't be there, Toni explained, because her sister had just had the baby. And Rhamie and Abigail had their indoor finals the next day, and had to keep in form.

Work friends alone like this are pointless, Marbie realised as she listened to Toni's explanations. *They only succeed as a team.* But she rallied and said in an upbeat voice: 'Can I get you a drink?'

Toni replied: 'I was going to get you a drink! But, okay. Gin, lemon and lime? I can*not* believe Tabitha piked. I mean, fair enough Abi and Rhamie, they were absolutely shattered last night, and their final's important. But I mean, the baby's not *going anywhere*, and this is when *you* need us, don't you?'

'Well,' said Marbie. 'But a baby.'

She fetched the drinks and took the long way back, nervously scanning for the aeronautical engineer. She wished she could scan for Vernon, but he had never been to the Night Owl Pub.

Toni began a story as soon as she returned, her elbows on the table and her fingers at the straw of her drink. Marbie lost the thread at once.

'. . . so he was going, and I was going, and Abi was thinking of coming as far as the bridge . . .'

'Mmm.'

'. . . I mean, I love her to death, she's an absolute sweetheart, but seriously, I just can't *stand* it when . . .'

'No-o.'

'. . . I mean, sure, maybe I *wasn't* up to scratch, but all they had to do was come and talk it through.'

'Obviously!'

'. . . And *Leila*, fairly obviously, is not up to it.'

Who is Leila?

Marbie risked: 'Absolutely!'

At which Toni shook her head a little: 'Not Leila, I mean Katerina, of course.'

Marbie nodded sagely: 'Of course.'

While Toni talked, Marbie remembered that Vernon would not be at the Meeting that night. Also, that Listen would not be there to watch a movie with Cassie.

She drove to her own apartment instead of her parents' place, and found the mailbox overflowing, and ten messages on the phone. They were all from Tabitha and Toni, seeing how she was.

She phoned her mother and said she could not go to the Meeting that night, and her mother said, 'But, darling, you and Fancy still haven't done the Maintenance Intrusion. And Project 78 . . .'

But Marbie was insistent. Then she sat in a beanbag and watched TV all night.

●

It's Saturday! So you're allowed to do the next Spell. Well done for waiting!

I hope you have been well.

This is a Spell To Make Someone Find Something Unexpected In A Washing Machine!

Go for a walk and shout: HOORAY whenever you see something that looks strange, or lovely, or orange.

The Spell will work in seven weeks or so. You can do the next Spell next Saturday.

●

In the second week of the school holidays, the weather men and women gave up hope of more snow. But it remained record-breakingly cold.

Fancy and Cassie fell into the habit of sleeping in, then deciding on an outing for the day while eating porridge with brown sugar in the kitchen. They had already seen all the holiday movies in the first week, and Cassie was beginning to complain about Lucinda, so they had to use their imaginations.

Of course, by the time they left the house each day, the Canadian had finished his breakfast and was nowhere to be seen.

•

Friday night at the Zing Family Secret Meeting, Fancy told Marbie she had run in to Vernon at Coles the previous afternoon. He was buying tangerines. He looked sad. He had bleached his hair white-blond with sprouting black roots and a jagged short cut. Also, he was wearing a long black overcoat which floated, moodily, to the laces of his ankle-high boots.

'How terrible,' Marbie said, about Vernon's bleached hair. 'I loved his hair.'

'No,' said Fancy, thoughtfully. 'No. It works. It's entirely sexy.'

•

'Vernon? It's me.'

'Oh, hello.'

'Don't hang up, okay? I just wanted to let you know that I'll get the mortgage payments on our apartment, okay? While you're – until you get back, I'll cover them, okay? In case you were worried. You know how it's due next week?'

'Yep.'

'Everyone misses you, you know. The meeting last night was awful without you, it was so – And Fancy says she saw you at Coles and you've changed your hair, and she says it looks good.'

'Okay. Two things. First, I told your sister not to worry about the Secret, so I'll tell you that too. It's safe with me, okay? Second, in relation to the apartment: when you can afford to refund my half of the deposit, send me a cheque, and I'll transfer my share to you. Everything else, you can keep.'

He had carved off most of his voice, and the leftover bit was as cold as a dental instrument. Marbie had to close her eyes.

'Uh–huh,' she breathed, with her eyes still closed. 'If that's what you think.'

'That's what I think.'

●

A dwarf pygmy seahorse is only about 3cm long. That's the size of my little finger. A blue whale can grow to a length of 28 metres. That's three times as tall as our school library.

●

'Hey, Vernon, it's me.'

There was silence.

'Vernon? Can you hear me? It's me. It's Marbie.'

'I know who it is.'

'I just forgot to say something when I called earlier.'

'What did you forget to say?'

'I forgot to say, um, happy Saturday. It's Saturday today.'

'Yes, Marbie, it's Saturday.'

'Can I speak to Listen?'

'She's busy.'

'I want to tell her good luck at Cassie's school on Monday.'

'She's in the caravan. She didn't want to be disturbed.'

'Vernon? Can I see you? So I can tell you how sorry I am?'

'Nope.'

Marbie was still staring at the phone, wondering at its power, when it rang again. It was the aeronautical engineer.

'Come for lunch?' he said. 'Today? I've got a picnic!'
'I haven't heard from you for two weeks,' she said.
'I know!'

•

A Spell To Make Somebody Eat A Piece Of
Chocolate Cake

1. Take up rock climbing!
2. Stop rock climbing!
3. Take it up again!

*This Spell will work in about six weeks or so. You can do
the next Spell in TWO MONTHS!*

•

The aeronautical engineer greeted Marbie at the door of his house and
said, 'At last! I get to see you again! It's been two weeks!' He did not try
to kiss her, but kept a respectful distance.

'I have to tell you something,' Marbie said at once.

'What do you have to tell me?' He ushered her into the living room,
where he had the following items set out neatly on a picnic blanket on
the floor:

    pickles
    sundried tomatoes
    two large radishes
    crackers and cheese
    bottled water
    corned beef sandwiches

boiled eggs
a salad made of spinach, crumbled bacon, and anchovies

'A lot of food,' she said, surveying this.

'What do you have to tell me?' He took her coat.

'I have to tell you about my family,' she said in a breathless rush, and then frowned at the voice in the back of her head, which was saying, companionably, *Marbie, where is your mind?* She would have to speak louder, to drown it.

'I HAVE TO TELL YOU OUR FAMILY SECRET!' she yelled, and he took a step backwards. 'OKAY, LISTEN FAST, IT'S THIS. We spy on a 2nd grade school teacher named Cath Murphy! WE HAVE A CAMERA INSTALLED IN HER DINING ROOM WINDOW and she *does not know that it is there.*' She quietened down in surprise at herself.

'Wo ho!' He was grinning at her, holding both hands to his ears like a comedian, and then gesturing that she should sit cross-legged on the floor, like him.

'Yes, yes,' she did as he instructed, 'so, we have a camera in her dining room window and another camera but . . . anyway, earlier this year, she knocked out the camera when she washed the windows, so we had to go in and replace it. Then she made it go blurry by throwing apple juice at it. So we had to go in again. It slipped *again* two weeks ago, at the start of the school holidays, *so we don't have a clue what she's been doing for the last two weeks.*'

'Marbie! Marbie! Why did I wait so long to call you?'

'And I don't feel like doing a Maintenance Intrusion to fix it.'

'You're a riot and I don't understand a word! Eat, my princess! Dig in!'

'No,' said Marbie, watching as a radish rolled across the blanket. 'I have to tell you more about the Secret.'

7

THE HOT AIR BALLOON

Once upon a time there was a physicist who thought he could invent a balloon. This was in 1783, and the physicist's name was Professor Charles. To his wife, the Professor made a promise: 'I shall build a balloon made of taffeta, twelve feet in diameter, covered in india-rubber, and inflated with hydrogen gas!'

'Oh!' said his wife, not understanding, until, early one rainy March morning, the Professor and his friends paraded the balloon through the streets of Paris on a wagon. They inflated it with hydrogen gas and let it loose. It rose to enormous heights, astounding a crowd, in the rain, on the *Champ de Mars*.

It is said that Benjamin Franklin (an old man at the time) was amongst that crowd on the *Champ de Mars*. Benjamin Franklin, as is widely known, invented such things as: bifocal glasses, a urinary catheter, and a 'long arm' for reaching books from the tops of bookshelves. Invention was an interest of his.

'What's the use in that?' exclaimed a passerby scornfully – meaning the balloon.

Ever wise, Benjamin replied, 'What use is a newborn baby?'

•

He meant, Maude understood, that newborn babies grow up to be men, just as balloons would, eventually, grow up into jet-engine planes.

Maude Sausalito was sixteen years old and the moon was just a slither tonight, a sliver of leftover soap. She was jogging gracefully, her high-heels in her hands, stockinged feet on the damp dewy grass of people's lawns. *The Mickey Mouse Show* chanted to itself from the window of every house she passed. A sharp piece of gravel glanced against her toe, and she slowed slightly.

She was not all that late. But her new boyfriend was coming to dinner at her family's place that night, and she wanted to make potato casserole. Her favourite thing, at the moment, was to peel and slice potatoes and layer them with salt, pepper and cheese. Then bake for 45 minutes.

The little white moon, Maude noticed now, was actually tucked into the corner of a big dark circle of moon. She was not pleased about this: it undid the idea of fresh and changing moons; plainly, now, there was just one moon, presenting itself like a dull set of slides, in differing angles of light. But at least it had the look of a chocolate cream biscuit, a curve of white cream at its edge.

At present, Maude was saving to buy herself a piano. Also, she was growing her hair (which now curled up around her ears) because she wanted it to swish down to her shoulders. She expected this would keep her warmer on cold nights, like a cheap and never-lost scarf.

She had a bag of mixed lollies in her pocket to share with her new boyfriend, after the potato casserole.

The new boyfriend's name was David. He worked in the novelty corkscrew shop next door to the bakery where she worked. He himself was vibrant, energetic, bouncy, and leapt about his life like the tail of a kite. But his *family*! His family was remarkable. Stretching back to great-great-greatness and beyond, *every single one was an inventor.* Every surface in David's house bristled with patent certificates.

Although the family had not made any money, Maude and David were both looking forward to David's first invention. They wondered what it would be.

Maude herself was reading a lot about balloons these days, and she secretly hoped that David might invent something balloon-related.

Also these days, Maude was spending a lot of time planning the journey in a hot air balloon which she would take on her honeymoon with David.

David, once he had grown up and invented a thing or two, would probably become a diplomat. Then he would propose to her. Floating along in their honeymoon balloon, they would play chess for long, languid hours. As the sun set each night, David would mix cocktails, gazing at her over slow, careful stirring with the swizzle stick. He would bite his lower lip seductively, and then wink, surprisingly, once.

•

As for the Professor's balloon, it landed in a field, where peasants found it and poked it with pitchforks. Upon smelling the horrible hydrogen smell, they panicked and beat it to death.

Consequently, the French government issued a 'Warning to the People on kidnapping Air-balloons'. *If you see a black moon in the sky,* said the Warning, *do not panic! It is not a monster, it is just a bag of silk.*

8

CATH MURPHY

On the first day of term after the holiday, Cath arrived to a brisk, blue-sky. She stepped over ridges of mud in the car park, and turned when she heard her name.

'Cath! Cath! How *are* you? How was your *holiday*? What about the weather! Were you cold?'

It was Suzanne, rolling down her window as she pulled into a spot. Cath waited as Suzanne spilled out of her car, and gave her a welcoming hug.

'Wasn't it *cold*!' Suzanne exclaimed, falling into step alongside Cath. 'My big old house was just *freezing*! How about your apartment?'

Cath explained that her landlord had installed central gas heating, with a vent in every room, just before the start of the holidays.

'Lucky duck!'

'Hello there,' a deep voice moved against the back of Cath's neck, like slowly warming sunlight. They both turned and there he was: Warren Woodford, smiling down.

'Warren!' cried Suzanne. 'How was your holiday?'

Warren explained that he had attended a K-2 Cognitive Learning Conference in Bowral for the whole two weeks, so it was not, in fact, a holiday. He then interrupted Suzanne's exclamations to ask after *her* vacation.

'Me? Oh, I spent a lot of time with Lenny, poor old Lenny – what was up with that anyway? They seemed so happy. I'm just *wrecked* about that fight. Hey, I left my briefcase in the car!' Suzanne rolled her eyes affectionately at her own forgetfulness, and skidded back toward the car park. She held a hand flat in the air behind her, meaning they should wait. Obediently, Warren and Cath stood side-by-side watching her.

'Well,' murmured Warren, without turning his head. 'I myself am not *wrecked* about that fight. I myself am fairly *stoked* about that fight.'

'You can't be glad,' said Cath promptly, eyes still on Suzanne, 'about two happy people having a fight.'

'But I am. I'm glad they had a fight, because then Lenny had a party, and then I went to your place, and then – and look who's back again!'

Suzanne hurried up to them, grinning and waving her briefcase.

In her classroom, waiting for the class to settle down, Cath watched the playground through the window. A long line of girls in blue tunics were marching out of the Assembly Hall in pairs. What was that all about?

Of course! It was the Year 7 students from St Carmel's, rescued from their flooded classrooms. She had forgotten all about them. And yet there was something *important* about them – something she herself had to do – what was that? She could not remember.

Marcus Ellison was tapping on her elbow. 'Ms Murphy, I've done my class play.' He handed her a neat manila folder. 'But we can start practising Cassie's first if you like,' he added, formally.

'Well, what a great guy you are, Marcus! Thank you *very* much. I can't wait to read it!' She looked around and noticed Cassie unpacking her bag at her desk. 'Hey, Cassie, how did you get on with your class play?'

Cassie looked up from her desk. She tilted her head to the side. She closed the desk-lid slowly and said, with some surprise, 'I forgot!'

'Oh well, never mind, Cassie, you just write it whenever you can, okay? We've still got plenty of time.'

'It snowed at my place in the holidays,' Cassie said, by way of explanation.

'How about that?' smiled Cath. 'It snowed at my place, too!'

Later that morning, they had News, so that everyone could tell about their holidays. It turned out that most of the children believed the snow had happened to them alone. While each child told an *amazing* story about waking up on the first day of the holiday and finding *snow* outside!, the rest of the class daydreamed quietly to themselves.

Cath recalled the first day of her own holiday, how she woke in a ruffled empty bed and looked for a single red rose.

'Well,' Warren had said, sitting on the side of her bed with one hand flat on her forehead and a takeaway coffee in the other, 'I promise I'll leave you a single red rose when I plan to say goodbye. But wild horses could not make me say goodbye. Let's say wild horses wanted to.'

Then they had run away together. They went to a K-2 Cognitive Learning Conference in Bowral. Warren was already going to the conference, because Breanna, it turned out, was on a psychology seminar herself. The strange weather meant there were plenty of cancellations, so it was easy for Cath to get a place.

They attended all the same lectures, sitting side-by-side and writing notes to one another in the margins of their handouts. They ate lunch and had coffees together. They walked the streets of Bowral, looking for the gardens and sweet shops that inspired *Mary Poppins*.

They never touched in public, except for one afternoon when they were caught in a downpour and had to cling together, to share the umbrella, as they ran for the shelter of a café. At the café, a woman said sadly, 'It's only rain.'

In the evenings, they said, 'See you tomorrow,' in the courtyard, in the presence of other conference attendees. Then they went their separate ways to their own rooms. Warren's room was in the north wing; Cath's room was in the east wing. There was a laundry in the basement, which was accessible from all the wings.

Each night, Cath went down to the laundry room in her pyjamas, and when there was nobody looking, took the staircase to the north wing. Each night she passed the same sign:

BOWRAL FUNCTION CENTRE LAUNDRY FACILITIES

- PLEASE REMEMBER THAT THESE MACHINES ARE FOR THE USE OF *ALL* CONFERENCE PARTICIPANTS.
- THE MACHINES TAKE $2 COINS ONLY – *NO* CHANGE IS AVAILABLE AT THE FRONT DESK.

• PLEASE CLEAN LINT FROM DRYERS AFTER
EVERY USE.

It was the sweetest, most emphatic sign she had ever read.

Cath smiled around her classroom, and decided she should listen for a while. Cassie Zing was standing out the front, talking to the class about fairy penguins and ice creams. Also, she was explaining that her mum had let her keep some snow in the freezer at home. She opened the lid of her lunch box to show off a little pool of water.

Cassie's mum was *always* writing notes. Cath wondered if there would be one today — perhaps about the incident in which Cassie scooped snow into the lunch box. Perhaps it would say, 'Sorry! I couldn't resist! Hope it doesn't spill all over the floor!'

Of course! That's why she had to remember the Year 7 students from St Carmel's. She had been asked to keep an eye on one. Some kind of relative of Cassie's? One with an unusual name. What was that name . . .?

She and Warren had not discussed what would happen now that they were back in the real world. Breanna would be down for the weekends, and they would both have school work to do in the afternoons. Perhaps it would all be over? Perhaps it was just a two-week interlude? But that was impossible.

Later that day, Cath was walking home from a dentist appointment at Round Corner when a rusty station wagon slid along the street beside her. She glanced over. The passenger door was opened from the inside.

'Get in,' said Warren, looking straight ahead like an undercover agent. Then he drove them to her place for the night.

Over the next few weeks they fell into a pattern. During the day they practically ignored one another, except for occasional acquaintance-friendly chats. But late each evening, Monday to Thursday, Warren found his way over to Cath's place. He returned to his own home early the next morning. When Warren had a soccer match, he arrived muddy in his soccer clothes and took a shower while Cath made dinner. When Cath had a law class, Warren let himself into her apartment and got dinner ready for her return. He liked to wrap things in filo pastry —

chicken, eggplant, goats cheese – and then bake it alongside a tomato. They watched movies, listened to music, and did school work sitting side-by-side at the dining room table. But mostly, they spent their time in bed.

Warren chipped a tooth slightly while at Cath's place.

They were cooking together on a Monday night, in Cath's kitchen, which was crowded with ingredients. She made him dance with her, to her favourite Suzanne Vega song, while the ingredients waited. They were sleepy, wearing bathrobes, drinking red wine and eating occasional olives.

Cath was telling a story which included an impersonation of Billson, the school principal. The impersonation made Warren laugh so suddenly that he bit down on an olive stone and chipped a tooth.

Later that night, Cath made Warren look through her family photo albums. He was very obliging, and remarked on such things as the healthy fur of their family dog, and the resemblance between Cath's and her mother's hair colouring.

At that, Cath unlocked her secret box and explained that she had been adopted. She only had this one photograph of her biological parents: they had been killed in a fire which burnt down their house in the outback. The photo was hazy, as if the smoke had seeped into its edges. Warren stared at it for a long time, and eventually said he could see that Cath's parents were in love.

The only other photo Cath had was one showing the firefighter who had rescued her, a sleeping baby, from the fire.

'Do you think we should stop?' Cath said occasionally in the early dawn light as Warren buttoned his shirt.

Warren always considered the question grimly, and always said the same thing: 'You're right. We should stop. We should stop soon. But I can't.'

And in the silence that followed, they would think the same thing:

This affair has parameters. It's only the weekdays. It's only at Cath's place. It's a secret from everyone else. We have plenty of chats about *guilt*, about *marriage*, about *lost opportunities* and *fate* ('if only we'd met sooner!', 'we're so *right* for each other!', 'I never thought I'd do this kind of thing'). This affair has an end date! Soon it will finish! The moment Breanna gets a job in the city, we will call the whole thing quits. But for now, why should we stop? The betrayal has already occurred: on the night of Lenny's party, the marriage was broken. If it's already broken, why stop? With parameters in place, why stop?

Two or three times, Breanna phoned Warren on his mobile late at night, and he pretended to be at home. 'Something's wrong with the home phone,' he explained. 'For some reason I don't hear it when it rings. Don't worry though, you can always reach me on my mobile.'

Then he and Breanna would talk as Cath waited in bed, staring at his naked back in the darkness of her hall. She could hear the chatter of Breanna's voice, saying things like 'Can't wait until the weekend! Oh God, I miss you!'

Afterwards, they were both silent for a while. Warren sat on the side of the bed with his head in his hands. Cath kept her body careful and separate.

Eventually, Warren would say, 'I'd better go home', and Cath would say, 'Yep', and he would dress in heavy silence and go home.

Thursdays, they made mulled wine to say goodbye for the weekend. Warren had a crisis and Cath agreed at once to end the fiasco. Warren always looked crestfallen and torn.

Then he decided: 'No. Let's keep going until she gets a job in Sydney. Why stop now when we have come this far? When she gets a job in Sydney we will stop. But until then, I just can't.'

Cath always said: 'Are you sure?'

And Warren said: 'Yes.'

Then, Cath had her own crisis. What exactly did he think he was doing? He was cheating on his wife! And every weekend, he was cheating on *her*! But the worst thing of all was Breanna's voice. When she heard the voice on the mobile phone in the hallway, it was as sharp to her as a papercut. But imagine if Breanna knew he was allowing his *lover* to hear those conversations! That was the worst betrayal, worse than the physical part. Breanna believed her voice to be safe within her husband's home, safe within their private married world – when instead it was here, on display, in the hallway.

He listened fiercely to every word, and agreed, nodding his head. She put special emphasis on the word 'lover' in her attacks, embracing the word, loving it.

He listened, and then he explained, over and over, how sorry he was, how shocked he was at his own behaviour, that he could not hurt his wife, that telling her would kill her. And Cath pounced, *I don't WANT you to tell your wife, I don't WANT you to leave your wife, I've never ASKED you to leave your wife*, and he said, *yes, but it's coming apart at the seams.*

It didn't have long, their marriage, he said, it was coming apart at the seams. Then she would relent, and they would look at one another and say, 'This is all so stupid, because you and I are *right* together.' And: 'I'm sure that it's going to work out.'

Cath spent the weekends pacing her apartment, trying not to think of Warren and Breanna, the closeness of their bodies and hands. In the dark of night, she would wake in a panic of disbelief. In the cold light of day, she would shake her head in wonder at her own behaviour. She had always been opposed to mistresses. She was a vixen, a villain, she was betraying her own kind. She was a home wrecker!

But she didn't really mean these lectures to herself, and quickly rallied to her own defence:

If she doesn't know, how can it hurt her?

I haven't told a single person!

If nobody knows then it's not really happening!

Besides, I only get him on the weekdays – she gets the fun days, the week-end days.

Why should she get him, anyway, just because she met him first?

And all the time, she was really just waiting until Monday, and her heart was beating quickly and excitedly, because she knew that it would all work out. Somehow, it would all work out, and nobody would end up getting hurt.

Sometimes, of course, she worried vaguely about the job in Sydney. 'I'll give you a rose as a poignant goodbye,' Warren joked, 'the moment she gets herself a job.' What if she did get herself a job? But really, Breanna had been looking for work in Sydney for months. She was probably not trying very hard. She probably didn't even want to spend the weekdays with Warren! Besides which, it *was* a joke. The idea of saying goodbye! It was funny.

Meanwhile, the weather grew steadily warmer and the only remnant of the Sydney snow was the fact that ski poles occasionally washed up on Bondi Beach.

Strangely, Cath did not think of the pact about the rose when she found a short-stemmed rose in her pigeonhole on Thursday afternoon. She simply blushed and thought: *that's a risk!* Because people would wonder where she got it from. Then she sat at the table ready for the Staff Meeting. She would slip the rose into her handbag when nobody was watching, as soon as the meeting finished.

Billson started with a joke about the Year 7 students from St Carmel's, and how nobody expected them to hang around *this* long! The one high school teacher attending smiled warily.

Cath kept her eyes away from Warren. She was talented at pretending there was nothing going on (he was always telling her this).

Billson suggested a new format for the School Newsletter, and a couple of teachers had far too many thoughts on this theme.

Cath wanted Billson to get a move-on. It was Thursday and they had to go to her place for their crisis and mulled wine.

'A temp is a temp, as fine a temp as Mrs Rory has been.'

Billson was nodding at the temporary 6th grade teacher: the emergency replacement for Lenny. Cath watched his face carefully for signs of a broken heart when he said Lenny's name. He seemed perfectly all right. Perhaps he was an *actor* like Cath?

'And as you all know,' Billson continued, 'we have put our heads to the wheel on this particular one.'

'Heads to the wheel,' murmured Warren from across the staffroom table, 'ouch', which gave Cath an excuse to look at him and smile.

'And Mrs Rory has agreed to become permanent! As you all know, she's had plenty of experience, she's rock solid, and she's loads of fun!' Mrs Rory smiled modestly, and everyone said congratulations.

'So!' Billson got a move-on, gathering his papers. 'So, that's the 6th graders taken care of! And –' He held both hands high, to still the stirring room. 'And, here's some news!' He had trouble keeping his smile in check. 'You remember how Lenny used to be 6th grade teacher *and* school counsellor? Well! Never let it be said that we don't fly with the times here at Redwood!'

The teachers paused with their bags and their coats at the ready.

'Guess what?' Now Billson was beaming. 'We have reached a decision to employ a *separate* school counsellor. A *full-time* school counsellor! And guess who we have chosen?'

Nobody could guess.

'A woman by the name of Breanna!' Billson practically whooped as he beamed his delight about the room. 'The psychologist wife of our very own Warren Woodford here!'

'Huh!' cried the room, and, 'Congratulations, Warren!'

Warren leaned back in his chair and took a bow.

FANCY ZING

Returning home after dropping Cassie at school the first day back after the holidays, Fancy paused just inside the front door and looked at the vacuum cleaner. She had placed it in the hallway, alongside the umbrella stand, as a cryptic message to Radcliffe that she knew about his affair.

The vacuum cleaner gazed back at her, its hose neatly coiled at its side. *I was once broken*, it said. *I choked on the shattered pieces of a marriage. A glass had been broken by the husband's lover; the husband used ME to clean it up. But no, I choked on his deceit. Now, the repairman has fixed me: can the same thing be said of the marriage?* So far, Radcliffe had not appeared to hear.

Fancy pushed it a little further out into the hallway: if it tripped him over, he would surely get the message. But, of course, her plan was more concrete than that, and now that Cassie was back at school she could set that plan in motion.

First, she ran upstairs and crawled around her bed, peering underneath into the darkness for further clues of the affair. As usual, there was nothing. She returned to the downstairs hallway and picked up the phone, her heart beating gently.

'Radcliffe!' she said, when he answered. 'Just thought I'd let you know that I'm going to the city for the day. I'm on my way out the door right now. Doing some work for Mum. So, don't bother coming home for lunch, will you? I won't be here *all day*.'

Radcliffe thanked her and she hung up, walked out the front door and sat down on the porch.

The way she walked out the door and sat down, with her head oddly tilted and her posture straight, it was as if she were a ballerina. *My husband is having an affair.* She smiled softly, and hugged her knees. She could have been wearing a gossamer gown.

The Canadian was not on his porch. She longed for it to snow again. Imagine this, she thought, imagine that this is now a *city of snow.* Imagine that *everything* has changed: there are reindeer, caribou, polar bears and squirrels. In fact, helpfully, Cassie had left footprints in the muddy front lawn, which could almost resemble claw marks. Bear prints!

Imagine this, thought Fancy: a black bear moving gracefully, as if the bear had glandular fever, or as if the bear's husband were having an affair, is making its way up the street. It passes open curtains, parked cars, and For Sale signs; pokes its snout into letterboxes; sharpens its claws on telegraph poles. Its movement is silent in the snow. It pauses now and then at distant sounds: a truck on the highway; somebody's screen door.

The fantasy was complicated slightly, Fancy realised, by the presence of a man in a pale grey T-shirt and jeans, standing inexplicably still by the side of the house next door. When the bear approached, that man would have to be warned.

It was the Canadian, looking at the wall of his house.

'Hello!' she shouted.

He turned slowly, and waved. 'Just checking for structural damage,' he called. 'I had a *minor* explosion in my basement just now. Did you hear it?'

'No!'

'Great!'

He turned back to the wall and stared some more. After a while, he turned back to Fancy, waved and smiled again, and then disappeared into his house.

Fancy waited on her front porch until 3 pm that day, but the Canadian did not reappear. Nor, for that matter, did Radcliffe or his lover.

Over the next few weeks Fancy's days fell into a pattern. She would drive Cassie to school, return home, phone Radcliffe and tell him she was out for the day, and then she would sit on her porch. After a few days, she remembered that Gemma-from-the-pay-office worked afternoons, so she decided she could stop around lunchtime. Any liaison must surely take place in the morning.

This was fortunate because she needed the afternoons to work on her prize-winning novel, or on the Zing Family Secret, or to go to the gym. Meanwhile, her sister Marbie kept arriving unexpectedly at dinner time and asking frantic legal questions.

Very occasionally, on her morning vigils, the Canadian would emerge onto *his* front porch and sit at his breakfast table. These days he was eating blueberry muffins and breadfruit with his coffee. He never seemed to wonder at Fancy's presence on *her* front porch, simply chatting to her about this and that, and Fancy felt that her neck was slender and that her hands, when she spoke, were like butterflies.

One day the Canadian had a small portable stereo alongside his blueberry muffin. 'Hey, Fancy,' he called, 'you want to help me out with this?'

'Okay!' she called back, happily.

It turned out that he was required, for some reason, to compare two different versions of a song called 'Love Cats'. One version was the original, by a band called The Cure. The other was a more recent cover, by a man called Tricky. Such a jumble of mysterious words and names! Fancy felt nervous and excited.

'Which one do you think is slicker?' the Canadian called. 'Which one is more powerful? Which is more beautiful? Which one makes you want to dance? Which one do you think is sexier?'

He played the two songs over and over, facing the stereo towards her porch, and the space between their houses filled with drumbeats. Fancy answered his questions solemnly, and he jotted down her words, nodding with interest.

'I like them both a *lot*,' said Fancy.

'Tell you what,' offered the Canadian, 'I'll make you a copy.'

'Thank you!' said Fancy, tears in her eyes.

Not once did Radcliffe's car appear in the driveway, and nor did Gemma arrive to reclaim her purple sock. Meanwhile, Fancy's prize-winning novel had stalled. She had re-read the book about love-and-leaves and had made a discovery. The author had done more than simply list leaves, he had also provided information about them – there were entire sections of the book devoted to pigmentation and photosynthesis.

It was not just lists that were required, Fancy realised, it was *language*. By the time that a reader reached the end of a prize-winning novel, she or he had to know a new language. For example: the language of photography, geography, topology. The language of fly-fishing, Malta, or bread-making.

Fancy was not sure she knew any languages worth teaching, and sensed that she ought to learn one. Meanwhile, each new prize-winning novel released took another language away – the better books, the *Booker*-winning books, often used four or five. It had to be an easy language, of course. Fancy was very busy. Antarctica could not be her language. She had neither the time nor the inclination to sail to Antarctica.

One day Fancy collected Cassie from school, and took her to the dentist for a check-up.

'This is not the way to the dentist,' said Cassie as Fancy took a right-hand turn.

'You have an excellent memory, darling,' Fancy declared. 'You're right. It's not the way. But we're going to try a *new* dentist at Round Corner. On the way, tell me how school is going.'

'Okay,' agreed Cassie. 'For one thing, I have to write a class play and I keep forgetting.'

'Would you like me to remind you?'

'Thanks.'

'And how's Ms Murphy? Do you still like her?'

'Uh-huh. She's pretty nice, actually.'

'Mmm. Do you think she's good friends with any of the other teachers at your school?'

'Well,' said Cassie, thinking and staring out the window. 'She's got two friends. Mrs Barker and Mr Woodford.'

'Mr Woodford, eh? Hmm. He's the other 2nd grade teacher, isn't he? What's he like?'

'He is *so* funny,' declared Cassie, swinging back around from the window. 'Everyone is always laughing at his jokes.'

At the dentist, Cassie's mother held out her toothbrush. 'Here,' she said. 'Run to the bathroom down the hall and clean your teeth.'

Cassie took the toothbrush, and the woman at the desk said, 'Cassie? Would you like a treat?'

By treat, the woman meant the tiny plastic zebra she was holding up. Cassie did not want a tiny plastic zebra, but she said, 'Okay.' The zebra could be a trick. The woman might have a Tim Tam hidden in her other hand.

Fancy sat in the dentist's waiting room and took out her mobile phone. She selected her mother's number.

'I'm here,' she murmured. 'Nobody else in the waiting room. Perfect layout. Now is good.' She hung up.

Almost immediately, the phone behind the reception desk rang.

'Round Corner Dental Centre,' the receptionist said. 'How can I help you? Uh-huh? Oh, gosh! Hang on then. No, I'll – wait right there and I'll be out!'

She stood up, and hurried out into the corridor. The lift doors opened and closed.

Fancy moved behind the reception desk, opened the top drawer of a silver filing cabinet, and flicked through manila folders. Her fingers landed on: MURPHY, Cath. She slid the folder out and glanced around the room. She opened the folder and held her wristwatch over the first document. Then she clicked the side of the watch. A flash flickered. She turned over to the second page, and clicked again. She closed the folder, returned it to the drawer, and sat back down in the waiting room.

She was reading a magazine when the receptionist returned. 'Huh,' said the receptionist to Fancy as she resumed her seat, 'a courier just phoned and said she'd backed her van into our service entry and couldn't get it out! But when I got down there, she was gone. Must have got out on her own.'

'Oh,' agreed Fancy. 'She must have.'

Cassie in the dentist chair felt small because the dentist was a giant. 'Well!' he giant-voiced, wheezing and buzzing a button which made the chair bend backward. Going to the dentist would be fine if the dentist wasn't there, and you could just be alone and play on the chair.

'Well!' the dentist boomed again, buzzing another button, which made the chair rise slowly upwards. It practically hit the spotlight on the ceiling. The ceiling itself was good, she noticed. It was painted green, like a jungle, with a lot of elephants, monkeys, lions and giraffes. So you had something to look at.

Cassie thought about offering her puffer for the dentist's wheezing. But then he would put it in his mouth.

'How old are you, Cassie? What is it: seven, eight, nine?'

'Seven,' replied Cassie from her sticky leather chair.

'Seven!' The dentist seemed to find this funny. 'Let's have a look here, shall we?' he chuckled, and leaned over her with a wheedley, 'Open wide.'

The dentist began to play with her teeth instead of the chair.

Cassie thought about the class play.

What was the play about? That was the trick.

'Rinse out,' said the dentist.

Cassie did not want to rinse out because the dentist's water was pink and warm, but you had to.

'Mrs Zing?' The dentist was wiping his hands on a towel at the doorway.

'How is everything? Everything all right?' Her mother appeared looking cheerful.

'A teeny little hole, just the one,' boomed the dentist with a chuckle, probably still thinking about her age.

'Ah well,' said her mum. 'Never mind. I'll make another appointment to bring her back.'

'I can do it now if you like,' suggested the dentist. 'Won't take a minute. Shall we have happy gas? And then the fluoride treatment and we're done.'

'*Fluoride*,' said Cassie from the chair. 'Mum, you know that makes me cry.'

Her mum just laughed, agreed to happy gas, and happily returned to the waiting room to wait.

Cassie breathed slowly into the happy gas mask, sank into the chair, and stared up at the jungle pictures on the ceiling. She took herself from the chair into the jungle for a moment, then she came back.

The dentist's booming voice became a food-processing buzz, and Cassie decided to ignore it. She thought about the class play again. She chose to sink through the chair to the floor. She climbed back up from the floor and floated to the ceiling. A pair of cheetahs ran side-by-side towards the edge of the ceiling, while the other animals ignored them and got on with their lives.

And there it was. The story for the class play. It had been there on the ceiling all the time.

●

During those first few weeks of the new school term, when Fancy spent her mornings on the porch, difficulties arose in relation to the Family Secret. Specifically, Marbie was refusing to attend Meetings or do any Maintenance. This meant that the camera in the dining room window of Cath Murphy's apartment remained broken. The other camera which they kept in the apartment had never been any use.

Meanwhile, Marbie kept appearing at Fancy's front door in time for dinner, and asking frantic legal questions.

'She's a *lawyer*,' she said, in the doorway, on one such occasion. 'Why have we never *considered* that?'

'She's not a lawyer,' Fancy pointed out, standing aside so that Marbie could come in. 'She's a school teacher. She's only studying law. And only *part*-time.'

'No difference,' declared Marbie, handing Fancy a bottle of wine. 'She's still going to sue. Can I stay for dinner again?'

'She's not going to find out,' said Fancy, 'so she's not going to sue. Of course you can stay.'

'If she does find out, she'll sue.'

'What for?' Radcliffe appeared at Fancy's shoulder – pressing his *chin* into her shoulder, in fact. 'What will she sue for? What's the charge?'

'Hey,' said Marbie ignoring Radcliffe and wandering into the kitchen, where Fancy's music was playing. 'Hey, you're listening to "Love Cats" again. I love this song.'

Another night, over spinach soufflé, Marbie said, 'As soon as she's a lawyer, she'll sue.'

'What's the charge?' said Radcliffe, predictably. 'What charge?'

'Who's going to sue?' Cassie had her hands around her strawberry and orange juice, just about to drink.

'Nobody, darling,' Fancy explained, giving Marbie a meaningful look. 'What do you think of the juice, Cassie? It's new! A new variety.'

'Wait,' said Cassie, 'I'll try it.'

'Ever heard of the Convention for the Protection of Individuals with Regard to Automatic Processing of Personal Data?' pounced Marbie.

'Gosh!' said Fancy. 'Is there really such a thing?'

'*That*,' said Radcliffe scornfully, scraping at the burnt bits of cheese on the edge of the serving bowl, 'that's to do with computer process-ing. Government databanks, that kind of thing. For big corporations. Nothing to do with us.'

'Oh,' said Marbie. 'Really? But I suppose it's illegal to break in to –'

'Who says we're breaking in?' Radcliffe interrupted. 'We're the landlords and it's all in the lease. In the fine print, I admit, but: "access shall be granted blahdy blahdy maintenance blahdy blahdy nice and vague".'

'It's not bad,' said Cassie, replacing her juice on the table and wiping her strawberry mouth. 'You try it.'

Fancy, Radcliffe and Marbie reached for their glasses.

Nobody knew what was going on with Marbie but they supposed it was connected with Vernon. The fact was, he *still* had not returned. They were all taken aback by that, so Marbie must have been reeling. She was probably worried that he might use the Secret against them somehow. He would never do that, they all agreed, uneasily.

Radcliffe offered to replace Marbie on the Maintenance Intrusion, but Fancy said she did not feel comfortable with the concept. She and Marbie worked so well together. Besides, she added kindly, Radcliffe had spent *hours* on the desktop publishing lately. Everyone agreed that the latest issue of *Elf Epistles* looked fantastic. Such glossy pages!

'Still,' said Radcliffe, 'I'm surprised at Vernon. I would have sworn he'd have forgiven her by now.'

'Would you just?' said Fancy, coldly.

'Well,' said Radcliffe, shelling pistachio nuts and piling the shells onto his thigh, 'wouldn't *you*?'

'I miss chatting with Listen,' sighed Fancy, unexpectedly.

Coincidentally, Fancy saw Listen at the gym the very next day. She had been climbing on the step machine for half an hour.

'Two minutes to go,' said the machine.

Well, I should hope so, thought Fancy, climbing the stairs.

The machine provided her with a WorkOut Summary, and released her, and she ran into Listen at the bubbler.

'Well, *hello!*'

'Hi, Fancy!' Listen seemed shiny-eyed and sweaty, cute in tracksuit pants and a singlet top, with a silver bangle at her wrist.

'You don't *work out* at the gym, do you?'

'No,' Listen explained, 'I'm doing rock-climbing classes. In there – see that colourful fake rock wall they have in there? I just climbed it.'

'Ha! How about *you*! Mission Impossible! James Bond!' They smiled at each other for a moment.

'Anyway,' said Listen, 'I'd better go now – Vernon's picking me up. Say hi to Cassie for me, would you? I see her around at Redwood sometimes but she always looks kind of busy.'

'Okay, sure. We all miss you so much, Listen, especially Cassie. I hope we get to see you soon.'

And Listen, running up the stairs to the gym's front doors, her pony-tail bouncing behind her, turned back and gave a funny grin.

•

Finally, after several weeks of sitting on the front porch, Fancy decided that she needed a new tactic. It was obvious that Radcliffe had moved his affair to a different location – perhaps the incident with the vacuum cleaner had been enough to scare him away? Dangerous, after all, to bring a clumsy woman like Gemma into his home. They were probably spending all their time at Gemma's place – breaking *her* crockery.

This realisation came to her one Thursday afternoon while she was sitting on the front porch and waving at the postman. He was wheeling his bicycle along, and had just pressed a handful of letters into their mailbox. Fancy stood, still waving, thinking to herself: *I need a new tactic*, and began to walk across her lawn to fetch the mail. It was then that she realised that her gestures were no longer graceful: they were awkward, uneasy, jerky, like a puppet on uneven strings. She blinked and even her blinking had an arrhythmic sort of a twitch.

Here was the problem, she thought, calming herself down, as she drew out the mail. She was about to lose her hold on the affair. Over the last week, there had been days when she wondered where she got the idea in the first place; there had been days when she doubted that a purple daisy sock could *really* mean so much; there had even been days when she *completely forgot* that her husband was having an affair.

She needed to focus, to give the affair the right sort of attention, to pin it down, to line it with sandbags. Otherwise, she felt, it would slip from her grasp, rise out of reach, and drift away forlornly like a helium balloon.

Looking down at the handful of mail, she saw her answer. It was on a flyer at the top of the pile of envelopes.

RELATIONSHIP COUNSELLING

- Affordable
- Discreet
- Confidential
- Guaranteed

Winston Hills Family Counselling Centre (see reverse for contact details)

Of course! The plan came to her in a tumble: she would set up some sessions with a counsellor. She would surprise Radcliffe with these sessions. She would tell him it was a kind of gift certificate for their marriage, like a trip to a health farm. In fact, the idea would be to ensure an anchor, a structure, a controlled environment. Within that environment, she could tell Radcliffe that she knew of his affair. The counsellor would ensure that the affair did not skitter away. It was 'Guaranteed'! She went straight inside to make an appointment for the following Tuesday.

Relieved, having restored the graceful swish to her movements, she decided to hang some laundry. It was breezy and sunny, the chill almost gone. She leaned and pegged, leaned and pegged, then crossed to the other side of the line where yesterday's clothes were ready to be removed.

Grevilleas were blooming she noticed as she unpegged a pair of her own underpants, sunny and dry, cotton underpants, apricot in colour. Spring was certainly here. The return of the graceful, floating feeling meant that her hands did not quite grasp at things, so that the wind, when it breezed by, found it easy to take the underpants from her fingers and fling them through the air. Whoosh! Up into the sky! Whoosh! Over the fence and into the neighbour's yard.

She ran to the fence in time to see her underpants blow into the face of the Canadian next door. They flattened against his face, and then dwindled toward the ground. He was surprised, but caught them before they hit the grass. He had a peg out ready himself, she saw, and was hanging his own laundry.

Specifically, he appeared to be hanging out three pairs of women's underpants: tiny, multicoloured g-strings, like colourful lizards. He turned to face her, smiling, holding up her underwear.

'And you,' she called, apologetically, 'with all that pretty underwear!' Then she wondered at what she had just said.

But he laughed and clumped over his lawn, companionably, to the fence. 'Your panties?' he offered, graciously.

She took them from him, thinking that the word 'panties' was the most intimate thing she had ever heard. She, a writer of erotic fiction. 'Sorry to blow them in your face,' she said.

He gave a little chin-lift of laughter, and leaned against the fence, and they both turned back towards his clothes hoist, to stare at the line of frilly panties. Which was when Fancy saw it. A single purple sock, hanging from a peg at the edge of his line, flickering slightly in the wind.

'Excuse me,' she said, 'but may I see that sock?'

'Well, sure,' he agreed, and clumped back over to his clothesline. Good-naturedly, he unpegged the sock and brought it back.

Yes, it was the one. It was the pair. A purple sock stitched with a daisy.

'Where did you get this from?' she said, realising that her voice quivered melodramatically.

'That's a funny question.' He remained good-natured. 'I found it in the bottom of my washing machine today. Unexpected. It belonged to my ex-girlfriend. Ex-*ex*-girlfriend as a matter of fact. I guess she left some of her laundry behind, and this sock was maybe stuck in the bottom of my washing machine for a while. You know socks.'

'Well, the thing is,' said Fancy, 'the thing is that I found the pair to this sock in my bedroom a few weeks back.'

'Did you *really*?'

They both stood still for a moment, while the wind dabbed at their clothes and at their hair. They found themselves gazing at the cotton underpants in Fancy's left hand and the purple sock in her right.

'I guess,' said the Canadian reflectively, 'that Tammy's sock might've got blown over the fence one time, just like your panties did today. I guess I might have hung the one sock up to dry while the other one was stuck in the machine, and the line one got blown over the fence, and mixed up with your laundry.'

Fancy was doubtful. She was caught up in much more vibrant explanations: a threesome between Radcliffe, his Affair and this *Tammy*, for example. Or kinky Canadian climbs into her bedroom in the middle of the night, and hides his girlfriend's sock under her bed.

'I guess that could have happened,' she conceded eventually. 'I *do* sort my laundry in the bedroom sometimes, so I guess I might have sorted it there and the purple sock fell and got kicked under the bed.'

Then they stood still for a moment while the sun sat on their shoulders.

'Funny,' said the Canadian, 'me finding the sock in my washing machine like that, on the day your panties blow over the fence.'

'Shall I get the matching sock for you?' suggested Fancy. 'So you can send them back to – Tammy?'

'Ah, forget it,' he shrugged, endearingly. 'Tammy can live without her purple daisy socks, I guess. She didn't turn out all that nice. Now, *Gina . . .'* he continued, looking back at the underwear frill along his line. 'But she had to go back to Naples in a hurry. I'm sending on her valuables,' he added vaguely.

'Say out and about,' said Fancy, out of nowhere.

'Out and about,' he obliged, at once. But then, as he strolled back to his clothesline, he turned and called, 'Oot and aboot!' and rolled his eyes, in a friendly way.

There is no purple sock, thought Fancy as she smiled her thanks at the Canadian. There is no purple daisy sock belonging to a woman from the pay office at Radcliffe's work. Radcliffe's affair – she thought next, with a strange little thud, like a book falling off a bedside table – Radcliffe's affair is over.

My husband is not having an affair.

MARBIE ZING

The day after the picnic on the living room floor, Marbie hit snooze on her alarm clock, just as the telephone rang. It was the aeronautical engineer.

'Don't call me *at home*!' she hissed, pretending that Vernon and Listen were still there.

'If your boyfriend had answered I'd have just hung up. Okay? Just chill, okay? Can you talk?'

'No.'

'Well, can you listen for a moment? Marbie, you are a riot. What *was* that yesterday? Showing up at my place, telling me a story about spying on a 2nd grade teacher, and waltzing right out the front door? You didn't even touch my picnic! I thought to myself, who *was* that?'

'Well,' said Marbie, 'it was me.'

'Okay, whatever, I just want to say one thing. I want to say that you are gorgeous, and I want to say how happy I am about the decision that I made, way back when I first met you at the Night Owl Pub.'

'That's more than one thing. And you didn't meet me at the Night Owl Pub. You met me at work.'

'Huh. Yeah, I remember that too. Your paper aeroplanes! Wo ho! Dodgy! But what I'm talking about here is my *decision*. At the Night Owl Pub? When I saw you sitting there? All your pals were gone and my car had just got towed. So I asked you what the time was and "five o'clock" you said, in that voice of yours – and right away I made a decision. The best decision I ever made.'

'What decision?'

'The decision to get a taxi. I thought – like out of nowhere, like *shazam!* – I thought: *I'll get a taxi.* I was running late for a meeting, see, and I knew I'd miss the bus if I stayed. So I was about to say, "see ya", but then I thought: *shazam*, I thought: a *taxi*, that'll do the trick! And it was the best decision I ever made.'

'Okay. Well, that's great. I think I should hang up now.'

'Sure. That's all I wanted to say anyway. Just that.'

'Okay.'

'Oh, and Marbie, you've got to come by my place tonight and explain what you were going on about yesterday. You can't tell a spy story like that and just leave me hanging. You hear me?'

'I can't?'

'No.'

'Because I was thinking that I could. I was thinking you could forget I said a word, and get on with your life. Okay?'

'No, because I heard every word, and now I need an explanation or who knows *what* might happen? See you tonight. Another thing, if there's anybody there with you now, just say that this was a wrong number.'

'That's stupid.'

'Okay, gorgeous. Bye.'

Marbie hung up and clutched her pillow tightly to her chest. Quite simply, she did not know why she had slept with the A.E. in the first place, let alone told him the Secret. She looked around the room in confusion. The night before, she remembered, it had suddenly seemed clear that she must tell him, and that this would be the answer. But how could it have been? Here she was, Marbie Zing, embracing an irrational existence. She looked down at the pillow in her arms and thought: *my existence is a pillow.* She did not even know what she meant.

She threw the pillow away and dialled Vernon's number, but there was no answer. She left a message saying that she just wanted to wish Listen good luck again, for her first day at Redwood Primary, and also, if Listen needed anything, well, she, Marbie, was right here in the apartment, except when she was at work.

•

The Year 7 St Carmel students were marching down the path at Redwood Primary School. They had been welcomed at the Assembly Hall and now they had to go to the demountables, which would be their classrooms.

'In pairs!' shouted the teachers. 'March in pairs!'

But actually the teachers did not care if they walked in pairs or not, and Chloe, who was next to Listen, faded back from her to join the two behind. Listen had just said, 'How was your holiday?' but at exactly the same time someone had shouted, 'GIVE ME MY HAT', so Chloe had not heard.

There were Redwood Primary kids at the windows of classrooms, opening their mouths to stare. Listen tried to huddle with the pair in front, so the kids would not think she was alone, but she couldn't because they patterned out and took the whole path.

Two's company. Three's a crowd. She thought this sadly, and then there was a glint of sunlight on the buckle of her school bag and she thought it again: two's company, three's a crowd! Of course! Let's say somewhere in her form there was a group of three friends? Well, two's company, three's a crowd. So, they would need a fourth. She could be the fourth.

The teachers tried to teach like a normal day, but the girls mucked around like a vacation. It should be a vacation; it was the first day back and this was a primary school.

'That doesn't mean you have to *act* like primary schoolers,' the teachers said, over and over. When the bell rang for recess, it was not a high school electric bell, it was a strange, clanking primary bell.

On the muddy grass outside the demountable, Listen pulled her jumper sleeves over her hands and said, 'Hi, Kelly.'

Kelly Favoloro, who was walking past, looked surprised and said: 'Hi.'

Listen said fast, in a metal-flat voice, 'Can I hang out with you guys, maybe, just today?'

Kelly looked around for her two friends, Amber Tang and Sasha James, and all three raised their eyebrows.

Then Kelly said, 'Sure, yeah, okay.'

Quickly and politely, the other girls said it too: 'Sure, Listen, yeah!'

Listen said, in a serious voice, 'Just say no if you want.'

'Don't be stupid.' Kelly twirled Listen's ponytail around her hand. 'Why would we say no?'

•

She would have to go to the A.E.'s place to begin repairing her mistakes. Maybe she could shout 'April fool!' and pretend it had all been a trick? But it was not April, and when she arrived, she saw that it was too late to pretend.

His eyes, when he opened the door, had a glittery, greedy look.

So, sitting straight-backed in his lounge chair, she explained the Secret again, more succinctly this time, and with emphasis on confidentiality. She spoke in a soft, serious voice, in order to imply that reverence was the appropriate reaction, rather than feverish excitement. He assumed a grave expression. She concluded by explaining that the Secret was an honour which was rarely bestowed. He smiled and assured her he was worthy of this honour.

Then he served the lasagne and things began to go wrong.

•

In the caravan that night, Listen had a bumping heart of frightened happiness. This plan could work. She had sat with Kelly and the others at recess and lunchtime that day, and Kelly had admired her hair. It's so soft and shiny, Kelly said. Then she wanted to do it in a French braid. Also, Amber told a long story about how her father lost his job during the holidays but then talked his boss into giving him a *promotion* instead. Sasha didn't say much, but Listen thought she could ask her some questions about ballet. Sasha loved ballet so much that she carried her slippers around with her all the time, like a long, drooping bracelet.

•

Marbie had a mouthful of lasagne when she noticed that the A.E. was frowning. He was staring at his fork and there were at least thirteen different cracks and creases in his forehead. It was unnecessary, that many cracks and creases.

'So, basically, you spy on this woman without any kind of government authorisation, or permit, or, I don't know, police protection? Right?'

'Right. It's just us. But "spying" is the wrong –'

'And basically, this woman is not only a 2nd grade teacher, she's also a lawyer, you say?'

'Not a lawyer. She just studies law part-time.'

His frown was like a freshly broken mirror. 'Studying law part-time? I've got to say, Marbie, you're playing with fire there. What happens when she finds out? Don't think a lawyer's going to pull any punches, do you?'

'Who says she's going to find out?'

'Well,' said the A.E. with a maddening shrug. Then, as he reached for more lasagne, he said, 'Come to bed with me?'

'No,' replied Marbie, 'thanks all the same.'

•

The second day of term, Listen felt both frightened and safe. At recess and lunchtime she sat outside in the late winter sun and chatted with Kelly Favoloro while Amber and Sasha arm-wrestled. She passed around her bag of Valerio Honey-Mustard Chips, and everybody took one.

Then, the next morning, while the History teacher read to them from the textbook, Judith Sierra, who had braces and a ruler-straight fringe, turned around and whispered, 'Listen?'

'Yeah?' Listen whispered back.

'Who d'you hang around with?' Carefully, Judith regarded her.

'Kelly Favoloro and Sasha and Amber.'

Judith looked concerned. 'Um,' she whispered, ''cause they were talking to me before school, and they're really worried. They thought you only wanted to sit with them for one day – they didn't think you meant, like, forever?'

'It was just until today,' Listen explained. 'They don't need to worry, it was just until today, and that's it.'

Judith looked relieved. 'I'll let them know. They were really worried. See, Kelly likes you but Amber and Sasha aren't so sure, so Kelly felt guilty about saying you could join.'

'Okay,' said Listen. 'Thanks.' She smiled for reassurance and Judith smiled back.

•

Over the next few weeks Marbie's days fell into a pattern. She would arrive home from work, phone Vernon, get his answering machine, and go over to the A.E.'s place. The A.E. would ask difficult questions about the Secret, and try to persuade her to go to bed with him. The next day she would go to Fancy's place to find answers to the A.E.'s questions, so that, on the following day, she could go to the A.E.'s place again.

It was exhausting but she could not see how to stop. The A.E. had the Secret, and he kept setting little brush fires with it. She had to go over and put them out.

•

Mopping the shop floor in the Banana Bar one late afternoon, Listen discovered that her mind was humming: *two's company, three's a crowd! Two's company, three's a crowd!* – in a cheerful, mocking tune. *All right*, she thought, *so the plan didn't work. You don't have to sing about it.*

She looked at Vernon, who was counting money at the register, and thought, with a thud: *two's company, three's a crowd.* That's why Vernon and Marbie broke up! Because *I* made them into a crowd!

She mopped savagely for a few moments, tears in her eyes. Then she calmed down, because she knew what Vernon would say if she mentioned that to him. She knew she was being stupid. She wouldn't even waste Vernon's time by raising it.

But she would ask him something one more time. 'Vernon,' she said, and he looked up, mouthing *twenty-three* as he did. 'Vernon, what did you and Marbie fight about?'

'Ab–so–lute–ly nothing,' said Vernon with a smile, and returned to his counting.

She squeezed the mop into the bucket. It was too much of a coincidence: A Spell To Make Two Happy People Have A Huge Fight Over *Absolutely Nothing*. Even when she reminded herself that there was no such thing as magic, and also that, as far as she knew, the first two spells had not worked (a spell to make someone decide to take a taxi, a spell to make a vacuum cleaner break) – it was *still* too much of a coincidence.

The only hope was the promise on the back of the book: *This Book will make you Fly, will make you Strong, will make you Glad. What's more, this Book will Mend your Broken Heart.* As long as she finished *all* the spells, the book would somehow fix its own mistake.

She wondered if the next three spells would work – as far as she could figure out, they were all supposed to happen at the same time in a few weeks. A spell to make someone give someone a rose (maybe Vernon would give Marbie a rose?); a spell to make someone find something unexpected in a washing machine (hmm); and a spell to make someone eat a piece of chocolate cake (maybe Marbie would drop by the Banana Bar for cake?).

At least, if those spells worked, they wouldn't hurt a fly.

•

'Playing with fire,' A.E. said, wanting to talk about the Secret again. 'Crash down on you like a house of cards.'

'What do you mean, exactly?' Marbie was slicing up an onion. 'The house of cards will catch on fire? Or the house of cards will fall on our heads. Because guess what, a house of cards *would not hurt a fly.*'

A.E. sat on his kitchen bench, drumming his heels against the cupboards and watching as Marbie chopped the onion. The frown was in the centre of his forehead again.

'Ton of bricks then,' he adjusted. 'Crash down on you like a ton of bricks.' Then: 'Don't think a lawyer's going to pull any punches, do you?'

'What's the charge?' pounced Marbie. 'What charge?' She spoiled the effect by sneezing seven times.

'Hayfever?' said the aeronautical engineer.

'So?' said Marbie, spitefully.

'You've probably got a cold. Not hayfever at all. As for the charge,' he continued, 'ever heard of a particular little document known as the Convention for the Protection of Individuals with Regard to Automatic Processing of Personal Data? Hmm?'

'What in the world makes you think I'd have heard of such a thing!' cried Marbie with a flurry of onion skins.

The aeronautical engineer simply breathed.

'You made it up,' said Marbie.

He turned his palms upwards. 'Did I?'

•

There were disadvantages to being at Redwood Primary. For example, there were no laboratories or kitchen facilities, which meant that, in Science and Food Tech, they did nothing but theory for the term. A lot of the girls complained about this and the effect it might have on their futures. Also, although Redwood was only five minutes' drive from St Carmel's, some teachers could not make it there in time for a class. So they often had substitute teachers, and once, they even had a Redwood teacher step in at the last moment to take Commerce. His name was Mr Bel Castro. His own class, he said, were doing gym.

'Excuse me, sir,' said Donna Turnbull, pretending to be polite. 'Can I just check with you about something?'

'Of course,' said Mr Bel Castro, also polite.

'What *grade* do you teach normally?'

'Fifth grade,' he said.

'So,' Donna continued, slowly, 'don't take this the wrong way or anything, but could I just ask, have you ever had any, kind of like, *experience* with teaching high schoolers – I mean, students like us?'

Anxiously, she looked around the room as if concerned about the fate of her class. Beside her, Caro giggled.

'Teaching students like *you*?' said Mr Bel Castro, pausing as he picked up a marker. 'Well, I don't know about students like *you*. I did spend five years teaching Economics to Year 11 and 12 students at Riverview before I came to Redwood. So, I don't know, which would you say are more like *you* – my senior students from Riverview, or my 5th graders here?'

Everyone laughed and someone said, 'Haaa, Donna, he got you good.'

Then Mr Bel Castro wrote his name on the whiteboard and moved straight on to teaching. Afterwards everyone said he was better than their regular high school teacher. In fact, he seemed to have a whole lesson stored in his head, which he taught by asking questions.

'You've been doing advertising?' he began. 'Consumer awareness and so on? Well, who here thinks that the Valerio Empire is messing with our minds?'

Then he smiled when everyone said, '*Huh?*', and soon had them shouting out Valerio products from their homes and their days, including Valerio toys, pies, cars, computers, TV shows, and cleaning products. Then he waited while they began reciting Valerio jingles, and lines from the recent Nikolai Valerio biography, which had outsold the *Harry Potter* series in the first two weeks of its release.

'Okay, you've got Valerio jingles jumping around in your minds, and Valerio's book on your shelves. You've got Valerio films on your TV screens, and Valerio junk mail in your letterboxes. Who thinks the Valerio Empire might even be invading their privacy?'

This led to a discussion about whether you could invade somebody's privacy by getting products and words inside their mind. Also, whether it made a difference if people chose to buy the products and watch the movies. Kelly Favoloro pointed out that you sometimes *couldn't* choose because Valerio shows were the only things worth watching on TV. 'Good point,' said Mr Bel Castro.

Then Angela Saville said, 'But isn't it really the other way around, and *we* invade the Valerio family privacy?'

'Ah-hah!' said Mr Bel Castro. '*Interesting*! Well, let's see how much we know about the Valerio family. Who's in the family for a start?'

Of course, everyone knew the Valerio family: Nikolai, his wife Rebekka, and their three handsome, grown-up sons. Nikolai and Rebekka had now retired of course, and liked to play tennis and gin rummy in their South Dakota mansion. They had their own bowling alley! Nikolai had been a beautiful young motor mechanic, working in New York with a smear of motor oil on his nose, when he was discovered by a movie producer. His seven films were generally considered the best ever made. He became a sex symbol and an icon immediately after his first film. He designed a line of Valerio underwear, which was an instant smash. When he married Rebekka, a Romanian model, after his first film, women all over the world threw themselves off buildings. There was a famous wedding photo of Nikolai and Rebekka dancing their bridal waltz in a buttercup meadow, *in bare feet*. Bees buzzed close to their naked toes, but the pair, being blessed, were not stung.

Nikolai and Rebekka's three sons, although still very young, now ran the family empire. Each of the sons had been troubled by drugs and shoplifting in the past, but had recovered after treatment in a Swiss resort. The eldest was only twenty-one, but was always Bachelor of the Year.

'So,' said Mr Bel Castro. 'Do you think Rebekka can paint her toenails without somebody noticing? Can Nikolai buy a hamburger? Could any of the three Valerio sons take up guitar without *you* finding out?'

'Yeah, that's a true point,' said Donna, 'but I'd put up with being watched all the time if I had about one quarter of the money they've got.'

'It's because they're like the royal family of the world,' said Angela, 'because Nikolai made his seven movies in seven different countries so it's like he spread himself all over the world, like peanut butter, and now *everybody* loves him.'

'But not everybody loves peanut butter,' somebody pointed out, wisely.

Listen was quiet, thinking about how much work it was to hide from the eyes of the girls in her year, and the teachers. She had to hide because whenever they saw her, they saw this: a girl who had no friends. Once they had seen her in that way, they could never see her any other way. She couldn't change it. She couldn't make it stop.

'I don't think it's worth it,' she said, without even putting up her hand. 'You'd forget how to be yourself.'

'Yeah,' said Angela. 'But Nikolai *chose* to be a movie star.'

'That's just one choice,' said Listen. 'After that, the world decided he and Rebekka were *perfect* people, who couldn't even get stung by bees, and they wouldn't let them change. They were like a king and queen because that's what everybody wanted. Then they had three sons so that's a fairytale. So now they're a fairy story family, and there's nothing they can do to make it stop.'

Everyone was quiet and surprised. Listen Taylor rarely spoke in class.

'Huh,' said Mr Bel Castro, 'sorry, I don't know anybody's name – you are . . .?'

'Her name's Listen Taylor,' said Angela.

'Her name's not actually Listen,' said Donna.

'It's *Alissa*,' Caro added. 'She just *calls* herself Listen.'

Mr Bel Castro looked from Angela to Donna to Caro, and then back to Listen. 'She just calls herself Listen?' he said. 'I like that.' He smiled at Listen, and nodded as if to congratulate her.

•

One night, watching *Law & Order: Criminal Intent*, the aeronautical engineer laughed at something Marbie had just said, and murmured, 'Maribelle, *you* are a riot!'

'Who's Maribelle?' said Marbie from the floor, where she liked to watch TV.

He continued to watch the screen, leaning back on the couch. After a moment he said, 'Isn't Maribelle your name?'

'No, Maribelle is not my name.'

'Well, what else could Marbie be short for?'

'What else?! And you call yourself a visionary. It's short for Marbleweed.'

'Marbleweed!' He laughed so much that he had to mute the TV. 'Why would your name be Marbleweed?'

Marbie explained about her mother – how she had wanted to give them gifts with their names. She gave Fancy the gift of *imagination*, and Marbie the gift of good luck.

'Good luck!' cried the aeronautical engineer. 'With a name like *Marbleweed*?'

Marbie explained that 'marble' was, in fact, *excellent* luck, according to a book on witchcraft which her mother once owned. If marble grew like weeds, her mother thought, you'd end up with a surfeit of good luck.

'*And*,' Marbie added, 'it worked. I've had *excellent* luck all my life.' Then she frowned for a moment, considering this, and cleared her throat.

'Marbleweed,' he whispered, shaking his head at her. Then he giggled, and began singing the name, over and over, humorously.

A few days later, the aeronautical engineer fell asleep, lying flat along the couch, while Marbie watched a rerun of *Survivor All-Stars* from the floor. When it finished, she tried to wake him to tell him that the Convention for the Protection of Individuals with Regard to Automatic Processing of Personal Data did not apply to the Zing family. It was irrelevant.

And even if it technically applied, she thought, exasperated as she tried to formulate this thought, even then, what did the law or legal documents have to do with her family and its meetings in the shed? The Zing Family Secret was a family matter, far too complex, emotional, private, fragile and delicate for the application of *rules*.

'Hey,' she said. 'Hey. Wake up.'

He gasped in his sleep, and said: 'Huh? What? Huh?' in a mumble, and turned on his side. A cushion fell off the couch.

'Wake up.'

He executed a gigantic turn to face the other way. She found the whole display affected.

'Oh *forget* it,' said Marbie, and went home.

One night, after dinner at Fancy's place, Marbie asked her sister when Vernon would return. 'You said he'd come back,' she accused.

'Well,' said Fancy, cheerfully. 'Has he had an affair with someone else yet?'

Marbie gasped.

'Because,' Fancy explained, 'he's allowed to now. And I don't think he'll come back until he's had an affair of his own.'

'But I only slept with the A.E. once!' cried Marbie.

'And you're not seeing him anymore, are you?'

'No!' she lied.

'Still, that's just a technicality. As soon as you slept with your aeronautical engineer, you gave Vernon the right to sleep with someone else. It's a rule.'

Although Marbie begged Fancy to change her mind, she refused.

'He *has* to,' Fancy explained, gently. 'Otherwise it's not balanced. Didn't you realise?'

'I would die if Vernon even touched someone else.'

'You should have thought of that before.'

'Stop it, Fancy, it's not funny. I don't *want* him to have an affair. Come on, please?'

'It's not up to me. Revenge is his right.'

Oh God! thought Marbie, breathless with panic. Vernon's hands on another woman's hands, Vernon's thighs against another woman's thighs! Vernon playing the astronaut game and moon-walking across another woman's bed! Why had she not thought of this before?

If he had to get revenge – and Marbie supposed that he did, because Fancy was generally wise – if he had to get revenge, then couldn't the revenge be something else?

The next day, Marbie slept with the A.E. again.

For weeks he had seemed perfectly content to ask her, now and then, if she would like to 'give it a whirl again'. Each time he asked, she would pretend to consider it, politely, and then say, 'No. Thanks though.' But on this day she arrived to find him wearing nothing but boxer shorts and a bow tie. He was carrying a bottle of champagne.

'Marbie,' he said, as she walked in the door and raised her eyebrows at him, 'Marbie, this can *not* go on.'

'Can't it?' she said.

'No, my beautiful, it cannot. You *cannot* sleep with me once and then not again. You *cannot* use those pouting lips to tell me your delicious family scandal and then keep your lips away from mine. You *cannot* come over, night after night, with those sexy legs and that husky voice, and *not* sleep with me again.'

She gazed at him for a few moments. 'All right,' she said. 'But not on the living room floor.'

So they gave it a whirl in the bedroom.

On this occasion, it seemed to Marbie that the A.E. was determined to demonstrate his sexual prowess. His prowess consisted of masterful choreography – elegant traditional rhythm cut through with surprising bursts of activity. For example, he would suddenly spin her over, jump onto the floor and beckon her over to the wardrobe. *Oh well*, she would think, *I was happy where I was.* But she played along. He kept going for almost two hours, often pinning her hands at the wrists, or catching her eye so he could gaze at her ferociously.

She understood that he needed to show off like this. That first time, on the living room carpet, with the ice storm building outside, he had not been very coordinated. To be fair, she herself had lacked her usual dexterity, since the carpet had made her sneeze.

So, she decided, doubtfully, as the A.E. danced around her, *the reason I agreed to do this was to give us both a second chance.*

In any case, she added crossly, what was the point of coming to the A.E.'s place every second day, and listening to his criticisms of her name, her family, and the Secret, if she was not, at least, having sex? Especially now she knew Vernon had to have an affair.

For the next few days, Marbie stayed at home. She explained to the A.E. that she had to do 147 Business Activity Statements for the various Zing Family Secret corporations. (This happened to be true: she had an excellent mind for corporate structures and formalities.) She phoned Vernon and offered to do the Banana Bar BAS, as usual, but he said he had found an accountant.

The next time she saw the aeronautical engineer, it was in the Night Owl Pub, after her work friends had gone. He did not even sit down. He whispered in her ear, 'Have a drink on me to our second time,' and placed a schooner of beer in front of her. Then he took out a curl of paper, tied with a pink ribbon, and added, 'One of my new visions', before he slipped away. Marbie opened the vision and read it. It left her somewhat cold.

THE VISIONS OF AN AERONAUTICAL ENGINEER
VISION # 1562

Trapped within the cobwebs of my counter-intuitive chin,
I see this, I see this, I see this.
I see, with startled clarity, for just a whispered moment:
Bi-directional Evolutionary Structural Optimisation.

The following Thursday was a difficult day for Marbie. Things such as this kept happening: she made a call to get somebody's number, scribbled the number on a sticky note, and then lost the post-it note. She ordered a salad sandwich for lunch and when the girl behind the counter said, 'Salt and pepper?', she replied, 'Just pepper, please', and the girl gave a glazed and rueful nod, meaning, *that's what everybody says*. She bit the inside of her cheek, by accident, on the first bite of her sandwich, and then kept biting the same spot. Also, her nose and her eyes were itchy, and she was always on the verge of a sneeze.

She was almost relieved when the A.E. phoned in the afternoon and asked her to slip out of work to meet him at a nearby café.

In order to change the nature of the day, she ordered a piece of chocolate cake.

'Whoa,' said the aeronautical engineer, when the chocolate cake arrived. The waitress smiled, as if it were a compliment. 'You gonna eat all that by yourself?' He himself had only ordered an espresso.

'You can share it if you like,' said Marbie, politely.

'Heeeee-uge,' whistled the aeronautical engineer between his teeth, and then shook his head: 'No thanks.'

Marbie adjusted her chair slightly, and took up her spoon.

'It's not *that* big,' she said after a moment, at which he chuckled slightly and said, 'You'd better get stuck in. I mean, we don't have all *day* here; sure, if you wanted to share it with a starving nation, you might just —'

She touched his thigh lightly to make him stop.

'Ho ho!' he said, looking at her hand on his thigh with a grin. 'Ho *ho*!'

When she returned to work, the day continued exactly as before. Worse even: one of her toenails seemed to have developed a sharp edge and was cutting into the next toe along whenever she walked to the photocopier.

Later that night, she drove to the A.E.'s place, to watch TV.

'I'm hungry,' she said, during an ad break.

'After that piece of chocolate cake!'

'That was hours ago,' Marbie pointed out.

He raised his eyebrows. '*I'm* not hungry,' he declared.

'I assume you realise,' said Marbie, spitefully, 'that your not being hungry doesn't make you a better person than me?'

He chuckled and leaned back on the couch, stretching out an arm as if to do a reverse park. Marbie stood up. She stared at him.

He gave her a little *oops* grimace. 'What's up? Feeling fragile today?'

Formally, she announced: 'I'm leaving. Sorry, but we have to end it now.'

'Come on,' he smiled wryly. 'You're ending it because of a piece of chocolate cake?'

'Because of a piece of chocolate cake,' she agreed, and she gathered up her handbag and her shoes.

FANCY ZING

When Fancy Zing was eleven years old, her father went to Ireland for a year. The day that he was due to return she sat at the kitchen table to write him a poem:

> 'Today! Today! My Daddy's Coming Home!
> At last! At last! Fetch the Cheese and Honeycomb!'

The thick black lead of the HB pencil slipped when the table wobbled, and the 'Cheese' spilled its 's' across 'Coming'.

Fancy examined the table. It was cracked and scribbled with words such as 'MARBIE ZING' and 'COW!' She lay her hands flat and rocked the table to pinpoint the wobble, tore a corner from her poem-paper, and crouched next to the table leg. As she crouched, she stopped and swirled her skirt, making the skirt touch the floor in a parachute circle. It was a brand-new skirt, to Welcome Daddy Home.

Her mother had said, 'New jeans?'

And Fancy had said, 'I think I'd like a skirt.'

'A skirt!' cried Mummy. 'Aren't we growing up!'

Then she took most of the money from the St Vincent de Paul box on top of the fridge, took Fancy's little sister, Marbie, by the hand, and all three caught the bus to Castle Hill.

Fancy's mother bought herself a pale green scarf, which floated in the air when she tossed it about, making up her mind whether to buy it or not (and she leaned toward Fancy and explained, 'A little pink lipstick and a pale green scarf, and you'll find you win any man's heart!' 'Will you?' said Fancy, surprised.) They bought a purple T-shirt for Marbie, and for Fancy, they bought a skirt in the colours of a rainbow lorikeet.

Now Fancy stood up from the floor, graceful, a flamingo, and felt the skirt rest against her legs.

The wobble was gone when she sat back down, and she took up her pencil again. But here was the problem. She could not write the poem too fast because she had to be there, writing it, when her father arrived. She had to be sitting at the kitchen table, her pencil chatting poetry, frowning as she worked on the last few words.

He would walk through the door and say, 'Fancy! Hi! Doing your homework?'

And she would say, 'Writing a poem to welcome you home.'

She would stand up, and her lorikeet skirt would fall against her legs in a great spray of colour, and he would say, 'You're all grown up!'

And she would say, gracefully, 'Welcome home, Daddy.' And present him with the poem.

So she sat at the table and drew tiny flowers in the space between the lines of her poem. Then she wrote the heading: 'WELCOME DADDY' in bubble letters, and made a 3D effect by shading around the edges.

The telephone rang and Mummy shouted from the laundry, 'Get that would you, Fancy?' But Marbie came skidding through the back door, and grabbed it from just beneath her fingers. 'Hello?' she said.

Fancy whispered at her sternly: 'Good afternoon, Marbie Zing speaking.'

Marbie shivered her muddy face and turned towards the wall. 'Yes,' she said to the receiver. Then, 'Ye-e-e-e-s! Of course!' Then, 'Uh-huh, uh-huh. Okay. Bye.'

Fancy said, 'You're all muddy, Marbie. Who was that?'

'Nobody,' said Marbie, squirming past and running down the hallway.

'It can't have been nobody,' Fancy murmured to herself. She followed Marbie at a more stately pace.

'Who was it?' Mummy asked.

'Guess.'

Mummy stood up slowly from the laundry basket, carrying a pair of

Marbie's shorts. She put her hands in both shorts pockets, one at a time, and took out crumpled tissues and dirty handkerchiefs. 'Look at you, Marbie,' she said, shaking her head. 'Look at your lovely new T-shirt.'

Marbie looked down and said 'Oops!' to see the purple T-shirt splattered with mud specks.

'Oops is right, young lady.' Mummy took an apple core from Marbie's shorts pockets.

'Who was it?' Fancy demanded. 'On the phone?'

Marbie licked her fingers and began scraping at the drops of mud.

'Stop that,' said Mummy. 'You'll only make it worse. Here, take it off right away and I'll put it in with this lot. Marbie, who was on the phone, darling?'

Marbie lifted her T-shirt up over her face and from behind the purple she said, 'Daddy.'

'Daddy?' Fancy cried.

'Hang on,' said Mummy. She had noticed something deep in the washing machine, and leaned way into the machine. Marbie and Fancy waited. 'Huh,' she said, coming back out and holding up a sock. Then she tossed it into the basket and turned around to reach for Marbie's T-shirt.

'Yeah,' said Marbie, 'Daddy. And he says he's still at the airport now because the plane was late, and he said he'll come home soon, okay?'

'Right,' said Mummy, bending to the basket once again. 'We may as well get dinner started. No sense in us starving, is there?'

'I'll start dinner, Mummy,' offered Fancy.

The chicken and chips were sitting on the bench, wrapped in a great white bundle. Fancy took the silver tray with its burnt biscuit stains, and let the chicken and chips tumble from their paper onto the tray. Then she switched on the oven, and the timer, and placed the tray in the centre of the shelf.

Ceremoniously, she moved to the table, took her HB pencil, and crinkled her forehead at the poem.

MARBIE ZING

When Marbie Zing was five years old, her father went to Ireland for a year. Every night that he was gone, Marbie crept into the school yard next door and took midnight swims in the pool. During the days while he was gone, she put the hose on the trampoline so she could jump with the splashes of water. Also, she sailed paper boats in the kitchen sink.

The day that her father came home, Fancy wrote a poem, Mummy washed the curtains, and Marbie turned the hose onto the vegetable garden.

It was Marbie who answered the phone when he called from the airport.

'That's Marbie, isn't it?'

'Yes.'

'Do you remember your old dad?'

'*Ye-e-e-s! Of course!*'

They ate chicken and chips for dinner, and their mother said, 'Let's get this place looking *perfect* for your dad!'

Fancy threw away the chicken bones, and Marbie, accidentally, threw away Fancy's poem.

Mummy hung freshly washed curtains in the kitchen windows and stood back. 'Girls, what do you think!'

Fancy said, 'Beeeautiful.'

Marbie said that the curtains looked crinkly.

'Did anybody see my poem?' said Fancy, shifting magazines around.

Mummy took another step back and bumped into Fancy. 'Maybe you're right. I should iron them.'

'They look beautiful, Mummy,' Fancy said. 'Leave them. But I can't find my poem. Did anyone see my poem?'

'Only I don't know if I have time.' Mummy looked at the kitchen clock, the curtains, and the closed front door. 'Oh dear.'

'Maybe you should just throw the curtains away,' suggested Marbie.

'That's not the answer, precious one,' said Mummy, then: 'Fancy! What are you *doing*?'

Fancy had the kitchen garbage tipped upside down. She was sitting amongst chicken bones, tin cans, paper towels, tuna-fish, carrot peels and corn.

'My poem!' Fancy cried. 'I can't find my poem!'

'The floor!' Mummy cried.

Headlights flashed through the kitchen curtains and an engine grumbled in the drive.

'He's *here*!' Fancy shrieked, and Mummy and Marbie jumped.

'And I'm all ruined, and I can't find my poem, and –' Then she found her poem.

'My *poem*!' Now she was crying properly. 'It's *ruined*, it's got *chicken grease* all over it, and LOOK AT MY SKIRT.'

Which is why, when Daddy got back from Ireland, the first thing he looked at was Fancy's new skirt.

'That's tuna or something on your skirt there, isn't it, Fancy?'

Those were his first words. He was carrying a large brown suitcase, and his face, Marbie thought, was like a fat pink balloon. Fancy stood up in a tumble of rubbish, and ran from the room in a sob.

'I hope you're not hungry,' Mummy announced. 'We've eaten all the chicken and chips.'

'Have you got presents?' said Marbie.

'Of course I've got presents!' said Daddy. 'I'll put my suitcase away, and then we'll all go sit in the lounge.'

'Come on, Marbie.' Mummy began scraping rubbish back into the bin. 'Help me with this.'

In the lounge, Daddy gave them presents: boxes of Smarties and packets of chips. They waited hopefully, but that was it, so they began to eat the Smarties. Daddy looked around the room and began picking up objects and putting them back down.

'Just leave that one,' said Mummy suddenly, but Daddy had put down a photo frame and picked up a magazine. When he did, a dried flower fell onto the floor.

'Oh,' said Daddy, 'sorry', and he tried to pick up the pieces of the flower. 'Just leave it,' Mummy said.

Meanwhile, Fancy sat on the carpet in her dirty skirt and sniffed. 'I wrote you a poem,' she said eventually, 'but it got thrown away and now it's ruined.'

'Here, come sit on my lap,' Daddy suggested. 'You can write me another poem if you like!'

'But I can't . . .' Fancy burst into tears and nobody heard what she said next.

'We can't hear you,' Marbie explained. 'You have to stop crying.'

Fancy kept crying anyway, and Mummy said, 'Hush now,' and leaned forward to stroke her hair.

'I can't sit on your lap, Daddy.' This time they heard Fancy. 'My skirt's too dirty.'

'Rubbish!' cried Daddy.

'Yes,' Marbie explained, 'it's rubbish. All over her skirt.'

'Come along.' Daddy patted his knees. 'I think on this special day you can sit on my lap, no?' So Fancy did.

'Where did you go for a whole year, Daddy?' said Fancy, wiping away her tears.

'I went to some islands, Fancy, off the west coast of Ireland.'

'How many islands, Daddy?'

'Three.'

'What are they called?'

'Inishmore, Inishmaan and Inisheer.'

'What are they like? Are they nice?'

'The soil is almost paved with stones,' said Daddy, clearing his throat, and continuing: 'so that in some places nothing is to be seen but large stones with openings between them, where cattle break their legs. The only stone is limestone, and marble for tombstones. Among these stones is very good pasture, so that beef, veal and mutton are better and earlier in season here than elsewhere.'

'Interesting,' said Mummy.

'Yes,' agreed Daddy.

'What did you do on the islands, Daddy?'

'I wrote my novel, Fancy.'

'Can I see your novel, Daddy?'

'No. Once I had finished my novel, Fancy, I took the pages, one by one, made each into a paper boat, and sent them all to sea. Because, Fancy, my novel took me away from my family. So I washed it away in the waves.'

'Daddy!' whispered Fancy, then: 'Welcome home.' She cried again, and threw her arms around him.

'Little Fancy,' whispered Daddy, 'little Fancy.'

Marbie sat on the carpet, ate her Smarties, and blinked her eyes to make herself cry. 'What's the matter, Marbie?' said her mother. 'Don't tell me you're allergic to this carpet?'

THURSDAY NIGHT

Late Thursday night, Cath closed the door on Warren, and sat down on her couch to imagine.

She had driven straight home from the Staff Meeting that day, without touching the rose in her pigeonhole, and had waited, breathless, for Warren to arrive. When he did, she threw open the door and said, '*What's going on?*' Then she laughed at her own melodrama: he was sure to have an explanation.

It turned out he did not. The truth was set out in his solemn face: Breanna had a job at Redwood Primary, beginning Monday. In fact, he could not even stay tonight – he had to go home and get the house in order. Her furniture would arrive the next day. The affair was officially over.

'Why didn't you tell me before?' she said.

'I didn't know until today that it was definite.'

'But why did I have to hear it from *Billson*?'

'I tried to warn you. I left you a rose.'

'But why didn't you *tell* me?'

'I'm sorry,' said Warren. 'You're so completely right. But it was up in the air until this morning, and I just didn't want it to be true. Really. I left you a rose.'

'But at *our* school! Why didn't you stop it from happening?'

'I couldn't stop it – how would that have looked? When it came up a couple of weeks ago, I didn't think it was serious. I really didn't think it could happen.'

They spent the evening sitting on the couch, while Cath tried to cry. She found that she could not. There was nothing to cry about. Here he was beside her. The idea of his not being there was absurd.

'It's just that I think I love you,' she murmured, eventually, into his shoulder. Then she panicked: it was the first time this had been said between them. It was the first time she herself had ever said it first.

'I think I love you too,' he replied, and stroked the hair behind her ears.

'It feels impossible,' she said.

Warren agreed. His voice was sad, but practical. 'I can tell we'll be together one day,' he said. 'Some day, soon, it will all work out.'

'You're married,' she reminded him, but in a teary, smiling voice.

'Yes,' he replied, 'but it's coming apart at the seams.'

Then he left, pausing at the door. They stared at each other fiercely, and then laughed, and he placed his hand on her forehead as if checking for fever.

Cath returned to the couch to imagine the affair being over. To help her imagination along, she pictured a train screeching to a halt with a jolt and a *tick-tick-tick* into silence. (Then the sound of a window squeaking open and a passenger blustering: what *now*?) But, in her vision, the train slid back into motion almost at once. She could not imagine it simply standing still.

It would be *intellectually* interesting, she decided, but otherwise would probably not hurt. It was not as if he was leaving *her*, he just had to return temporarily to his wife.

She would miss spending nights with him, of course, and the sex. They had always agreed that contact would cease when Breanna moved to Sydney. Otherwise they would have to sneak around like people having an affair. And, although she would miss his body, this would be altogether different to broken hearts of her past. After all, she and Warren were in love. They had admitted it. Shortly, the marriage would unravel.

Warren would still be around. She would be able to see him, talk to him, tell him her secrets. 'It will be fine, won't it?' she confirmed with her cat, Violin.

•

Late Thursday night, Fancy stood at the long narrow window by her front door and gazed out across the dark lawn.

Radcliffe had driven to the corner shop to buy milk, and Cassie was asleep in bed. For the first time that day, Fancy had a moment to consider how she felt about the end of her husband's affair.

Instead, she thought about hotel foyers.

Ah, she thought, *hotel foyers!* The smooth integration of elevator doors, marble floors, and granite reception desk!

The concierge behind his helpful little glasses, which glint in the chandelier light. The glass shop fronts with their indoor plants and neat subtle lettering: *Armani, Gucci, Dolce & Gabbana.* The wine bar in curving stainless steel with dashes of electric blue (martini glasses!); and the bathrooms, especially the bathrooms! Their frosted glass and their clever taps, towels folded into neat white piles, dried flowers and sensors! Everywhere the sensors! Hand driers, toilet flushers, doorways!

As generally happened when she thought of hotel foyers, Fancy's breathing slowed. She calmed enough to return to her own front hallway. *Your husband is NOT having an affair*, she reminded herself. But watching the front lawn, and hearing the occasional gear change of passing cars, she felt herself jolted back to the imaginary foyer.

Immediately, she ran into a man in a pale grey T-shirt. This had never happened in her hotel before.

She thought she might kiss him deeply. No! She would lean in to kiss him and he would turn away! She saw him, the man (not quite his face, more his T-shirt), and she longed for his touch; please, put your hand on my wrist! But he refused.

Jolted again, she was back in her home. She shrugged deeply, feeling the spasm of the stranger's non-touch by touching her own arms with her fingertips.

Was that him now? Had he followed her out of her dream? That was a car!

She peered beyond her reflection into the night. A car *was* pulling in to the driveway. There was a succinct click as the headlights turned off. The engine was quieting. It *was* him! The man from the hotel foyer! It was *his* strong hands unbuckling the seatbelt, his thumb on the button of his keys: *Bip-Bip!*

His shoes were on the gravel – a quiet crunching, a few running steps up the stairway – and now he would knock! 'That was you in the hotel foyer,' he would accuse, enigmatically.

'Won't you come in for a drink?' she would reply, breathless, and –

Fancy jumped as keys rapped on the window.

'Fancy that!' cried a voice. 'My Fancy is at home!'

Radcliffe leaned around the door with a grin, holding up a carton of milk.

•

Late Thursday night, Marbie drove home from the A.E.'s house, relieved she had finally ended the affair.

She walked down the hallway of the empty apartment, switching on lights and checking behind doors for intruders. Then she sat down on a beanbag in the living room to think.

The A.E. was not attractive, kind, intelligent, poetic or interesting. In fact, he was mostly annoying. Despite that, she had slept with him twice, told him the Secret, and spent several nights in his home. All the time, she had been conscious of a mild yet persistent voice asking, *Excuse me, but where is your mind?* She had treated the voice in the same way you might treat a person asking, *What's that burning smell?* You might look vaguely towards the kitchen and then turn back to the TV.

Now she would suffer the consequences. She would wake each morning, conscious of the fact that she had failed to pay attention while her house burned down.

9

THE HOT AIR BALLOON

Once upon a time there was a man named *Monsieur Blanchard*, who fell in love with hot air balloons. By lucky chance, he also fell in love with a woman (*Madame Blanchard*), who herself was enamoured of balloons. Together, they cast their ballooning spells, performing sky shows all over France.

Madame Blanchard was a sensitive soul who could not stand the clamour of noise. Often, of an evening, she took her balloon into the sky, and remained there, with the moon, until dawn.

Sadly, Madame Blanchard died in a balloon crash. It was during a fireworks display over the Tivoli Gardens in Paris. From the basket of her balloon, Madame Blanchard sent gold! and silver! in cascading stars to the delight of the crowd below, and then she sent a great burst of fire. The crowd cheered happily, not understanding that this burst of fire was an error, and signified disaster: in fact, the balloon was on fire.

She crashed onto the roof of a house in the rue de Provence, and broke her neck.

•

Maude Sausalito, now older, and married (and in fact not Maude *Sausalito* anymore), wore her hair long and flat like a shawl. She was telling her husband about the Blanchards, the legends of ballooning, while he polished his shoes. She herself was icing cupcakes on the one clear corner of the kitchen table; he had spread newspaper across the remainder and was nodding as he dipped a brush in polish. He had just been promoted to Assistant Manager at the menswear store where he worked, which is why shiny shoes were important.

When Maude told how Madame Blanchard took to the sky of a night, her husband, David, chuckled to himself, and said, 'Not a bad idea!'

They both glanced down at their first child, Fancy, who was sleeping in the bassinet. Lately, she had been teething, so that their nights had become precarious affairs: they did not sleep so much as teeter in suspense. The baby's cries were so sharp they both felt the cut of the tooth.

Maude and David had married two years before, and honeymooned in the Hunter Valley. Maude had secretly arranged a dawn balloon ride for the second day of the honeymoon, but, during the wedding reception, David's brother made several jokes about his vertigo.

'What's vertigo?' Maude whispered.

'A fear of heights,' David whispered back.

He had never told her! Secretly, she cancelled the balloon ride.

They never mentioned his vertigo, but both acknowledged it silently – for example, when Maude's kite got caught on the chimney, she herself climbed up to retrieve it while David watched, trembling and pale.

Generally, David was happy to hear her balloon stories, but when Maude finished the story of the Blanchards, he said sternly, 'She died in a balloon crash? That's not a nice story, Maude. Why tell me that story?'

'Okay, here's a nicer story,' said Maude at once. 'About *Monsieur* Blanchard. The husband. About how he crossed the English channel in a balloon! Just bounce the bassinet a bit with your foot, would you? We'll kid her to go back to sleep.'

As she told the story of Monsieur Blanchard, Maude daydreamed about the journey they would take in a hot air balloon, once David was cured of his vertigo. (If she told enough balloon stories, then surely . . .?)

The pilot would have long curling hair, almost to his shoulders. In the creaking basket of the balloon, one night, he would point out a powerful owl. 'Is that actually a bird?' David would say. 'Isn't it just a bit of dust?' But the pilot, his muscular arm reaching up to tug a rope, checking the wind with a private little nod, would steer them closer to the dust, which would turn into a powerful owl. He would glance at her reaction, shy for a moment, but then he would grin, mischievously, and turn to the care of his balloon.

Blushing, she would look down at the slice of lime, perched on the side of her martini.

10

CATH MURPHY

The following week, Cath found out how it felt, the end of her affair.

It felt: suspenseful, frightening, surprising, confusing, obvious, outrageous and eventually like despair. These emotions arrived individually or in clusters, and sometimes one would brush the surface for a moment before eliding into another. On the first day, Monday, the primary emotions were SUSPENSE and FEAR.

Three significant events took place that day:

1. seeing Breanna for the first time;
2. being introduced to Breanna; and
3. having coffee with Breanna.

At Monday Assembly, she sat in her usual place, mistaking the suspense and fear for an exciting arriving-at-the-theatre sort of feeling. Warren ran in late, as usual, and sat beside her, with a friendly yet restrained 'hey, hey'. His face was grim and grey, and her excitement increased. She ignored Billson's introductory remarks, but then tuned back in when she realised he was no longer talking but was breathing, unpleasantly, into the microphone.

'I'm *waiting*,' he said, holding up his left thumb and then his pointer. He was going to count ten fingers, while the children whispered and giggled. 'All right,' he said, growing bored with the game. 'Let's show our newcomer how well behaved we are at Redwood! A round of applause to welcome our new school counsellor, Breanna Woodford!'

And there at last was Warren's wife. She was moving forward to the front of the stage, and she was, on first impression, cheerful and breezy – but then, Cath realised, she also looked extremely nervous about being on a stage. This gave Cath the strangest stab, and she had to look away.

After the assembly, on her way across the playground to her class-room, Cath felt terrified as Billson approached, beckoning Breanna to follow him. Breanna would surely see the truth in her eyes! Or hear it in her voice? Or sense it in the way she held her shoulders?

'Oh, *you're* Cath Murphy,' said Breanna, friendly. 'I've heard so much about you!' She swung her right arm forward, as if to shake hands, but instead clapped her own hands together, as if she were very excited.

Recklessly, Cath said, 'I've heard a lot about you too!'

'I was really looking forward to meeting you at the Carotid Sticks?' said Breanna. 'Remember? It was such a shame I couldn't make it down in time.'

'I know!' exclaimed Cath, but Billson was bored by their chatter and wanted to whisk Breanna away to meet somebody else.

'Do you want to have coffee after school today?' Breanna called, over her shoulder, to which Cath replied: 'That's a great idea!'

Watching Breanna hurry away, Cath felt another strange stab. 'I know!' she had said about the night when they almost met. And 'that's a great idea!' about coffee. It was all so cheap and deceptive.

At coffee, Breanna chose a couch instead of a hard-backed chair, and slumped in it, as if determined to relax. They were in the shopping mall across the road from the school, with a view over the highway.

'I'm so relieved to get this job,' said Breanna, stirring her coffee. 'I didn't know how much longer I could stand being away from Warren for the weekdays. Do you know what I mean? I don't know if it's good for a marriage, for a start.'

Cath breathed in for a moment, her mind looping backwards on itself as she tried to figure out a response. *What would I say, in this situa-tion, if this situation were what it's meant to be?*

'Mmm,' she said, and then tried to change the subject. 'So, you've worked with kids before, have you?'

'A few years ago,' said Breanna. 'And actually mostly with teenagers, but my thesis was on nine- to twelve-year-olds.'

Cath prolonged this for as long as she could, asking after Breanna's thesis topic, where she went to university, who her favourite teachers were, whether she took good notes. She enjoyed the conversation. She almost forgot who Breanna was, but the FEAR and SUSPENSE always buzzed just below the surface.

'Anyway,' said Breanna, 'Warren tells me —'

'Oh, hang on!' panicked Cath. 'Have you heard there are some Year 7 girls from a local high school at our school? Because their classrooms got flooded? Do you think you'll be *their* counsellor too?'

Breanna knew about the Year 7s but she didn't know if they were part of her job description. They probably had high school counsellors of their own.

'The thing is,' said Cath, 'I've been watching one of these girls, because she's somehow related to a girl in my class. And every time I see her she's alone. I think she might not have any friends.'

'Well,' said Breanna, 'I don't see why I shouldn't try to help. Do you know her name?'

Oh God, thought Cath, *there is nothing to dislike. She is kind and obliging, she has pretty eyes and nervous hands, and there is nothing, nothing, nothing to dislike.*

But then Breanna took the subject back to Warren. 'Warren's as excited as I am about me moving down to Sydney,' she said. 'He's like a little boy. You know what? He even secretly went and bought a new bed to welcome me! And he surprised me with it! A four-poster. He put a sign on it saying "WELCOME HOME". Isn't he gorgeous?'

After these three distinct events, the week fell into a haze, and Cath walked around a step or two behind herself.

On two separate occasions, she saw Warren take Breanna's hand, and together they ran across the road. Once, she saw Warren beckon Breanna across the playground, and then tip up a small bag of chocolate sultanas, filling Breanna's palm. She also saw Warren demonstrating the staffroom coffee machine. Breanna stood beside him, concentrating so hard that he laughed and told her this was not life or death. Breanna also laughed, embarrassed, and shook her shoulders to loosen herself up.

Meanwhile, the other teachers stopped talking about 'Warren' and started talking about 'Warren-and-Breanna'. They kept telling Cath what a nice person Breanna seemed to be, and how fun it was to meet Warren's 'other half'.

Cath began to feel that the ground was shifting slightly, and that the sky was not quite fixed to the earth. *Now then*, she thought, trying to stay calm, *who am I? Where do I belong? Who are my friends again?*

She thought of her three best friends from high school, who, oddly enough, had all ended up moving to remote, exotic locations: Lucy to Nepal, Kristin to Mongolia, and Sarah to the Sahara. She decided to write a long e-mail to the three of them, telling the story with the subject header: 'HELP!' But Lucy, Kristin and Sarah rarely got access to the Internet, so she did not expect an answer for a month.

An image kept recurring in her mind, of a man on a TV cooking show, sharpening a pair of knives. The screen was filled with a flurry of glints and clashes. At night, she did not go to bed. Instead, she sat up on her couch watching TV until she fell asleep.

She tried to study her law notes, but could not concentrate. For example, when she read the chapter on *Larceny*, she decided to steal Warren from his wife:

> 'A asked B to lend him a shilling (she read). B agreed and handed A a coin. Both thought it to be a shilling, but later it emerged to be a sovereign. A kept the sovereign.'

Ah-hah! (She looked up from her book.) She would ask Breanna for a loan of a *sovereign*, and by mistake, Breanna would hand over *Warren*. Cath would carry him away on a white horse, wicked laughter echoing; too late Breanna would discover her mistake!

There was one day during that week – possibly Wednesday – which she thought of as the Day of Letters. The first letter was handed to her in the playground before school had begun. Cassie Zing, sprinting past,

suddenly skidded to a stop and said, 'I forgot to give you Mum's note!'
She took an envelope out of her pocket and handed it over.

Dear Ms Murphy,

*Just a note to let you know how very much I am looking forward to
meeting you at the Parent-Teacher Night this Friday.*

> *Very best wishes and kind regards,*
> *Fancy Zing*

Cath looked up in surprise. This note was so warm and unnecessary!
Such a kind, pointless thought from a stranger! She felt suffused with
comfort – *all would be well.* But then she saw Breanna smiling at her and
she had to crunch the letter in the palm of her hand. *You do not deserve
such kindness*, she thought.

This was confirmed when she checked her e-mail and received a
reply from Kristin in Mongolia: 'CATH!! YOU POOR BABY.
DON'T FEEL GUILTY. THIS IS NOT YOUR FAULT. IT WAS HIS
CHOICE. IT'S ALL HIS FAULT. WILL SEND LONGER EMAIL
SOON. AM RUNNING OUT OF MONEY!!!!!!'

But it *is* my fault, she said to the computer screen. She had never tried
to stop him. He had asked her to be strong.

Then, in her staffroom pigeonhole, she found a large pink envelope,
addressed in swirling purple. At first she felt excited, but then she
opened it and read:

Dear Ms Murphy,

I know something about you.
> *Something secret and unforgivable.*
> *Meet me Friday, 1 pm, at the Valerio Couch Potato Café across
the road from your school.*

> *A Stranger*

So it was true. She was evil and she could not be forgiven. She felt
a crawling of self-loathing down her spine.

Then she read the note again and panicked: what was this letter about? *Was it suggesting blackmail?* She and Warren had been so convinced that nobody knew! They had even been proud of their subterfuge! How had they been caught out?

It must be someone from the school. Who else could possibly know? She hunched over her pigeonhole, examining the letter, and then glanced furtively around the room: Heather Waratah was eating a blueberry muffin. Jo Bel Castro was reading the paper. They both looked innocent.

She thought she should search for Warren, and show him the letter, but decided against it. The only thing that she and Warren had left now was their secret. Also, it would be unbearable to see him panic about Breanna finding out. She, Cath, would deal with the blackmail on her own.

That night, Cath arrived home and found a fourth letter in her mailbox. This one was from her landlord, and said that the landlord had purchased the two apartments adjoining Cath's. He intended to knock down the walls between all three, creating one grand apartment. Naturally, Cath would be welcome to continue living in the grand apartment, which would, incidentally, include a sewing room and a sauna. The letter continued:

> *Of course, renovation can be noisy and inconvenient! We therefore offer you free accommodation in a penthouse suite at the Winston Hills Tudor Arms for the duration.*
>
> *Rest assured that, despite the additional comfort which we endeavour to provide with these alterations, your rent will remain as it is for the remainder of your lease.*

Cath read the letter over. A sewing room! A sauna! What would she do with such things?

But it was exciting, and she reached for the phone to call Warren. Of course, she remembered, she could not.

It occurred to her that this was a common feature of break-ups – the not being allowed. When boyfriends had broken her heart in the past, she recalled, the worst of it, when she saw them again, was not being allowed to touch. Not being allowed to smooth their eyebrows, or take their hand at the traffic lights, or touch the end of their nose. Not being allowed to phone up and say, straight off: 'Well! You're not going to *believe* what's happened!' Instead, you had to explain yourself. You had to say, 'Hello, this is Cath, how are you?' And that was assuming you were allowed to phone at all.

Of course, all along she had been denied the right to hold Warren's hand in public – but now she was not allowed to see him on weeknights and she was forbidden to phone.

She re-read the letter, to comfort herself – *at least her landlord seemed fond of her* – and noticed, as she did, a pale little footer in the bottom right corner of the page. 'Project 78', said the footer.

Project 78. Now what did *that* remind her of?

She ran into the kitchen, opened a few drawers, leafed through recipe books, and found it: a letter she had received a few months before, offering a free course in Healthy & Delicious Cooking for the Young and Young At Heart. (She had not taken the offer, but had abandoned it in her recipe drawer.)

And there it was – a pale little footer in the bottom right corner of the page. 'Project 75', it said.

She had a strange, scary feeling for a moment – *how was her landlord connected with a local cooking school?* – but then she smiled: what a coincidence!

The coincidence comforted her. It suggested a world in which everything was connected by faint dotted lines. There was a grand scheme to things, a gentle, controlling destiny. Life was a series of projects – project 75, cooking; project 78, renovations.

She returned to the dining room table and re-read the letter about the proposed renovations. She traced the letters of *Project 78*: things that were meant to be would happen. Some day, somehow, it would all work out.

She almost reached for the phone again, to call Warren and let him know.

After the Day of Letters, Cath found that her week was clenching into RAGE.

'What's going on?' she said to Warren in his empty classroom, at the beginning of recess. He was tacking paintings on the wall, ready for parent-teacher night the next day.

'I think,' said Warren, 'I think it won't be too much longer. Things are just falling apart. Bree and I are both sensing something's wrong.'

'Mmm,' said Cath. Then, as he continued tacking paintings to the wall, she said: 'If it's falling apart, why did you buy a new bed? And put a sign on it saying: Welcome Home Breanna.'

'She told you that?'

'Uh-huh.'

Warren was silent now, gazing at the thumbtack which was lying on its side in his palm.

At lunchtime that day, Breanna found Cath in the staffroom, sat down beside her and said briskly, 'I just wanted to let you know that I spoke to that Year 7 girl, the one named Listen Taylor? The one you were worried about? I spoke to her yesterday.'

'Wow,' said Cath. 'That was quick.'

Breanna looked pleased, so Cath continued to praise her: 'Seriously, thanks so much for doing that. That was really nice of you. And you are so efficient!'

'Anyway,' said Breanna, opening up a packed lunch, 'I think you were right. She seems unhappy to me – not that she would admit she didn't have any friends. Her big brother brought her up, you know – apparently her parents died when she was a baby. Poor kid.'

Then Breanna gasped slightly and said, in a low voice, 'Oh, Cath, I'm so sorry. Exactly the same thing happened to you, didn't it? Your parents died when you were a baby, too, didn't they? In a house fire?'

'Yes,' said Cath, frowning slightly, and trying to turn the frown into a smile. 'But I wasn't raised by a brother – I was adopted.'

'And the only thing you've got left of your real parents is a faded photograph? Is that right?'

'Mmm,' said Cath. Then she remembered that she should be back in her classroom preparing for the parent-teacher night.

When Warren saw Cath at the doorway to his classroom, he said, 'You okay?'

'Sure,' said Cath, with a *snap* like a ring-binder. 'You told her I was adopted. You told her about the photo of my parents.'

'I'm sorry, Cath. I didn't know it was a secret.'

'You didn't know it was a secret? I told you at three o'clock in the morning. I got out the photo of my parents from a locked jewellery box. We *both cried*. And that didn't seem like, I don't know, a *confidence*?'

'Cath, all I can do is say I'm sorry.'

'Stop saying my name,' snapped Cath. 'You both keep saying my name. You and your *wife*, she does it too.'

Warren looked surprised, and Cath said, 'You can't *do* this' – her voice became trembly – 'you can't have an affair with me, and then go back to your wife, you can't say that it's coming apart at the seams and then buy a four-poster bed. It's not *allowed*.' She reached towards him, and he took one step back.

'I'm sorry, okay? I can't do anything about it now – it would kill Breanna. I know this sounds arrogant but the fact is she's really in love with me.'

'Oh cut it out,' said Cath. 'She's not in love with you. She doesn't even *know* you.'

'Well,' he said gently, 'we've been married for three years.'

'She doesn't know you,' Cath repeated. 'You're a man who cheated on his wife. She doesn't know that, so she doesn't know you.'

He bowed his head while Cath's shaky breathing filled the room.

'I can't leave her,' he whispered, after a moment.

'I'm *not asking you to leave her*,' she almost shouted. 'I *like* her, she's *nice*. I *don't want you to leave her*. You said it was *falling apart*.'

'It is,' he said. 'I swear, we just have to wait.'

'Well, while we're *waiting*, do you have to keep *touching* her? Do you have to keep holding her hand? I saw you *massaging* her *feet*. Have you *thought* about how *that* makes me feel?'

'Please don't cry,' he said.

'This doesn't make me cry!' Haughtily, she stalked out of the room.

That afternoon, she tried to study Criminal Law but decided, instead, to murder Warren Woodford. She would smother him with cross-stitched bookmarks, or watch, with a smirk, as he drowned in the syrup of his words. She chose her defence in advance: Provocation

(Chapter 5). The accused, transported by passion, was simply not mistress of herself.

Later that night, sleeping on the couch, she dreamt that Warren told her he was in love with Breanna again. 'It's over between you and me!' he confided, warmly, happily. 'I'm in love with my wife again!'

She shouted at him and punched his chest: 'You are *not* in love with your wife! You're in love with me! Warren, don't you understand? It's not real! You *think* you're in love with your wife, because she's so *happy* and so *bright* and so *nervous* and so *sweet*, whereas me? Look at me! I'm so *cold* and so *angry* and so *bitter* and so *sad*, but I'm *not*, Warren, if you'd just come back to me, *I* would be the happy person that you want, if you'd just, if you'd just, I'm *not* this brittle, this – Warren, this *does not count.*'

On and on she argued in the dream: passionate, ferocious, eloquent, ingenious. Her arguments sliced the air like glinting knives. But still he smiled his contented smile and shook his head.

By Friday, she had settled into DESPAIR.

Watching through her classroom window in the morning, she saw Warren and Breanna walking from the car park. *I hate you*, she thought. He was facing away from her. *Look at me*, she thought, *turn around*.

But he reached his hand back like a beckon, and Breanna hurried forward like a reply.

I love you, Cath thought, plaintively. He was swinging Breanna's hand.

At lunchtime that day, Cath sat calmly in the Valerio Couch Potato Café and waited for her blackmailer. She took one sip of coffee and slammed it down on the table, thinking: *I hate these Chain Store Coffee Shops! Why couldn't the blackmailer have met me in a REAL café?* But really she was thinking: how dare Warren tell his wife my secrets!

She remembered the night she told him she was adopted. He had played soccer that afternoon, and had come straight to her place from the game, his skinny legs streaked with mud, and socks pulled lumpy over shin guards. He carried two cold beers, opened one while he talked and handed it to Cath, opened the other for himself, and sat down on the couch. Then he stood to explain how a tackle went wrong and his knee twisted around during the game.

'You see?' he said, pressing his muddy knee against her knee, to demonstrate. 'You see what went wrong?'

They had made pasta together, and he had chipped his tooth on an olive. She had shown him the photo of her real parents later that night. He had run his finger gently over the outline of her parents, and that of the brave burly fireman, and tears had formed in his eyes.

Cath's eyes blurred as she looked at her watch. It was two o'clock and the blackmailer was nowhere to be seen.

Later, while her class was doing Music, she tried to read her lecture notes from Principles of Statutory Interpretation.

'*Ejusdem generis* (she read), "of the same type",' and then she had written, cryptically: 'is a crowbar the same as a mask, disguise or letter?'

Her notes did not explain themselves. Instead, they descended into pictures. She had drawn an elegant mask; a swooping cape; a letter sealed with wax; and a crowbar. Her crowbar was set aside slightly from the other more romantic objects.

It is a crowbar, thought Cath, sadly: it will never belong to the same club as a mask, a disguise, or a letter sealed with wax. All this time she had believed that her affair was something wonderful and clandestine: a detective novel, a cloak-and-dagger mystery. But an affair, she realised now, is as blunt and as common as a crowbar.

That afternoon, she sat in the staffroom correcting school work, waiting for parent-teacher night to begin. Just along the table, Warren and Breanna leafed through Ikea brochures, and giggled at furniture pictures.

'No,' murmured Breanna. 'No, you can't have chrome in the living room – we've got a pine coffee table, remember?'

'You're right,' agreed Warren. 'I just really like the look of those shelves.'

'Tell you what,' suggested Breanna. 'What about the study?'

'Or too big?'

'No! Look. Here's the measurements. See the scale?'

'EXCELLENT WORK' Cath wrote in an exercise book. 'WELL DONE!' and she made a monster tick across the page.

'Hey, Cath,' said Warren, turning in his seat beside Breanna. 'We should be getting over there now, shouldn't we?'

Cath agreed – it was almost five, and the parents would soon begin arriving.

Breanna said, 'Oh, Cath, before you go – I wanted to tell you something. I was showing a new Year 7 girl around the school this afternoon, and anyway, I introduced her to your Listen Taylor. You never know. Maybe they'll be friends?'

'Huh,' said Cath, 'that's great, Breanna. Thanks.'

'See you at home, okay, Warren?' Breanna was picking up her bag. 'I'll stop by the hardware store and surprise you with curtain rings!'

The 2nd grade interviews were held in Cath's classroom: Room 2B. Warren set up a table at the back of the room, and Cath used her own desk.

The first parent to arrive was a man who introduced himself as Radcliffe. 'I'm Cassie Zing's dad!' he said, before he had even entered the classroom. He was wiping his feet on the doormat. 'Call me Radcliffe. And you must be Ms Murphy.'

'That's right,' agreed Cath, and looked around Radcliffe. 'Your wife?' she said. 'She's not coming? She writes a lot of notes . . .'

'*Does* she?' cried Radcliffe, pausing, and placing his hands on his hips. Then he grinned and walked into the room. He stood still before Cath and continued to grin, shaking his head slowly. Then he remembered himself: 'Ah yes, Fancy, my wife. Well, something's come up, I'm afraid, and poor old Fancy couldn't come. Cassie got – well, we had a little incident with Cassie, but she'll be fine. Fancy took her to the doctor.'

His words seemed blustery, overexcited, and they hurried in a stop-start shuffle. He picked up a chair, spun it around, and sat down with his arms around the chair back.

'Well,' said Cath, straightening her voice. 'Thank you so much for coming in then, Mr – ah, Radcliffe. We all adore Cassie – she has a great deal of character. In reading, she –' But she stopped, as the man was gazing at her face, and rocking slightly on the chair.

'So you're Cassie's teacher then?' he said abruptly, as if she had not just spoken. '*Cath Murphy*, eh? Wonderful to meet you.' He reached out as if to shake her hand, but she was too surprised to offer her own. 'Not giving you any trouble, I hope?' he tried, settling back into his happy rocking motion.

'Trouble,' repeated Cath, with an effort. 'Well, no, not really.'

'Not really!' He beamed at this.

'I just worry a little,' Cath explained. 'She seems, sometimes, to be – angry at the world? And she uses – inappropriate words. She *chants* inappropriate words.'

'Oh that *game* of hers,' agreed Radcliffe. 'I know! Where she chooses a word and then repeats it? My wife and I don't have a clue what to do about that.'

'I've tried several different strategies to deal with it,' said Cath – someone had to be the professional here – 'but nothing has worked so far. Also, I've done a bit of reading, and I found that children sometimes develop a sort of obsession with things that seem *forbidden*, if they are excluded from – if there is – sorry, I don't mean that this applies to *your* family – but, this sometimes happens if there is some forbidden, shadowy region of family knowledge?'

Radcliffe continued to gaze at her.

'Anyway,' she added, embarrassed, 'they're the words that were used in the article I was reading and I like them – the words – the forbidden, shadowy –'

'Is that right?' Radcliffe interrupted, his voice fascinated. 'You're saying that kids pick up on family secrets and get – what was your word? Obsessed with things that are forbidden? Is that the case?'

'Of course,' blustered Cath, 'I don't mean that *your* family has a secret, I just wondered if . . .' She tried to change the subject. 'I was pleased when Cassie offered to write a class play for us. Her writing skills are really coming along. Although she doesn't seem to have started the play yet . . .'

But the man was simply staring at her. She looked down, searching for other topics, but when she looked back up, he was standing, as if it was all decided. Or as if he was too excited to keep still. *Good heavens*, thought Cath, and also stood up.

'Look,' said Radcliffe, reaching into his pocket. 'Here's my business card. Any time you need to talk about our little Cass, give me a call at work. My advice is to leave my wife well out of it. She's under a lot of stress at the moment – so best, by far the best, if you call me. All right?' He pressed the card into her hand. 'Just *wonderful* to meet you!'

And then he was outside the classroom door, but facing inward and wiping his feet on the mat, confused. 'Ha ha,' he said, pointing down. Then he spun around, waving, calling, 'Looks like rain!', as he headed out into the night.

'Good grief,' murmured Cath, and glanced to the back of the classroom.

Warren did not have a parent with him yet, and had been bowing his head, listening to the interview. He grinned now, opening his eyes wide, and she opened her eyes wide in return. Then he pulled one of those faces of his, one side of the mouth down, the other side up.

Oh God, thought Cath, laughing. *I am still in love. He is still in love with me.* Then a gathering of parents arrived.

Afterwards, while the last parents were opening their umbrellas at the doorway, ready to run into the rain, Warren joined her at the front of the room. Outside it was dark and heavy with rain. Inside it was warm with a strange orange light. Cath felt his breath and his body next to her, and believed he was going to kiss her. As soon as the parents' voices faded, he would close the space between them.

But when the voices faded, Warren remained apart from her, watching the rain. In a slow, heavy voice he said, 'I don't know what to do.'

'No,' agreed Cath.

But she did: close the space, Warren, that's all.

Warren stood still at the edge of the space, and Cath stood beside him, her arms by her side, and waited.

FANCY ZING

The idea was in the jungle on the dentist's ceiling, but she did not know how you *ended* an idea.

'Can I go back to the dentist, Mum?'

'Whatever for?'

They had just pulled up outside the school gate on Monday morning, and the engine was running.

'Nothing,' said Cassie. 'But can I?'

'Does your tooth hurt, darling? You must tell me if it does.'

'Which tooth?' said Cassie.

'Any tooth, Cassie. Any tooth at all. Have you got an umbrella? Have you got your note for Ms Murphy?'

'Yes,' said Cassie, listlessly.

'Yes umbrella? Yes note? Don't forget the note now, will you? Give it to Ms Murphy the moment you see her, okay? Darling, your uniform's skewiff!'

Cassie, standing on the footpath outside the car, untwisted her uniform until her mother was content. After her mother drove away, she twisted it back around again. It was warmer that way.

•

On Monday afternoon, outside the grocery shop, Fancy watched as a fat man in a charcoal suit strode along the street and spotted, in the opposite direction, a thin man. The fat man opened his face and arms wide, stopping in the middle of the footpath. Simultaneously, the thin man called, 'Hi!', casual, unsurprised, although friendly enough, and continued his stride. In fact, the stride was so brisk that he had to glance back over his shoulder for the second half of the 'Hi!' – and noticed only then as he glanced back that the fat man had stopped and had both arms out ready to embrace. The thin man *chose*, considered but *chose*, not to stop, and instead strode on with a grin, slightly apologetic, slightly wry. The fat man readjusted his arms and carried on.

On the drive home from the grocery store, Fancy wept for the fat man.

In Fancy's opinion, a choice had to be made when your husband said something unkind. Specifically: be cruel, be strong or sulk.

'Be cruel' by saying an unkind thing straight back.

'Be strong' by firmly choosing not to mind. But to do this, you have to use up a bit of the love that you have for your husband. You have to shave off enough of the love to forgive. After a while, the piece might grow back, but sometimes not. And if you shave off all the soft curves, you'll be left with sharp-edged love.

'Sulk' by sulking. In effect, sulking is simply delaying the choice to be cruel or be strong.

Watching TV on Monday night, Fancy said, 'That is so disingenuous, the way they do that.' She was referring to a TV talk show host who was pretending to be alarmed at the arrival of a small turtle on the set. The turtle was followed by its owner, proud but nervous, ready to talk about the turtle.

'Do you know what I have noticed?' said Radcliffe. 'When you use the word 'disingenuous', you get a funny smug look around your mouth. You're pretty proud of yourself when you use that word, eh?'

Be cruel, be strong, or sulk? Fancy usually chose to sulk.

On Tuesday morning, Fancy woke and remembered she had made a counselling appointment. She lay in bed sadly for a moment, realising that she ought to have cancelled it – there was now no point in going.

Radcliffe was not having an affair. Still, she thought, it was odd she had *believed* it for so long.

And then, almost immediately, she found herself imagining a discussion with a counsellor. 'I set up this meeting because I started to think that my husband was having an affair. Stupid, isn't it? I had absolutely *no reason* to think it, but I just couldn't stop!'

In response, the counsellor flinched slightly and said, 'Oh, *Fancy,* I'm so sorry to tell you this, but women *do* know when their husbands are cheating. Even if there seems to be no evidence, you just *sense* it.'

'Really?' Fancy said, tearfully.

'Really,' the counsellor confirmed.

With a flutter of hope, Fancy called out to Radcliffe in the bathroom: 'Radcliffe! I need to ask you something. Are you busy today? I need to talk to you.'

Radcliffe was surprisingly cheerful about the marriage counselling, even at such short notice. 'Huh,' he said, naked, both hands on the shower taps. 'A *refresher* course for the marriage, eh? Why not?'

But in the apple-green office of the Winston Hills Family Counselling Centre, it did not go according to Fancy's plan. For a start, the counsellor was a pale, thin, bald man who crossed his legs, and then twisted his ankles as well. It was as if he wanted to plait his legs.

Bravely, Fancy began her speech: 'Well, I set up this meeting because I started to think that my husband was having an affair. Stupid, isn't it? I had absolutely *no reason* to think –'

Beside her, Radcliffe was gaping. '*Fance,*' he began, 'what on *earth* –'

The counsellor interrupted by slowly unplaiting his legs. 'Well,' he said, smiling kindly at Fancy, 'that's *one* thing for us to work through. First, let me assure you, Fancy, that irrational fears like this are common at this stage in a marriage. You're approaching middle age, and I'd guess you're fearing that your husband is losing interest in you. You fear that he may be growing bored, looking elsewhere – am I right?'

Radcliffe and the counsellor both gazed at Fancy, waiting for her response. 'Approaching middle age,' she murmured. 'I'm only thirty-four, you know.'

The two men took this to be a joke, and laughed appreciatively.

The counsellor spent some time asking Fancy about her days, and about her coping mechanisms.

'My coping mechanisms?'

'The place you go to when you start to panic about things like approaching middle age?'

Fancy admitted that she liked to imagine herself calming a pair of angry seagulls. Also, she liked to imagine herself in a hotel lobby. Finally, she sometimes liked to remember Radcliffe's marriage proposal.

The men were very quiet as she listed her 'coping mechanisms', and when she reached the marriage proposal, she felt a hand squeezing her shoulder. It was Radcliffe: she turned and saw that his eyes had become misty.

'This is just the opener session,' the counsellor reminded them. 'Please don't expect *everything* to be solved today. Fancy, we will work through your stresses, be assured, and we'll work on your coping mechanisms. For now, we're just laying the table.' Then he gave them each a notebook and pen and asked them to write letters explaining the things they disliked about the other.

'*Dis*like?' cried Fancy.

'Dislike. Trust me, okay?'

Fancy and Radcliffe sat side-by-side in the counsellor's office, resting their notepads on their knees. Radcliffe chewed on the end of the pen, chuckled quietly, and began to write. Fancy hesitated. It could not possibly be right to set out the things that she disliked. Did the counsellor realise the impact that might have? Radcliffe would have to choose to be cruel, be strong or sulk. As would she. If either chose to be cruel, the cycle could go on forever.

You were probably supposed to answer cleverly, pretending to say what you disliked, but actually revealing the depth of your love. Like in a job interview, when asked about your weaknesses.

On the other hand, the counsellor wanted the 'table laid'. Perhaps he meant them to 'express' their irritations, for their own good? Very well, she would express herself, but she would do so in such a way that Radcliffe could never understand.

Dear Radcliffe,

All over! All over!
Leave it! Leave it! I'll do that.
Tap, tap, tap.
Tap, tap, tap.
Fancy! Ha! My dog –
Fancy! Grrr, just clear my throat!
Leave it! Leave it! I'll do that!
Tap, tap, tap.
Tap, tap, tap.
All over! All over!

Lots of love,
Fancy

Dear Fancy,

I would much prefer to say the things that I like about you, Fance. But unfortunately the assignment is the things that are annoying. So, here goes.

- To be frank, I am not fond of your moles.
- Occasionally, you don't ask me how my day was.
- You shouldn't sigh so much while washing up. Either do it or don't, but don't sigh.
- I don't like your sultana cake.
- It's wasteful the way you don't drink all the wine that I pour into your glass. Is it hygienic to tip it back into the bottle? No.
- You are sometimes a bit boring and repetitive.
- You very rarely wake me with a blow-job.

All my love,
Radcliffe

On Wednesday, Fancy dropped her car off at Valerio Auto for a wheel balance and alignment, and caught the bus home.

While she was waiting on the bus stairs to pay her fare, she noticed the driver's ID photo, hanging from his rear-view mirror. The photo showed a man in his fifties with a handsome, well-structured face, and a winning smile. But when it was her turn to pay the driver, Fancy saw a *different* man. That is, she saw the same man with the handsome, well-structured face – only the face had a glowering scowl.

For the entire bus trip, Fancy watched the driver and his expression remained the same. She imagined to herself the time when the photograph was taken: how the man was perhaps delighted to get the job, how maybe all his life he had wanted to be a bus driver, and here was his dream come true! They were giving him his uniform, and taking his ID photo: he was joking with the photographer and grinning in joy!

And then, what happened? Was it a personal tragedy? Or was it just the daily grinding of the gears, the folding and unfolding of the doors, the beeping of buttons telling him to stop, of tickets, inspectors, teenagers pretending to be younger than they were to get cheap tickets, people leaning forward to ask where to get off, feet on seats, and spilling Coke cans. Was it just the day-to-day that did this?

Fancy cried the whole way home.

On Wednesday afternoon, Fancy was working on her prize-winning novel. *Look for characters from everyday life.* She remembered reading that somewhere.

She thought of the scowling bus driver and wondered if *he* could be a character. It could be a sort of public transport novel. *Transport* could be the language that she taught her readers! Excitedly, she began to research 'transport' on the Internet. She scribbled down the addresses of various useful sounding websites: why not just list the URLs at the start of every chapter? Why not – and here she became even more excited – *why not just refer her readers to Google*? 'If you are interested in any of the topics raised in this novel, please enter the following search terms in Google: bus, train . . .'

'Hmm.' Fancy paused in her frantic scribbling and looked up, frowning to herself.

A faint sound caught her attention. Cassie, she realised, had been standing at her office door knocking gently for some time.

'Hello, Cassie!' she said.

'Hello, Mum,' replied Cassie, nodding. 'Can I paint my bedroom ceiling, please?'

'What colour would you like to paint it?' said Fancy, spinning around in her office chair.

'A lot of colours,' Cassie explained. 'It has to be like a jungle. There have to be monkeys, elephants, cheetahs . . .' Cassie listed the animals on her fingers, but her voice drifted away.

'Well!' said Fancy. 'Why not?'

She and Cassie drove to the hardware store and bought paint, brushes, and a small stepladder. Then they spent a very pleasant afternoon standing side-by-side, and painting. Fancy persuaded Cassie that they should put the jungle on one of the walls, rather than the ceiling, so that they would not have to strain their necks.

She was standing on the top step of the ladder, painting in some stars in the jungle sky, while Cassie was cross-legged on the floor, adding lady-beetles to the jungle grass, when Radcliffe arrived home.

They heard his car in the driveway.

Then they heard his voice at the front door: 'Fancy that! My Fancy is at home!'

Cassie held her paintbrush still for a moment, and looked up. 'Mum,' she said. 'How come he never says, "Fancy that, my Cassie is at home"?'

Fancy looked down at her daughter.

'Or else,' said Cassie, beginning to paint again, '"*Cassie* that, my Cassie is at home." How come he doesn't say that?'

'That's a good question, Cassie,' said Fancy.

Early Friday morning, Fancy took some routine ZFS documents into the Castle Hill Kwik Print Shop, to get them copied.

A young bearded man with tapered cheeks and lacquered hair sat behind the desk and smiled enthusiastically as Fancy walked through the door.

'First customer!' he said.

'Thanks!' said Fancy, inappropriately. Then: 'I'd like to get these copied, please.'

'No problemo,' said the man. 'Follow me.'

To Fancy's surprise, he led her up some stairs, unlocked a door, and walked her in to a small dark room. He began flicking switches, murmuring, 'What the heck? Where's the light?'

Fancy began to feel nervous, but then he found the right switch and the room filled with light. It was also, Fancy saw, filled with photocopiers. The man chose a machine and pressed the on–button.

'It might take a while to warm up,' he apologised. 'I'll come up now and then and check on you. You have a lot to do?'

'Well,' explained Fancy, slowly, 'I didn't really mean to do it *myself*. I usually arrange for somebody *here* to do the copying for me.'

At this, the most awful, unexpected embarrassment flared on the young man's face. He switched off the machine and the light, and hustled Fancy out of the room and back down the stairs.

'Sorry about that,' he said, somewhat coolly, when he was back behind his desk. 'It's my first day here.'

For the rest of the day, Fancy cried on behalf of the man in the photocopy shop. *It's all right*, she comforted him, *it was just a mistake. You don't need to lose your enthusiasm. Please stay happy with your life.*

She tried to comfort herself by recalling that today she was going to meet Cath Murphy. *For the first time ever, I am going to talk to Cath face to face.* But this made her cry all the more.

That afternoon, Fancy was choosing earrings to wear to the parent-teacher interview, when Cassie appeared at her bedroom door, sneezing quietly to herself.

'Hello, Cassie!' said Fancy, seeing her in the mirror. 'I thought you were playing outside.'

'Hello, Mum,' said Cassie, and coughed.

Fancy continued to hold various earrings against her ear.

'Mum?' said Cassie, after a moment.

'Yes, darling?'

'Can I show you my foot?'

'I've already seen your foot!' Fancy joked, and then, when there was silence, she turned around and looked at her daughter. 'All right then, let's see your – my *God*, Cassie, *what have you done?*'

Cassie's right foot was the size of a large loaf of bread.

'I got stung by a bee,' explained Cassie. 'And I'm allergic to bees, aren't I, Mum?' Then she slid down the doorframe to the bedroom floor, whispering, 'I can't breathe very well.'

Radcliffe arrived home from work just as Fancy was carrying her daughter out the front door.

'Bee sting,' she called, jogging across to her car in the driveway. 'I'm taking her to the hospital.'

Radcliffe slammed his car door. 'Did you give her the injection?' he said.

'And she's had an antihistamine,' Fancy nodded. 'She's already feeling better, aren't you, darling? We'll just get the doctors to make sure.'

Radcliffe approached and opened the car door for Fancy. 'But her eyes! Cassie, are your eyes all right?'

'They're just a bit itchy,' said Fancy breezily, closing the door on her daughter.

'They're getting better,' Cassie called through the window.

'Just relax there, Cass,' suggested Fancy, getting into the driver's seat.

Radcliffe hovered, anxiously, and said, 'I'll just stay here, shall I? Or shall I come along?'

Fancy put the car into reverse and pressed the accelerator to the floor.

When they returned it was ten o'clock and Cassie was fast asleep. Fancy carried her into her bedroom, changed her into pyjamas, and then sat on the edge of the bed and watched her daughter sleeping.

Radcliffe hovered, whispering, 'She's all right?'

Fancy nodded.

They went into the kitchen for a cup of tea. 'By the way,' said Radcliffe, filling up the kettle. 'I suppose you're pretty upset about missing the parent-teacher night?'

'Oh,' said Fancy, remembering.

'Well,' said Radcliffe, 'good news! I called the school and managed to speak to Cath. I explained that you couldn't make it, and I asked if you could have another appointment. She promised to call you back to arrange it.'

'You spoke to her!'

'Only for a moment, and only on the phone,' said Radcliffe firmly. 'Don't worry yourself, Fance. Just as we all agreed, *you'll* be the first of us to meet Cath in person. All right? And you'll get to do that *on your own.*'

'Well!' Fancy was moved. 'Thank you so much, Radcliffe.'

Radcliffe nodded, and looked earnest for a moment. 'Like your mother says,' he declared, 'the restraint you've shown this year has been commendable. It would have been so easy for you to make an excuse to meet with her. But no. You exercised caution and waited till the proper time. All you have to do now is wait a little longer, and she'll give you a call.'

Fancy blinked. There were tears in her eyes.

'But tell me more about this hospital fiasco, would you,' said Radcliffe. 'They kept you waiting all this time?'

'Yes,' said Fancy. 'Can you believe it?'

MARBIE ZING

Monday lunchtime, Listen wandered, pretending she was going some-where, but in her mind she was climbing the outside wall of the Redwood central building. She could see hand- and foot-holds all over that wall – window ledges, jutting bricks, water pipes – and she was getting very fast at her rock–climbing classes.

Imagine this: there is a 1st-grade girl trapped on a window ledge up there; Listen climbs the side of the wall and rescues the kid in an instant; most of Year 7 watches in awe from the school yard below.

Then, after lunch, at her Science class, imagine this: an intruder surprises them, planning to take the class hostage; silently, Listen slips out of her seat; 'Stay down!' she whispers, and girls hunch over their desks with startled eyes as Listen runs and leaps – a flying side kick across the *entire* classroom! It ends with a dramatic thump of her foot against the whiteboard, which sends the board spinning. This distracts the intruder so that, next, she overcomes him with a series of spinning hook kicks, chair splits, side kicks (straight up), fly-ing back kicks, and double knifehand guarding blocks.

Breathless, one foot on the chest of the astonished intruder (now lying flat on the floor), Listen glances back at the class. They are weep-ing with fear and relief, but also applauding.

Another thing: that Redwood teacher – Mr Bel Castro – he happens to be taking the class, by chance, and he gazes with admiration and says, *I like that.*

•

Dear Vernon,

This is just a note to tell you something, as you keep hanging up on me when I phone.

Well, this is what I want to tell you: you are funny, kind, clever and attractive, and when you frown there is just that one little line, like a 'Y' between your eyes.

Lots of love,
Marbie

Having posted a letter to Vernon, Marbie sat in her beanbag, as usual, and reflected, against a backdrop of growing alarm, on just how much she missed him.

She remembered a time when she had arranged to meet Vernon and Listen in Castle Hill but, half an hour before the meeting time, she had seen them in the distance, by chance. Vernon had also seen her, and had stopped still, dropping his shopping bags to the floor, opening out his face and his arms in an enormous, wondrous smile, shaking his head, as if to say: '*Look* who's *here!*' while Listen giggled beside him.

Also, she remembered how patient he was with her nightmares and sleepwalking. How she would wake in a panic from a nightmare and, from the darkness beside her, Vernon would speak calmly, in his daytime voice, and say, 'Marbie? Are you okay?'

She remembered that when she touched him on a knee or on a forearm, he continued with conversation, but casually, as he talked, he would cover her touch with a touch of his own, the tiniest pressure from his thumb.

She remembered also the bursts of love she had experienced when she saw him hunched over papers, working on ideas for the Banana Bar. Or when she saw how kind he was with his sister – how seriously he took her education, and how he knew all the names and hobbies of her friends. He had been disappointed this year when Listen stopped talking about school and friends, but had reflected on this issue late one night, and concluded: 'I guess she's growing up now and I have to make sure she has her own private life. Even if I really miss her stories, it's got to be up to her whether she tells them or not.'

Now Marbie knew it was time to confront herself. Why had she started an affair with an aeronautical engineer? She sank deeper into the beanbag and closed her eyes. (Somebody once told her that ideas and answers emerged as you fell asleep.)

Certainly, although the A.E. was not objectively attractive, there had been a strange low buzz between them which she supposed was 'chemistry'. Why had she not had the strength to ignore it? You just had to wait, keep yourself apart, and the attraction would eventually fade. There had to be something else.

She made herself consider Toni's theory. 'It's because you had just moved in with Vernon and his sister,' Toni had informed her. Could it have been about *Vernon*? Had she been reacting, subconsciously, to all the indications that here was the rest of her life? After all, she had bought an apartment with him *and* she had told him the Zing Family Secret. The level of commitment was impressive, and perhaps overwhelming.

That's just nonsense. I was ecstatic about life with Vernon. I considered him perfect. I was *terrified* of losing him! I thought I had to concentrate on keeping the luck – I was obsessed with ladders and black cats! I was afraid of making the simplest decisions – what to wear to work; whether to leave paperclips under my desk – just in case one tiny thing would end it. I could hardly *breathe* I was so afraid! I saw catastrophe at every corner, and the suspense was killing me.

And there it was.

Marbie's eyelids fluttered as she shifted slightly in her beanbag. It was clear to her just for a moment. If she was going to lose Vernon at some unknown moment in her future, she had better make it happen at once. If a catastrophe was flying at high speed towards her, she would move to be directly in its path.

She found she was drifting towards sleep. Already, her revelation was splintering into confusion. She fumbled for its words, but found there was nothing in her mind anymore except small sharp images, the pinpoints of tiny paperclips skimming through the air.

•

On Wednesday morning, Listen was summoned out of rollcall by a woman in a cardigan and wooden earrings. 'Might I borrow Listen Taylor?' said the woman from the door, and the rollcall teacher said, 'Why not?'

The woman introduced herself to Listen as they walked across the school. Her name was Mrs Woodford and she was the Redwood counsellor. Her office was very small – the size of a broom closet – but every surface was covered with paper lanterns, paper swans, paper bears and paperweights. There was also a picture of a fox on the wall.

Although Mrs Woodford seemed like a nice person, Listen was confused about what she was doing sitting in her office.

After chatting about how warm it was getting, how summer was approaching, and how difficult it was to remember the snow, Mrs Woodford asked what Listen's parents did for a living. Listen explained that they had died in an accident when she was a baby, and that she'd been brought up by her big brother, who ran a Banana Bar. Also, she added, since the counsellor seemed keen to hear more, also, they used to live with her brother's girlfriend, Marbie, but recently they had to move back to the caravan.

'*Oh!*' Mrs Woodford was upset about that.

In fact, she was so upset that Listen had to reassure her: 'It's okay. I don't really mind living in the caravan. I mean, I miss Marbie and that. But it's fine.'

Mrs Woodford played with a square of construction paper, and turned it into a rose.

'Cool,' said Listen. 'How did you do that?'

'So,' said Mrs Woodford, not answering. 'How's school for you?'

Listen looked at the rose and said, 'Fine.'

'Uh-huh. Plenty of friends to muck around with then?'

Muck around with, thought Listen. What did that mean? 'Yep,' she said, staring at the paper rose, which she now thought was maybe just a cabbage.

'I go to Tae Kwon Do and also rock climbing after school. So I've got some good friends there.'

'And friends at this school?'

'Well, this is a primary school, so it's all kind of different,' she tried.

'No, but I mean in your year? Your own year?'

'Yep,' said Listen, 'plenty.'

After that, Mrs Woodford chatted about how happy she was to be a school counsellor at Redwood Primary, and how Listen could come and see her *any time she liked*, and then she was allowed back to class.

It was true that she had friends outside of school: she had two new friends. At Tae Kwon Do, she sometimes talked to Carl Vandenberg, who was a black belt. The other day she had noticed a Bellbird High emblem on his bag, and she told him she used to visit the house next door to Bellbird every Friday night. Carl said she should look out for him because he stayed back late on Fridays for violin. She didn't get a chance to explain that she had actually stopped going to the Zings on Friday nights, because the others at Tae Kwon Do were laughing at Carl for being a black belt who played violin.

Furthermore, at rock climbing, there was a girl named Samalia Janz with a ponytail, who always said 'Hi' and 'See you', as if Listen were a regular person. Listen was pretty sure that they would soon be friends.

After school that day, Listen collected the mail from their post office box, but there were just two letters for Vernon.

She walked the letters back to the Banana Bar, and did not press the button at the traffic lights. Instead, she ran to the middle of the road, waited as a truck skimmed past her, and then ran again.

Vernon was eating a chocolate-coated banana in the empty shop. He was sitting on the counter and swinging his legs. 'Whatcha got?' he said, trying to see the envelopes.

'Nothing.' Listen sat up beside him on the counter.

He leaned back and got her a chocolate banana of her own.

'Hey,' he said, when he had opened the first envelope. 'This is from your school. Did you know they were going to do this?'

'Do what?'

'A camp,' said Vernon. 'They've fixed your classrooms – so you'll be able to go back in a couple of weeks. And they're taking you all to the mountains the weekend after next, because you've been good sports. Good sports. It says it right here. See that?'

'How about that,' said Listen.

'I always knew you were a good sport, Listen,' said Vernon. 'And now here it is in print. Wait a second. Now it says they're going to do some extra lessons at the camp, to make up for the classes you've missed. So, the camp's also compulsory.'

'Compulsory?' said Listen. 'It can't be.'

'Which is it?' said Vernon. 'Is it a special treat because you're such good sports, or is it compulsory because you're behind in school work?' He held up the letter and shook it: 'Make up your mind!'

'Who's the other letter from?'

Vernon picked up the second envelope – it was brown with strange pieces of bark and string embedded in the paper.

'Nobody,' he said, and put it in his pocket.

●

Dear Vernon,

Well! I hope you got my last note. And I hope you like these 'natural' looking envelopes. Strange, aren't they?

I just wanted to write to remind you how sorry I am, about cheating on you, and to tell you that I really wish I hadn't. I think you're so amazing that it makes me cry.

Love,
Marbie

●

On the doormat there was a large pink envelope, addressed with the single word 'Marbie' in swirling purple ink. 'More poetry,' she frowned, recognising the A.E.'s style.

Inside the envelope, just as she suspected, there was another of the A.E.'s visions.

THE VISIONS OF AN AERONAUTICAL ENGINEER
VISION # 1563

Deep inside the turnpikes of my crispy fragrant duck,
I see this, I see this, I see
ANGUISH, a BROKEN HEART!
Abandonment!
Also, I see a man with a hat upon his head.
And a cat upon the hat,
And a mat upon the –
No. Wait. That's not mine.
Look. Forget I said a word.

'Well,' said Marbie aloud, 'so much for *his* broken heart.'
Then she found a small typed note glued to the back of the vision.

Marbleweed! I miss you! Come back to me!
   In the alternative, please see the following:

RE: YOUR FAMILY SECRET.

*I HAVE ARRANGED A MEETING WITH CATH MURPHY
AT 1 O'CLOCK THIS FRIDAY. AT THAT MEETING, I
INTEND TO TELL HER EVERYTHING I KNOW!*
   *DELIVER $50,000 IN CASH TO MY HOUSE BY NOON
TOMORROW AND I WILL STAND HER UP.*
   FAIL TO DELIVER AND THE GAME WILL BE UP!!!!!!!!!!!!
   THE CHOICE IS YOURS.

'Uh!' said Marbie, and sneezed hayfeverishly. She had suspected it
was too much to hope, that she could simply walk away from the A.E.
and all his little brush fires.

She stood in her doorway now, re-reading the letter. Certainly, she would not allow him to blackmail her like this. That much was clear. She supposed she would have to resume her evening visits to his house. She would have to watch TV with him, and eat his crunchy lasagne, and argue with him about the Secret. 'But I don't want to sleep with him again,' she pointed out, firmly.

Then she realised with a slow shock that she would *have* to sleep with him again. If she resumed her visits, eventually he would greet her in his boxers and bow tie again, and say, 'Marbie, this can *not* go on.'

'No,' said Marbie, raising her eyebrows, '*it cannot.*' He *had* been blackmailing her. She just had not seen it.

She walked back into the house, clapping her hands together softly, which was her way of thinking. Then she sat at her computer and began to type.

Sir:

I write with respect to a patient of mine (Marbleweed Zing). Ms Zing informed me recently that she had commenced a 'relationship' with you. I was delighted to hear it — her condition generally frightens the fellows away.

As she will have informed you, Ms Zing suffers from severe paranoid delusions, generally revolving around her parents' garden shed. When suffering from these delusions, she believes such things as: the shed appears only when it rains; the shed is used as a base for spying on a 2nd-grade school teacher; aliens have eaten the shed (catalogued delusions: #32, #49 and #102) — and so on.

I hope that Ms Zing has not succumbed to any of these delusions in your presence; however, she can be absent-minded and occasionally forgets to take her medication.

It has occurred to me that you might like to assist her in this manner. Occasional, gentle reminders can do a world of good — as you no doubt know, she is somewhat embarrassed by her pills (they are inconspicuous, small and red) and conceals them with her hayfever medication. Take them out of the plastic! Dangle them good-naturedly before her nose! Tap her on the head with the box! *Little things like this can only help.*

Finally, Ms Zing mentioned that you write 'visions' because you have a sort of artistic 'beast' tearing away at your insides. My professional view is that you give up the poetry and try a sport instead. Have you considered hunting?

Please do contact me if you have any queries regarding Ms Zing. Together we can work to crack this nut!

Yours sincerely,
Doctor Arthur G. Gravestein MD, PhD, FRACS, FACS, FHKAM (Psych.)

Fortunately, Marbie had sufficient software, precedent letterheads, thick white stationery, and authoritative stamps to make the letter look genuine. The Zings had stockpiles of such equipment.

Also, fortunately, she was accustomed to breaking in to other people's homes. In fact, Intrusion and Maintenance used to be *her* field of expertise, until Cath got the cat, which made Marbie sneeze and affected her work.

Although the A.E. was a nuisance, she was pleased about doing another break-in, for old time's sake. She drove to his neighbourhood at 2 am, parked a block away, broke in through the bathroom window and planted, in the back of his top bathroom drawer, a box of her hayfever tablets. Inside the box she had hidden two small red pills.

Down the hallway, she could hear the A.E. mutter and grumble in his sleep. 'Tch,' she said to herself, and climbed back out into the street.

She was home again by 2.15 am.

Afterwards, when the adrenaline had faded, Marbie lay in bed alone, wondering at herself. It had been foolish enough to get involved with the A.E. in the first place, but why had she entangled herself further by telling him the Secret? She had never told anyone before Vernon, and requesting permission to tell *him* had seemed such a turning point. Her mother and Fancy had formed a sub-committee which decided, rapidly, that she was sufficiently committed to Vernon, that he was sufficiently in love with her, that he was an all-round wonderful guy, and that therefore she could tell him.

It was as if she had announced her engagement. Everyone congratulated her, and Radcliffe said, mysteriously, 'You'll keep him forever now, you know – the Secret's got a lot of pull with your average bloke.'

Her memory of telling the A.E. was less clear. She recalled a sensation of urgency; a compulsion to tell him. Yet she must have known the risk. He could have used it to ruin her family. Had she *wanted* to ruin her family?

Her drowsy mind began to toss images about: her mother pulling the shed door closed; her father, squinting at surveillance equipment; Fancy leaping smartly from a window to a tree. She was confused. There was something, she thought, so exquisitely fragile about these images. Her family, it seemed to her now, were always on the verge of catastrophe.

Of course they were. Their entire life was built on the foundation of a Secret. All it would take was one small slip of the tongue, and the foundation would collapse. *The suspense*, said Marbie's mind now, *was killing you.*

This was a familiar idea. Pre-empting disaster by welcoming it. Perhaps, she reflected, a lifetime of suspense about the Secret had found its way into every corner of her life.

Marbie's ideas began to fragment again: she saw sea urchins sink beneath sand on the ocean floor; she saw Fancy, a teenager, standing in the beach house, declaring she had done something incredible. A chalkboard stood outside a beachside takeaway: rain fell against it languidly, washing away the specials.

•

Dearest Vernon,

I'll tell you one of the many things that I love about you.
    The way you can take two cans of Coke from the fridge in a shop, and carry them to the counter in one hand. You can hold two cans of Coke, one for me and one for you, in a single, outstretched hand.

    Love,
    Marbie

•

Early on Friday morning, Listen remembered she was allowed to do the next spell. Vernon was already in the Banana Bar, so she had the caravan to herself. There were only a few pages left in the book, she realised, and the spell began by declaring itself to be the third from last.

> Yep, only two more Spells after this one! And then?
> All will be well! Why, you may ask? Ask no questions
> and I'll tell you no lies. Curiosity and the cat, eh? No
> use crying over spilt milk? No use at all! Go ahead
> and mop it up! By the way, after this Spell, you can
> do the *next* Spell on Thursday week!!

What had happened to the Spell Book? It was getting manic.

> Anyway, here is A Spell To Make A Person Get Stung
> By A Bee.

Listen paused. She had been determined not to do any more spells that could hurt people, and bee stings stung.

Still, there were only two more spells, and *all would be well*. And people were always getting stung by bees – it was no big deal.

<u>Ingredients</u>

- You
- A Complete Stranger

<u>Method</u>

Introduce yourself to the Complete Stranger by shaking the Stranger's hand, saying 'Hi!' and giving your name. Now, say the following things to the Complete Stranger (in the following order):

- Are you the sorcerer?
- Do you, possibly, have the flying carpet?

- Do you happen to have the ingredients for carrot pie handy?
- Consider this, Stranger: I have hardly even caught your name, and yet I feel I know your every thought. What can it mean?

'Oh, come *on*,' said Listen, and she threw the book onto the caravan floor.

Later that day, the final bell was ringing when the counsellor put her head in the door of Listen's classroom and called, 'May I borrow Listen Taylor again?'

Listen followed her across the school playground but this time they did not go to her office. Instead, they stopped outside the library door. The Redwood School Library was one small room with plate glass windows, through which you could see pictures of cartoon hippopotamuses glued to the wall. A large stuffed-toy zebra ate leaves from a crepe paper tree, and picture books were opened on display.

A girl stood just outside the library door. Her fringe was so long it almost covered her eyes and she was wearing torn jeans and a small gold stud in her chin.

'Here you are again,' said Mrs Woodford, smiling at the girl as though she did not have a gold stud in her chin.

'Listen Taylor, I'd like you to meet a new Year 7 student – this is Annie Webb. She's just moved to the area and will be joining your school next week! I've given Annie a quick tour, but I thought I might let *you* tell her all about life here at Redwood, not to mention life at St Carmel's. Okay?'

'Okay,' agreed Listen, politely.

Mrs Woodford smiled at them both and hurried away toward the staffroom.

Annie Webb stepped away from the library door, so now they were standing in the middle of the path, staring at one another.

'So,' said the new girl, and scratched the skin around her chin-stud. They both turned and watched Mrs Woodford crossing the playground.

'Mmm,' agreed Listen.

'Whatever,' said the new girl.

They both laughed.

'What was your last school like?' Listen tried.

'A shit-hole,' said Annie.

'Yeah,' said Listen. 'Well, this one is too. It's only temporary, because of the flood, not that St Carmel's is any better.'

The new girl nodded slowly, and swivelled on the heel of her shoe. 'I might not be coming to your school anyway,' she said. 'I didn't tell that teacher, but my mum and me are checking out a couple in the area today. So we can make a proper decision. Anyway, what did she say your name was again?'

Well, thought Listen, *I have nothing to lose.*

'Hi,' she said, holding out her hand to shake the new girl's hand. 'I'm Listen Taylor. Are you the sorcerer? Do you, possibly, have the flying carpet? Do you happen to have the ingredients for carrot pie handy? Consider this, Stranger: I have hardly even caught your name, and yet I feel I know your every thought. What can it mean?'

Annie Webb was staring. Eventually, she whispered, 'Did you just ask for the ingredients of carrot pie?'

Listen bit her lower lip.

'Wow,' said Annie, shaking her head slowly: 'You really think you know my every thought?'

Listen was not sure how to answer or explain without breaking the spell. She tried to put a mysterious expression on her face.

'I have to go now.' Annie walked backwards away from her. She didn't seem to need to see where she was going; she continued to watch Listen carefully as she walked. 'My mum's waiting, so I have to go. Maybe I'll see you next week if I choose this school? Though I've got to say, I probably won't choose it. The uniform sucks.'

Listen nodded.

•

Anaphylactic shock, said Marbie to herself. It was late Friday night, and Fancy had phoned her from a hospital pay phone to let her know that Cassie had been stung by a bee.

'But she knows she's allergic,' Marbie said. 'What was she doing outside in bare feet?'

Fancy explained that she had actually been wearing sandals, but, according to Cassie, the bee had *wanted* to sting her.

'What I don't understand,' said Marbie, 'is why a bee would want to sting someone. Don't they die as soon as they use their sting?'

Fancy agreed that it was odd, but suggested that the bee did not know.

Now Marbie sat in the beanbag and thought about bees, wasps, peanut dust, and funnel web spiders hidden in sneakers. She thought about how you could run over the cord of an electric lawnmower, or slip on an ice-cube and knock yourself out, or accidentally leave the gas on and fall into a coma. A beach umbrella could stab you between the eyes. You could suffocate in this very beanbag.

THURSDAY NIGHT

Two weeks later, almost midnight on a Thursday night, Cath Murphy lay beneath her featherdown quilt and waited.

'We just need to wait,' Warren had promised, again, that morning. 'It's seriously coming to a head – Breanna and I don't love each other anymore. It's gone. The love is gone.'

Cath sat up now on the side of her bed and stamped in sudden fury on the floor. Then she calmed herself and climbed back underneath the covers. She lay still, patiently.

A steamroller started at her toes and clanked against the bolts in her knees. Her thighs and her stomach were flattened now, and her neck and her face quite crushed.

•

Almost midnight on the same Thursday night, Fancy Zing sat on the living room floor and studiously turned the pages of a prize-winning novel.

Radcliffe wandered into the room, in boxer shorts and sports socks, nodded at her on the floor, and picked up the crocheted blanket from the couch.

'That's the ticket!' He lay down on the couch, carefully positioning the blanket over his body, and closed his eyes.

'Haven't heard from Cath yet, have you?' he said, after a while.

'No,' she said, and turned another page. 'I'm still waiting.'

'Well, she promised she'd call. I'm sure she will. Good night then.' He snuggled into the couch.

Fancy read on for a moment. Then she looked up at Radcliffe: at his socks with their ribbed ankles, and the hole where his big toe poked out. His elbows seemed to stretch at the blanket. His eyes seemed self-consciously closed.

'I love you, Fancy,' said Radcliffe, unexpectedly, in a sleepy drawl, without opening his eyes.

'Thank you,' she said, politely, and then she took a breath and added, 'Me too.'

Radcliffe chuckled and turned to face the wall. The blanket slipped slightly to the floor.

•

Meanwhile, Cassie lay in bed and reflected on the crankiness. There was so much around that she could hear it.

First, it had happened at school: Ms Murphy had talked in a loud smile like an ad for Kmart. 'Well now!' she had said. 'Let's say we talk about dinosaurs!'

'Let's say we bring in some dinosaurs for show and tell!' said Mark Baxter.

Ms Murphy screamed as if Mark had shown her a tarantula. But the scream turned out to be a laugh.

At home, her father had talked all night about pedestrian crossings. Her mother lined up all the mugs on one side of the dishwasher, threw the dishcloth onto the floor, and moved all the mugs to the other side.

Now Cassie could hear the scritchy, angry noise of crankiness. It was a sound that scrabbled around the edges of all other sounds. When she turned over in bed, for example, the rustle of her sheets and the elastic bounce of the mattress were exaggerated. Even the sounds she made herself – she made a 'hmm' sound to test it, and clapped her hands together – even these sounds were louder than usual, collecting the crankiness around them. It was like those days when she had asthma and didn't notice at first – she'd be walking around happily, and then would realise that an extra sound, the sound of her own wheezing, was scrabbling around the edges of her breath.

●

Almost midnight on the same Thursday night, Marbie twitched and clicked in her sleep. She was dreaming of a letter she was writing at work: the penultimate paragraph, in this dream, had dislodged itself from the rest of the letter, and its words were clattering like marbles to the floor.

Marbie woke with a gasp at the sound of the marbles, and peered into the deep spring darkness of the room. She waited for the shadows to take shape.

●

In the caravan behind the Banana Bar, Listen lay awake and thought of: recess, lunchtime, after school, before school, choose-a-partner, form-a-team, and worst of all, she thought: *school camp*.

The school camp would begin tomorrow morning. It would span the weekend and half of Monday. She had tried to persuade Vernon to send an excuse letter, but he took her education too seriously.

'I could stay and help in the café,' she had offered, 'and catch up on my homework. In the long run, it would be better for both of us.'

'I'm not letting you miss out on a camp to help in the café,' Vernon had replied calmly. 'What kind of a brother would I be? Don't worry, you'll have a great time. Donna and the others will be there, won't they?'

Now Listen's head was so heavy she was surprised that the pillow could hold it. She thought she might go outside, climb a telegraph pole and get electrocuted. Or else climb under the caravan bunk-bed where a snake might poison her. Anything was better than a weekend full of bus seats, cabins, free time, night time:

- Bus seats – she would walk down the aisle of the school-camp bus past girls with their bags and their legs curled beside them, meaning: *this seat is saved for a friend.*
- Cabins – girls would crowd around bulletin boards filling in *ten* names, *ten* friends for a cabin.
- Free time – 'Okay,' the teachers would say, 'everybody off now, out of our hair, *for the entire day*!' and girls would rush to the bush, to the bathroom, to the lake.
- Night time – 'Okay,' the teachers would say, 'lights off, everybody quiet!' and girls would cluster together for séances or smoking or climbing out through windows.

The clock-radio, which they kept on the caravan sink, said 11.56 pm. She had gone to bed at 10 pm, and she was still not asleep. Only four more minutes until Friday, she thought sadly.

Then she realised that meant four minutes left of Thursday, and *she had not yet done the next spell.* The second-last spell in the book. She had been so distracted by the school camp she had completely forgotten it. Now it would be too late. She could never do a whole spell in four minutes.

Unless it was one of those short spells, of course. She took the book from under her pillow, and picked up her reading torch from the caravan floor.

●

In her sleep, Cath waited, hopefully.

●

Fancy looked up from her novel and remembered one of her favourite conversations with the Canadian next door. It had happened just after the snow storm.

'Did I tell you my mother swept up all the snow on her front porch with a dustpan and broom?' she had said to him one morning. 'She tipped it into the kitchen tidy bin.'

The Canadian laughed. 'Wait till I write home about that,' he said.

'Where is home anyway?' she asked.

'Canada.'

'No, but where in Canada?'

'Where is Canada?' He looked concerned.

'No, no! Where *in* Canada?'

'Oh!' He was relieved. 'I grew up all over, but most recently Montreal.'

'Montreal? Does it snow in Montreal?'

The Canadian laughed again. 'Does it snow in Montreal?' he repeated to himself, quietly, affectionately.

'Okay, then,' said Fancy, 'what's it like, in Montreal, when it snows?'

Obediently, he reflected. 'Sometimes,' he said, 'you get as much as a two-metre snowfall. That's not just decoration when that happens. That changes everything. It changes the terrain.'

'The terrain,' agreed Fancy, pleased: 'it changes the terrain.' Then, since this reminded her: 'I made a chocolate *terrine* last night. Would you like some with your coffee?'

He was surprised, but agreed, and they each ate a piece of chocolate terrine, sitting on their own front porches, watching the melting snow.

Of course, that was back when Radcliffe was having an affair with a woman in purple daisy socks. All that was over now.

She returned to her novel: she was on the last page. The book was about an old married couple, and there was a moving final line, in which the old man declared his love for the woman, despite her senility, and she, in a rare flash of sanity, replied that she loved him too.

It was a sad and beautiful moment, if you knew the characters as Fancy did.

She stood up and walked across the room, not looking at Radcliffe on the couch. She could hear him breathing very deeply tonight, using up everybody's oxygen.

●

Cassie got out of bed, switched on her bedroom light and took her exercise book from her school bag. She wrote the end of the class play lying on her bedroom floor, the cranky noises gathering around her pencil as it moved its way across the page.

●

Marbie fell asleep again, thinking, unexpectedly, of sharp little bird beaks, thumbtacks and pieces of cuttlefish bone.

She sneezed and clicked her throat in her sleep.

●

A Spell To Make Someone Catch A Cold!

Simply place this Book under your Pillow, and Think, inside your Head, of Three Small Sharp Objects.
You can do the Next Spell – the *Final Spell* – *tomorrow morning!*

Listen did as the Spell Book said, just before the clock flicked to midnight. Then she fell asleep, thinking: *bird beaks, thumbtacks, cuttlefish bones, bus seats, cabins, free time, night time, bird beaks, thumbtacks, cuttlefish bones.*

11

FANCY ZING

Shortly after her father returned from Ireland, Fancy's family went to the seaside for a month. They stayed in a house on the hill.

Each morning, the family gathered their towels, buckets, spades, suncream, T-shirts and beach umbrella, and tumbled down the hill to the beach.

Each evening, Fancy stood with her back to the mirror and turned her head to see her shoulders. She wore a purple sarong, which she tied in various ways: between her legs, over her shoulder, or around her waist so it flapped low against her silver ankle chain. Her shoulders, as she watched, turned golden brown.

But one day, Fancy's parents told her to take her sister to the beach on her own. 'We'll just be doing some cleaning here in the house,' said Mummy, 'don't worry about us.'

'Only swim between the flags,' said Daddy.

'Or in the rock pool?' said Marbie.

'Right,' agreed Mummy. 'And I've made you some buttered sandwiches, so you can buy hot chips for your lunch. Give them some money, David.'

'Stay at the beach until they take the flags down,' Daddy reminded them.

Two lifesavers in yellow-red caps marched past the girls, flagpoles on their shoulders, and Marbie said, 'Are the flags down now?'

Fancy, who was making Marbie's towel into a shepherd's veil, agreed, 'Yes. Let's go.' She frowned at her golden shoulders, which were peeling.

'Can I peel some of your skin?' said Marbie, swinging her shepherd's veil.

Fancy allowed her to take three pieces of skin.

They washed the sand from their feet and ankles, and walked on the gravel road home. Fancy was carrying the suncream, the flippers and the beach umbrella, and Marbie was carrying her thongs.

'Put your thongs on,' said Fancy, 'or you'll kick your toe.'

'No,' said Marbie, 'because my feet are wet and that makes the thongs slippery. Whose car is that?' ·

From the bottom of the hill they could see their house, but it looked strange and unfamiliar. A long silver car stood in the driveway. They approached slowly, and saw that the car was shiny, its windows dark. A sticker on the back window said: 'SEA LION'. Another sticker, on the bumper bar said, 'If you can read this sign, back off'.

They ran up the stairs to the verandah and paused at the living room window. Inside, they could see their mother, sitting on the couch with a straight back and a small, interested tilt to her head. Next to her was their father. And seated in a row of kitchen chairs, their backs to the girls, were three men dressed in black. One of the men, Fancy saw, was tapping a polished black shoe on the floor.

Fancy and Marbie stood at the window and watched as Daddy coughed into his fist, Mummy laughed, and the three men in black each picked up a briefcase from the floor. There was a scraping of chairs and a shaking of hands, then the front door opened so that voices and light spilled out onto the verandah.

'Oh!' said Mummy from the front door, seeing the girls.

'We waited till the flags came down,' said Marbie.

The three men stepped out and lowered their heads. One of the men said, 'Girls,' with a nod at Fancy and Marbie, but the others did not appear to see them. One man unlocked the car with his keys, and opened three doors, politely. The men got into their car.

Then the Zing family stood in a mosquito-slapping row on the verandah and watched as the car slid away.

'Who were they?' said Fancy.

'Nobody,' said her father.

MARBIE ZING

Shortly after her father returned from Ireland, Marbie's family went to the seaside for a month.

Each day, Marbie's sister Fancy made Marbie's beach towel into a turban, a crown, or a shepherd's veil. She had to hold her head straight or the towel fell into her eyes, making the world a soft, speckled white. If she shivered slightly, it brushed against her shoulders like long hair.

One day, Fancy and Marbie were allowed to go to the beach on their own until the flags came down. Another day, they woke up and their mother was gone.

Their father was sitting at the head of the table waiting for them. He had placed the box of Coco-Pops in the centre of the table, alongside the milk. He had laid the table with three bowls, spoons in straight lines beside them.

Formally, he explained: 'Mummy had to go away for a few days. She will miss you very much.'

'Has she gone to Ireland?' said Marbie, and her father chuckled.

The three of them went to the beach, as usual, and had fish and chips for lunch. Daddy wanted to participate in their beach games: he helped with a sandcastle, but wanted to build it higher than was necessary, and also wanted to decorate the castle with sea-grapes and Paddle Pop wrappers. The girls grew bored and went for a swim.

As they walked home together that day in the cooling light, Marbie said, 'Will Mummy be home when we get there?'

'No. Just a couple of days and she'll be back.'

In the kitchen, Fancy set the table for dinner while Marbie spun in circles. She bumped into a chair, spun away from the chair, and landed with her feet apart for balance. Then the room spun itself, the windows tipped, the couch capsized, and the clothes hanger draped in swimming costumes jumped.

She fell against the chair, which crashed to the floor.

'*Marbie*!' cried Fancy.

Daddy stood at the kitchen door and said, 'Stop it, Marbie. You'll make yourself sick.'

But it never made her sick.

They had sausages for dinner, which Daddy fried with smoke, a tea-towel and a frown. They pulled out their chairs and sat down, quietly. Daddy took a fork and put sausages on each plate, then cut a tomato into three chunks. Fancy and Marbie looked at each other about the tomato.

That night Marbie lay in her bed and thought that the sound of the waves on the beach was the sound of the silver car bringing Mummy home. Daddy was out in the kitchen, clanking the plates, rinsing the knives and forks, sweeping the floor, and switching off the lights to go to bed.

The next couple of days were similar. At the beach, they were allowed Splices, Chocolate Hearts and Chiko Rolls. Daddy built his sandcastles higher and higher. The girls swam between the flags but returned occasionally to admire Daddy's castle.

Mummy came home in a taxi, at breakfast time one day.

Fancy and Marbie ran outside in their nighties, and Daddy emerged slowly behind them. The taxi driver was more excited than they were. He was chattering, laughing, and opening car doors.

Mummy's voice came from inside the taxi.

'Girls,' said Daddy, 'wait a moment.'

He leaned down to Mummy. When he stood back up he was holding something like a pink shopping bag. Marbie thought it might be presents.

'Here we go!' cried the taxi driver. 'Look what we've got! Look, girls, look what your mummy's brought home for you! Here's your bag, and here's the box, here it is. Look what we've got!'

Fancy took one step and said, '*It's a baby.*'

'Not just any baby!' cried the taxi driver, but he had to stop as Daddy wanted to pay him the fare.

'Whose baby is it, Mummy?' Marbie said. 'Where did you get a baby from?'

'Just a moment, precious one,' said Mummy.

The taxi driver talked his way around to the driver's door, '. . . congratulations! . . . All the best! . . . You take care of Mummy now!' He seemed to continue talking as he drove away.

Daddy said, 'Do you think you can manage that box between you, girls?'

Fancy and Marbie carried the box, Daddy carried the baby, and Mummy carried nothing.

Inside, Fancy and Marbie sat on the couch and took turns holding the baby. Marbie grew a little bored: the baby simply lay in its blanket and you couldn't scratch your knee. But Fancy crinkled her eyes and sang, '*Hello*, little baby, *hello*, little cutie baby, *hello*, little baby.' Mummy sat beside her, leaning over, watching.

Daddy and Marbie opened the box and it turned out to be a new basket for the baby. Daddy found baby sheets and nappies in a cupboard which Marbie had never noticed.

'I didn't know you were pregnant, Mum,' said Fancy, grown up and casual, twelve years old.

'That's because I'm quite plump already,' explained Mummy. 'It doesn't show so much, see? Nobody knew, darling. Don't worry.'

'Is it *our* baby?' Marbie said.

'Well,' said Mummy, 'it is and it is not. This is where you have to listen carefully, now.'

Fancy was on the couch with the baby in her arms. Marbie was sitting by the empty box on the floor, and Daddy was standing at the kitchen door with his arms folded.

'This baby,' said Mummy, looking closely at the girls, 'is a secret baby. Do you understand?'

Fancy and Marbie said they understood.

'No,' said Mummy. 'It's more important than that. It's more important than anything ever before. It's a special Zing family secret. Okay?'

Fancy and Marbie nodded.

'This baby,' continued Mummy, 'can only stay with us for one week.'

'*No!*' cried Fancy. 'Only a *week!*' She kissed the baby's forehead.

'I hope you will help to take care of her this week,' said Mummy.

'Of *course*,' said Fancy.

'Okay,' said Marbie, thinking: *what about the beach?*

'What's her name?' said Fancy. 'What's the new baby's name?'

Mummy looked at the baby and straightened the folds of the blanket. After a minute, she said, 'I have decided to give this baby the gift of a normal life. So her name is Catherine.'

'Is it?' breathed Fancy.

'Yes,' her mother replied.

12

THE HOT AIR BALLOON

Maude was making pastry when her husband, David, announced that he was leaving.

It was not surprising that she was making pastry: she was always making pastry in those days. She had become the official pie chef for the local cake shop, three nearby coffee shops, and two city restaurants. She could no longer look at a circular object without thinking of its use as a pastry cutter: teacups, breakfast bowls, steering wheels, balloon baskets.

'Hmm,' she said, vaguely, when David made his announcement. She was rubbing the butter into the flour, her favourite part of pastry making, fluttering her fingertips as fine crumbs emerged, neither flour nor butter.

'I'm so sorry,' said David, softly. (It was after midnight and the girls were asleep.)

Now Maude paid attention. 'You can't *leave*,' she cried.

He explained that he had no choice, and as he talked – about how he needed time alone to figure things out; how he hoped it would not take long, the figuring out; how he also hoped, when it was done, that she would take him back, but he understood she might not – as he said all this, Maude slowly sank into a kitchen chair, and thought: *of course*.

Her pie-making must have distracted her. Her husband was fading into nothing. Where was the vibrant, vivacious boy with excited expectations of invention? She recalled how he used to spring down the aisles of department stores, looking for inspiration; then how he took to wandering, more slowly and thoughtfully. The wandering grew listless, and now he never wandered, except down the hallway of their home. Now and then he picked up one of Fancy or Marbie's toys, turned it over distractedly, and put it back down on the carpet.

He had never lost his gift for electronics and gadgets, nor his thoughtful approach to life. He used the gadgetry skills to repair the girls' clock-radios or install deadlocks on the doors. As for the thoughtfulness – just the other day, when Maude had been ill with the flu, she had woken to find a note in David's handwriting on the carpet: 'THIS WAY FOR BREAKFAST' with an arrow pointing to the bedroom door. She followed the arrow to the hallway, where several other 'THIS WAY' notes directed her to the kitchen. 'THAT'S RIGHT!' said a note on the kitchen floor, 'YOU'RE ALMOST THERE.' And then a triumphant 'BREAKFAST!' alongside a tray on the table, which contained a boiled egg, a saucer of strawberries, and a little note explaining that orange juice was in the fridge door.

David's talent had been consumed by his family life, Maude saw now. And here he was, a grown-up Zing who had never invented a thing. His parents and relatives commented on this now and then, but were friendly and forgiving. The inventiveness had to stop *somewhere*! they said. Why not with David? He had, after all, created two lovely girls. That was enough for them!

But David spent hours watching TV, or playing Fancy's Donkey Kong game. His vertigo grew worse instead of better – these days, he could not even go to the movies. The seats were at such a steep gradient, he said, he feared he would fall into the film.

As David talked and apologised, Maude considered all this, and played with her flour-dusted wedding band. Eventually, she pulled it off her finger and dropped it on the table between them. David breathed in sharply, and buried his head in his arms. Maude regarded the wedding ring, imagining its use as a pastry cutter. Thousands of tiny pastry circles for thousands of tiny pies.

'Well,' she said, surprising him with the kindness in her voice. 'Well, I understand you have to go. But we'll say that you're going to Ireland. We'll say that you plan to paint pictures or write poems, or maybe a novel.'

Why Ireland? David wanted to know.

Maude thought it was the romantic sort of place where people ran away to do creative things. 'That way,' she explained carefully, 'if you happen *not* to invent anything, you can come back to us, without –'

'But people will ask me about Ireland when I get back,' David pointed out, changing the subject.

'You can look it up in a library book,' suggested Maude. She stood up again, and returned to the counter where her pastry was waiting. Then she changed her mind and sat down on the kitchen floor to have a cry.

As a goodbye present for the girls, David hung a swing from the highest branches of the scribbly gum out the back. This tree had no low-lying branches. He stood a ladder against it to reach the closest branch, and then climbed the rest of the way up. This was the bravest thing he had ever done.

Fancy, who was a formal little eleven-year-old, waved him off in the taxi, wishing him the best of luck on his trip to Ireland. She hoped he would write a good novel. She hoped he would come back soon. She would miss him *very* much. But Marbie was only five, and didn't wish him anything.

While David was away, Maude stepped up her pie-baking business. She pinned notices to community bulletin boards, and visited several cake shops. But it was only by chance, looking for a new vacuum cleaner one day, that she found the ad in the *Trading Post*: 'WANTED: Twelve Pie Chefs for Short-Term/Full-Time Baking'.

●

It is well known that Nikolai Valerio's second movie, *Pie in the Sky*, was secretly filmed in the western suburbs of Sydney. Indeed, despite careful secrecy, news of the shoot leaked to the press as filming neared completion, and mobs of hysterical fans began to form. They had to whisk the cast away to Lord Howe Island to wrap up.

322

The movie is a timeless classic – gentle, yet ambitious; dangerous, yet ineffably sweet. As with all of Nikolai's movies, it swept the pool at Cannes and at the Oscars that year, and many Valerio critics rate it as his best. He had been polished and toughened by his first movie – yet he still exuded the naiveté of the oil-smeared motor mechanic. Later, he lost some of the innocence and, although his acting remained superb, *Pie in the Sky* was vintage Valerio.

Of course, Maude knew who Nikolai Valerio was and, like most women, had seen his first movie several times. Like most women also, she had engaged in secret fantasies in which she imagined Nikolai, the famous smudge of motor oil on his nose, greeting her at the auto shop. But when she auditioned for the pie chef position, she had no idea it was for a Valerio film – that was still a secret. She thought she was going to help with a series of TV ads for Mama's Frozen Desserts.

Eighty pie chefs auditioned for the job, and twelve were selected. Maude was asked to pass a national security check and told to sign five separate Confidentiality Agreements. She began to suspect that this might be more than a series of ads for Mama's Frozen Desserts.

•

Maude was wearing a silver Alice band in her hair. Her daughters were asleep and she was sitting in the living room, watching through the window. Her husband, David, had been away (*in Ireland, writing a novel*) for almost a year, and she, Maude, was having an affair. Specifically, she was having an affair with Nikolai Valerio.

Technically, Nikolai Valerio was also having an affair with her: he had recently married Rebekka. But, really, Maude thought, when you are as famous as all that, the same rules do not apply.

The affair consisted of odd fragments: messages in code; a fireplace in a sandstone pub; wet shaking hair; a compliment about a cherry pie; a frangipanni flower which she pressed between the pages of a magazine; kisses in a claw-foot tub; silk sheets; Egyptian cotton bathrobes.

In her living room now, Maude was recalling her first days on the film set. All twelve pie chefs had been jittery with excitement until it emerged that their days would be spent in one dark trailer, seated together around a long table, ingredients and cooking utensils set out at each place, sweltering in the heat of baking ovens.

At break times, they stood around on the dry, dusty grass, trying to get a glimpse of Nikolai. Only it turned out that movie stars were rarely there when movies were made. Most of the day, the dull film crew walked around, measured things, talked to each other, set up equipment, looked at papers, frowned at the sky, shouted commands – as if building an imaginary skyscraper.

Nikolai and the other stars were whisked onto the field in dark-windowed cars only when the sets were ready for them. Even then, you could only see fragments – the top of a head, an arm reaching out – through the clusters of cameras and assistants.

It was not until the third week of shooting that Maude saw Nikolai's face. She had been asked to help place some pies in the shot – *Pie in the Sky* called for a general backdrop of pies. As any film student will tell you, apple pies, pumpkin pies, cherry pies and pecan pies, each with golden crust, were artfully scattered in the distant background of every camera shot in the film.

Maude was carrying a steaming cherry pie in each hand when the limousine paused beside her. A window was rolled down. Nikolai Valerio was smiling at her.

A woman seated beside Nikolai leaned around him. 'He wants a piece of your pie,' she called. 'Can you give him a piece?'

Everyone in the car laughed, while Nikolai continued to smile at Maude.

'I'm sorry,' he said in his movie star accent, 'I'm sorry, I keep seeing these pies everywhere I look. You make all these pies?'

Maude explained that she was only one of twelve pie chefs. He tilted his head to the side, interested, and asked, 'Do you think I may have a piece of one? It doesn't have walnuts, does it? I am allergic and my lips will swell to the size of a balloon!'

She shook her head about the walnuts, but then she didn't know what to do: she had no knife for cutting, and no saucer or spoon on which to place a slice of pie.

'Here,' he said, reaching his hand out of the car window. 'I'll just tear off a corner if you – ow, this is a very hot – and I'll just – oh, this is cherry pie, I cannot explain how happy that – my god*father* this is a beautiful *pie*! – and now, I will just straighten the edge, and *so*! It is still fine now . . . like nobody has touched it.'

The people in the car quietly watched all this, and then they laughed and said, 'All right, Nikolai?'

'All right,' said Nikolai, smiling at Maude again. 'And the best cherry pie I ever ate, did you make this cherry pie or was it one of the other eleven?'

'Me,' said Maude.

'And you are?'

'Maude,' she said. 'Maude Zing.'

Then the car moved away from her again.

She did not see any more than fragments of him for the next few days, until one night, when most of the cast and crew had left. Nikolai and the leading lady remained for the long, leisurely, midnight boating scene. Maude also remained – she had left her girls with a neighbour for the night – along with one other pie chef, and the two were extremely busy. The river had to be lined with pies. Furthermore, each pie had to look freshly baked, a twirl of steam rising from the neatly scored lines in its lid.

It was exquisitely intimate, this filming with only the two main actors and a skeleton crew: for the first time, Maude was able to watch and hear the slow unfurling of a scene. Furthermore, she was *part* of that unfurling. She heard an assistant comment, 'That coffee smells *great*,' and he meant the coffee she herself had just brewed!

Then the two actors and the collection of crew wandered over to where Maude was laying out the pies.

'Hello, Maude Zing,' said Nikolai, remembering her name, and holding the name, for one breathless moment, in his accent.

The leading lady was less friendly, and seemed to be complaining to the director. 'Come over here,' said the director, in a low voice.

Nikolai and a make-up lady tried to persuade Maude to let them eat one of her pies, and she jauntily refused. She found she was no longer nervous of Nikolai. He was an ordinary person with an accent. She was chatting with him! She was making him laugh!

Then there was an angry shout from the leading lady and she strode into the distance.

'Oh, come off it!' called the director. 'This is nothing. We're fighting about *nothing*. Come on, you've got to be kidding me!'

But the leading lady refused to return, and disappeared in a long black car.

The director was distressed. The moonlight sprinkles were perfect on the river, and the scene was almost done.

Maude was trying to gather up her pies, to keep them hot in the oven, when she realised the director was staring at her. 'Turn your head slightly,' he instructed, 'now back, now left, now right.'

It turned out that Maude's hair, the back of Maude's neck, the smooth curve of Maude's cheek, all precisely matched that of the leading lady. She would be the double, they informed her.

Which is how it came to be that Maude spent most of the night in a long slender boat being punted up and down the river by Nikolai Valerio. Nikolai chatted as he punted, applying his disarming accent to every word he said. He asked questions about Maude's daughters and about her life, and he told short, witty anecdotes about Hollywood actors who were his close personal friends.

The night grew colder so the director let them drink glasses of port to keep warm; the port made them clumsy, so that when Nikolai tried to cross the boat toward Maude, to fix a strand of her hair, he capsized the punt. This resulted in shaking wet hair, huddling together under blankets, shivery giggles, and patient amusement from director and camera crew, all packing up to go home.

Nikolai suggested that Maude accompany him in the limousine to his hotel room, to bathe and to sit in a robe by his fireplace, and dry her hair with his towel. Which was how the affair got its start.

In her armchair now, some weeks later, Maude felt that she was floating just above the chair. Nikolai would visit any moment. They had spent several elaborately secret nights in his hotel suite. She had bathed in his claw-foot bath while he watched, turning the hot water tap with her toe. He had listened to her stories of hot air balloons, and had sworn he would fly her away in a gold-trimmed balloon one day.

Now he was insisting on seeing her in her own home. He wanted to know everything about her, he said, as his hands traced the curves of her body. He seemed, genuinely, to love her body.

He had arranged to come in a plumber's van, labelled 'EMER-GENCY – 24 HR PLUMBING SERVICES', so the neighbours would not be suspicious. He was going to drive himself. He was going to wear a moustache and blond wig. She was going to make him pancakes in her kitchen while her daughters slept.

They were in love, she and Nikolai, but knew that their affair could not go on. Often, they spoke in wonder of the strangeness of the affair: it was essential but impossible. It must cease to exist for it floated between their two unbridgeable realities. His reality was his career and his beautiful wife. Hers was her pie-making, her daughters, and her husband, David, who had recently phoned to ask if she would take him back.

Yet, although Maude blinked tears from her eyes, knowing the affair had to end, she did not believe it ever would. The realm of the affair was too exquisite. Why, any moment he would arrive and help her make pancakes: he would watch in his reverent way as she cracked eggs, and measured out flour. That was all that their realm required. Such moments, with him, in her kitchen. She loved him so much she felt that *they*, together, would become the pancake batter. Intertwined, they would spill into the pan, and together they would breathe with slow new bubbles.

Now, waiting for Nikolai, she amused herself by comparing him to a man she had often read about, a hero of ballooning named Vincent Lunardi.

Vincent Lunardi was the dashing secretary to the Neapolitan Embassy in London, and was also, more or less, the first man to fly in English skies. His flight was made by blue-and-red balloon on 15 September 1784. In his balloon he carried a pigeon (which escaped), a cat, a dog, a bottle of wine, and a leg of chicken.

His courage, his excellent bone structure, the success of this flight, his *ability* to fly – all of this made Vincent Lunardi the subject of a thousand daydreams. Across England, hearts fluttered, eyes closed, and women took to wearing a specially designed bonnet called *the Lunardi*.

By winning the heart of Nikolai Valerio, Maude felt that she had, effectively, won the heart of the great balloonist, Lunardi. It was equally essential and impossible.

She, Maude, leaned into Lunardi's shoulder (his face, in the fantasy, was Nikolai's, of course), her right arm pressed against the edge of the basket (later, there would be interesting ridges pressed into that arm as a result), her left arm raised in a wave. Below, the other women wept and yearned, with only their bonnets to comfort them.

The moon tonight, Maude thought idly as she flew the night skies with Nikolai, was as round as a tablet. It would do very well for cutting pastry. As a matter of fact, so would Fancy's hula hoop, which she could see through the window, luminescent on the lawn. Or her own watch face, here on her wrist, showing Nikolai to be an hour late.

The next day she received a note from the Set Decoration Supervisor. It was pinned to an artificial rose and it informed her that *Pie in the Sky* had been moved to a secret location. Although she would be missed (the note continued), her pies were no long required.

13

FRIDAY MORNING

Early Friday morning, the sun just touching the sky, Listen read the final spell by torchlight.

> **Here it is!**
> **The Final Spell!**
> **Once you have completed this Spell, all will be well!**
>
> **It's A Spell To Make Two People Fall In Love Again**
>
> **Gather up the following things:**
>
> • **An overnight bag**
> • **Four candles**
> • **Flowers**
> • **A bottle of wine**
> • **Bread, cheese, olives and chocolate brownies**
>
> That's it! Just by gathering these things together you will make the Spell take effect. (And by the way, you will *know* when the time is right to *use* these things!)
> Goodbye then. It's been a lot of fun.
>
> (In the next few hours, when you've completed this Spell, you should be sure to throw this Book some place you will never see it again.)

Listen crept out of bed and gathered everything on the list, packing them together in her overnight bag while Vernon slept. By lucky chance, she found bread, cheese and olives in the Banana Bar fridge, chocolate brownies in the caravan cupboard, and a bottle of wine in a crate underneath the table. She added the Spell Book to the overnight bag, so she could throw it away somewhere later that morning, and she got back into bed, trying to sleep while her heart beat wildly.

When she woke again, Vernon was already up and gone. She was so excited she could hardly dress or clean her teeth. Maybe he was *already* with Marbie! Maybe he had driven straight to her place when he woke up!

Walking from the caravan to the back door of the Banana Bar, she tried to stay calm but felt the sun on the back of her neck, saw the pale blue curve of the sky, and thought: *it's the beginning of everything!*

As she walked into the shop, the phone was ringing, and she reached for it, but Vernon, who was behind the counter, called, 'Just leave it.'

The answering machine switched on, and there, as Listen knew it would be, was Marbie's voice. She reached for the phone again, but Vernon said, sharply, 'Listen.'

So they both stood quietly while Marbie chatted: 'Vernon! Sorry, it's me. Sorry to bother you. Sorry, I'm sniffing, I've got a cold, and that's why I'm calling you, not really, that's not really why. But I decided I shouldn't go to work today and then Mum called and said she and Dad are going away for the weekend, to this Festival of Balloons somewhere in the Hunter Valley, and I thought, seeing as I'm not going to work I might as well go away for the weekend with them, and I thought, well! maybe Vernon and Listen want to come along! I thought it could be fun for you guys to see the balloons, and you know, and anyway, give me a call if you're interested. We're leaving in the next hour or so, so it's spontaneous. Okay? Great. Hear from you soon, I hope.'

The machine clicked and whirred backwards. Listen looked over at her brother with shining eyes. Here, now, it was going to happen.

'All packed?' said Vernon.

She raised her overnight bag and swung it around slightly.

'You need to leave now or do you have time for breakfast?' he asked next.

'I guess I need to go now,' she said. 'But I've got a minute if you want to call Marbie back.'

'That's okay,' he said, and switched the sign on the Banana Bar door to BACK IN TEN MINUTES. 'Hang on,' he said. 'Left my keys in the caravan.'

Listen stood on the path in front of the Banana Bar, the hot wind brushing at her face. She leaned against the glass door to wait.

When Vernon pushed the door open again, jangling his keys in her face, she said, 'So, are you going to call Marbie?'

'Nope.'

She watched his back as he opened the car door.

'What do you mean "*nope*"?'

'Listen, I'm sorry, I'm not going to call her.' He was standing with the door open, waiting for her to come across to the car.

'You should go to the balloon festival,' she said, beginning to panic. 'You *have* to go to the balloon festival. Don't you get it? Vernon, it's perfect. I'm going away for the weekend; what are you going to do if you don't go to the balloon festival?'

'Run the Banana Bar, for one thing,' he said. 'Listen, I'm sorry, baby, I thought you understood. I'm not getting back with Marbie. Not ever. It's over. Finito.' Then he slammed his car door closed.

They drove toward Redwood Primary, where coaches would collect the girls to take them to the mountains for their camp. Listen watched her brother's profile, but it was set and calm. There was nothing she could do to change it.

She looked into her overnight bag, at her pyjamas, shorts, T-shirts, swimming costume, and beneath them, the glint of a bottle of wine, the lid of the jar of olives, the white of the candlesticks.

She was not going to the school camp.

And now she knew where she was going. It was just like the Spell Book had said. You will know when the time is right to use these things.

The time was now. She was supposed to hear Marbie's message, not because it meant Vernon and Marbie would fall in love again, but because it told her that the Zings were going away. She would hide in their place for the weekend. She would hide in their garden shed. She would live on olives, bread, cheese and chocolate brownies for the next few days.

But what were the candles, flowers and wine for? They suggested some kind of ritual. Did she have to perform some ritual? She pictured the Zings' back garden: the large green shed, the sagging trampoline, the scribbly gum with its old rope swing. She thought of the old rope swing, how it swayed sometimes, white against the night time, when she watched through the Zings' kitchen window. She thought of rituals with candles and flowers.

She thought: *two's company, three's a crowd.*

She thought: *you will know when the time is right.*

She thought: *this book will make you strong.*

And the whole thing fell into place.

•

'It's two hundred degrees in the shade, Dad.'

'Kiddo, I think you'll find it's not.'

'Yes, Dad, it is. I heard it on the radio just then.'

'No, Captain Cassie, you did not.'

'I was right about the snow. Remember when it snowed?'

'You were right about the snow, but about this, Casso, you are wrong. It's hot, I will give you that, but not so hot as you think.'

'Well, anyway, I finished my erotic fiction.'

'You finished your what?'

'My class play. I finished it last night. You want to read it, Dad?'

'Well, I can't read it, Casso-tobacco. I'm driving.'

'Yeah. How come you're driving me to school anyway?'

•

Fancy found it too hot in the kitchen, and took her breakfast to the porch, for the breeze.

She sat on the edge of the porch, which burned her thighs, and carefully set her breakfast bowl, orange juice and coffee around her. Radcliffe had offered to drive Cassie to school on his way to work, which was unusual. But she expected him back any moment. He had forgotten his lunch: she had just seen it in the fridge.

She was thinking vaguely of her prize-winning novel. The book she had finished reading the previous night, about the elderly loving couple, had employed a lyrical tone. The one she had finished last week was written with startling coarseness. You had to choose your tone, she realised. That was one of the rules. You chose cursing, coarsing, slap-stick, pastoral, melancholy, magical, lyrical, poetic or flatulent. But, she wondered, wouldn't you *increase* your chances of a prize if you com-bined some of these?

She began to formulate a sentence: 'pressing its delicate hoof into the mist-curling grass of the copse, the deer breathed the stench of gingivitis –' But then Radcliffe's car turned into the driveway, and he called through his open window: 'Hey, Fance! Can you grab my tuna sandwich?'

When she opened the front screen door again, carrying his sandwich in a brown paper bag, she had an *aren't you silly?* expression ready on her face. But he was standing on the porch.

'Oh,' she said. 'I was going to bring it to your car.'

The shape of him was dark against the sunlight.

'Right,' he said. 'But, Fancy, I've got to tell you something. I can't stand this deception.'

She felt the familiar leap of excitement – *he's having an affair!* – but was so weary of that leap that she dispelled it with a breath of mocking air. 'Ye-e-s?' she said, almost tauntingly.

'Can we sit down?'

Obediently, she sat beside him on the edge of the porch.

He swivelled towards her, and began, haltingly: 'The reason I offered to drive Cassie to school this morning was that – now, you might think it was nice of me to make that offer, but the *reason* was that . . .'

'Ye-e-es?'

Then he told her his secret in a breathless rush. 'The reason was that I didn't want you to see Cath Murphy! Because you're waiting for a call from her and maybe you would say something to her about it, but you're never going to get a call, Fancy, I made the whole thing up. *I went to the parent-teacher night in your place!* When Cassie got stung by a bee, and you took her off to the hospital, well, that's what I did. I just went. And I'm sorry, but I couldn't help it. I just couldn't stop thinking that the bee sting had happened for a *reason*. The reason being that *I* was meant to get to meet Cath. *Me*. A non Zing family member. The first of us to meet her. *I* wanted to talk to her, to see her, to have *her* see me. *I* wanted *her* to meet me! Fancy, I am *so so* sorry.'

Fancy stared at her husband. She shifted away from him slightly. 'So, I didn't get to meet Cath first,' she said. 'And Cath is not going to call me. Right?'

'Right,' he agreed. 'I am so sorry.'

'Fine,' she said, 'it's fine, Radcliffe. But can I just check something with you. When Cassie got stung by a bee – our Cassie, our Cassie who is allergic to bees, our Cassie who could die from a bee sting – when that happened, Radcliffe, all you could think about was going to the parent-teacher night?'

'Mmm,' he nodded mournfully.

·

Marbie left her message for Vernon, hung up the phone, and breathed in sharply. The sound of the phone clicking back onto its hook had struck her with the truth. Vernon would never call her back.

She could send as many letters as she liked, she could leave apology messages, and messages inviting him to hot air balloon festivals, she could invite him on a trip to the moon, but Vernon was never coming back.

Then she had to stop this unfurling chain of thought because she was sneezing. Her sneezes were immense, dramatic and shivery. She thought she might just get back into bed for a while before she packed for her weekend with her parents.

She saw herself in the bedroom mirror – ruffled hair, bleary eyes, pink nose – and gathered her bedclothes around her.

She had used up a whole box of tissues in the night, but felt around the cardboard bottom, hoping for a single loose tissue. She found something odd and crackling.

What was this crumpled piece of paper doing in the bottom of a tissue box?

•

Cath arrived early on Friday morning and sat on a bench in the sun.

The weather reminded her of her early meetings with Warren: the day he stood at the opposite end of the 2nd grade balcony and pulled his funny face; the day he brought her a coffee, saying, 'white, no sugar, yes?'

Such a soft warm breeze, such a tender blue sky. It was early summer and the weather had relented, promising gentle surprises. The warmth made her long for the touch of Warren's hands and, for the first time in a while, she was confident of that touch. Today could easily be some day!

Here was Cassie Zing, waving a manila folder at her.

'Ms Murphy. I finished the class play in the middle of the night last night.'

Cath smiled to herself, thinking, *see, things are happening today! This is a day of new beginnings.*

'Ms Murphy, did you hear me? It's me. Cassie.'

'So it is,' laughed Cath. 'Thank you, Cassie. I can't wait to read it.'

She took the manila folder, and Cassie instructed her sternly: 'Read it now.'

Obediently, Cath opened the folder, and Cassie nodded and walked away. But before she had read the first words, a voice behind her said, 'White, no sugar, yes?', and a coffee appeared in the air.

Warren Woodford straddled the bench like someone riding a horse, and now he was facing her shoulder.

'Thank you,' she said, tilting her head, taking the coffee and smiling at him.

He smiled back. There was something so generous in his smile that she almost wept with relief. 'Cath,' he said, 'I need to tell you something.'

She continued to trust in his smile.

'This morning something happened,' he explained. 'Something amazing. Bree and I woke up really early, before it was light even, and we looked at each other, and I'm sorry, Cath, but we fell in love again.'

'Ah-hah!' she said, kindly, as if a child had shown her a magic trick.

'I'm so sorry about all this, Cath, but I've got to say, for me, it's a relief, I couldn't go on this way much longer. It just happened, out of nowhere, we fell in love again.'

'You're not in love,' Cath began her speech, carefully but firmly. 'You're not in love because she doesn't know what you've been —'

'That's the thing,' said Warren. 'I told her last night. She knows the whole thing, and she's pretty upset, but we talked and talked and we both cried and it was so great. It was like we'd never talked before. And that's why, this morning, early, we woke up and fell in love again.'

'That's why, is it?' she said, suddenly outraged. 'Lessons on how to save a marriage by Warren Woodford. Lesson one, cheat on your wife. Lesson two, tell her about it. She'll fall head over heels! You just *talked and talked* and then you *cried*, and now, well done, you're both in love, and I really really think you should *trust* that feeling, Warren, that must be *so real*.'

She saw his expression, panicked, and adjusted her face. 'Warren,' she said, 'come on, seriously. I see how it must feel like a relief, but she *can't* love you now she knows. She must hate us both.'

'I'm sorry,' he said again, now in the voice of a teacher who needs to repeat a simple lesson. 'I'm sorry, but it happened. It's real. I seriously thought it was gone, that our love was gone, but early this morning it came back. I am so sorry.'

So she tried brisk: 'It's fine, Warren. I knew what I was doing. I never meant you to leave her unless it was really over. And I think it *is* over, Warren, this is just some kind of false hope. I'll still be here. I'll still be waiting but please God tell me that Breanna isn't at school today. Because if she's not blaming you, then I swear to God, she must be ready to scratch out my eyes.'

'I'm sorry,' he said again. 'She's in the staffroom. Probably watching

337

us right now. She's angry, Cath, but I don't think she would hurt you.'
He was standing up and backing away.

'What happened to the seams?' she called.

'What?'

'Forget it,' she said. 'I'm trying to work.'

She opened Cassie's play and pretended to read.

CASSIE'S PLAY

CLASS PLAY
by Cassie Zing

THE PLAY IS CALLED A EROTIC FICTION: FUCK.

Seen 1
Man Teacher: Good morning boys and girls.
Class: Good morning Mr Wort.
Man Teacher: Melinda. You be in charg. I'm going to see my girlfreind
for haveing sex.
Melinda: Yes Mr Wort.
Class: GIRLFREIND! FUCK.
Man Teacher: Good by boys and girls.
Class: Good by Mr Wort.

Seen 2
Lady Teacher: Good morning boys and girls.
Difrant Class: Good morning Miss Mop.
Lady Teacher: Mindy. You teach the class. I'm going to see my
boyfreind for having sex.
Mindy: Yes Miss Mop.
Difrant Class: BOYFREIND! CUNT.

Sceen 3

They walk away. They get a bed and get in to bed.

Man Teacher: I love you and I love you.

Lady Teacher: I love you.

Man Teacher: Here is my penus.

Lady Teacher: What is a cunt?

Man Teacher: What will we do?

Lady Teacher: Run away off the seeling!

Seen 4

They are running off the seeling together.

Seen 5

New Lady Teacher walks in.

New Lady Teacher: CHILDREN. Where is Mr Wort?

Children: They ran off the seeling.

They come back.

Man Teacher: Help! It's my wife.

He hides.

New Lady Teacher hits Man Teacher. They all jump up and down on the bed together.

Class comes in.

Class: Hooray!

THE END

THE CHASE

On the edge of her wooden bench, Cath sensed the gleams of light on the staffroom windows, each window gazing fixedly at her. She had yearned to be seen and now felt the shock of exposure. Children's shadows crossed her body. *Here is the teacher who had loved another teacher*, the shadows said, placidly enough, *here is the teacher who planned to run away with him, but his wife arrived and she had to come back to the seeling.*

What was 'the seeling'? Some strange sealing of her fate? Somehow, everybody knew and the whole school was watching her. The child, Cassie, had taken on the task of warning her with this play.

Meanwhile, the Wife was moving from window to window, stalking her, judging her, despising her, and all with perfect right. The sun was not gentle and tender at all, it was a spotlight. She hunched over Cassie's play, unable to make herself look up.

•

On the 2nd grade balcony, Cassie stood outside her classroom, watching the playground. Ms Murphy was reading her play. Ms Murphy loved her play so much she was curling her shoulders around it. The bell was ringing for school to start, and Ms Murphy hadn't even moved.

'You go inside,' Cassie told Lucinda. 'I just have to stay here for a minute.'

•

Fancy, alone on the porch again, now with a new cup of coffee, listened to the fading engine of Radcliffe's car. He had left for work with a final beseeching request that she forgive him. *Was that possible?* she mused now.

All her life she had longed to meet her baby sister – her mother had promised that she would be the first – and Radcliffe had stolen that away.

Still, she thought, did it matter? She could meet Cath another time. She almost felt embarrassed for Radcliffe, as if he had revealed that he ate the last of Cassie's chocolate Easter eggs, and secretly, guiltily, elaborately covered it up. It was childish and greedy, but what was the big deal?

She thought she could forgive him. Which made her think: what else could she forgive? If Radcliffe *had* been having an affair, for example, would she have forgiven him? *Should* she have forgiven him? Wasn't she supposed to get revenge?

Be cruel, be strong, or sulk.

Of course! She had forgotten. Revenge was just one of the options. The rules were more complex than that.

All this time, waiting for confirmation of Radcliffe's affair so she could pounce with a counter-affair, she had forgotten she might have to be strong. As a matter of fact, strength was a more appropriate response when you were a grown-up with a house, car, garden hose, and child. She sipped her coffee and felt the mug tremble in her hand.

Then again, she thought, as the coffee fanned out in her head, if you chose the 'strong' option you had to shave off a piece of love as fuel for the strength. And if great strength were needed, she might have used up all her love. But would she be *allowed* to –

Oh, stop it, she thought angrily, slamming the coffee mug onto the porch, and burning her hand with the splash.

•

The paper crushed into the bottom of the tissue box was covered in Listen's curly handwriting. It was entitled, 'Things That Make Me Sad', and the text began: '*Donna has a table tennis table in the basement of her house, and once Sia's mother made us all eat spaghetti squash.'* Even before she had finished the page, Marbie was reaching for the phone.

'Vernon,' she said into his answering machine. 'Sorry to call again. I know you won't come to the Balloon Festival, it's okay, it's not that, it's about Listen. I don't know how long ago she wrote this but there's stuff in here that's scaring me, maybe you know all this now, but if you don't, you should, and she says she can't find any friends, and she says, she says she's going –'

'Marbie?'

Marbie jumped at the sound of Vernon's voice.

'I'm here,' he said.

'Oh,' said Marbie, 'okay, hi, Vernon, well I just found this paper that Listen wrote, like a kind of diary, and did you know that Donna and those others from her primary school threw her out of their group?'

'What are you talking about?'

'I'm just reading this and it's full of how she's trying to make new friends and how she wants to cross highways in front of cars and she walks through long grass hoping to get bitten by a snake, and switches on the power with wet hands, and I think she's going to hurt herself, so where is she, Vernon? I really need to speak to her.'

'Okay,' said Vernon. 'You have to calm down. I just dropped her at school for a camp. Hang on, I've got a customer.'

•

When she finally raised her head to confront the staring eyes, there was nobody looking at Cath. Children were running towards their class-rooms, teachers were chatting in the doorway to the staffroom, even the staffroom windows had a blank, unseeing look.

The vulnerable, exposed feeling receded slightly, and she decided to be sensible. It was unlikely, for a start, that *all* the children knew. Cassie Zing must have guessed somehow, but even if she'd told others they would not have believed nor understood. Most of them did not have Cassie Zing's grasp of the erotic.

And maybe, now that she thought about it, even *Cassie* did not know. She remembered that Cassie's mother wrote erotic fiction: maybe Cassie was just stealing from her mother's writing, and applying this to the school yard?

She would have to destroy this play, but there was only one real problem, if she was going to be sensible.

The presence, in the school, of Breanna.

At least for today, she would have to run away.

Warren was emerging from the staffroom again, calling out something to somebody inside, and heading across to their building.

'Warren,' she called, 'can you take care of my class for the morning?'

'Of course,' he said, grim, solemn, apologetic and gentle all at once.

'I just have some *work* to do,' she scolded, and then, as he waved and hurried on, she saw two coaches pull in to the school driveway. In fact, the entrance to the driveway appeared to be crowded with girls and sleeping bags.

It was the Year 7s, she realised, from St Carmel's, heading off for their camp in the mountains. And there was that girl – Listen Taylor – the relative of Cassie Zing's. Listen was taking something out of her bag, crouching down and pressing it under a rock in the garden which edged the driveway. Strange. Was it a book? Now she was pointing out her name to a teacher with a clipboard, and was stepping back into the crowd.

Watching Listen, Cath felt a rush of guilt. She had asked Breanna for help with this girl – now that Breanna knew about the affair, asking her for help seemed unforgivable.

She looked again for Listen in the crowd but could not see her. She was turning, then, about to head to the teachers' car park, but something caught her eye.

Listen Taylor was slinking towards the school's front lawn – and had just ducked underneath the fence.

•

From her hiding spot on the 2nd grade balcony, underneath the bag rack, Cassie watched the Year 7 girls for a moment. Dressed in jeans, they were kicking pillows at each other.

Then she turned back to Ms Murphy.

Ms Murphy was gone from her seat. She was running through the front school gate. Trying to escape!

Cassie clambered out from beneath the bag rack and rushed down the 2nd grade stairs.

●

Stop it! Fancy thought. *Stop with these childish games and rules! You can't wait for permission to have an affair! You can't wait for permission to leave!* You have to be grown up and make things happen on your own. You have to face the truth: *there is no love left.*

Now, trembling on the front porch, Fancy struggled to argue back, setting up the cue cards of her love for Radcliffe. But all she could see were squabbling seagulls, the inside of a hotel lobby and the neat italic typeset of that recurring sentence: *how is your ocean bream, my love? How is your ocean bream?*

●

Marbie, pressing the phone to her ear, waited through a malted milk-shake transaction. She heard a brief exchange about cricket and the jangling of cash register and change.

'Marbie?' Vernon's voice was there again, and she could hardly breathe. 'Marbie,' he said. 'So, this sounds bad, but you know, she's at the school camp so . . . Could you post me that paper she wrote?'

'Okay,' whispered Marbie. His voice had turned cold and final again.

'Anyway,' he said, even colder. 'Why so interested in Listen? You haven't exactly been thinking of her up to now.'

She tried to hold on to her tears.

'Marbie?' he said, now sounding almost rough.

'Vernon, I've thought of Listen constantly through all of this.' She made herself speak, and as she did, her voice began to build. 'I hate myself for what I did to you, but I wanted to be like a *mother* to Listen and look what I've done. Haven't you noticed that I love your little sister as much as I love you?'

Now Vernon was silent, breathing quietly. 'You know, Marbie,' he said eventually, 'I'd have forgiven you almost right away if it hadn't been for Listen.'

There was the distant sound of a jangling door and Vernon shouted, 'WE'RE NOT OPEN.' His voice returned to the phone, softer and quieter. 'See,' he said, 'I'd have given you years to make up your mind about me, and to have affairs, if it wasn't for Listen. I can't put her through that uncertainty.'

'But I've *made* up my mind,' said Marbie breathlessly. 'I know it didn't seem like it, but I didn't *want* to have an affair, I was always sure of you. If I could see you, I could try to explain how it happened. But I would never never do it again. Never. I can't believe how much I miss you.'

'Are you sure you should be going away this weekend?' said Vernon. 'You sound like you've got a cold.'

'I know,' said Marbie. 'But I told Mum I would go to this festival, and she loves it when we show an interest in balloons. I think you should come too.'

Vernon was silent. 'So you met this guy at the Night Owl Pub?' he said, eventually.

'He asked me to play a game of tennis.'

'Tennis. How was he?'

'Well, pretty good, a lot better than me. He said he played C-grade competition. But you played A-grade, didn't you?'

There was a strange clanging noise, which could have been Vernon stacking and unstacking silver cups.

After a while he said, 'You think there's a tennis court someplace near your mother's festival?'

•

Cath thought of calling out to Listen Taylor, but it seemed the wrong thing. Somehow, it seemed more professional to take the entry gate of the school and follow at a lurking crouch.

The girl darted across the street, and Cath darted not far behind her.

Now she walked fast along the footpath, turned down a side street and stopped at a bus stop.

Cath stepped back behind a hedge.

●

When she thought of squabbling seagulls, Fancy thought of Radcliffe being childish and greedy.

When she thought of hotel lobbies, she thought of herself, running from Radcliffe, checking in to glamorous hotels.

When she thought *'how is your ocean bream, my love?'*, she pictured, suddenly, an ageing couple in a restaurant. The man was asking his wife, in a loving, interested voice: *how is your bream?*

And Fancy understood. She herself would never be part of such a couple, because Radcliffe would never care about her ocean bream.

Panicked, she reminded herself of Radcliffe's wedding proposal: the shoe polish mud, the winding trees, and Radcliffe clicking a photo of her: *'I would like to marry you and everything about you.'* She waited for the usual rush of contentment – her husband loved her and everything about her! – but instead was amazed. Why had she never thought of this before?

I would like to marry you and everything about you.

He meant the Zing Family Secret.

He meant the Friday night meetings, the hidden cameras, the network of suburban spies. He meant the edicts from Nikolai Valerio, the labyrinthine corporate structure, and the romantic ideal of Cath: a more beautiful, meticulously sculpted version of Fancy herself. He loved the Secret more than he loved her. He loved it more than his own daughter. He was so overcome with the thrill of meeting Cath he hardly gave a thought to Cassie's bee sting.

It was settled. Fancy was going to have to leave him.

•

The 382 pulled up and Listen climbed aboard. Cath leapt from behind the hedge and knocked on the closing bus door, which reluctantly opened to let her aboard. She slipped into the front seat and bowed her head.

•

Cassie skidded through the gates of the school in time to see Ms Murphy hop on to a bus. The bus pulled away at high speed.

Nice try, she thought, with a grim little nod, and began to run.

It was the Olympic run. It was the run she had started on the iced-over playground, and *now she was going to finish it*. She would run as fast as that bus.

She pounded the footpath ferociously, her eye always on the bus. Sometimes, she had to run across three lanes of traffic as a shortcut.

•

When Listen got off the bus, Cath got off behind her. Listen skittered around a corner. Cath stopped at a real estate agent to smile at the pictures in the windows, but after an agonising moment, she gave chase again.

Listen, she saw, had arrived at a blond-brick house, alongside a local high school. But the girl did not go to the front door. She lowered herself to a crouch and darted around the back of the house. From further along the pathway, Cath waited for a few minutes. Then she also lowered herself and darted to the back of a house.

There was a large back yard lined with a wire fence through which you could see the empty grounds of the school next door. In one corner of the yard there was a tall gum tree with a swing. A few metres away there was a large timber shed, painted olive-green. The yard was empty. The girl must have gone into the shed.

Cath ran across the lawn. She stopped, looked around embarrassed, and knocked on the door.

There was no reply, so she opened the door. She wiped her feet on the 'WELCOME' mat and walked into the Zing Garden Shed.

THE GARDEN SHED

'But I just got to work,' said Radcliffe, reasonably.

Fancy, however, was insistent. She needed to meet him right away, at the Muffin Break in Castle Hill. He eventually agreed.

'I asked you to meet me,' said Fancy, taking a deep breath, 'because I want to talk about *us*.' She stirred her cappuccino into chocolate swirls. At a table nearby, two young women were looking through a pile of photos.

'They've been to Fiji,' Radcliffe said, nodding at the women's table. 'Lots of tropical island shots.'

'How do you know it's Fiji? It could be Tahiti.'

Radcliffe turned back to Fancy, and assumed a concerned expression. 'This is about the parent-teacher night, isn't it?' he said. 'I thought you were a bit too quick to get over that this morning. But seriously, Fance, I'll do whatever I can to make it up to you.'

'This is not about the parent-teacher night. This is not about Cath.'

'See that?' said Radcliffe. 'They've taken some panorama shots. Doesn't Fiji look great?'

•

Vernon drove while Marbie curled in the passenger seat with a fresh box of tissues. They followed Marbie's parents, and at every set of traffic lights, her mother waved excitedly in the rear-vision mirror.

•

Cath was vaguely surprised at what she saw. She had expected spider webs, rusty nails, mud-encrusted shovels. Also, possibly, red-bellied black snakes curled inside of gumboots. Instead, the shed was a spacious, post-and-beam construction, with a high ceiling and polished floor-boards. A cluster of high-backed wooden chairs were set up in the centre of the room and there was a slightly raised platform at the far end. On the platform was a microphone, and a white screen on a stand. The wall stretching away from the entrance was lined with filing cabinets in unexpected colours such as spearmint and lilac. A bank of television monitors was set up along the opposite wall. Also, there were pot plants in corners and vases of yellow tulips scattered about.

On either side of the doorway where Cath now stood, there were slender, ornate bookshelves, holding rows of photo albums and piles of manila folders. On the top shelf of each bookcase, two white candles stood in saucers, flickering dimly. The candles seemed curiously point-less because the room was lit like a film set with bright track-lighting. There were no windows, although a beam of sun from a single skylight hit the far wall.

Just below this skylight, and behind the platform, the girl, Listen Taylor, was sitting on the floor and staring at her.

'Hello!' called Cath, squinting down the room.

'Hello,' said Listen, shifting slightly so that she was in the shadows.

She decided she had better approach Listen, but as she made her way across the garden shed she felt oddly foolish, like someone heading up to the spotlight with nothing to perform.

•

Cassie ran along calmly. She was several blocks behind the bus but that was not her fault. A car had blocked her path when she tried to cross the highway and she had had to run back to the traffic island.

Anyway, the bus was no longer important. She had seen it stop a few moments ago, and two people had stepped into the street. One of them was Ms Murphy. Also, she had seen the corner where Ms Murphy turned: it was the road where her grandparents lived.

•

Cath saw an overnight bag on the floor by Listen's feet, and standing neatly alongside the bag: a bottle of wine, a loaf of bread, cheese, olives and chocolate brownies.

'Hello!' she said again, standing opposite Listen, awkwardly.

The girl looked up at her.

'Having a party?'

She shook her head.

'I'm from your school!' said Cath, suddenly realising that Listen might not know her. 'I mean from Redwood. I'm Cassie's teacher, you know Cassie Zing? I'm her teacher, Ms Murphy. And I saw you – I noticed you running away.'

Listen, she realised, was not looking at her. She was staring just over her shoulder, towards the doorway of the shed. They were both silent.

After a while, Cath said, 'Did you light those candles?'

Listen nodded. 'I'm not going to drink the wine, you know.'

'Okay. Are you *meeting* somebody here?'

Listen shook her head. She was leaning against the wall of the shed, her legs stretched out before her, and now at last she looked Cath in the eye.

'Well,' began Cath, 'are you planning to spend the weekend here?'

'No.' The girl was barely whispering. 'No, I'm not staying, I'm just – *can you please leave me alone?*'

•

Fancy told Radcliffe she wanted a *trial separation*. The girls with the Fiji photos raised their eyebrows at one another, and bowed their heads sideways to listen.

'Nonsense,' said Radcliffe, jocular. 'I said I was sorry. I'm going to fix it, Fancy. I'll set up a meeting with your sister somehow.'

'You don't understand,' said Fancy, 'this is not your fault.'

'Well whose fault is it then?' he said crossly.

'I think we should go home.' Fancy pushed her chair back.

'I need to go to work.' Radcliffe looked distracted.

'I'm trying to leave you, Radcliffe.'

'No you're not.'

●

'I'm not going anywhere,' said Cath.

'It's okay,' said Listen. 'I'm allowed to be here. This shed belongs to a family I know called the Zings. They're Cassie's grandparents?' She tried to shrug, casual, but stopped at the sound of a knock at the door.

A tiny figure stood in the doorway, dark in the sunlight.

'*There* you are!' she cried, pointing at Cath, and now they recognised her.

'Cassie! What are you doing here?'

'I didn't know you were here, Listen. We're not allowed to be in here, remember?'

Cassie wandered into the shed. '*Finally*, I get to see it.' She gazed up at the high ceiling and along the walls. 'Who's the girl in that photo? Is that me?'

'Cassie, did you run away from school?' said Cath. 'Did anyone see you leave the school? How did you *get* here?'

Cassie had wandered over to a small framed photograph sitting on top of a filing cabinet.

'I don't think it's you, Cassie' said Listen, joining her at the cabinet. 'It looks a bit like Fancy or Marbie though.'

'Look,' said Cath, getting up as well, and marching over. 'Why don't we all get a tax – who did you say that girl was?'

●

In the living room, home again, Fancy tried to convince Radcliffe that she wanted him to move out for a while.

'Like a holiday?' he said, not taking this seriously, little dimples around his mouth. 'You want me to take a holiday? Fance, girl, aren't you the one who needs a break?'

'I need to stay and take care of Cassie!'

'Well . . .' He put his thumb to his mouth, and played with his lower lip, thoughtfully. 'I suppose I could go and stay in Vernon's caravan out the back of the Banana Bar. No! That's no good. Vernon's living there, isn't he? Marbie and Vernon have split up. Marbie had an affair.'

Fancy realised he was trying to give her a complicated message. 'I *know* you didn't have an affair,' she said. 'I know there's no reason. It's just something I want you to do.'

●

'Hey,' said Marbie. 'It looks like Mum and Dad are stopping.'

'You sound like a girl with a cold,' said Vernon, pulling over behind the Zings.

'She's pointing at that café,' said Marbie. 'We'll have to cross the highway to get to it.'

'Oh well,' said Vernon.

Cath was staring fiercely at the photo in the frame when Cassie began opening filing cabinet drawers.

'I had a denim skirt just like that,' Cath said. 'And I'm *sure* I had earrings like – and that *background*, can you see what that sign says, Listen?' Politely, Listen examined the photo.

'Pets,' announced Cassie from the filing cabinet. 'Knee. Broken here – broken hee-arr. Broken *hearts*.'

Cath and Listen looked up from the photo.

'Cassie, are you allowed to be looking at those things?' Cath said, but as she spoke, she was wandering over to Cassie and the filing cabinet. 'I mean,' she said, while she moved her eyes over the files in the drawer, 'do you know what your grandparents use this place for? I guess it's probably private!' She glimpsed two labels as she closed the drawer: 'Nightmares' and 'Potential Recruits'.

Cassie, undeterred by Cath, opened the next drawer down and pulled out a handful of papers. 'Can you read this for me?' she said, handing a small piece of cardboard to Cath.

'Maybe you shouldn't,' murmured Listen.

'It's some kind of ad,' said Cath, taking it in a teacherly manner, and beginning to read. 'Wouldn't it be better to know what's going on in your home or office at all times? Now you can! Our top-of-the-range pocket radio receivers provide superb sound sensitivity, so you can listen even to whispers! Range is up to 500 metres.'

'I wonder if we should be looking at this,' said Listen.

'Are they *spies* or something?' Cath said excitedly, opening another cabinet drawer and quickly closing it again. 'Listen, do you think you could get into the house and phone up Redwood? To tell them that Cassie is here? In case they're worried.'

'Okay,' said Listen, 'but I don't think we should look at this.'

'Hey,' called Cassie, who had moved to one of the bookshelves. 'I just found a whole lot of photos of that girl!'

●

Radcliffe yawned, stretched, and said: 'I suppose I should fetch my toothbrush!'

He glinted at her, but Fancy said, 'All right then,' and they narrowed their eyes at one another for a moment.

Radcliffe walked down the hallway at the slow, steady pace of a bridesmaid.

'It's not a joke!' said Fancy, behind him.

'Of course not!' agreed Radcliffe, and grinned. 'It's a *holiday*!'

She watched as he packed his toiletries bag. He packed toothpaste, toothbrush, shaving cream and razors, and three cotton buds from the pack.

'I've been using this to paint the wart on the back of my heel,' said Radcliffe, picking up the nail polish remover. 'Mind if I take it along?'

'A trial separation,' he repeated to himself, moving into the bedroom to find his overnight bag. 'I suppose you'll want me to finish that desk-top publishing I'm doing at work?' he called from deep within the wardrobe.

Fancy stood at the bedroom door, and Radcliffe emerged and smiled at her. 'Because I don't know if I *should* be working on the Secret,' he said, raising an eyebrow, 'while we're on our *trial separation*. What do you think?'

At last Fancy understood. He was threatening her. He could not take this seriously because he had the trump card: he knew the Secret. She could never end their marriage: he would go straight to the press. *Of course* he would. She could never leave him.

'Hmm?' prompted Radcliffe, cocking his head to the side.

●

Cath was scrambling around the floor of the shed, surrounded by opened drawers and spilling paper, books and cardboard. The photos that Cassie found were *all* of her. Now she opened and closed folders in a frenzy, grabbed at papers and dropped them. 'This is my *dog*,' she cried, 'my *school* report . . . my *string art*!' Cassie, sitting on the floor nearby, was turning the pages of another photo album, every now and then looking up at her teacher steadily, and then looking back at the photos.

•

Radcliffe moved around the house again, carefully packing random items: a CD from the shelf; a kiwifruit from the fridge. He was bluffing. He knew that at any moment she would have to laugh, apologise, and tell him to stop.

Fancy felt a rising helplessness. The telephone rang and she jumped.

•

Climbing through the kitchen window into the house, Listen thought she had better call one of the Zings. Not Redwood Primary at all. There was something strange going on in that shed, and she was the one who had started it. She looked at the auto-dial buttons on the phone, each neatly labelled, and remembered that Fancy lived nearby. So she pressed the button labelled 'FANCY'.

'Listen! Hello, sweetheart, how are you?' Fancy sounded odd.

'Who is it?' That was Radcliffe's voice in the background.

'It's Listen! Listen's on the phone!'

'Fancy, I have to tell you something. I'm at Grandma and Grandpa Zing's place, and Cassie's here too.'

'Oh, honey! Well, they're not there. They've gone to look at some balloons! What did you say about Cass – how did *Cassie* get there? Why isn't she at school? Can you put her on the phone for me, honey?'

'I can't,' said Listen, bravely. 'She's in the garden shed out the back. She's okay though, because her teacher's there too. I think her name's Ms Murphy?'

Fancy was silent for a moment. There was the sound of breathing, and then clicking fingernails on the receiver.

'Who did you say was there?' she said eventually.

'Ms Murphy. Cassie's teacher? She's in the garden shed with Cassie.'

'Listen? Can you get them out of there? I mean, right away?'

Now Listen was silent for a moment. 'Well,' she admitted, 'it's tricky. Ms Murphy is looking in the filing cabinets at the moment. I tried to stop her.'

Fancy took an immense breath of air and began to laugh: 'Ha ha ha!' It was a high-pitched laugh, and she repeated it: 'Ha ha ha!'

'What *is* it, Fancy?' Radcliffe's voice was in the background again.

'Oh well, Listen,' said Fancy in a fluting voice, 'the game's up now! Tell you what, I'll call my mother back from the balloons. You sit tight and I'll be right over. Thanks for calling, sweetheart!'

Listen hung up and stared at the phone.

THE FIRE

Radcliffe was standing on the porch, his overnight bag over his shoulder, waiting for Fancy. She approached the front door and he grinned back at her.

'I should go now?' he called. 'Check in to a hotel?'

'That was Listen on the phone,' Fancy replied in her musical voice. 'And then I had to call my mother. Guess who's in the garden shed going through the cabinets?'

'Can't guess.'

'Try.'

'The *police*?'

'No, Radcliffe. Better! It's Cath Murphy! *She's in the garden shed*!'

Radcliffe turned pale grey. '*Cath*?'

'Yes!' cried Fancy, dim in the hallway. He tried to squint her into shape.

'Then the Secret is out?'

'Yes! And, Radcliffe, I want a divorce!'

A gust of wind slammed the front door closed.

•

A gust of wind blew Marbie's hair all over her face, so that, for a moment, she was blinded. The same gust blew Mr Zing's eyes into narrow squints. It tangled Mrs Zing's shouts: 'We have to go BACK!' she was shouting. She had been shouting in to her mobile phone as they ran across the first three lanes of the highway, and now she was waving the phone above her head: 'That was FANCY! We have to go BACK!'

All four stood in a row on a slender median strip as cars raced by in both directions.

'But the café's over there!' said Marbie, hair in her eyes, taking one step forward.

'Marbie!' cried Vernon, pressing her back so abruptly that she did not stop on the median strip, but tripped into the lane behind. She fell into the path of a sports car.

•

A gust of wind skidded across the yard and through the open door of the shed. It tossed papers in the air, extinguished three candles, and knocked the fourth onto the WELCOME mat, where the flame took hold of a loose fibre.

Cath and Cassie, at the far end of the room, grabbed at the fluttering papers and photos and continued reading.

•

Amongst the papers and manila folders, Cath found: lists of every movie she had seen; charts showing her growth patterns from birth; an Excel spreadsheet of her favourite foods, colours, dance steps and magazines. Everything she touched was connected to *her*.

There were butterfly paintings she had done when she was six. There were dozens of close-up photographs of her face, aged eight or nine, hair in a high ponytail, leaning forward at her school desk. There were photos of her ankles. Photos of her walking home from school, swinging her school bag. Photos of her, aged twelve, talking to a horse named Buck, and offering a secret carrot. There were lists of her favourite books, along with her own observations on these books. In one drawer, there was an actual collection of each of her favourite toys.

Although she continually gasped and murmured, 'Who *are* these people?' and 'What *is* this place?', she also murmured, 'That's *right*,' and 'I *loved* that doll!' She found herself feeling elated. Here it was! All of her! Here in this garden shed.

•

As she climbed back out of the kitchen window, Listen felt her eyes begin to sting. She looked up at the sky which was a strange yellow-grey colour, as if someone had stretched a pair of nylons across it. Tendrils of black smoke were wafting through the open door of the shed.

She looked around for Cath and Cassie, but they were nowhere to be seen, so she ran across the yard. 'GET OUT OF THERE!' She ran around the outside of the shed, thumping on the walls. 'GET OUT OF THERE! THE SHED'S ON FIRE!'

•

Cath was leaning over Cassie's shoulder as the child turned the pages of a photo album. 'That's me on a jet-ski,' she said.

'Okay,' agreed Cassie.

'. . . me riding a pony . . . me winning a medal at Brownies. That's me eating an ice cream . . . that's me behind that sunflower . . . that's me at a law class – who *took* that?'

Cassie quietly turned the pages, coughed and rubbed her eyes. Cath coughed, thinking vaguely that she ought to open a window, and looked up to see if there were any.

The shed doorway had vanished behind clouds of smoke.

•

'Help!'

Listen stopped thumping on the shed walls. A tinny voice was calling from somewhere deep inside the shed.

'Help! Listen, can you hear us? We can't get to the door!' The voice was the 2nd grade teacher, Ms Murphy.

'Call a fire engine!' That was Cassie's voice.

Listen backed away from the shed to look at it again: there were no windows and no back door. She ran towards the open front door again, and saw that it was shrouded in black. The only sound was a low, industrious rustle, and the heat pressed her away.

Next she ran to the garden hose which was neatly wound on a spool by the garden tap. She wrenched it out of its spool, turned the tap to full, and pelted across the yard dragging the hose behind her. The hose reached its limit well before she had reached the shed, and jolted her onto the grass. In any case, looking down at the slender plastic, and feeling the weakish water dribble from the nozzle, she knew it would not have worked.

She stood again, squinting through the smoke at the burning shed. There must be another way out. Her eyes drifted up and caught a glint of sun on the skylight. It was too high for them to reach, but if she could somehow get *on to* the roof, and lower a rope down to them, she could help them out. Where would she find a rope?

Her eyes swung to the gum tree and its old rope swing. She would climb the tree, untie the ropes, and climb on to the roof of the shed.

But the shed had such slippery high walls, she knew she could never climb it.

She would have to jump from the top of the tree to the roof of the shed.

The tree was smooth but the ropes of the swing were helpful. 'Use your feet,' the climbing instructor had always shouted. Her sneakers slipped on the bark.

Panting, she straddled a branch near the top of the tree, dragged the swing seat up to her level, and began to untie the knots. They were tied in re-threaded figure eights which was what they used at climbing. She wound the rope around the seat, and looked over at the shed.

Black smoke billowed from the doorway and crept through cracks in the roof. Beyond the roof of the shed she could see the grounds of the school next door, where a small group of students was gathering. Now they were moving slowly across the yard, watching her.

There was no time to stop. She stood up on the branch and tucked the swing seat, wound in its own ropes, under her arm. The leaves above her tangled with her hair and twigs scratched at her neck, but she knew she had to start in the right position: one knee raised, the other bent, one arm forward, the other back.

There was only room on the branch for two and a half steps of the starting run, but she used them, bumping her head on the branch above, and leapt. She was rising into the air. There was a rush of wind in her face. Her legs were steady as a dancer's: for the briefest moment, she was flying.

She landed by the skylight with a self-conscious kick, which was the correct way to finish a flying side kick.

There was a small metal handle on the side of the skylight, which burnt her hand when she touched it. She pulled an edge of her T-shirt to cover the handle and wrenched it open, so that the skylight lifted high into the air. Then she was on her hands and knees looking down into blackness.

●

Cath crouched against the far wall, pressing her arms, her T-shirt, her skirt against her face, but nothing would stop the smoke. She was clutching Cassie tightly to her body, the girl's face pressed hard into her stomach. *This is how my parents died*, she remembered. She looked around again for a way out. It was too high to climb to the skylight. Flames were hurtling around the room, excited by the scattering of papers and folders, melting into the plastic covers of photo albums. There was a shrieking wrench as timber crashed on to the floor. The heat felt tight, like a rubber glove.

There was a shout from above.

●

Listen lay flat on her stomach and lowered the swing seat through the open skylight and down into the shed. The ropes of the swing were looped around her wrists and gripped in her palms, but she had no idea if she was strong enough.

Cath saw the swing above her and reached for it, but then stopped to gather Cassie close again. With one hand, she caught the swing seat.

'Wrap your arms around the seat,' shouted Listen, 'and use your feet on the wall.' Cassie's eyes were tightly closed against the smoke, but she nodded, and wound her arms around the seat. With Cath's help, she placed one foot high against the wall, and looked up towards Listen.

Listen slid back, pulling the swing ropes as she did, and burning her knees on the shed roof, until the ropes were tight. Now she was dragging the weight of Cassie: she started flat on her stomach, inching back along the roof, and then lifted herself onto her elbows and knees, until she was finally standing up, leaning backwards and pulling, arm over arm. Below, the shed was so dark with smoke that Cath was only a pale shape.

When she was high enough, Cassie reached a hand up and Listen helped her scramble out. They both fell back onto the roof for a moment, and looked around. Smoke billowed out of the skylight.

Cassie crouched close to Listen while Listen lowered the swing again. Below, now pressed into a corner by flames, Cath grasped the swing and looked up doubtfully.

But this time, Listen felt the strangest surge of strength. She dragged at the rope with both hands, again sliding back from the skylight on her stomach, and within moments Cath's hands appeared at the edges.

Now all three huddled together, looking for a way to get down. They could hear the shriek of a fire engine; also, they could see that the Zings' back yard was crowded with Bellbird students from next door, shouting and waving at them.

'JUMP! JUMP!'

Cassie straightened up, coughed once, and jumped. A flurry of hands caught her.

Cath and Listen looked at each other and down at the school kids below, and then, feeling the heat burst around them, they both dived into the crowd.

•

Listen felt hands all over her stomach, arms and legs, and found herself carried in a tumbling rush to the front lawn, away from the heat. There was a bustle of shouting and excitement, and she was lowered onto the grass while students asked where it hurt and whether she was burning.

'Give her space!'

'Get some ice!'

'No, not ice!'

'Get the hose!'

The students backed away from her in a circle. They were quiet for a moment, watching, uncertain, as she lay coughing and staring up at them.

She tried to focus on the students, to stop them from shifting in her gaze. Just before she passed out, she saw three distinct faces: Carl Vandenberg, the black belt from Tae Kwon Do; Samalia Janz, the girl with the ponytail from rock climbing; and Annie Webb, the new girl with the gold stud in her chin. All three wore Bellbird High uniforms.

Although she knew that this must be a dream, she also felt a soft rush of gladness.

14

SLEEP

Cassie dreamed of roasting mice on sticks around a bonfire. She dreamed of explaining to Lucinda, very slowly and precisely, that her skin would turn to ashes unless she drank her Fanta.

Listen dreamed that she had to climb the walls of Redwood Primary, which scratched her knees like bark. 'It's okay if you let go with both hands,' explained Samalia, her ponytail swinging in the wind. 'See?' She flung her hands into the air, and ran up the wall like Spiderman.

'Thanks,' said Listen, doubtfully.

Cath Murphy dreamed she was teaching a class of teenagers. 'Vituperative and scornful rejection,' she said wisely, 'of the applicant's connubial advances.'

The teenagers turned to one another, nodding earnestly. 'No ice,' she heard one say to a friend. 'No ice, no butter, no toothpaste, no tomato.' The friend nodded: 'And don't touch the burn with your hands.'

•

Fancy and Radcliffe arrived at the Zing house to a clamour of fire trucks, school children, and smoke. There were sirens and ambulances parked at jaunty angles, and there seemed to be girls on stretchers everywhere they turned. Shortish men in uniforms leaned briskly over these stretchers.

'Cassie?' called Fancy, but no sound emerged. She watched vaguely as Radcliffe hurried into the jostle, throwing questions around him. After a moment, he returned and told her to get into the car.

They arrived at the hospital at the same time as Mr Zing, Mrs Zing, Marbie and Vernon, which caused some confusion in the revolving door. The confusion intensified when they found their way inside and were directed, variously, to Accidents & Emergencies, the Children's Ward, and the Burns Division. Also when they noticed that blood was slowly spilling from each of Marbie's knees.

In the lift, Mr Zing said to Radcliffe, 'We drove straight back to our place like Fancy said we should, and followed the ambulances here. What's going on?'

'I spoke to an ambulance officer,' Radcliffe told him, watching the lift buttons grimly. 'Apparently, Listen and Cath Murphy were climbing the tree in your back garden, which caught alight, and Cassie had to rescue them. All that smoke, eh? From a single tree!'

In a corridor, Mrs Zing explained to Vernon, 'I don't think Listen was involved, Vernon. Cassie had an asthma attack, that's all, because of the smoke from a bonfire in the school yard next door. Now is this the right direction?'

On a stairway, Fancy said to Marbie, 'What have you done to your knees?'

'I fell into the path of a sports car,' Marbie replied. 'But it swerved.'

In a waiting room, a doctor said to Fancy and Radcliffe, 'We suspect that Cassie may have smoke inhalation poisoning.'

'What do you mean?' demanded Radcliffe.

'We understand she was trapped in the burning room – a shed, was it? Or a garage? In any case, she was trapped for some time. She's under ten. She's exhibiting difficulty breathing. And there is some slight discolouration of her skin. These factors add up and tell us smoke poisoning is likely. Now, she suffered only very slight burns, and we have already begun treatment – in those circumstances, the prognosis is good.

But I must impress upon you that a condition like this can be extremely serious, and the major cause of . . . there *is* a chance . . . I must ask you to *prepare* . . .' The doctor's voice seemed to fade in and out.

'She's asthmatic,' Fancy tried to say.

In a small office, a nurse said to Vernon, Marbie and Mr Zing, 'Now, it's *Listen*, did you say? Right, well, she has some bruising, cuts, some minor burns and grazing on the palms of her hands and her knees. She's dehydrated and exhausted, and she's resting right now, but otherwise she's fine. We're keeping an eye on her for smoke inhalation, but am I right in thinking that she wasn't actually in the shed? She was the one who helped the others out?'

'The *shed* was on fire?' murmured Mr Zing. 'Has anybody told my wife?'

In a corridor, a doctor said to Mrs Zing, 'She's sleeping now, but we've treated her for second degree burns on her arms – it looks like she was wrapping her arms around the little one, protecting her from the fire, like so . . . You need me to explain second degree burns? No?'

•

Cassie dreamed of porridge. 'Never put porridge in your nose,' she told Lucinda, who only coughed in reply.

Listen dreamed that she was performing a magic trick with a handful of balloons. The Zing family watched and clapped while, hazy in the background, Carl Vandenberg went through the motions of his black belt pattern.

Cath dreamed that her cat, Violin, was evil, and she had to save him. It was too late: Violin was treading through dried brown grass towards nesting plovers which would pluck out his eyes.

'Violin!' shrieked Cath, but her cat gave a snort of contempt and ran his claws slowly down her forearms.

She dreamed a defence for Violin. She scrambled through her law notes, passing pregnant fishwives, eggshell skulls, snails in ginger beer bottles, and landed with relief on the defence of *necessity*.

'But twelve voted in favour of conviction,' explained Mr Billson, apologetic in the school playground, 'twelve in favour of acquittal. There being no majority in favour of reversal, the conviction stood.'

This meant guilty.

●

For a while, the family moved about between hospital rooms and sleeping girls in a state of agitated confusion, but eventually they settled down.

Radcliffe and Fancy sat by Cassie, watching her without a word. Once, Radcliffe cleared his throat and said, 'Fancy, the doctor mentioned that her asthma might be worse now, worse than ever.'

'Forever?' breathed Fancy.

'Than ever,' corrected Radcliffe.

Then they were silent again.

Vernon, Marbie and Mr Zing sat in a row by Listen's bed, occasionally chatting amongst themselves about the contents of the hospital menu, or the fact that Vernon's sneakers had a squeak. Mr Zing suggested he try beating them with a stick, or drowning them in a bucket of water for a day or two. He swore that these techniques were effective. A nurse noticed Marbie's bleeding knees and chastised her before carefully washing and dressing them.

Mrs Zing, meanwhile, sat alone by the sleeping Cath, gazing at her steadily.

'Now, Cath,' she murmured eventually. 'If it's true that the shed burned down, I don't know what might be left of our garden there. Which is a shame, as I think you'd like that garden. We have so many flowers! Let me think. We've got sweet peas, begonia, pansies, petunias, snowdrops, cyclamen, daisies, and orchids. No roses though, because of the thorns. We've got port wine magnolias, camellias, dahlias and azaleas. We've got a vegetable garden too, you know. Broccoli, carrots, beans and peas. Corn, cauliflower, lettuce, parsley, strawberries, tomatoes, mint and thyme. And there's David's little lemon tree, of course. You might have noticed that.'

•

Cassie dreamed about breakfast cereal, stale in the bottom of the box. She tried to explain to her father how to tip the box so the stale cereal would not spill, but he was distracted.

Listen dreamed of pieces of silver glimmering in the tortoise pond.

'As a reward!' said the principal, happily, 'for all your squeaking sneakers!'

'Bravo,' said a voice. It was Annie Webb.

'It's silver,' Listen explained.

'Bravo,' Annie said again, more quietly.

Cath dreamed that a frightening rabbit stood in the centre of the road. It was ordinary sized and ordinary shaped, but there was something incredibly scary about it. For a start, it was surrounded by piles of broccoli, carrots, beans, peas, corn, cauliflower, lettuce and parsley.

•

Cassie gave a single, high-pitched wheeze, which surprised her. She turned her eyes towards her mother on the seat by the bed. 'I can run as fast as a bus,' she whispered, hoarsely. Her mother burst into tears.

Listen opened her eyes and saw Marbie, Vernon and Mr Zing, sitting by the side of her bed. 'Sorry,' she said. Mr Zing leaned forward and gave her a friendly tap on the head with the hospital menu.

Cath woke up. A plump woman was sitting by her bed. 'Hello,' said the woman. 'Are you all right? The painkillers are working? I hear you've seen our garden shed!'

15

CUCUMBER SOUP

Six weeks had passed since the fire, the holidays had begun, and Mr Zing had built a gazebo on the site of the garden shed. It was here, for symbolic reasons, that the Zings held their 'explanation lunch' for Cath.

While in the hospital, she had been extremely confused by everything Mrs Zing said, so that, in the end, she spoke in her law student voice to say, 'Why should I not call the police about your shed, please?'

Mrs Zing asked that she wait until she was home and felt better, and then they could hold an explanation lunch, and *then*, if she still wanted to, she could telephone the police. It was not clear what she could say to the police even if she did call them (the Zings could deny the contents of their burned-down garden shed), and what she really wanted was an explanation. So she had agreed to Mrs Zing's request.

Cath Murphy sat at one end of the table, and Mr and Mrs Zing at the other. The table was draped in a new white cloth, and was surrounded by elegant garden chairs. Bellbirds chimed in the bush behind the Zings' back fence. A kookaburra rested on the fence itself, silently watching the family as they in turn regarded their cucumber soup and reached for their serviettes and spoons.

Cath had been introduced to each of the Zings on the way out to the garden, and now she sat with her back straight and surveyed each Zing in turn. On her right sat the girl, Listen, who had rescued her from the fire, then Listen's older brother, Vernon, and Vernon's girlfriend, Marbie. On her left sat Cassie Zing, then Cassie's mother, Fancy, and Fancy's husband, Radcliffe. Occasionally Cassie whispered an observation to Cath. She had already whispered that her parents were getting a divorce, and that her mum didn't really want her dad here today. Now she was whispering something about the mint sauce.

'Well,' declared Mrs Zing, in a ringing voice, and people drew their hands back from their spoons.

'I thought I would begin with a general explanation,' she said. 'Then, if you have any questions, we can do our best to answer them.'

'Mmm,' said Cath faintly.

Mrs Zing breathed in deeply and began. Her narration was punctuated by clinking spoons, chiming bellbirds, and the occasional chuckle of the kookaburra or whip of a distant whipbird.

'Several years ago,' Mrs Zing began, tilting her head slightly as if to remind herself of the details, 'my husband, Mr Zing' (here, Mr Zing raised a hand to identify himself) '– yes, Mr Zing here, went to Ireland to write a novel. While he was away, I got a job on the set of *Pie in the Sky*. I had an affair with the star of that movie, Nikolai Valerio – yes, Nikolai Valerio. I had an affair and became pregnant with his child. Then he left me with nothing but an artificial rose. Then my husband returned.'

She paused and everyone looked at Cath, who was smiling gently.

'Nikolai's career relied, or so he thought, on his loyalty to his wife, Rebekka. His image was that of perfection. There were already rumours surrounding Nikolai's friendship with me – it was known around the set that my husband was away – so Nikolai's people rushed me, David, and our daughters, Fancy and Marbie –' (Fancy and Marbie raised their hands, solemnly) '– that is, the whole family – to a secret location by the sea. There, they offered me a deal.'

'A deal?' prompted Cath, humouring her. She had not touched her soup spoon.

'Right. Valerio's people would arrange for you – you understand, of course, that *you* were the baby – yes, they would arrange for you to be adopted, and *I* could secretly monitor your upbringing. They set up a company structure through which I would communicate with Nikolai, report on your progress, and make requisitions for anything you needed. The corporation paid Mr Zing and me a salary for our work.

I'm sure you can never forgive me for giving you up, Cath, but let me assure you, I did it for your own sake. I wanted you to have a normal life. If anyone had known who your real father was –'

At last, Cath interrupted. 'My real parents,' she said firmly, 'died in a house fire. I have a photograph of them at home, and I can assure you my father is not Nikolai Valerio. Nikolai Valerio! Of course,' she continued, her voice growing strident, 'I have adoptive parents who I consider to be my parents. They live in Perth and know nothing about what I found in your garden shed, because I knew it would upset them, but don't think for a moment that I won't tell them if I need to! I don't want to hear another word about Nikolai Valerio. I *know* who my real parents are! I'll show you the photo if you like. But I want one sane person to tell me *right this moment* why you people had all that information about me. I mean, right now. Or I'm calling the police.' She held up her mobile phone, impressively.

'Ah!' said Mrs Zing. 'The photographs of your "*real parents*"! I'd almost forgotten. Yes, we arranged two photos. One, if I remember rightly, was of a young blondish couple, the other of a big firefighter who was supposed to have rescued you. All three were extras in Nikolai's movies. We made up the fire story so you'd never go looking for your past.'

'Your adoptive parents seemed like very nice people,' said Mr Zing. 'It's probably a good thing that you haven't upset them with this.'

'About the shed,' Fancy put in helpfully. 'Well, we kept all our records about you there, as well as the photos. Medical, dental, educational . . .'

Cath gasped so hugely she almost choked.

'Oh,' said Fancy, sadly.

'It was like this,' tried Radcliffe, leaning his elbows on the table. 'Here's an example. You remember when you had that skiing accident when you were sixteen or so?'

'You needed reconstructive surgery for your knee,' Marbie reminded her.

'Oh yes!' said Mrs Zing. 'We all learned as much as we could about knees and knee operations! We became quite the experts! All the information is –'

But Cath had stopped listening. 'How do you know about my photo of my real parents?' she demanded, but her voice trembled. 'They *did* die in a fire. They're not *extras* in a film. How do you know about my photos?'

Mrs Zing suggested that they go inside and watch the DVD of *Turntable Troubles*, Nikolai Valerio's fifth movie. Radcliffe pointed out, as the movie began, that Cath had the same fine cheekbones and bump on the end of her nose as Nikolai. She ignored him. Mrs Zing paused at the spot in the movie when each of Cath's 'mother', 'father', and 'heroic firefighter' appeared as extras in the background.

It was confirmed that *Turntable Troubles* had been made five years after these people were supposed, by Cath, to have 'died'.

EXTRACTS FROM THE ZING GARDEN SHED (Burnt Fragments)

Suggested Reading Material
Comito R.B., 'Compression Pin Fixation of Articular Phalangeal Fractures' Royal Bartholomew Orthopaedic Review, Vol. XII, No. 2, February 1989;

RECURRING NIGHTMARE NO. 4

A very scary rabbit stands in the centre of the road. It is ordinary sized and ordinary to look at, but there is something very scary about it.
Number of Reported Recurrences: 3
Subject's Age: 11
Reporter: newspaper delivery boy

SURVEILLANCE EQUIPMENT – CONSIGNMENT

Pencil sharpener with hidden camera, transmitter, and receiver.
Retail Price: $250
Your Frequent Buyer Price: $225

ROAST LAMB, POTATOES, PEAS AND MINT

Cath was staring at Cassie, who was spearing peas onto her fork. She had three peas on each prong of her fork, and was trying for another.

'All right,' Cath said finally, looking up around the table. 'Just *assuming* that this story is true —'

'Oh, it *is*,' interrupted Radcliffe, buttering a slice of bread vigorously.

'Just assuming,' repeated Cath sternly, and Mrs Zing nodded encouragingly. 'Well, how did you get all that information about me? You had photographs of me at my desk in primary school. You had photographs of me in my law classes! In my *dining room*! You had photos of my ankles! You had my *academic records*!'

'Well, good question,' said Mrs Zing. 'We had three main avenues of enquiry. First, and most importantly, we had spies. Second, we had gathering techniques. Third, we had one or two hidden cameras.' She raised her voice slightly, so she could pretend not to hear Cath blustering: '*Spies*? Hidden *cameras*?'

'In relation to spies, we chose people around the edges of your life. Your postman, the dental nurse, the school secretary, the local florist, colleagues, acquaintances, and so on. They had to engage you in conversation, ask routine questions, take secret photos of you, and so on. We recruited them by hinting that this was a top secret, yet slightly shady organisation — you know, we played up to their thirst for adventure. They didn't know anything about the Valerio connection, of course. And they had to sign very strict confidentiality agreements. We paid them so well that it was hard for them to refuse. Also, easy for them to ignore any pangs of conscience . . .'

'Mum did most of the recruiting,' said Fancy. 'She always knew exactly the right people to approach. She never got a refusal.'

'In relation to gathering techniques, well, Fancy and Marbie developed all sorts of methods for getting access to school offices, dentists, doctors, physios, and so on, and taking photos of your records. We were meticulous about maintaining up-to-date information. Cath, you really should eat. You need protein and carbohydrates to help recover from burns, I read that. Vernon, help Cath to the gravy, would you?'

'Of course,' said Vernon, politely.

'And in relation to the hidden cameras?' said Cath, coldly, ignoring the hovering gravy boat. Vernon set it down next to her plate.

'Well, don't worry yourself too much about that,' said Mrs Zing. 'They never had sound recording devices, so we didn't hear what you said. We had several around your house when you were small.'

'We should let her know that her adoptive parents didn't have anything to do with this,' said Mr Zing.

'You're right,' agreed Mrs Zing. 'This had nothing to do with them. They never had a clue. That was a golden rule. But anyway, we cut back on the number of cameras as you got older, to protect your privacy. From the age of twelve, we stayed out of your bedroom, for example – that's the age when I stopped going into Fancy and Marbie's bedroom, so it seemed about right.'

'You cut back on the number of cameras,' said Cath, 'to *protect my privacy*?'

Everyone looked down at their food, except Listen and Cassie, who both stared silently at Cath.

EXTRACTS FROM THE ZING
GARDEN SHED (Burnt Fragments)

INTERIM SURVEILLANCE REPORT
AGENT: ELLA HIETZKE (SWIM COACH; OLYMPIC
MEDAL WINNER)
SUBJECT: CATH MURPHY
SUBJECT'S AGE: 11

Oh! She is very sweet little girl but cannot swim to save a life. I always think she is drowning but it's just her breast-stroke. Today I say again, 'You want to be a lawyer? Why not be a lawyer? You make lots of cash!', and she say she wants a horse. 'A horse?' I say. 'What you want with a horse?' She had a little cold, but not too se

INTERIM SURVEILLANCE REPORT
AGENT: LEONIE MARPLE-HEDGINGTON (FELLOW
STUDENT AT UNIVERSITY)
SUBJECT: CATH MURPHY
SUBJECT'S AGE: 19

I have today engaged in further dialogic exchange with Subject in order to derive/arrive [at] conclusions/suppositions in relation to her current (un)state of 'mind'. Subject applies discourses of 'fear' and 'anxiety' to [imp]ending end-of-year exams and her first practical teaching assignments. Subject [un]consciously accepts dictates of patriarchy (eg 'What are you supposed to *wear* when you teach 2nd graders?!') I invited

INTERIM SURVEILLANCE REPORT
AGENT: SUZANNE BARKER (TEACHER, GRADE 1A)
SUBJECT: CATH MURPHY
SUBJECT'S AGE: 23

As requested by you, I invited Cath and her new boyfriend to my place for dinner at the weekend. I gave them a nice roast but the potatoes came out floury and I don't know, maybe I overcooked the carrots? Cath seemed happy enough but I didn't take to the boyfriend. He is some kind of environmentalist and goes on about swamps and whatnot, and I thought: 'well, hang on, is that interesting to the rest of us.' My kids were pulling faces behind his back which is a good sign – kids seem to have a sixth sense about things like this. He is just morbidly fascinated with swamps and he'd leave Cath for one in a second.

I saw Cath looking hopefully at the bread basket while he was talking, and he could have noticed and passed it over, but oh no, not him. Anyway, I don't think she had the aura of someone truly loved and

INTERIM SURVEILLANCE REPORT
AGENT: DOCTOR DAVID CARMICHAEL
SUBJECT: CATH MURPHY
SUBJECT'S AGE: 23

Subject appeared emotional and somewhat unstable in my class today. Of course, she could simply have been bored to tears, but I do try to keep my lectures lively. Photographs of Subject at her Desk (taken with Turban Cam) are attached, and, as you c

INTERIM SURVEILLANCE REPORT
AGENT: KATIE TOBY (TEACHER, KINDER A)
SUBJECT: CATH MURPHY
SUBJECT'S AGE: 23

This Report is about something VERY IMPORTANT which happened today!! I was in the school car park and I saw CATH MURPHY and the other 2nd grade teacher, WARREN WOODFORD together. He is married, I should add! Anyway, they were about to go to a movie together and they seemed VERY nervous. Could something be going on between them?!!! STAY TUNED and I'll keep you post

INTERIM SURVEILLANCE REPORT
AGENT: DEBBIE HARLAND (CORNER STORE
EMPLOYEE)
SUBJECT: CATH MURPHY
SUBJECT'S AGE: 24

No more dreams to report and I'll be off on my overseas trip
from next week, *but* . . . (suspenseful drumroll) . . . I just wanted
to tell you a brief event from last night. Cath and a *man* came into
the store, around midnight, in the middle of the Snow Storm.
'What have we here?' I said to myself, but it turned out he was a
teacher from her school and they'd just come from a party. They
bought chips and salsa. He took a mobile phone call while they
were in my shop, and he said something like: 'Breda! Hi! Don't
even worry yourself. No taxis so I'm staying at Cath's. We're just
on our way. You warm enough?'

Then he smiled happily, and told me fairly proudly that that
was his wife.

In the circumstances – he was honest and loving with his wife;
Cath seemed more keen on the snow than she did on him etc etc
– I didn't sense any romance and I'd say things were all above
board. And that's all, folks!

DESSERT

'Now,' said Mrs Zing, 'at least try a piece of Fancy's famous chocolate terrine!' She was slicing it up and passing dessert bowls down both sides of the table.

Cath was pale and silent, so Mrs Zing continued: 'The final thing we must explain is *why* we were gathering this information. There were two reasons, Cath, one minor and one major. The minor reason was this: you may find this hard to imagine but your father, Nikolai, adored you. He was greedy for information about you – you are, after all, his eldest child, and his only daughter. So we compiled the information into regular reports, with photos affixed, along with the requisitions for certain funds – and this kept him happy.'

'And kept him happily sending us money to carry on,' Radcliffe pointed out.

At this, Listen accidentally interrupted by saying, in a disbelieving voice: 'Nikolai Valerio.'

'Exactly,' agreed Cath, nodding at her.

'But the *major* reason was that we wanted to make your life wonderful,' Mrs Zing continued. 'We wanted to give you gifts. We wanted you to have every opportunity. We wanted you to be happy, and to develop your potential. So! Let's think of some examples, everyone!'

'Well,' said Fancy, shyly, 'Marbie is a great swimmer but she never got swimming lessons when she was young. We thought you might have the same talent and we wanted to make sure it wasn't wasted. So we found a way to get rid of the mediocre swimming teacher you had and replace her with a former Olympic champion.'

'Any time you were sad,' said Marbie, 'we tried to think of a present for you that might cheer you up – like a trip to Disneyland or a new puppy dog or a Hoyts Gold Pass or a pair of designer sunglasses. And the same whenever it was your birthday.'

'Nikolai gave you birthday presents too,' said Mrs Zing. 'But you probably never noticed them. He always got us to find out who your favourite singer was, and then he would write a song for you and get them to put it to music and release it on the date of your birthday. You remember Kylie Minogue's hit, "Blue-Eyed Blonde Beauty" which came out on your twelfth birthday?'

'And there was that Eminem song on your twenty-first birthday,' said Marbie. 'I loved that song. About the teaching student with the pet cat? Eminem added all the swearwords though, which really annoyed Nikolai. I always wondered if you noticed the similarity to your life.'

'Not really,' whispered Cath. 'I didn't listen to the words.'

'Huh,' said Vernon.

'And we had *projects*,' added Radcliffe, 'for more major things. I remember when we decided that it would be good to broaden your horizons, so we tried to put you in the way of trips or jobs in exotic locations such as Mongolia and Nepal! That was Project 53, wasn't it?'

'Project 55,' corrected Mrs Zing.

'The funny thing about *that*,' continued Radcliffe, 'was that your friends kept swooping in and stealing the offers! It just goes to show, you can't –'

'The spies were supposed to find out what you were unhappy about,' Vernon cut in. 'Or what you *really* wanted. And then we thought up ways to get those things to you.'

'Nikolai was also keen to steer you in certain directions,' added Mrs Zing. 'It wasn't just us. Occasionally, he would send an *edict* – a special request for us to concentrate on some aspect of your life. For instance, he wanted you to be refined – a woman of resources. It was his idea to get you horse-riding lessons, and then that wine appreciation course when you were older? Remember?'

'Ah yes!' said Radcliffe. 'And he was so keen that you become a lawyer! His dream was for you to eventually become the managing corporate lawyer for the Valerio Empire! We tried *everything* to –'

'Anyway,' interrupted Marbie, 'the challenge was how to get these things to you without being obvious.'

'That was the fun part,' agreed Fancy.

'We used scholarships, prizes, raffles, free offers – things turning up on your doorstep – anything we could think of.'

'The magazines were the stroke of genius,' smiled Mrs Zing.

'Fancy wrote most of the content,' said Marbie, 'and Radcliffe did the desktop publishing at work – we all thought up the competitions.'

'We tried hiding things in taxis,' said Vernon.

'But you kept not noticing them!' cried Radcliffe.

'Or when you did,' said Mrs Zing, 'you gave them to the driver. You were so honest.'

Cath was breathing in, ready to unleash a stinging rebuke, when she realised they had stopped looking at her. They were chatting animatedly amongst themselves, reminiscing.

EXTRACTS FROM THE ZING GARDEN SHED (Burnt Fragments)

(FROM 'MINUTES OF ZFS MEETING')

- F and M both adamant that C should be reading *Cosmo Girl* rather than *Dolly* if she wants to be 'cool'.
- F has noticed that C's skin is breaking out and thinks she should try Clearasil Daily Face Wash.
- R suggests a door-to-door make-up consultant offer free advice and free samples.
- Resolved *that sub-committee be formed, consisting of*

(FROM 'MINUTES OF ZFS MEETING')

- M thinks we should have Project to make her wear more blue – thinks she looks great in blue and it brings out her eyes.
- F proposes a Project to get her to try Pilates, says she herself never has time to try it but

---

SURVEILLANCE EQUIPMENT – CONSIGNMENT

Sunglasses with hidden camera, transmitter and receiver.
Retail Price: $450
Your Frequent Buyer Price: $435

COFFEE AND CHOCOLATE STRAWBERRIES

Cath was feeling pale.

She sat with her chair a little distant from the table, and her chin a little distant from her neck. The Zing family's explanations meandered around her while her forearms stung faintly and her vision blurred.

'Here,' said Fancy quietly, sliding the milk jug towards her. 'Coffee stays warmer if you add the milk straight away.'

'Does it?' said Cath, strangely elated for a moment by this glimpse of everyday, practical truth.

Fancy nodded: 'The milk is like a little white blanket.'

'Oh!' cried Mrs Zing, from her end of the table. 'I've forgotten the chocolate strawberries! Hang on there while I get them.'

Everyone watched as she crossed the lawn, and listened to the gentle thud as she closed the back door behind her.

The family set down their coffee cups and watched Cath.

'I don't believe any of this,' said Cath. 'I wouldn't believe it at all if I hadn't seen that garden shed. But okay, just assuming it's true, even if you might decide to keep an eye on a baby when you give it up for adoption, why did you all keep going? Why didn't one of you *stop* this? I'm grown up now. I've got a job. Why did this go on for so long?'

'Well,' said Radcliffe, heartily, 'you didn't know it was happening, so how could it hurt you? There wasn't really anything *illegal* about it. And to be perfectly honest, it was a lot of fun! All the exciting subterfuge and espionage and so on!'

'Also, it was all for you,' added Marbie. 'It was to protect you because, you know, if it had come out that you were Valerio's daughter, you'd never have had a normal life. The media would have watched you more than we ever did, *and* they'd have put it in the papers. We only put it in the garden shed.'

'Maybe that was my decision to make,' said Cath.

'We gave you a lot of presents,' Radcliffe pointed out.

'Maybe I didn't want them.'

'Besides,' said Marbie, 'it was part of our life. It was what we did on Friday nights.'

'Right,' agreed Fancy. 'Once you get your filing system up, it's hard to stop working on the files.'

Mr Zing cleared his throat. Everyone turned to him, a little surprised. He had hardly said a word for the entire meal. 'It's like this,' he said, holding out the palms of his hands. 'Some people are good at changing things by seeing them in just the right light. Let's say, for example, a man has a mid-life crisis. He thinks he's destined for greater things than a family, and he runs away to a one-room apartment in West Ryde. Let's say his wife makes that event into something else. Let's say she calls it an *artistic mission*, a trip to Ireland to write novels. Now, take a look at that! He's not a selfish fool anymore, he's just a dreamer. See what I mean? Call a thing by a different name and you change it.'

Even the kookaburra was surprised into silence.

'Okay,' continued Mr Zing, clearing his throat. 'Now let's say this woman gives up her baby. Oh, she does it for all the right reasons – she thinks she's giving the baby a better life, she thinks she's saving her family. But the fact remains, she gives up her baby. So let's say she calls this event something else – a *Zing Family Secret*. A complicated secret with subterfuge and spies, but most of all, a secret which is all about *taking care* of the child. Let's say we ever put a stop to that. We might have had to see what it was.'

Quietly, he pressed out his final words, 'It was a bribe, Cath. She gave up her baby and they paid her off. That's what it was.'

Somewhere, in the bush behind the fence, a whipbird commenced a long, suspenseful toooooo which ended in a sharp whip-crack. Then the back door slammed and Mrs Zing emerged with the strawberries.

16

THE HOT AIR BALLOON

Although Maude set out to be scrupulously honest in her narration of the Zing Family Secret, she did not tell Cath everything. For example, she did not tell her that once Cath had been transferred to Valerio's people – after which the Zings returned home from the seaside – she had not considered the garden shed for weeks.

Instead, she lay in bed, and only got up to do the ironing. David slept on the living room couch at this time. He made sausages and tomatoes for dinner each night and did the girls' homework for them.

In the bedroom, Maude lay still with her eyes open wide, exhausting her imagination by forcing it to hold, steady on her chest, the image, weight, fragrance and warmth of her baby girl. A soft little cat pressing itself ever closer.

When she did fall asleep, she dreamt that she was standing in the basket of a hot air balloon. Behind her was her baby, strapped into a small bassinet, and Maude, without pausing, gathered up the bassinet and tipped it over the side. A parachute opened from the bassinet as it fell, and Maude caught her breath: *the child is saved!*, but then she saw that the parachute was upside down. The bassinet crashed to the ground and was smashed to pieces.

Day after day, Maude lay in bed, snapping in and out of this nightmare: the balloon, the bassinet, the baby rushing to the ground. Each time she woke in horror at the sound of the crash, wept into her pillow, and rebuked herself sharply for throwing the baby overboard. Then she fell into a fit of yearning. If only, she yearned, if only in just one of these dreams the bassinet could catch an up-draught! If only the up-draught could carry it high into a zinging blue sky, over a hill of whipped butter, across a maple syrup pond. And finally, gently, deposit the child on a buttermilk pancake bed.

Until one night, after such a dream, she regarded the circle of the moon through her bedroom window – so sharp-edged it would sever the tendons in your hands if you reached up to hold it – and she thought: *I'll make her one.*

Maude wrote the entire Spell Book on her bedroom floor that night.

First, she stapled a set of blank pages together with some lime green cardboard, folded at the edges for a cover, and she printed the words 'SPELL BOOK' on the front. Then she sat back on her knees and considered the issue. She knew the language of spell books, having read plenty in her herbal remedy phase, and, at a pinch, she could draw on the language of her recipe books. But what was she hoping to achieve?

As soon as she asked herself this question, she turned the book over and wrote on the back cover:

'This Book will make you Fly, will make you Strong, will make you Glad. What's more, this Book will Mend your Broken Heart.'

She had sent Cath over the edge, and she would always be crashing to the ground. If nothing else, decided Maude, this book would provide a soft landing.

Opening the first blank page, she decided she must recreate the important events – her love affair with Nikolai; her broken heart and abandonment – and then she would write a resolution.

It all began, she recalled, efficiently, on the day that her husband, David, called a taxi and left her (*A Spell To Make Someone Decide To Take A Taxi*). Then she had discovered the pie-chef job in the *Trading Post*, when looking for a new vacuum cleaner (*A Spell To Make A Vacuum Cleaner Break*). She had won the boat-scene role in the film when the leading lady fought with the director (*A Spell To Make Two Happy People Have A HUGE Fight Over Absolutely NOTHING*) and in such a way the affair had begun. The affair had ended, effectively, when the set supervisor sent her the artificial rose (*A Spell To Make Someone Give Someone A Rose*).

Now, bravely, she considered her broken heart. She looked at its anatomy closely: her yearning for Nikolai's return; her anger with him; her hatred of Nikolai's wife, for having got to Nikolai first and for keeping him from her. Thus, she included her fantasy that someone might find some evidence of the affair – a note, perhaps, from his jeans pocket – so that the marriage would end (*A Spell To Make Someone Find Something Unexpected In A Washing Machine*). She had also imagined him eating chocolate cake laced with walnuts, so that his lips might swell like balloons (*A Spell To Make Somebody Eat A Piece Of Chocolate Cake*). In her lowest moments, she had thought of the famous wedding photograph in which Nikolai and Rebekka pranced barefoot in the fields (*A Spell To Make A Person Get Stung By A Bee*).

The end of the affair had been sealed, in her mind, when her husband returned from his apartment. He had caught a cold, which turned into a fever, and in a delusional state he had finally seen the truth: he would never become an inventor, and in pursuing this fruitless path, he was losing the only things that mattered. As soon as his voice came back, he had phoned Maude, apologised, and begged her to take him back. Knowing that the affair with Nikolai was only a fiction, thinking of the girls, remembering that once she had loved him, Maude had agreed. He arrived home two weeks later, phoning from Strathfield station when his train was cancelled, and pretending that the plane had been delayed. So: *A Spell To Make Someone Catch A Cold*.

Now, Maude paused again. She had reached the final Spell. Where was the resolution? It was too late to get her baby back. All she could really do for Cath, she thought slowly, was to secretly watch over her, find ways to solve her problems and guide her through her life. She had access to Valerio funds for this reason, but how could she put it to use?

She would need her husband. David would know how to modify cameras and microphones, to conceal them in shirtsleeves and collars. He would know about zoom lenses and bugging devices. She would recruit the spies and he would fit them out. He would gather the information;

she would study it and make the requisitions. He could insulate the shed; she would set up the filing system.

They would work closely together. Fancy and Marbie would have their parents back. The Zing Family would be intact. At least in this small way, the sacrifice of Cath might have been worth it.

She trembled as she wrote the final spell. (*A Spell To Make Two People Fall In Love Again*.) She closed the Book, climbed into bed, and fell into a deep dreamless sleep.

She thought she would post the Spell Book to Cath on her eighteenth birthday, but shortly after she wrote it, she threw herself into the Secret: painting the garden shed and making some early recruitments. In the midst of this practical excitement, she began to see that the Secret was the *real* way in which she would take care of Cath. The writing of the Book, she saw, had really been for herself, a sort of desperate, feverish therapy.

In fact, flicking through the Book one day, she realised that it reminded her of a self-help book she had once read, which suggested humming exercises to combat stress. She looked up the humming book and smiled, remembering how the endorsement on the back cover had persuaded her to buy it. 'This book really truly works,' said Elinor Daisy Weaver of Jacksonville, Alabama. 'You've got to do all the exercises of course but boy oh boy! Until I did those exercises, I was the unhappiest girl in the State.'

On a whim, Maude copied this endorsement word for word (with slight adaptation – 'exercise' had to be 'spell') onto the inside flap of the Spell Book.

Then the Book got lost, probably mixed up with Fancy or Marbie's school things, and she forgot all about it. She only ever performed one of the Spells herself.

17

CATH MURPHY

The evening following the Explanation Lunch was a still and balmy one. Cath's apartment blinked, apprehensively, when she threw open its front door. She gazed at her living room with such contempt that it drew up its chin defensively.

In her arms she held a Tupperware container filled with Mrs Zing's meringues, and a brown paper bag of lemons from Mr Zing's tree. These she appeared to notice now with startled exasperation, and she allowed them to tumble to her feet. Then she marched straight to the dining room window, and ran her fingers up and down the frame. It took only a moment to find the camera, although it was smaller than her smallest fingernail.

At the Explanation Lunch she had deliberately calmed herself, and set herself apart, by finding the Zing family absurd. *I don't believe a word of this*, she had said to herself now and then, comfortably, *but it's very amusing!* But even as she reassured herself, the contents of the Zing Family Shed had drifted across her memory so that her heart began pounding again (*if not this nonsense, then how to explain that shed?*).

And now, here was a camera in the palm of her right hand.

Was it all true? Had this tiny object been observing her all this time? Could something so slight as this have shaped her life? Had fat Mrs Zing watched her eat dinner, making notes about what she might need? Had those strange smiling Zing sisters slipped into her home and replaced or repaired the camera when she wasn't home? She brought her palms together hard, crushing the camera. When she opened her hands again she almost expected to see a drop of blood, as if she had killed a mosquito.

She began a frenzied search through the apartment, without knowing quite what she was looking for: more of the fingernail cameras, of course, but also anything electronic or odd, anything she might recognise from movies about spies or surveillance. The Zings had assured her that the only equipment in her apartment was the dining room camera, but she thought she had also caught odd half-references that day, to one additional camera, which only ever photographed her ankles. So she ran a knife along the skirting boards, prised open electrical outlets, and even turned her socks inside out. Her cat, Violin, watched.

Finally, she collapsed onto the living room couch, but found that her head was shaking back and forth in disbelief. Her hair was getting caught on the fabric.

She sat up and gazed around the room, from the low bookshelf to the standing lamp, to the plasma TV on its chrome stand. At that moment her eyes caught the shape of a small green 'V'. It was the 'V' on her TV remote control. There was a similar 'V', she saw now, on the side of the leather-bound box which sat by the DVD player. It was her collection of Valerio Classics.

Valerio! She had almost forgotten. The Valerio Empire had been funding the entire thing!

Well *that* part, she thought scornfully, was *certainly not true*.

Valerios connected to her mediocre life? It was ridiculous enough to think of the Zing family examining her ordinary days, but the Valerios! She had studied Nikolai's films in high school Social Studies! She owned a Valerio electric toothbrush, and used Valerio conditioning treatments on her hair! She loved to eat Nikolai Gingerbread Men and she had recently signed up for the Valerio Young & Fit Health Plan. That small green 'V' filled her life!

She reached for the leather-bound collection of classics, opened it, and took out the movie at the top of the pile. Nikolai Valerio smouldered up at her from the photo on the front cover. There was the trademark smudge of motor oil, and there were the elegant cheekbones. Unconsciously, she touched her own cheekbones. *I am the daughter*, she thought, doubtfully, *of Nikolai Valerio*. It was like thinking: *I am a princess*.

It's not true, she reminded herself, as Violin skirted her ankles. But just in case, she took the movie collection down the hall and hid it in the linen closet. Even as she pressed the cupboard door closed, she was distracted by the small green V on the side of her coat rack. Her eyelid began to flicker.

18

THE HOT AIR BALLOON

When Maude lay in bed for several weeks, she only got up to do the ironing and to write the Spell Book. David, who was sleeping on the living room couch at that time, saw only her closed bedroom door. He placed arrangements of food at the foot of the door – a bottle of orange juice alongside a bowl of black plums, for example – but otherwise left her alone.

The day after she wrote the Spell Book, Maude got up. David, seeing her at the breakfast table, pretended she was there every day and offered her the coffee. Fancy and Marbie, in their school uniforms, followed his example.

Maude and David scarcely knew each other. They had spent more than a year apart, and David had returned to the news of Maude's affair and pregnancy. Accepting that he was at least partly to blame, David had tried to be calm and understanding. Once, he questioned Maude's resolve to accept the Valerio offer, and suggested he raise the child as one of his own. But Maude, oddly detached and determined, had declared that the choice had been made. Then they had both been distracted: the house by the sea; the visits from Valerio agents; legal documents and large sums of money; the terrible handover day; and then the return home and Maude's several weeks in bed.

Now that she was up again, they worked on the Secret together. They chose a colour for the garden shed, and bought clipboards, maps and cameras. They researched baby carriages, and their first major gift to Cath, presented as 'market research', was a cutting edge stroller. They were polite and friendly with each other, but David continued to sleep on the couch.

At last, after some months had passed, he knocked on the bedroom door and walked into the room. It was late and the girls were asleep. He pressed the door quietly closed behind him, his right hand still clenched from the knock.

There was no moon and the room was deep in darkness. He stopped still in perfect helplessness.

'I'll get the bedside light,' offered a voice from the bed. There was a click and a small glare of light, pooling itself on Maude's hair and the edge of her arm. She sat up against the headboard.

'I hope I didn't wake you,' David said. He sat on the far edge of the bed, in the shadows by the bumps of her feet. Their voices were cheerful yet measured.

David edged his way along the bed, until he was gazing at Maude's pale face. She studied his face also. They were silent, conscious that now they must speak. Their words would be soap operatic.

Maude would say: You left me for a year!

David would respond: That may be, but while I was away, you fell in love with someone else.

Maude would cry: But how could I know you would return?

David might be silent and torn.

Maude would admit, a tremble in her voice: I don't know if I love you anymore.

David would murmur: How can I convince you that you do?

Maude would whisper: My heart has been broken by another.

David would say, bluntly: He's a movie star. Get over it.

Maude would say: I gave away my child.

The final truth would eclipse the other truths. In a soap opera, it would give way to an ad break.

Instead of speaking, they continued to stare at one another. David unclenched his fist, and there was a small, crackling sound. He revealed a folded square of glossy blue and handed it to Maude, who moved it into the light.

'That's next weekend,' said David, in a voice like a challenge.

The paper was a pamphlet, advertising a Festival of Balloons at

Berowra. 'But you're not even interested in balloons,' said Maude, and then added, pointedly: 'You're afraid of heights.' She caught his eye and they both acknowledged that this might be the only truth spoken.

'That's true,' he agreed. 'But that doesn't mean I wasn't interested in your balloons, Maude.'

'You didn't even listen to my stories.' Her tone was tear-filled, defiant and teasing all at once.

'Oh, I didn't listen, did I?' He chose the teasing tone. 'Lie down,' he instructed. 'And close your eyes.'

She moved back under the sheets, so she was flat on her back, her head in the centre of the pillow, watching him. 'I'm not closing my eyes,' she said.

'But I've decided to tell you a story,' he said. 'And next weekend I'll take you to the festival. Look at this.' He took the pamphlet back from her. 'They've got balloons in every shape you can imagine. Rabbits, cats, cars and Pepsi cans. And they'll have arts and crafts for sale, those doily things you like, and they'll have steak and onion sandwiches, I bet, and fairy floss.'

Maude did not look at the pamphlet, but at his face. 'What story?' she said.

It had been more than a year since Maude last told David the story of Monsieur Blanchard, the first man to fly the English Channel. But that night, sitting on the edge of her bed, he repeated the story the way she liked to tell it, almost word for word: 'Now, Jean-Pierre Blanchard was determined to be the first man to fly the English Channel,' he began. 'And he wanted to do it alone. Even the American physician who financed his trip was not to be allowed to come, although the doctor, in point of fact, loved the idea and, in second point of fact, insisted.

'Close your eyes,' said David, interrupting himself.

'Am I making you nervous?'

'I'm not nervous. It's supposed to be a bedtime story, that's all.'

He ran two fingers from her forehead over her eyelids, so that they closed, but she opened them at once.

'Jean-Pierre tried all sorts of tricks to stop the doctor from coming. One day, he wore a lead-lined belt in his trousers, so that the balloon seemed to sink beneath their weight. 'We're too heavy!' he exclaimed, sadly, to the doctor. 'I'm afraid you'll have to get out!' But the doctor smelt something fishy, and made him turn down his pants.

'Look at this,' said David. 'The fitted sheet's come away. No wonder you can't sleep. Move over a moment.' Maude moved to the other side of the bed, and David dragged the bottom sheet back where it belonged, pulling it over the mattress corner. He straightened up the quilt, placing it carefully around her shoulders. Then he swung his legs onto the bed, and sat up in her place. She closed her eyes.

'Eventually, they sorted out their quarrel, and Jean-Pierre agreed that the doctor could come along. It was January 7, 1785 that they set off from the Dover cliffs, carrying with them the following:

> barometer
> compass
> thirty pounds of ballast
> flags
> anchors
> cork jackets –'

Here David paused, repeating the words to himself: '. . . flags, anchors, cork jackets . . .'

'A packet of pamphlets, a bottle of brandy,' prompted Maude.

'A packet of pamphlets, a bottle of brandy, some biscuits, some apples, a pair of silk-covered aerial oars . . .' He had taken her wrist, as if it helped him remember, and as he listed each item, he tapped her wrist bone once with his thumb.

'A rudder,' provided Maude.

'Hush,' said David, and tapped her wrist again. 'And a useless, hand-operated revolving fan.'

'Which *later* –' she began.

'Which *later*,' he reproved, raising a finger to silence her, 'which later would be useful as an aeroplane propeller.'

Maude nodded, satisfied. She turned onto her side, her head pressed into her pillow.

'The flight went very badly. The balloon zipped up and down like a yoyo, and they began, calmly at first, to throw bits and pieces overboard.

Yes, they had to throw the brandy and the apples! By the time they reached the French coast, they were frantically hurtling more and more, and Jean-Pierre, most likely, eyed the doctor longingly! Instead, he took off his trousers and threw them overboard.'

David curled a strand of Maude's hair around his finger, let it slide away again, and said, 'I didn't listen to your stories, eh?' She smiled without opening her eyes. He had been sitting up on the bed, with his knees propped up before him. Now he lay down close to her and continued.

'The story has a happy ending.' He spoke the words into her hair, and kissed her head once. 'They landed safe in the forest of Guines. They were entertained, as heroes, for weeks afterwards by the French.'

•

The Berowra Hot Air Balloon Festival was the first of several attended by Maude and David over the years. Later they took to bringing one or both of their daughters along, but this first festival they attended alone. Maude packed an overnight bag containing: four candles, flowers, a bottle of wine, bread, cheese, olives and chocolate brownies. She scarcely knew why she did this, but it appeared to do the trick.

19

CATH MURPHY

Cath spent the morning of the Redwood Sports Carnival holding one end of the finish line ribbon. She spent the afternoon supervising novelty events. The novelty events were anarchic and unstructured: it was something to do with the pointlessness, Cath thought, of running with legs tied together, or with potato sacks strapped around your waist, or an egg-and-spoon thrust out before you. She did not supervise closely, but allowed small episodes of chaos to erupt and subside while she considered her life.

It was the first week of the new school year. Warren and Breanna Woodford had resigned over the summer, and Lenny D'Souza had returned as full-time counsellor. Lenny and Billson were back together, and rather cloying. Cath herself refused to speak to those who had been Zing family spies, such as Suzanne Barker or Katie Toby, but she also said little to anybody else.

What was there to say? She had no personality. She had watched the accumulated records of her life burn to cinders in a garden shed. In a gazebo, under the blackened bark of a scribbly gum, she had learned the explanation for practically every important event, surprise, or success in her life. She was nothing. An imaginary character. An elaborate Zing family fiction, *brought to your TV today* (she liked to add, with bitter humour) *by Valerio Soap-on-A-String!*

All that was real, thought Cath, were these burn scars on her forearms and this incessant sensation of burning in her cheeks. The feeling of being watched.

She had moved to a new apartment, choosing one through a reputable agent. She had discarded all her furniture, and bought everything new from Ikea. She had washed down the walls and windows of the apartment and padlocked the doors. She had also threatened the Zings with legal action if they so much as glanced her way. But still she narrowed her eyes if a sales assistant asked her how she'd been, and flinched when she saw a camera.

She could tell the police, of course, or the media, but what was the point? Even if they believed her, her life would just be theatre once again.

She stepped backwards, absent-mindedly, and landed on an egg. Nearby children, seeing this, shrieked and jumped up and down.

The complication was this: that, sometimes, in the darkest part of the night, she wished that the Secret continued. While her cheeks burned, angry and humiliated by their surveillance, somewhere in her heart was the cold recognition that now she was truly alone. It was almost as if, all her life, she had intuitively known they were watching and had basked in the limelight.

Children, she knew, imagined themselves to be performers. She remembered once when she was five or six turning cartwheels on the sideline of a cricket game. She had believed that the cricketers were secretly watching her acrobatics, far more impressed by her skill than they were by their game. But children eventually realised they were part of a crowd.

Now she almost panicked when she woke in the night, alone and broken-hearted, and realised that no-one was paying the slightest attention. She might never get over Warren. *She might never fall in love again.* And she had to face this alone: the yearning she felt when she greeted this year's class on the 2nd grade balcony; the starkness of the staffroom without him in it; her splintering memories of Warren: a glimpse of his shoulder through a moth-hole in his T-shirt; feet tapping, side-by-side, on the dark wooden floorboards of a jazz café.

Also, the broken heart was complicated by guilt, self-loathing, and the knowledge that she had been there from the start. She hated him, but also she felt a powerful longing to have him back, and she begged each night: *Come back to me. Leave your wife. Find someone else, Breanna. Let me have him.*

As far as she could tell, the Zings had not known about her affair. But she wondered if eventually they would have found out. Would they have gathered in the garden shed, worried, and arranged to send flowers and a 'Cheer up' note? (That had been them last year, and not the former boyfriend in New Orleans, after all.)

The final of the three-legged race collapsed into fits of giggles, and Cath caught a sudden glimpse of herself in a memory. It was the first week of her affair with Warren, and they were running through the streets of Bowral together in the rain. They ran with their arms held tight around one another's waists, towards the shelter of some shops in the distance, their legs keeping time like a dance.

The three-legged race was not pointless. You used these skills when you ran in the rain with your arm around your lover's waist.

The carnival, she realised, was closing down and thinning out. She caught the eye of Fancy Zing, opening a car door. Fancy smiled and waved, and then leaned to talk to her daughter.

Cath did not wave back. She stared and turned away. But even from this distance, she thought, Fancy's smile was warm.

FANCY ZING

Fancy walked across Redwood Primary School oval, and a small flock of pigeons rose into the air. She smiled to herself, modestly.

It was strange how things worked out – there was Cassie, running towards her. Although she still had asthma, she had recovered from the smoke inhalation and her breathing today, as she ran around the field, was so pure it was almost silent.

Marbie had taken a day off work to watch Cassie win the races. 'It turns out,' she had confided, 'that Vernon doesn't need to have a revenge affair, because he already *got* his revenge.'

'How?' wondered Fancy.

'He pushed me in the path of a sports car!' Marbie's eyes shone.

It was even possible that Fancy's mother would win Cath around. She had been phoning her occasionally, and Cath had been hanging up. But now Mrs Zing had a plan: she would suggest that Cath *herself* carry on with the Secret. Nikolai would still be expecting reports, ready to authorise funds. Why not let Cath draft the reports?

'Would she really want to report on herself?' Fancy asked, doubtfully.

'Who said she had to tell the truth?' replied her mother.

Fancy reached her car, opened the door and, coincidentally, there was Cath, way across the oval, staring at her. She waved and smiled but then Cassie reached her, ribbons and trophies spilling everywhere.

Cassie's friend Lucinda was panting a few steps behind, trying to keep up.

'Okay,' said Cassie from the back seat, polishing a trophy on her T-shirt as they drove home. 'Okay, Lucinda. Never eat an apple and jump up and down.'

'Why not?' said Lucinda.

'The apple goes up your nose.'

'I'm going to try it as soon as I get to your place, Cass.'

'*Never*. Did you hear me, Lucinda? NEVER. What did I just say to you?'

'Take it easy, Cassie,' said Fancy, checking in the rear-view mirror.

'You could just get some apple and put it up your nose, if you wanted,' Lucinda commented. 'You wouldn't have to jump up and down.'

'*Lucinda*,' murmured Cassie, shaking her head.

Fancy turned in to her driveway, and pointed the remote control at the garage door. It rose.

While the girls ran in to the house, she wandered down toward her mailbox. A mynah bird was pecking at her lawn, so she detoured slightly and approached the bird, watching with pleasure as it fluttered out of her way. This was Fancy's new regime. She *made things happen*.

She went to shopping centres as often as she could, so she could march towards automatic doors and dry her hands in the bathrooms. She raised her right hand to make taxis stop. When she passed dog-walkers on the street she said, 'May I?' and then, holding a single finger in the air, she said, 'Sit!' Usually, the dog would.

Also, she had made her husband leave, simply by saying the words: 'I want a divorce.'

Such small gestures led to such grand results!

Radcliffe had been surprisingly compliant once the Secret was burned to the ground. (At present, he was living in the caravan out the back of the Banana Bar, but she was thinking of making him move on from there. It was no place for Cassie to visit.)

All her life she had been so caught up with rules, she had hardly had space in which to live. She used to wear her blazer in her bedroom, because the school rules said the blazer must be worn whenever 'out-side the school gates'. Once, at the gym, she felt a *frisson* of fear when a police car flashed by a window, and she realised that her arms were not swinging. As if the police might arrest her for failure to achieve a complete cardio workout.

The only freedom in her life, she realised now, had been in her foolish fictions.

She glanced over at the Canadian's house, and *tched* at herself. What a fool she had been about him! She didn't even know his name! He was a figment, a fantasy, constructed of chocolate terrines and lingerie!

Fondly, sadly, she recalled a particular fantasy she had developed around something he had said. He had come to her door to offer a cake, apologising for something rude his friend had said. She herself had blathered that it didn't matter, that she wrote erotic fiction, that the only person she had ever slept with was her husband. At which moment, the door had squealed and the Canadian had said, 'I could fix that.'

Days later, she had begun to believe that this was a cryptic message. That he was referring not to the door, but to her desolate sex life! What a dreamer! What a fool she was!

She laughed softly, and opened her mailbox. Its lid hung loose from its hinge and she wondered vaguely if she could replace it with a remote control cover. Then she could *make* it open.

There was a metallic clang nearby. It was the Canadian. He was standing at his own letterbox, and had just let the lid drop closed.

'Nothing,' he called.

'Oh,' she replied.

At least, she admitted to herself, she had not imagined his darkly tanned skin, nor the brightness of his eyes behind their spectacles.

'How about you?' Now he was walking towards her, companionably. His feet were bare, and the edges of his jeans were frayed.

'Well,' she glanced down. 'This might be a copy of my latest book.'

'The erotic fiction?' he enquired politely. He was standing right by her shoulder, and she found herself beginning to chatter.

'Yes! It'll be my erotic fiction! I *know*, it's such a cliché! Me, a housewife in the suburbs, writing this sort of trash! This one's full of multiple orgasms, you know, and I've never even *had* a multiple orgasm . . .' She dropped the letterbox lid and it swung crookedly.

'I could fix that,' said the Canadian.

He was gesturing at her letterbox, but when Fancy looked up, and into his eyes, she saw that they were dancing.

MARBIE ZING

Marbie and Vernon sat on the front porch of their apartment, drinking iced tea and waiting for Listen to get home from her first day at school. The afternoon was hot and the neighbourhood children were playing with a garden hose.

During the summer, Marbie had taken some time off work to spend a few days with Listen. Together, they repainted the apartment and drove up the coast.

Side-by-side on their beach towels one day, Marbie told Listen about the day when a beach umbrella almost killed her.

'See my scar,' she said, proudly.

Listen had heard the story before, but this time Marbie told it differently. 'I wasn't concentrating,' she said. 'Everyone was shouting, look out for the umbrella! And I was just sitting there staring out to sea. Why didn't I get out of the way? And that's the thing, Listen, most bad things can be avoided if you just *pay attention*.'

'But what if you concentrate really hard,' said Listen, 'and everything still turns out bad?'

Before Marbie had a chance to respond, Listen continued, 'Like, for example, if somebody didn't have anyone to sit with at school, even though they tried hard to find friends.'

'Well,' said Marbie, scraping her heels slowly along the sand. 'I guess you know that the person would have to go back to school next year and try again. Somewhere at the school there would be friends for that person, if she just kept on trying.'

'Right,' agreed Listen quickly. 'Okay. I know.'

'So that's what you know,' said Marbie, 'but here's what I think. I think St Carmel's have had their chance with that person. I think that person is much too precious to go back to the school. I'm not letting that school anywhere near that person ever again.'

'You're not?'

'No way in hell. We're tracking down a different school. For that person.'

'Well,' said Listen, casually. 'Bellbird High seems like the kind of school a person could try.'

'So she could,' said Marbie.

And she did.

20

THE SPORTS CARNIVAL

Cath Murphy (teacher, Grade 2B) stands at the carnival coffee table. Paper cups are set out in orderly rows, like a choir about to perform, and each has already been filled. How long has the coffee been sitting there, open to the breeze?

'Milk?' says Mrs Nestle (tuckshop lady).

Too late, thinks Cath.

The oval is almost empty. The last children are climbing onto buses. Mrs Nestle begins tipping coffee onto the lawn.

Cath heads to the staffroom which is empty and still. She glances at the corner kitchenette: the sandwich maker which she and Warren bought; the coffee machine, where Warren teased Breanna for self-consciousness.

She collects her mail and handbag, locks the staffroom windows, and imagines, for a moment, her evening: the new apartment with its bare linoleum and the fridge that squeals when she opens the door; her feet on her new coffee table; Violin, like a teasing scarf, climbing across her shoulders to sit on his side of the couch.

Outside in the school car park, Miss Waratah sings, 'Farewell, Cath!' Mr Bel Castro straddles his motorbike and kicks aside the stand.

She drives towards the gate, but brakes slightly, as something in the rock garden catches her eye. It is the corner of a lime green book, hidden underneath a rock. She puts her car in Park, opens the door, and pulls the book from under the rock. She waves it in the air, and smiles self-consciously at Mr Bel Castro, who is waiting patiently, revving his motorbike behind her.

She tosses the book onto the passenger seat, and drives toward home.

THE HOT AIR BALLOON

Once upon a time there was a confectioner who flew in a hydrogen balloon.

This was in 1810. He invited a friend from Bristol and the flight began well enough: they drifted over the Bristol Channel towards Cardiff.

Four miles off Combe Martin, however, they crashed into the sea.

But they did not break their legs or drown; they did not catch alight and burn.

Instead, something extraordinary happened: the basket bobbed on top of the waves, the balloon billowed out behind them, and presto! *they were saved*. They spent an hour wafting along in this manner, and were rescued by a boat from Lynmouth.

Maude Zing has always preferred the confectioner's story to the tale of the watercolour painter whose parachute was upside down.

She likes to imagine how the balloon must have looked, floating on top of the sea. The tiny basket, the immense sphere of cloth, the hopeful little men, the great expanse of water and sky. So strange, so lovely, so mystical, as with all unlikely, dreamy things such as whales, flying fish, pavlovas, and unexpected snowfalls.

But the confectioner's story was more. It was disaster transformed. A sailing ship conjured from a capsized balloon.

EXTRACTS FROM THE ZING GARDEN SHED (Burnt Fragments)

SURVEILLANCE EQUIPMENT CONSIGNMENT

Covert collar camera: Just fit collar to cat/dog/mouse *etc.* Collar houses Pinhole Camera with crystal clear resolution & super sharp audio. Pinhole placement is a tiny ½ mm wide. Collar is plain design. Also available in COLOUR and with BELL.

The Turning
Tim Winton

In the 1980s Tim Winton made his mark with tough, spare stories about youth and promise, of early parenthood and the challenges of loyalty. Now, almost twenty years since his last collection, he returns to the form with seventeen overlapping stories of second thoughts and mid-life regret set in the brooding small-town world of coastal Western Australia.

Here are turnings of all kinds – changes of heart, nasty surprises, slow awakenings, sudden detours – where people struggle against the terrible weight of the past and challenge the lives they've made for themselves.

Brilliantly crafted, and as tender as they are confronting, these elegiac stories examine the darkness and frailty of ordinary people and celebrate the moments when the light shines through.

From the internationally acclaimed and bestselling author of *Dirt Music* comes an outstanding work of fiction that will resonate with readers everywhere.

Temple of the Grail
Adriana Koulias

France, 1254.

On a mountain high in the Pyrenees, the monastery of St Lazarus is a
forbidding place. Behind its ramparts and battlements, heretical acts are
said to take place. There is also the rumour of a secret – a secret so
important and so dangerous that its keepers would be prepared to kill
before permitting its revelation.

At the end of a bitter winter, a delegation arrives to investigate the
monks of St Lazarus. Andre, a Knight of the Templar Order, and his
young scribe, Christian de St Armand, have been sent by the King of
France to oversee the investigation. When an elderly monk dies under
strange circumstances, Andre and Christian start to unravel the mystery
at the heart of St Lazarus.

Hampering them at every turn is Rainiero Sacconi, the Pope's ambitious
inquisitor. He seems determined to condemn the community of monks.
But why?

By the time the secret of St Lazarus is revealed, hypocrisy and violence
will be exposed. And for Andre and Christian, the investigation will turn
into a fight for not only their souls, but for their lives.

In the tradition of *The Name of the Rose* and *The Da Vinci Code*, this is
historical fiction at its gripping best.